BOX

Alex Shearer is a professional screenwriter and lives in Bristol. This is his first novel.

ALEX SHEARER

BOX 132

HarperCollins*Publishers*

HarperCollins*Publishers*
77–85 Fulham Palace Road,
Hammersmith, London W6 8JB

A Paperback Original 1997
1 3 5 7 9 8 6 4 2

ISBN 0 00 649825 6

Set in Postscript Linotype Meridien by
Rowland Phototypesetting Ltd,
Bury St Edmunds, Suffolk

Printed and bound in Great Britain by
Caledonian International Book Manufacturing Ltd, Glasgow

For Netta

ONE

It was best to come straight to the point.

Happily married man, he wrote, *seeks affair. No strings attached.*

He sat and read over what he had written. No, maybe on second thoughts it was too broad. Perhaps he should be a little more specific. Age for example.

He started again. *Happily married man seeks affair. No strings attached. With woman aged twenty to forty.*

He read that.

Hmm. Too narrow maybe. How about if he dropped the lower age limit to the age of consent? Or was that just a bit too – yes. Well, eighteen then. After all, if you were old enough to vote, you were old enough to make your own mind up about whether you wanted to have an affair with a married man or not.

Eighteen to forty then? Or was that still too narrow? Maybe he should raise that upper limit a little. There were some wonderfully well-preserved women around these days. And why deny yourself the benefits of experience? He wouldn't want to miss out. And an older woman might be more discreet, and appreciative, and divorced, with her own flat, and her own bank account, and able to pay for lunch.

Eighteen to sixty then? No. Why, his mother wasn't much older than that. It smacked a bit too much of old-age pensioners. Fifty-five then? Yes. Maybe fifty-five would be all right on a dark night, or with subdued lighting and the curtains drawn. And better a well-preserved fifty-five than a gauche and unkempt twenty.

It was a lucky dip, really. You never knew what you were going to get.

Happily married man seeks affair. No strings attached. With woman aged eighteen to fifty-five.

1

Now what about the rest of it? G.S.O.H. was a great favourite in the Lonely Hearts advertisements – a good sense of humour. Now, did he want to have an affair with a woman who had a good sense of humour, or didn't he? Hmm. It needed some thinking about. Plainly a good sense of humour was an advantage in some situations, but was that the case when what you were really after was serious sex? Maybe not. And besides, if her sense of humour was too good, she might see through to the whole comical absurdity of the situation, and laugh herself so silly that sex would never get on the agenda at all. You didn't want them laughing at you in your boxers the moment you took your trousers off and your knees made an appearance. No, forget the sense of humour then. They could be downright miserable if they liked, just as long as they were G.I.B.

Yes, G.I.B. – good in bed. You didn't see that one in the Lonely Hearts very often. A bit too explicit really. So, should he include a G.I.B. or not? He mulled it over for a while and then finally decided not to put it in. It wasn't so important that the woman concerned had to be *good* in bed. As long as she was actually *in* bed, that was the main thing. Good would be along the lines of a bonus extra. Even if she was mediocre in bed, he wouldn't mind. Even terrible in bed would be something. The point is that she would be in there, and hopefully he would be in her! That was the main thing. Everything else was bunce.

He looked at the roughed-out advertisement again. What else should he say? *All letters answered* – yes, that would probably be a good idea. Nothing more off-putting than thinking that your application hadn't arrived or wasn't being properly considered. It was a bit like applying for a job, really. That frustrating, empty limbo period when you traipsed down to the doormat to pick up the morning's post, only to find, yet again, that there was no news. And far from no news being good news, no news was extremely depressing.

So, all letters answered then? Fine.

Now, what about photographs?

It had always seemed a bit of a cheek to him somehow.

There you are – god knows what you look like – asking other people to send in their photographs, so that you can sit in judgement on their appearance, when, for all they know, you might have a face like a gargoyle on the front of a cathedral, the sort that frightens the devils off and stops dogs from peeing on lamp posts. But then, unsuitable candidates had to be weeded out. (Assuming there *were* going to be candidates of course. There was always the risk that it might be a vacancy for which no one would apply.) Looks weren't everything, admittedly, and you don't look at the mantelpiece when you're poking the fire, as his grandfather used to say. (To which his grandmother would answer 'No, and you don't look at your bottom when you're brushing your teeth'. Though he had never quite worked out to his satisfaction exactly what that meant. And he doubted that she knew either.)

Photographs would be useful, if only as guidelines, even though the camera could be a bit of a liar. And even when it wasn't, well, a pleasant face wasn't everything. And a pleasant face didn't always mean a body to match, or even a nice personality. And many plain, or even downright ugly faces belonged to bodies of great sensuality, and minds of great sensitivity. Pity sensuality wasn't something that you could easily photograph. There ought to be some kind of X-ray machine for measuring responsiveness to touch.

So, *All letters answered. Please send photograph – if possible.*

How was that? The 'if possible' made it, he thought. A nice touch that. It took the pressure off. Send one if you want to, if not, don't.

Only, if you don't want to send one, that must mean that you've got something to ... hide, perhaps? Like your two heads, or the fact that you once won first prize in the Elephant Man Look-alike Competition?

Please send photograph.

That was better. No 'if possibles'. Just send it, or else. Be there, or be square.

He tried to put himself in the mind of the kind of woman who might reply. How did he imagine her? Difficult to say. He had certain types, certain categories, already visualized, but

3

whether they actually corresponded to any kind of reality he had no idea at all. In fact, if he did have an idea, he probably wouldn't be doing this. What he lacked, what he wanted, was experience.

Happily married man seeks affair. No strings attached. With woman aged eighteen to fifty-five. All letters answered. Please send photograph.

Now, how much was that lot going to cost? He didn't want to stint on it, but he wasn't made of money. These ads could be expensive. And it wasn't good to make them too long. Lonely Hearts ads which said too much were as bad as the ones which said too little, or next to nothing at all. They smacked of garrulous desperation, when what he wanted to convey was the casual attitude – the take-it-or-leave-it, easy-going approach of the elegantly cynical, seen-it-all, done-it-all, took-the-photograph, sent-the-postcard-and-bought-the-T-shirt, man of the world.

An ad with an attitude, that was what he needed, the soft, cajoling, insinuating sell – an ad with a twinkle.

Hmm. Maybe he could afford a few more words after all.

It was strange really, he thought, how complicated the prospect of infidelity was. From the divorce statistics you would think that everyone was at it. Well, he wasn't, and never had been. Never so much as the smallest hint of opportunity. Not once, not even at the office Christmas party, had so much as a drunken receptionist come up to him, with smeared lipstick and runny mascara, and said 'You know, Giles, I've always fancied you. How about coming back to my place tonight?', before collapsing in a pile of half-digested mince pies on the carpet.

Where were these opportunities that never came his way? It was like trying to hitch a lift on a dark, rainy night, when no one wanted to stop and pick you up, and desperation set in, and the more desperate you looked, the longer you had to wait, as the more untouchable you became.

Maybe it all evened up in the end. Some sowed their wild oats when young, and then settled down, and sowed tame, legitimate, monogamous oats thereafter, all carefully planted in the field of matrimony. Others went on sowing them for-ever. Others never were wild boys. They just seemed to miss out somehow on all the youthful sex, drugs and rock'n'roll. They were the ones who'd had steady girlfriends, possibly the same steady girlfriend, from school days onward. It wasn't that these girls were prudes, it wasn't that they refused to sleep with you or hesitated to undo the fly of your Levis in the darkened cinema, they just seemed to expect, well, a kind of constant fidelity.

It was all so very old-fashioned – or so you would think at first glance. But on closer inspection you saw that old-fashioned, for some people, never really went out of style at all. It was always there, like country-and-western music, or the Church Of England. Permissiveness came and went, the social climate changed, and morals went round the barometer. Marriage was replaced by living in sin, living in sin then stopped being sin, and just became normal, everyday living. The divorce rate soared, and the world was full of broken homes, single mothers, sugar daddies, children who wondered where or who their father was. People re-married and re-re-married, and had extended families with relationships so com-plicated that you needed a professional historian with a magnifying glass and a chain saw to dissect the family tree. Family tree? There were family forests now.

And yet, creeping out of the woodwork, came that steady, unwavering bunch of monogamists to which Giles seemed destined to belong. This lot didn't have affairs. These couples stayed together. These mums and dads never got as far as divorce. They stuck together like glue, and made the best of the good years, and just tried to survive the bad. And on the face of it you might have thought they were happy, that they had it licked, that they'd got it made.

On the face of it. But under the skin there was that itch. That itch which was keeping Giles awake at night, driving him into Ann Summers shops to browse through the catalogues and propelling him to reach to the top of the magazine rack in the newsagents.

Those yearnings.

What other word was there? Look in the thesaurus and you got longings, hankerings, pinings, achings – but they were just other ways of saying the same thing: the hunger for something different, for a bit – well, he knew where – on the side.

A man might have to do what a man had to do – or, looked at another way, he might not. But he couldn't help feeling what he felt. And if he felt that somewhere along the line he had missed out, and was even now missing out, and that unless he did something about it he would always be missing out until the day he died, and that they would etch on his tombstone the words HERE LIES GILES, WHO MISSED OUT, then what choice did he have? He seemed to live more and more these days in a state of abject nostalgia – mourning not only what was lost, but also mourning what would never be found.

Pull yourself together man!

But he'd tried that.

Count your blessings.

He'd counted them – one, two, three. Good job, nice house, nice wife, nice children, nice car, nice holidays, contributory pension scheme, no worries there save ill health, accidents, and unemployment. Otherwise everything was nice and fine and cosy. And yet who would ever have thought the rules of mathematics would decree that when nice is added to fine is added to cosy, the product is usually something rather unpleasant and disagreeable. You couldn't make a life like that. It was like trying to make concrete without sand, any structure you made out of this sandless concrete would crumble and fall apart. That, or you ran around like a blue-assed fly, trying to hold the whole thing together, patching up the holes with assurances and regularly murmured 'I love you's when what you really wanted was –

Well? What was it?

He looked down at his advertisement.

Sex with strangers, to be honest. Abandonment in hotel rooms. The sound and the smell and the excitement of sex – with someone who wasn't your wife.

Yes, sex with another woman, that was it. No, correct that, sex with other *women* – plural. No, correct that again – sex with another woman *might* do. He'd have to see how he felt. Maybe just the once would be enough. But the bottom line was that it was not possible for a man to die happy, knowing that the only woman he had ever slept with in his whole life was the one he was married to. The prospect of a lifetime's fidelity – it lay on your chest like a tombstone, and on your stomach like an old pork pie.

He looked at his advertisement again. It seemed a bit stark and clinical now. Which maybe it was. But you couldn't say he wasn't being honest. *Man seeking sex with stranger seeks woman seeking same*, that was the nub of it. He wasn't kidding himself that it was a decent or honourable sort of advertisement, but it was legal, and it was truthful.

And it had to be done!

Or did it?

He'd thought that over too. And it came to this: if he stayed faithful to her, he'd be untrue to himself. If he tried to be faithful to himself, he'd be untrue to her. Hobson's choice, in fact. Damned if you do, and damned if you don't. But if he was unfaithful to her, at least he'd only hate himself. But if he was unfaithful to himself, well, he'd hate her. And that would never do. So in a way, it was as much for her sake as for his. *More* for her sake!

Who was he kidding.

Of course, other people didn't have these problems. It seemed so easy for other people. But then that was probably another conjuror's illusion too, the way that someone else's life always seemed better organized, better run, better maintained than your own. Other people had it all sorted and figured out, they had it wrapped and taped and sitting with a stamp on it, all ready to go. Other people's lives flowed like rivers, unimpeded, to the sea. They never got diverted or burst their banks. And other people's lives and cars and houses always seemed better than your own, and you were always sitting in the wrong vehicle driving in the wrong direction going home to the wrong kind of front door in the wrong part of town.

But it *did* seem easier for some people. Roy, for example. Happily married for seventeen years. Adoring wife. Pleasant children. And he was having an affair with not just one woman, not just two, but three, *three* women, simultaneously. And one of the affairs had gone on undiscovered for seven years. And they weren't just anybody. They were lookers, all three of them, attractive, professional women. All unaware of each other's existence. Married as well, two of them, plus one divorcée. In fact, Roy had written a computer programme especially to handle all his extra-marital appointments, to ensure that there were never any slip-ups, double bookings or unpleasant discoveries.

Little messages would pop up on to his computer screen:

>**Tina's birthday today. Send flowers. (Use florist in High Street.)**
>**Restaurant today. Joyce does not like steak!**
>**Wedding anniversary. Send large bunch of flowers. (Use florist in Park Row.)**

And he was working to make it even more sophisticated.

No, you couldn't say you approved of Roy, you couldn't say it was a nice thing to do. But you couldn't deny that he had a life. He definitely had a life. He would probably go to his grave thanks to a heart attack brought on by all his extra-marital fornicating. But he was certainly alive. He lived with both feet in the here and now, no doubt about that. While Giles was doing no more than existing, marking time, living in the now and then, the if and maybe, and the perpetual perhaps. He felt that even his name was against him sometimes.

Men don't make passes at girls who wear glasses.

But not even girls with glasses made passes at Giles.

He got up from the work station and went to pretend to look out of the window. But he wasn't really looking out of the window, he was looking at his reflection, peering to see the question mark which surely hung over it. He saw a face looking back at him which was not unattractive. But that was the trouble: the double negative. Not *un*attractive. Neither attractive, nor unattractive, just somewhere in the middle, an area of neutrality. On a scale of one to ten, he was a five, or a four-and-a-half. But on a scale of one to ten, Roy was probably a minus six for looks, and yet it didn't stop him. Far from it, it made him worse.

So. So where was he? Where had he got to? Ah yes. Who might reply. The young, free and single, maybe, in search of that change which would be as good as a rest? The older, married and bored? The freshly unattached and newly liberated? The widowed and lonely? Or the just plain honest and downright lustful and horny.

Yes siree! Let's hope so!

Perhaps he ought to say a few words about himself to sell the idea. You couldn't, after all, rely on the desperation of others and the national sex shortage which gave rise to personal ads in the first place. Though maybe it was more of a local than a national drought. He had thought before that the division of sex must be like the division of wealth, where twenty percent of the people were getting eighty percent of the orgasms, while the remaining poor and needy had to get by as best they could, with whatever they could lay their hands on – even if it was only themselves.

Maybe he could say what his star sign was. Things like that meant a lot to some people. If they thought you were compatible, then that was it, they were on to you like a limpet. Just as long as you were Pisces and they were Taurus, or whichever way round it was, you were away. He had heard about things like that. Seen it in a TV documentary once. People meet in a disco, and she says 'What's your star sign?' and he says 'I'm Aquarius the water carrier' or 'Leo the lecher', and before you know it, they're round at her place on the water bed, as it was written in the stars.

Destiny.

But on the other hand, it could be a turn-off too. Some women would run a mile rather than meet a Pisces on a dark night. And if it was a Sagittarius, they'd do the marathon. Or if you were on the cusp somewhere between one sign and another, they'd probably phone the police.

No, he'd avoid any mention of star signs, he didn't want to arouse any hostility. Or any suspicions.

Arouse!

He was away again. Dreaming filled the day. Dreams of one leg on another.

Curious word, really, arouse. And not just the word itself, but the things you applied it to. Suspicions and hostilities and sexual desires, things which lurked like sleeping dragons in caves, waiting to be prodded into life. *She aroused my suspicions.* You could almost picture them growing, like multiple erections. He could see his name listed in the *Guinness Book of Records* as the man with seventeen penises, whose suspicions had all been aroused at once, and here was the photographic evidence to prove it.

No, he couldn't have any suspicion-arousing going on. Discretion was the key word in the advertisement. He didn't want any marriages busting up, or anyone getting hold of the wrong ends of any innocently proffered sticks. A quick affair, a brief encounter, some wham, some bam, some thank you very kindly ma'am, and goodbye, page turned, book closed, episode over, life goes on.

It was like bungee jumping, or going up in a hot air balloon, or leaping out of an aeroplane with a parachute – you only had to do it the once. And then once you had satisfied both desire and curiosity, you could stuff that beast back into its cage, and it would return to being docile, and never want to be fed again.

Would it?

He read it through again: *Happily married man seeks affair. No strings attached. With woman aged eighteen to fifty-five. All letters answered. Please send photograph.*

Now how much was that going to cost him? He worked it out from the rate card. And then there was the cost of a box number. He added that on. He'd better go round and collect the letters, when they came in. Or have them sent on to him at the office, marked *Personal, Private and Confidential.* Or maybe that would arouse suspicions in the mail room. Hmm. He'd have to think that one over and work something out.

Yes, he'd have to make arrangements to pick up the letters when they flooded, trickled, dribbled (delete as applicable) in.

Maybe even rent a post office box. It was an additional expense, but never mind – safety first. He certainly couldn't have the replies sent to his home. He and Holly opened each other's correspondence as automatically as they opened their own. And why not? They had no secrets. They were all but Siamese twins. They were joined at the bank account.

Here, one for you, from your brother. He says he's changing his job again.

One for you, from your sister in Australia, she says she's going in for an operation.

No secrets, no skeletons, no locked cupboards. Everything split right down the middle. It was a complete partnership, complete togetherness, complete, suddenly smothering, stultifying, togetherness.

Yes, a bit less togetherness and he might not be contemplating this.

Right, a few brief, apt words about himself, but no star signs. So what should he say? No false modesty, no false vanity here. What could he say about himself? There was still *not unattractive* as a possibility. No. You wouldn't even buy a socket set on that sort of recommendation. *(A not unattractive socket set. A far from ugly set of spanners. A not entirely hideous collection of table mats.)* How about – nice? Nice! No. The damnation of faint praise. Not bad-looking then? In possession of two eyes, one nose, and a complete set of testicles?

What did other people say?

He glanced through the listings. *Gorgeous guy, handsome hunk, good-looking type, into body-building.* Yes, well, whatever else they were into, they certainly weren't into modesty. All these handsome hunk types probably went about with portable full-length mirrors, checking their appearance every step of the way, and setting up new branches of the Narcissus Society where the intersections converged.

Ah – here was one. *Man. Thirties*, it said. *Nicely-shaped head, seeks sincere woman for relationship.*

Nicely-shaped head? Hmm. He looked at his reflection in the window. Could you call it nicely-shaped? Or was it more on the lumpy side? No, receding hairline was more like it, and

11

he wasn't going to put that into any advertisement. Why do yourself down when you didn't have to. There were plenty of others who'd do that job only too happily on your behalf.

Well-groomed. Now how about that? He saw the phrase in an ad placed by a *Well-groomed businessman seeking companionship with view to possible long-term relationship with mature, motherly lady with large bosoms.*

There was something honest and endearing about a man who knew his own mind.

Well-groomed. Was he well-groomed? Well, he would be if he got his hair brushed out. It did have certain horsy connotations, but stables aside, well-groomed was also a phrase which seemed to express cleanliness, and talc, and Cussons Imperial Leather. He felt that there must be something reassuring to a woman in the expression. Well-groomed. She'd know that she was on safe territory and that she hadn't fallen amongst perverts, or men with unchanged, month-old sheets, and unwashed, week-old armpits.

Well-groomed and nice-looking then? Or pleasant? Yes, pleasant would be better. He re-wrote the ad yet again: *Well-groomed, pleasant-looking, happily married man seeks woman, 18 to 55, to have affair with. No strings attached. All letters answered. Please send photograph.*

How was that? Not bad. Maybe he should have written *woman with whom to have an affair.* He seemed to remember from his school grammar lessons that you should avoid ending a sentence with a preposition or conjunction. But then pedantry was the hallmark of a bore. So he left it as it was.

Right. How much was that lot going to cost him? About fifteen quid with the magazine box number. Okay. Right. He'd do it then. That very afternoon. Just for fun. I mean, not seriously, not really meaning it, more just to see what kind of response he got, and then take it from there. He didn't have to do anything; he might not get any replies, and even if he did, he didn't have to respond to them, he could tear the whole lot of them up. It would all disappear into the ether, down a hole into the void of Things That Came To Nothing, flushed down the toilet of Things I Started But Never Quite Finished, consigned to the barren world of Ambitions Unfulfilled. And there were plenty of those. Plenty of those everywhere. We needed a garbage disposal plant to recycle all the waste.

He paused. A last thought. Should he put anything else in? Maybe something about his interests? Something about liking good music and walking in the country. He didn't particularly like either of them – good music was never as good as it was cracked up to be, and wherever there was a walk in the country there was a cow pat not far behind, but it seemed like the thing to say. It wasn't just sex that people wanted these days, it was sex with a bit of culture, a little intellectual content maybe. Yes, women seemed to want to go to bed with men who had listened to a spot of Beethoven and who had read a bit of Shakespeare. Unless they were set on someone a bit rougher, the type who used Swarfega at the end of the working day. And even then, Shakespeare would probably find his way into it somehow or other. Over the postcoital ciggies or cups of tea, Beauty would lean over to Beast and say, 'So you left school at sixteen, did you, Beastie?'

'Yes, didn't like it there,' Beastie would say, as pleased at knocking off a bit of quality street as his partner was at getting a bit of rough-side.

'So you never did any Shakespeare?'

'Didn't like Shakespeare,' Beastie would say. 'Boring.'

'Ah, well, Shakespeare can actually be very interesting, you know,' Beauty would tell him, and would set to the task of unburdening Beastie of his ignorance and prejudice as willingly as an old lecher would unburden a schoolgirl of her virginity. And then she'd get her reward afterwards, when he introduced her to his tool kit.

So? To do, or not to do?

Yes, why not? It couldn't do any harm, and besides, it gave things a personal touch. And more importantly, it was totally misleading. Nobody who knew him would describe him as interested in either music or walking, so it threw them off the scent. The fewer people who knew what he was up to, the better. The ideal person to be was Mr Nobody, Mr Anonymous, Mr Never Guess It Was Me.

Well-groomed, pleasant-looking happily married man seeks partner, 18 to 55, to have affair with. No strings attached. Interests: classical music and walking in the country. All letters answered. Please send photograph.

That was it then. That would have to do. Cast your bread upon your waters. *Mesdames et messieurs, faites vos jeux.* The wheel was spinning, place your bets.

Chuck your maggot into the old canal, and see what fish rise to nibble.

TWO

Computers? That must be interesting.

That was how it had been, once upon a time. The job had a certain amount of kudos then, back in the old days of punch cards and coding pads, and punch-card girls – oh, those young, nubile punch-card girls, sitting on typists' chairs, with their buttocks straining the thin fabric of their summer frocks.

Steady on, Giles. Get this flow chart done for the new stock control system.

Now where was I?

Oh yes, the thin fabric of their summer frocks, that was it. With the outline of their panties clearly visible to the casual observer – and there wasn't a man in the whole computer department not adept at the art of casual observation.

'Could you just punch this a minute, Fiona –'

Or better still, could you take it in your hands and –

Steady on, Giles. He shook his head to clear it and focus his thoughts. What was happening to him? He had a suspicion that he knew. He had gone beyond reaching man's estate and was now moving into fresh territory – dirty old man's estate – and there was nothing he could do to stop himself.

Now, of course, the punch-card girls had gone, and the punch cards had gone with them. You did it all yourself now, with your own keyboard and terminal sitting on your desk. The punch-card girls with their summer dresses and tantalizingly half-visible panties, Aladdin's caves of hidden delights, had gone the way of match girls and land girls and milkmaids and upstairs maids. They belonged to another time, to another era, a time of nostalgia, back in the golden age of computers.

Computers? That must be interesting.

Not likely, not now.

It was now more *Computers? That must be dead boring.*

15

And your fellow party-goers edged away from you, as though they had just discovered that you were a child molester, or a secret train spotter, or that you had inoperable problems with your sweat glands.

People were too familiar with them now. They were no longer so esoteric, the province of the great mind and the scientific intellect. Familiarity bred contempt faster than rabbits bred other rabbits. Computers impressed nobody these days. Eight-year-olds knew more about them than Giles did – not that he was going to admit that to anyone. People had them at home, they saw them in banks, building societies, school classrooms, even on trains.

Yes, everyone knew all about computers now. Everyone knew what computers were. They were a pain in the ass.

Yes, there had to be change. True, there had to be progress. But how could change equal progress when it meant the end of punch-card girls and their wonderful panties.

'What you doing, Giles?'

It was Roy. His usual laid-back and laconic self. Giles sometimes wondered if he wasn't trying to promote being casual into an art form.

'Stock control system,' Giles said, hurriedly covering up the specification paper with his elbow. Where he should have drawn a diamond-shaped flow chart decision box, he seemed to have somehow drawn a pair of panties. Inside the sketched outline he had written DO YOU NEED TO REORDER? A YES arrow came out of the left leg, and a NO arrow came out of the right.

Too late, Roy had already seen it.

'Dear, oh dear. Fantasy time already? You don't want to let Lavinia see that mate, she'll have your testicles for a toothbrush.'

Giles wondered about Roy, and the more he listened to him, the more he wondered. What did he have? What *did* he have? What did his harem see in him? He wasn't especially good-looking, or well-built, or even well-hung. Giles had seen him in the shower room at the squash club and had made a quick visual comparison. Roy had come off the worse, with a mere apology for a penis. And yet women went for him.

It wasn't as if he was particularly intelligent or witty either. Popular wisdom had it that when a man was not all that physically attractive he invariably had a great sense of humour, or a quick and ready wit with which to laugh women into bed. But Roy didn't. Have your testicles for a toothbrush was his limit. Take the old clichés and stand them on their heads. Keep the formula, but just change either side of the equation. Have your guts for garters became have your testicles for a toothbrush. Give a dog a bad name became give a cat an unfavourable appellation. Red sky at night was a shepherd's knee-trembler. No place like home became no establishment like chez nous. The inability to organize a piss-up in a brewery became he couldn't arrange a wank in a massage parlour. And so it went on. And yet Roy's conversation in no way impaired his prospects. Enhanced them, if numbers were anything to go by.

'Missed the gusset,' Roy said.

He took a pencil and sketched a gusset in. 'Something about a gusset, isn't there?' he said. 'Just the word alone. Something erotic about it. Gusset. It always reminds me of mail-order catalogues and those pages where they have photos of undies for the fuller figure. Gusset,' Roy mused, savouring the sound of it. '*Reinforced* gusset! I used to pore over them when I was a lad. They used to think I was up in my room looking at the toy pages and deciding what to have for Christmas. But no, I was at the gussets.'

It amazed Giles really how little the incidental conversations of his life had altered over the past thirty years. At school he and his contemporaries had spent their morning breaks talking of sport and sex, of football and underwear. And here he was now, a grown man, and very little had changed.

'Did you go to the game on Saturday?' Roy asked.

'No,' Giles said, 'I didn't.' He never went to football matches. He hated football. He had told Roy this on numerous occasions, but he still persisted in asking him if he had been to the match.

'I took Doris One to it,' Roy said.

17

'Isn't that dangerous?' Giles asked. 'You might be seen.'

'No,' said Roy, 'only dangerous if it's on Match of the Day, and even there it's pretty safe, as the wife never watches that. It's only Doris One's husband I have to worry about then, in case he sees us on the terraces. But it's not that likely. Mind you, he'd be sick as a flamingo if he did.'

Roy rarely referred directly to the women in his life, usually he used the code names of Doris One, Doris Two and Doris Three. Dorises One and Two were the married women, Doris Three was the divorcée. Calling them all Doris seemed to make them easier to handle and to organize. It made them all uniform and standardized, a bit like a juggler's clubs, easier to keep all in the air at once. It was possible that he didn't even know their real names, that such things had deliberately never been exchanged, so that if anyone was ever captured by the enemy, true identities could never be revealed.

'Yes, I took Doris One to the match, and then after we went back to her place. Her husband's a Newcastle fan, so he'd gone north for the big one. So I had tea round there, then I told her I ought to be getting home to the wife, so I went off to meet Doris Two for a drink, down at the Rose.'

'And what about your wife?'

'What? Doris Four? Well, least recollected soonest repaired there. No, she thought I'd gone to Luton for that other match and so wouldn't be back till the small hours and tiny minutes. So I dropped Doris Two home – I didn't go in, as her husband –'

'Husband of Doris?'

'That's it, he was out with his mates, and she was supposed to be out with hers –'

'You?'

'Yeah, me.'

'Mate of Doris?'

'I suppose so, yeah. So I popped round to see Doris Three then, who was all on her ownsome –'

'And where did she think you'd been?'

'Oh, at home, with the wife. It's a great excuse when you've got a wife, Giles. Covers a multitude of peccy-dildoes, that does. All you have to say to your Dorises is "Sorry, couldn't make it, I had to stay in with the wife'', and it's no enquiries postulated. In fact, if it wasn't for the wife, Giles, I don't know how I'd manage to have all these affairs. In fact, if I wasn't married, I'd probably end up monogamous.'

Giles attempted to wrap his mind around the concept. It was computer logic, and there was undeniably a certain sense to it, but it was logic taken to extremes and thus rendered completely illogical.

'You drinking at lunchtime?' Roy asked.

So that was why he had come over.

'It's not Friday though,' Giles said. He and Roy usually had a pub lunch or went to a wine bar on Fridays. Coming back to the office a bit fuzzy-headed didn't seem to matter much on a Friday afternoon, when not a lot of work got done anyway.

'No, but I've got to meet Doris Two on Friday,' Roy said, 'so I thought you might fancy a half today instead.'

'Em . . . I would,' Giles said, 'but I've got to –' He hesitated as the words died in his mouth. Dust and ashes. Dust, ashes and dry cream crackers, nor any drop to drink.

If the truth be told.

Well, actually, Roy, I've first got to visit the post office to see about setting up a perfectly legal but totally illicit box number for the receipt of various and sundry correspondence, the exact, precise and anticipated nature of which I won't reveal just at this moment, if you don't mind. And once that's done, I then have to make my way round the corner to the offices of *Scene Around*, the well-known city listings and small-ads magazine, where I intend to place a personal advertisement. I won't say what it is, Roy, but you may surmise that I am of the mind to make friends and strike up new acquaintances, and possibly even influence people with the view to coming to bed with me. Now, you won't mention that to the wife, will you, Roy? Or to any of the Dorises?

No, I thought so.

Yes, I knew I could trust you.

And to make doubly sure that I can trust you, I'm going to tell you bugger all.

'Sorry, Roy, I've got to meet the wife.'

19

'Ah! Fair enough.'

Roy certainly knew his business. A wife was a damn fine alibi in matters of mendacity and deception. Why, if you didn't have a wife, you wouldn't even have anyone to be unfaithful to.

Computer logic.

Chop, chop.

'Well, we'll probably have to skip it this week, as I can't make Friday.'

'Next week then,' Giles suggested. 'Or maybe a game of squash. Thursday?'

Yes, maybe a game of squash. Perhaps he could sneak another look at Roy's plonker in the showers, just to reassure himself that it wasn't any bigger than his own, and that he therefore had no reason to doubt his ability to tackle what lay ahead. If Roy's bunch of keys could turn the lock, then there was no reason why Giles's couldn't cope equally well.

'Aye, aye. Hide your gusset. Here she comes.'

Giles looked up. Weaving her way through the work stations, apparently heading towards his section, was the power-suited and artificially broad-shouldered figure of Lavinia Stephenson. She had a file of documents in her hand and as she passed the desks around her, she glanced at the workers sitting by them, and the work-in-progress upon them, with the air of a master chef who surveys menial underlings chopping up vegetables in readiness for the banquet she is soon to prepare.

Roy followed her progress inconspicuously, with semi-averted eyes.

'Ballbreaker,' he muttered to Giles out of the corner of his mouth. Giles waited for the inevitable embellishment. 'Ballbreaker. A real gonadgripper that one. I bet she knows how to squeeze the scrotum. I don't know about her husband, she probably did for him with the potato peeler and carries it round on her key ring as a lucky souvenir.'

There was a certain amount of career-envy in Roy's voice, but his description was not completely inaccurate.

Lavinia – though it was hard to imagine it now – had started off as a punch-card girl. One of those very same, with the thin summer dress and discernible panties. But unlike many of the others, she was curious about computers, and began to work her way up from punch-card girl to computer operator to programmer to systems analyst to section head to departmental leader.

No panties were visible now. Just power dressing from Jaeger and Austin Reed. Or maybe there simply were no panties, maybe they had been dispensed with. That was the frightening thing. Perhaps she no longer bothered with them – Lavinia had that air about her.

It was all a bit like the peasant's revolt. There was Roy and there was Giles, the natural heirs to the throne of the computer department, who had been usurped by this forceful and self-made woman who had fought her way up from the ranks.

Once it had been, 'Here you are, Lavinia. Could you have these ready by four o'clock?' and not so much as a 'please'. But now the shoe was on the other foot. (*The garter's round the other leg now, old mate*, as Roy would feel compelled to say.) Now it was Lavinia who came up to them and demanded that they have it ready by four o'clock, with not so much as a 'if you can manage'.

In an obscure and cryptic sort of way, Giles felt that it was women like Lavinia who explained all the Dorises. The Dorises were Roy's revenge, his way of getting his own back on all the women who had risen to positions of seniority which once would have been naturally his by virtue of his genitalia.

Meritocracy – there was something so unfair about it.

What about the rest? The ones who had no merit to speak of? Why should they be denied? There should be a new social movement – Mediocrity's Lib. Time-serving Mediocrities of the World Unite! You have nothing to lose, as your promotional prospects are nonexistent anyway.

But meantime, there were Roy's affairs to keep him going. He was like the child at the back of the class, the one fate has not chosen for distinction, and who therefore occupies his hours with extra-curricular activities.

*   *   *

21

'Giles.'

'Yes!'

There was a snap-to-attention tone to Lavinia's voice.

'Giles –'

'Yes?'

At ease.

'How's the design of that system coming along?'

'Fine, fine, fine.' A moment of uncertainty and hesitation. 'Em – which one?'

'The stock control of course! What else?'

'Oh, that one, yes, of course, yes. Fine. Just working on the flow charts.'

'Can I see?'

It wasn't a question, of course. It was a command that just happened to come with a question mark.

Gimme! Gimme now! That was the subtext.

Giles reluctantly moved his elbow away from the flow chart he had drawn. Lavinia looked at it, starting at the top and working her way down through the structure of decisions and logic, until she came to the decision box which Giles had drawn as a pair of panties, and to which Roy had so kindly added a gusset.

'What's this?'

'It's DO YOU NEED TO REORDER,' Giles said.

'Do you need to reorder? A pair of panties? With a gusset? I thought this system was for canned goods?'

'Well, it was . . .' What? Knickers in a tin, maybe?

'It was what?'

He had been about to say it was Roy's gusset, but decided that there was no sense in dragging him into it too.

'It was – a mistake. A doodle – you know.'

'A doodle?'

'Yes, Lavinia, just, a doodle.'

Giles felt himself go red. How far away were those punch-card days. Who'd ever have thought that little Lavinia, with her thin summer dress, and the outline of her –

'Giles, how old are you? Forty?'

'Not quite.'

'Thirty-eight?'

'Thereabouts.'

'You are a section leader, Giles, a section leader in this department, and what do you spend your mornings doing? Drawing panties on your flow charts! Well, it's a bit early for the male menopause, Giles, or is it just puberty coming late?'

Roy was right. A ballbreaker. Giles could all but feel his starting to crack. He gave a shamefaced shrug and said feebly, 'Well, you know how it is.'

Lavinia put a clean piece of paper down in front of him. 'Perhaps you could do it again,' she said. 'This time without the lingerie?'

'Of course,' Giles said. 'Slip of the pen, that was all.'

'Mere slide of the pencil,' Roy said. 'You know how it is.'

'No, I don't,' Lavinia said. 'I'm afraid. And what might I ask are you supposed to be doing, Roy?'

'Gussets,' he said, startled to be suddenly asked a question.

'Gussets!' Lavinia said.

'That is – systems! Systems support,' Roy said, 'or gussets, as I call it.'

Lavinia looked at him witheringly. 'Perhaps you should get back to your own section, Roy,' she said, 'and get on with some work.'

'Yes, right, fine. Just came over to ask Giles something.'

Perhaps you'll get back to your own desk, Roy, and stop disrupting the rest of the class.

Giles felt hot and embarrassed, as much for Roy as for himself.

If you act like schoolboys, I shall treat you like schoolboys.

It wasn't said, but it didn't need to be. Roy nodded to Giles and shuffled back to his desk, like a dunce heading for the nearest available corner.

This was what it was all about. Giles saw it clearly. Because they weren't boys, they were men. It was all about the affirmation of masculinity in what was increasingly a woman's world. And maybe a man didn't automatically get the bigger wage packet and the better job now. But he could still bag his share of Dorises before he died. Rich man, poor man, beggar man, thief, salary man and manual worker. It didn't matter how much you earned or the nature of your occupation. Truth, unfaithfulness, betrayal, infidelity – none of these really came in to it. It was the simple assertion of the primeval masculine values of polygamy and promiscuity, and the right to have a harem. It was all part of the desperate search for identity. That's what Roy's Dorises gave him – a sense of worth, of value, of going forward, of being someone.

And that was a feeling which Giles hadn't had in a long time.

THREE

It was with a lighter heart that Giles stepped out into the crowded lunchtime high street and made his way to the post office.

Inside, a conga of would-be customers waited their turn for attention, queuing by a zigzag of ropes. A video screen at the head of the queue regaled them with advertisements for pensions, retirement plans, Saga holidays, stairlifts and discreet remedies for incontinence.

'You're next!' a voice called, and it almost sounded like a prophecy. Giles received a peremptory nudge in the back with an umbrella handle and made his way to the position that was free.

'Yeeearse?' the woman behind the counter yawned, displaying a set of teeth, the shape of which customarily denoted gormlessness in their owner.

'I'd like . . .' he felt himself colouring already. Bugger this sensitivity. There was a long way to go yet and far greater deceptions to be perpetrated than this. If he was going to blush all the time at the drop of a hat (*At the fall of a fez, old mate, ha, ha!*) he'd never even get started.

'Yeeearse?' Goofy repeated.

'I'd like to take out a box number,' Giles said.

The clerk looked at him blankly.

'A box of what numbers?'

'No, a box number. A post office box number. A post office box number to which letters may be sent and which I may then collect.'

'Why?'

'Pardon?' Giles said.

'Why do you want a box number?'

'To be frank, I don't see that's any of your business.'

'Haven't you got a door? With a letterbox?'

'Of course I've got a door with a letterbox!'

'Then why do you need a post office box number when you've got a perfectly good letter box? Unless you've got something to hide!'

'I haven't got anything to hide. I simply wish to make enquiries about a box number.'

'Oh, make enquiries,' the woman said. 'Yes, it starts with *you* making enquiries, and it ends with *other people* making enquiries, I shouldn't wonder.'

People in the queue were starting to stare. Giles felt hot and uncomfortable.

'I just happen to be asking on behalf of a friend, as a matter of fact!' he announced, in rather too loud a voice.

'Oh, friend, yes, a *friend*,' his toothy adversary said. And the way she said friend made the whole concept of friendship sound positively lewd.

'Well?' said Giles. He had come this far and he would stand his ground. 'How do I go about getting a post office box number then?'

'You'll have to go to the Royal Mail,' the woman told him.

'This *is* the Royal Mail, isn't it!' Giles said. He didn't even need to look at his watch. He knew instinctively. It was exasperation time.

'No, it isn't,' Goofy gleefully explained. 'This is Post Office Counters. You can't get a post office box number at the post office, you have to get it at the Royal Mail.'

'Then why is it called a post office box number then?' Giles demanded. 'Why isn't it called a Royal Mail box number?'

'Because that would only confuse people,' the woman said.

'What do you think *this* is doing?' Giles almost screamed. 'I only came in for a box number. I didn't want a mental breakdown! I can get one of those at home!'

'Sorry, you'll have to go to the sorting office,' she said. 'You go and see them, they'll soon have you sorted. Just tell them that you feel a bit out of sorts.'

'Oi, get a move on!' a man in the queue shouted rudely. 'I want to cash me giro before it goes mouldy!'

'Right. Thanks for your help,' Giles muttered, and he didn't just inject sarcasm into his voice, he gave it an overdose. But did she notice? Did she ever.

'You're welcome,' the woman smiled, 'glad to be of assistance. Next!'

And Giles was on his way.

He didn't have time to go to the sorting office as well during his lunch hour, so he rang them from the office.

'That's not a personal call, is it, Giles?' Lavinia asked, as she also returned, closely followed by Roy, who made suggestive, buttock-grabbing gestures behind her, which would probably have resulted in the immediate termination of his contract, had Lavinia had eyes in the back of her head.

'No,' Giles lied. 'Just following up on some correspondence.'

'Ah, right, fine. Because all personal calls must be logged, you know, and paid for.' And Lavinia went on her way, pausing only to look at the calendar on Roy's work station. It seemed rather incongruous for him, being a *Cuddly Kittens* calendar, with a photograph of different cuddly kittens for each month of the year.

'That's better,' she said. 'Much better. Nothing there to offend anyone.'

Well, plenty there to offend anyone with artistic and aesthetic sensibilities, but nothing of a controversial nature, certainly.

The war of the calendars had begun shortly after Christmas. Roy had a friend in the car trade who had given him a present of an old-fashioned, out-and-out sexist, romper-stomper of a calendar. G-stringed lovelies with breasts that could feed multitudes cavorted about on tractor tyres, or gazed longingly at suggestively-held radiator hoses with half-open, glycerined lips. He had hung it up on the inside of the partition which divided his work station from the rest of the office. Lavinia had spotted it within the hour.

'That's disgusting.'

'It's a bit of fun.'

'It's demeaning to women.'

'Says who?'

'It's got to come down.'

'No it hasn't'

'It's offensive to the women in this office.'

'It's inside my work station. Personal consumption only. I'm the only one who can see it.'

'What about the cleaners?'

Roy pointed to a lovely on a tractor tyre. 'That *is* one of the cleaners!'

'I'll go to management.'

'Do what you like.'

Lavinia hadn't gone to management however. She had gone to a nearby branch of Adult Books and had returned to the office with the aptly named *Fun Girl's Calendar of Whopper Choppers*, and she had pinned it up on her work station wall, at the head of the office.

All – or at least most – of the women had thought it was great. It was sauce for the gander all right, and chilli-hot at that.

But it gave rise to a certain air of ribaldry. There were sexist and downright offensive remarks. Comparisons, while odious, were inevitable.

After a few days of this, Roy summoned a meeting of the other male analysts and programmers.

'A joke's a joke,' he said, 'and a laugh's a laugh, and there's nothing wrong with a bit of fun. But you can go too far. And pictures up on the wall of blokes in the buff with plonkers on them the size of elephants' trunks – nigh big enough to pick up buns with – is going far too far, in my opinion.'

'I can't concentrate,' Chris from development said.

'I'm getting an inferiority complex,' said Brian from operations. 'It's degrading to men.'

'I don't mind it, myself,' Donald, one of the freelance programmers, said.

'That's only cause you're a homo!' Brian said.

'So?' Donald said. 'You asked my opinion, didn't you?'

Both calendars – girls with tractor tyres and men with big ones – were anonymously defaced over the next few days, with the unsubtle additions of extra appendages or the removal of existing ones. Finally Roy and Lavinia agreed on a truce and the calendars were taken down. Lavinia replaced hers with *English Country Gardens*. And Roy had got *Cuddly Kittens* for half price.

But only a few short years ago, *Girls With Tractor Tyres* would have gone up on the wall automatically, and no one would have complained about anything.

It was one more field of masculinity turned over to the plough.

Giles got through to the Royal Mail.

'Hello, Customer Service, Belinda speaking, how can I help you?'

Giles wondered if she'd like an affair. It would save a lot of money. He wouldn't need to advertise then, or go to all the bother and expense of a box number. He opened his mouth to ask her, but no, he didn't have the nerve.

'I'd like to enquire about a post office box number please.'

'Certainly, sir. For letters only – it would be letters only?'

He hoped so.

'For letters only, it will be fifty pounds for a year or forty pounds for six months. You can collect your correspondence from here at the sorting office on the production of your authority card, which we shall issue on receipt of your cheque. Would you like us to send you an application form?'

'Yes, please.'

'To where shall we send it?'

He almost gave her his home address.

Wheels within wheels.

Boxes within boxes.

It isn't a tangled web we weave, when first we practise to deceive. Rather we assemble a Russian doll, with one little old babushka inside another.

Chicken, egg, chicken, egg, chicken, egg, chicken.

Or is it egg?

On face?

He really needed a box number to which they could send his application form for a box number. He could hardly have it sent to his home. Holly would open it, sure as anything.

'Giles –'

'Umm?'

'Funny thing, but this form came this morning, addressed to us – well, you really – a form about opening up a post office box number.'

'Did it? Did it really? How odd, strange and peculiar. Must be some mistake, officer.'

'Shall I return it?'

'No, just chuck it in the bin.'

The truth was that in order to properly cover your tracks, you had to start planning your deceptions from an early age – preferably from birth. It was best to come into the world under an assumed name, with a collection of plastic hospital ID tags round your skinny wrist and a complete spectrum of birth certificates.

By the time you left school, you should have acquired several false driving licences, a useful selection of passports, a box of false moustaches, and have opened bank accounts under a variety of aliases with all the major banks.

It was the only way.

Then, armed with all the tools of fraudulent behaviour, you could deceive your partner with a clear conscience and with every consideration for his or her feelings.

What hope was there for honesty in relationships when deceit was such a complicated business. There ought to be safeguards to preserve the institution of marriage, and the issuance of a free and anonymous post office box number to every citizen would be a good start.

'Better send it to me here,' Giles said into the phone, 'at my place of business.' And he gave the office address. 'And better mark it *Personal*,' he added, 'just in case.'

'Certainly, sir,' said Belinda, 'we'll pop that in the post for you straight away.'

Pop it in the post.

Was Giles imagining it, or was there something suggestive about those words? Didn't they conjure up images of voluptuous, but softly-spoken widows, whose kitchens smelt of freshly baked cakes, muttering to you in the morning, 'You stay where you are, I'm just off to pop it in the post'. Or the oven. Or the fridge. Or wherever it was they popped it.

And then they would slip out of bed.

Slip out of bed.

Was Giles imagining it, or was there something erotic about those words? *Slip* out of bed. Slip, slipping, slippery. Weren't these words the very vocabulary of sex? Just *slip* these off. Just *slip* into something more comfortable. Just *slip* my hand under here. Oh, my, isn't it slippery.

It almost made your mouth water.

Made your mouth water.

Was it Giles's imagination or was there –

'All right, Giles?'

Slap!

Roy got him jovially between the shoulder blades.

'Here you are, mate. Got you a cup of coffee.'

He put a dun-coloured plastic cup of lukewarm liquid down on Giles's papers.

'Thanks!' Giles said. He moved the cup and mopped up the spillage with a tissue. Roy had left a ring on his new flow chart. He couldn't be bothered to start a new one so he just put it on the radiator to dry off.

'Whoops, sorry mate! Mucky pup. Bit of an unclean kitty-cat there, eh?'

What did they see in him? What *did* they see in him?

'Good lunch then?'

'What?' Giles looked at him.

'Lunch. With the missus. Meeting the missus for lunch, weren't you?'

'Oh, yes, fine thanks Roy, fine.'

Roy pulled up a chair and sat down uninvited. He sat on it the way cowboys did in old westerns, when they twisted the chair round, made the back the front, and leant on it for effect.

'Never guess what,' Roy said.

'What?'

'Had lunch on my own.'

'What, in the canteen?'

'No, decided to go out. Just for a half. So I went into The Plume, you know, where we usually go, and got a drink and the mutton curry, and looked for somewhere to sit down.'

'Yes?'

'And there's this woman at a table, on her own. So I ask if I can sit down, and we get to chatting, and –' *No, no. Please god, don't let it be. It would be too unfair. One more injustice in an unjust world.* ' – and so there we are, chatting away, and I suddenly think – why don't I ask her out? So I do. And she says yes. Yes, mate. So I reckon I'm in there! If you ask me, mate, I think I've found her!'

Found who, Roy? Miss Right?

But no, it wasn't Miss Right, was it. It wasn't Miss Right at all. In fact, Giles knew exactly who it was going to be, long before Roy told him.

'Doris Number Four, mate, I reckon it's Doris Number Four!'

He'd soon have one for every day of the week.

Sickening.

Quite sickening.

Giles would definitely have to get another look at Roy's tackle in the squash club showers. There must be something special about it.

Maybe he'd painted it blue.

FOUR

Softly softly.

That was the catchee monkey way.

There was no point in Giles blundering into this new world of sexual adventures and infidelities and leaving clues all over the place as to where he might have gone.

Making his way home on the train that night he congratulated himself on the double box number ploy. To his knowledge, it was a method which had not been used before, but which was perfect for covering all tracks. It was worthy of Frederick Forsyth and *The Day of the Jackal.*

In fact, the post office box number system was nothing but a fornicator's charter. And viewing it as a would-be fornicator, Giles could only approve.

Once he had got his post office box number in operation, he would then go down to *Scene Around* and put his ad into the personal columns, and he would pay for another box number there. Those responding to his magazine advertisement would then write in to the magazine box number. Once the magazine had received these replies, they would, under Giles's instructions, forward them on to his post office box number, and Giles would go along and collect them in due course.

It was foolproof, and, as far as he could see, undetectable. He would have two levels of protection against discovery. It made things as safe as if you were wearing two condoms – with spermicide.

Condoms!

Giles made a mental note. He would have to buy some. He and Holly had been using other means of contraception since the birth of their second and last child.

I would like another one, Giles, but I don't think I could stand the pregnancy.

Nor me, Giles agreed. He couldn't stand another pregnancy either. Nor another three years of sleepless nights.

Holly had gone back on to the pill for a while, and then they had tried various other methods of contraception, including the cap, the coil, and turning their backs on each other for six months.

Giles knew that all marriages went through the odd bad patch, but how long was a patch supposed to be? Six months seemed rather on the large side for a patch. With patches that size you were getting to the stage where it would be better to throw the old patched one away and get a new tyre.

But normal relations had ultimately resumed.

Once or twice a week plus extras.

'I never thought I'd end up as a manual worker!' Holly would say, as she helped Giles relieve himself of his mid-week frustrations.

It was her little joke.

Intercourse was more of a week-end, Friday or Saturday night thing, when they had more time for it and Holly felt she could relax.

'Somehow, Giles, I just can't seem to relax until I know I've done the ironing.'

And then it was the kitchen as well.

'Somehow, Giles, I just don't seem to enjoy it until I know I've done the ironing and put some bleach down the sink.'

Then the vacuuming.

'Somehow, Giles, I just don't seem able to enjoy sex these days until I've done the ironing, put bleach down the sink, vacuumed the carpets, got rid of the cobwebs – we must buy a new feather duster – wiped down the surfaces, and hung up all the coats.'

Soon, the way things were going, she'd have to repaint the entire house first as well.

Sex, therefore, had become an increasingly protracted affair, in which an hour-and-a-half of housework had taken the place of foreplay.

It was no wonder, really. It was no wonder at all. It was no wonder he was thinking of having an affair. The only wonder was that he hadn't thought of it sooner.

The reason Giles left it to Holly to ensure that no further children were born was because he had suddenly developed a severe allergy to condoms.

He didn't know what caused it exactly, whether he had developed an aversion to latex rubber, or some other reason, but one night, a few hours after making love, he had woken up with the most horrendous itch in his private parts. He had given them a good scratch and fallen back to sleep, only to wake an hour later to find that his penis had swollen to about four times its normal size. He put on the bedside light and shook Holly awake to get her to look at it.

'Look,' he said. 'Look at the size of that!'

'No, really, Giles, not at the moment, I've got to get up at seven.'

'No, no! Something's happened to it. Look – it's all swollen and red and itchy, and it's throbbing like a bus at the traffic lights.'

'You'd better go to the doctor's.'

'Yes, right.'

He went there first thing and sat uncomfortably in the waiting room with a newspaper on his lap, to disguise the true extent of the problem and to prevent any misunderstandings. After forty minutes, Doctor Moorhead (*Please, call me Jim*) summoned him in, and, after some humming and hawing, Giles presented him with the problem.

'Yes, now, that is a big one,' Doctor Moorhead agreed. 'I've not seen many like that, not in twenty-five years of practice.'

'Do you know what it is?' Giles asked, anxious that it might have to be amputated.

Dr Moorhead looked at it for a second.

'Yes,' he said. 'It's a penis.'

He was definitely one of the old school.

He hesitated. Maybe he was going to send out for a second opinion. No. He picked up a pencil and poked at the problem with the blunt end.

'Do you use condoms?'

'Yes, sometimes,' Giles admitted, not sure that it was quite the married thing.

'Hmm. Could be you're allergic to them. Try it without.'

'But we don't want any more children,' Giles said. 'We've got two already, and I almost cracked up with the first one.'

'Try an alternative method.'

'Like what?' Giles said. What was Dr Moorhead thinking of? A rubber band and a plastic bag? Was Giles allergic to clingfilm? Not that he knew of.

'Maybe your wife could go on something. Or perhaps you could become Catholics.'

'That's a bit drastic, isn't it?' Giles said. 'Catholicism?'

'Well, it's up to you, of course,' Dr Moorhead said, 'but going by the look of that thing, if you carry on with what you're using, there's a good chance that it might explode. Maybe you'd better put it away now.' Dr Moorhead obviously didn't want it exploding on his desk. 'I leave it entirely up to you Mr West, but I can certainly tell you that it's the only one you've got. And if anything happens to that one, you're not likely to get another in a hurry. At least not on the National Health.'

'Thanks,' Giles said. 'I'll think about it.' And he made himself decent and went on his way.

As he left Dr Moorhead's surgery and the door closed behind him, he heard Dr Moorhead barking into his intercom which connected to the waiting room, 'Next!'

Next.

Just like this afternoon with the woman behind the post office counter. That was how it was these days, get rid of one member of the public as quickly as you could, and then on to the –

Next!

So Holly had gone back on the pill for a while, and Giles had put his condoms down the waste disposal unit in the kitchen. He could simply have thrown them into the bin, but Ella or Lyn took the lids off everything, and he wanted to avoid answering as many awkward questions as possible.

The condoms broke the unit however and they had to get a plumber round. He had dismantled the unit and cleaned it out.

'Seems to be something rubbery in here,' he said. 'And bits of packets. With Durex written on them.'

'Kids,' Giles said. 'You know how it is!'

Not to the point of putting your Durex down the waste disposal unit, the plumber's expression seemed to say. I wouldn't let my kids do that! But his lips, like his bath taps, remained sealed.

Once off the condoms Giles's condition rapidly improved, and he was back to normal by the end of the week.

'Not so big now, is it?' Holly said, peering at it through her contact lenses. 'In fact, you forget how small it is, really. That is, I don't mean small, Giles, it isn't small, I just mean – you know – not as big as it was.'

Just to ensure that it really was the condoms that were doing it they used one a few weeks later, with exactly the same result. Worse, if anything. Giles's reaction was even more dramatic. The itch kept him awake till dawn, the swelling was twice what it was the first time, and there was also a florid rash, which travelled north as far as his navel and south as far as his knees.

'You look like one of those surfers, in the long funny shorts,' Holly said.

'Never again,' Giles said. 'That's the last time the London Rubber Company gets any change out of me.'

The train rattled on into the Home Counties. Its swaying motion was soporific, and Giles felt himself unwind and relax.

He should be worried, really. His allergy to contraception would be a serious obstacle in the way of any infidelity. It would be a dead and absolute giveaway. Holly would only need to take one look at it and she'd know instantly what he'd been up to.

Yet Giles wasn't worried. He felt at ease, sanguine, optimistic. Condoms must have come a long way since he'd last used one. Who knew – maybe they were making them out of new materials now. Maybe you could get them in an aerosol and just spray them on. Perhaps he'd give a different brand a go. He might not be so allergic to them. He'd maybe try a packet of Jimmy's. Jimmy's was the latest brand of condom to appear on the chemist's counter. Jimmy's were promoted not only as a means of avoiding unwanted pregnancies and reducing the transmission of diseases, but also as a philanthropic enterprise – Jimmy's had been launched by a socially-minded entrepreneur who generously donated all profits from sales of the condoms to the financing of daily drop-in centres for single mothers.

Yes, Giles would lash out on a couple of Jimmy's and see what effect they had on him. He could even tell Holly about it. She'd have no reason to be suspicious. He'd tell her that he was trying to shoulder his share of the nuptial burden.

'You could always have a vasectomy,' she'd said to him once.

But Giles had a dread of the knife. Especially down there. What if the surgeon sneezed when he was midway through the operation? Or was just about to do the delicate bit when he suddenly developed hiccups, and Giles ended up with chopped pork?

No. Giles didn't want to risk it. He didn't want his gonads looking as though they'd been through the office paper shredder, thank you very much. No, he'd stick to the old-fashioned, user-friendly, low-tech methods.

He didn't want hands-on in this instance.

Hands-off was fine.

The train stopped at the station and Giles walked to his car. He kept an old, battered Mini for the run between his house and the station car park. Holly used the decent car to get herself to her part-time job and to take the children to school.

When he got in Ella was in the bath and Lyn was doing homework. They had got beyond the stage of being pleased to see him when he got home. Once, and not so long ago, they had run to the front door at the sound of his key and jumped up and put their arms around him and clung around his neck.

They had even fought and argued and cried sometimes for the privilege of his attention.

'Me, me! You're not doing that to me!'

'I want to sit on daddy's knee!'

'It's my turn!'

But now, alas, such times were over. It was the monosyllabic reception now.

'Hello, Ella!'

Grunt.

'Good day?'

Grunt.

'Hello, Lynnie.'

Mutter.

'Good day?'

Mutter, mutter.

The eyes turned heavenward. The please-go-away. The wanting to tell him everything had turned into the need for secrets and the search for self and the wanting to tell him nothing.

How sad.

Or was it?

How often, when they were small, had he tried to extricate himself from their now greatly missed embraces? How often, when they had demanded his attention, had he wanted them only to go away and leave him in peace with the remote control and his drink and his paper?

And now his wishes had come true. And of course they were sand and ashes, vinegar and sawdust, call it what you would. You couldn't wait for today to be over. And yet tomorrow, you would long for it back, with a full, nostalgic and sentimental heart.

'Hello!'

'Hi!'

He went into the kitchen where Holly was sitting reading a magazine while food cooked in the oven.

'How was your day?'

'Fine. Get a paper?'

'Yes, here.'

Every night, the same. One night he wouldn't bring the paper. What then? Riot, famine, pestilence and commotion.

Every night, everywhere, in how many houses, in how many kitchens? Men to women, women to men. *Hello, hi, how was your day? Did you get a paper? Hello, hi, how was your day? Fine, yours? Did you get a paper?* Variations on an invariable theme.

It was no wonder people had affairs. And, in a way, infidelity had nothing to do with it. It wasn't lack of love, it was lack of life.

Get a life!

Some strange expressions came out of America, somehow able to encapsulate in a few words the longings and undercurrents of a whole society. All the things that bubbled under the surface.

We should all have a life.

Or get one.

That was the problem. Giles didn't feel that he had a life any more.

Been there, done that, get a life.

Yes. Only how? Join an evening class? Join a gym? Learn the piano? Take up country dancing? But that was all sublimation, all of it. Every hobby and interest was but one thing: a substitute for sex with strangers.

And that even included gardening. All that spade work. Nudge, nudge. Say absolutely no more. We all get your meaning.

The girls had already eaten, so Holly and Giles ate alone at the kitchen table. Holly worked part time in a local clothes shop as a colour co-ordinator. She sized people up according to a number of criteria taken from a manual, told them what colours suited them best, and then hopefully sold them a large number of expensive items in their particular shade of suitability.

They talked together about their days. It was almost like the quiet murmuring of monks, Giles thought, in a strange, mixed and almost sexless religious order. Brother Giles and Sister

Holly. He back from the hives and the honey-making, she back from her labours in the convent laundry, sitting, murmuring together about this and that and nothing in particular.

All passion spent.

Or maybe not so much spent, as safely lodged in the building society, and presently unobtainable, but hopefully accumulating interest. That was what Giles needed, to make a small withdrawal from his passion account.

As they ate and talked, Giles studied her face. It was a nice face. He had always liked it, from the first day he had seen it, all those years ago. A nice face and a nice figure. A little lined, a little less firm, but still – very nice.

Tasty.

He checked himself. What a word to come into his mind. Tasty. It made her seem like a lamb chop.

Of course, she didn't know. How could she know? There he was playing his part, chatting as on any other day, while he was actually plotting and scheming her betrayal and his own infidelities. For a moment he wanted to tell her, wanted to explain that he still loved her and always would, that all this came from somewhere else, that it was really nothing personal. But how could you?

When it came to their husbands sleeping with other women, some wives just simply weren't very understanding. They seemed to take it so personally. That it meant there was something wrong with the marriage itself.

Women. They just didn't understand.

Believe me, Holly, this really doesn't mean anything. And if I could stop myself, I would.

But I can't.

While they were having coffee, Ella and Lyn came in to say goodnight. For once, they were both in good humours and devoid of complaint, and they weren't fighting or bickering. They hugged and kissed Giles as they said goodnight, and Holly watched and smiled. And Giles smiled back.

He felt like Judas. Betraying family life, hearth and home for the sake of thirty bonks – if he could get them. Thirty bonks though, imagine, thirty bonks with thirty different women. Yes, first let's have the thirty bonks. He could go and hang himself with a halter later.

There was plenty of time for remorse. That's what old folks' homes were for, weren't they? And better to regret what you had done than what you hadn't.

Sins of omission. Now Giles knew what that meant. It meant all the sins you had omitted.

Yes, he did feel a little guilty, he did feel a little sad. But he knew that tomorrow morning his application form for his post office box number would be on his desk. And then he would go and put his advertisement in *Scene Around*. And buy a packet of Jimmy's.

Yes, he did feel very sorry about everything. He felt terribly sorry about everything that was going to happen.

But he wasn't going to stop.

FIVE

The next morning when he arrived at the office, a letter in an envelope marked Royal Mail was waiting on his desk. Giles opened it surreptitiously and took out a document headed Private Boxes, which was stapled to an application form for a box number. He quickly filled in the form, wrote out a cheque, put it in the reply envelope so thoughtfully provided, and then dropped the envelope into the mail tray.

Then he took it out.

On second thought, he'd post that one personally. Or better still, take it round to the delivery office during his lunch hour and see if he couldn't sort the matter of a box number out in person.

Lavinia passed his desk, as brisk and brusque as ever.

'Giles.'

'Lavinia.'

And that was it.

Then Roy shuffled over, looking rather bleary, as if the weight of all the Dorises in the world was resting on his shoulders.

'I'm having a bit of a problem, old mate,' he said. 'Bit of a Doris problem to be honest.'

'Oh, yes,' Giles said. He found it hard to feel sympathetic towards Roy's Doris problems. It was rather like asking someone on Income Support to sympathize with the problems of the rich.

'That computer programme I wrote can't handle them. I only really designed it for three Dorises plus the wife. But now that I've got four Dorises plus the wife – five in total – it doesn't seem able to handle it.'

'You need an upgrade,' Giles suggested.

'Reckon I do, mate, reckon I do. Because it's mixing up all

my appointments, and I've had to go back on the manual ledgers, pro-tem as it were. If I'm not careful, I'm going to double book myself. And then it'll be the revenge of the Dorises, mate, no doubt about that. I'll have to write a new programme. Something able to handle up to ten, maybe twenty, Dorises at once.'

Roy looked at Giles as though a serious money-making thought had just come into his mind. 'You think I could sell that?' he said. 'You think I could market that as a commercial proposition? You know, for the ordinary PC user? I mean, there must be loads of blokes needing a bit of organizational help with the old bits on the side. The old tangled webs, eh, the old knotty spider silk, as I call it. What could I call it now? How about the Doris Manager? Yes. Pithy, succinct, to the point. *Manage all the Dorises in your life with Doris Manager. Avoid domestic friction and upset with Doris Manager. Doris Manager — for the Dorises in your life.* It sounds like a winner to me, mate. I'll get cracking on it straight away.'

What did they see in him?

What *did* they see in him!

Roy decided to work through his lunch hour on the Doris Project, as he had now christened it, so Giles was not obliged to make excuses as to why he couldn't go down to the pub.

He was instead free to make his way to the Royal Mail offices, where – despite her protests that it should all be done through the post – he managed to persuade a Mrs Simpkinson to issue him with his post office box number, then and there.

It was funny how the Royal Mail only wanted you to write to them. It was a bit like Telecom, only wanting you to ring them up.

'It's not a key,' she said, 'it's a card. You must produce your card every time, or we won't be able to give you your letters.'

'Fine,' said Giles. 'And I can start using it straightaway?'

'I don't see why not.'

'And it is . . . confidential?'

'As long as you're not doing anything illegal. I draw your attention to paragraph four, which states that "A private box will not be used for any illegal or fraudulent purpose".'

'Right,' said Giles. 'That's fine then.'

Fraudulent or illegal? Well, it wasn't either of those, exactly. More just sort of . . . immoral.

Armed with his new box number, Giles made his way along the mile and a half of streets which separated the Royal Mail from the back-alley offices of *Scene Around*, the listings magazine. His advertisement was at the ready in his wallet, *Happily married man seeks affair . . .*

He passed a branch of Millets on his way, and went in to buy a hat, the sort of anonymous, suicidal-green waxed cap which found favour with country walkers and horse trainers and blokes on the buildings. Having purchased one a size too large, to make sure that it could come down well over his ears and cover most of his forehead, he proceeded to the *Scene Around* building and pushed open a door marked Ads.

Giles had given considerable thought to the right medium for his message. He had toyed with the idea of a small ad in the *Guardian*, but thought maybe this would be casting the net too wide. Obviously he didn't want an affair smack bang on his doorstep, but he didn't want one in the Outer Hebrides either. It was certainly the *Guardian* reader he was aiming for though. Giles felt that something about the articles in the women's pages denoted a sexually-active and experimental readership. He felt there was a lack of inhibition there which wouldn't be found, say, among the readers of *The Times*, or the *Telegraph*.

He could be totally wrong, of course. In fact, often the more conservative a person's politics the more abandoned their sexual antics – a quick glance through Hansard would tell you that. But Giles did feel that it was more of a free spirit he was looking for, a bit of a liberal, the sort who would read the *Guardian* for the confirmation of their prejudices, or the sort who would subscribe to *Scene Around*.

Scene Around carried more than listings of what was on in and around the city, it also carried some very right-on film reviews, some right-on interviews with some right-on minor actors, some right-on politicking, and its editorials were invariably sympathetic to travellers, the homeless, free festivals, theories about corn circles, sex, drugs and rock'n'roll. Despite this, it also had a high middle-class readership, who maybe only took the magazine because it was as near to sex, drugs, or rock and roll as they ever got.

The only other paper Giles had momentarily thought about was the *Evening Argus and Star*. (*The Arse'n'Guts*, as Roy liked to call it.) This had a very popular and very full Lonely Hearts page, teeming every night with widows seeking solace and single men (52) who didn't mind a lady with children. It reached a wider audience than *Scene Around*, but possibly an audience that was less discerning.

'What a rag!' Roy liked to say, although he bought the paper at least three times a week. 'What a rag! I mean, who reads it! Who reads this stuff? I'll tell you who, mate – toenail-clippers, that's who. They only buy this paper so they can clip their toenails on it. It's a dog's bottom of a newspaper this.'

Well, that had more or less decided Giles. Whoever he ended up having this affair with, he certainly wasn't going to have it with a dog's bottom.

Giles put his cap on and pulled it down over his ears. Then he slanted the peak downwards, so that it hid most of his face from view. No one would recognize him in this. He pushed open the Ads door, and went in.

Business was lackadaisical, and if Giles had been worried about looking strange in his pulled down cap, he could have saved his anxiety. They were all weird. Customers and staff.

'I'd like to put an ad in for Tarot card reading,' a woman in rainbow-coloured leggings was saying to a man behind the counter, who had a tattoo on his nose reading PICK HERE. 'My husband's a farmer,' she added, irrelevantly. 'He's got a psychic tractor.'

'I'd like to put in an ad for a sex slave,' another customer (male) was saying. 'Preferably a non-smoker. But I don't mind if they're from Cardiff.'

Giles bucked up at the sound of this. He was clearly among friends. Why, compared to this lot he was almost normal.

'Next!'

There it was again. The call of the bureaucrat. The call of the counter clerk. The call of the conveyor-belt world.

'Next!'

'That's me, I think,' Giles said, going to a booth where a young woman in purple and black, with several layers of mascara and four earrings, all in the one ear, was waiting to do his bidding.

'I'd like to put one in!' Giles said in a loud voice. Confidence was all.

What had he said?

God. Sometimes confidence was too much.

'That is, I'd like to put an ad in – in your magazine.'

'Yes, sir. Which section?'

'Personals – please.'

'I'm sorry, sir, I can't quite hear what you're saying, the peak of your hat seems to be in the way.'

Giles tweaked it up a bit.

'Personal – please.'

'Oh, right. How many words?'

'Em – thirty-one.'

'Thirty-one. And what does the advertisement say, exactly?'

'I've got it here.'

Giles shoved his bit of paper across. The girl looked at it. 'You are supposed to write in on one of our forms, sir. Never mind, I'll copy it over.' She did so, quickly and efficiently, with no apparent interest in what it said. 'I'll just check it through with you sir, if I may.'

'Yes,' Giles said, keeping his voice low and throaty. 'Of course.'

'Are you all right, sir?'

'Yes, fine. Just a bit –'

He meant to say hoarse. He knew he did. He meant to say it. Why didn't he? But for some reason, for no reason, or maybe from pure nerves, he said, 'Yes, fine. Just a bit – deaf.'

Why had he said it? Why? He had twenty-twenty vision and twenty-twenty hearing to go with it. Why? Why!

'Don't worry, sir, I'll speak up. You tell me if I've got anything wrong.'

'No, really, it's all right, I –'

'So the advertisement you wish to insert reads –' and then she started to shout. 'WELL-GROOMED, PLEASANT-LOOKING, HAPPILY MARRIED MAN SEEKS PARTNER, 18 TO 55, FOR AFFAIR –'

May the end come now, Giles thought, may it all soon be over. Sweet hole in the ground, swallow me up. Sweet garden shovel, fill the hole in. Sweet grass seed, come and grow right here and eradicate all traces.

She went right on to the end, shouting out every last sordid, shameful detail for all the world to hear.

'PLEASE SEND PHOTOGRAPH. There, sir, is that right?'

'Perfect.' He was the colour of strawberries.

'How many insertions would you like, sir? It's three for the price of two just now.'

'Eh, right, sure, yes, why not, okay.'

Act nonchalant Giles, act nonchalant. What if they are all looking? A man's entitled to put a small ad into the personal columns, isn't he? They're all at it anyway. You're just being upfront about it, that's all.

'AND DO YOU WANT A BOX NUMBER WITH YOUR AD, SIR?' the girl screamed in his ear. 'IF SO, THAT'S ANOTHER FIVE POUNDS.'

'Yes, okay.'

'And where do you want the replies sent on to?'

'I've got a post office box number. I'd like the replies sent there.'

'Very well, sir. We'll send the box number replies on to your post office box number, if that's what you want. So that's £31.50 altogether, and here's a copy of our code of conduct. Your magazine box number will be 132. Thank you.'

Giles left the offices of *Scene Around* with the peak of his waxed hat pulled down so low it was like a drawn venetian blind. His face was cherry-coloured, with what was not so much a blush as a volcanic eruption of embarrassment.

It was all so sordid. So sordid. But why?

Why wasn't it sordid when other people did it? It wasn't sordid for Roy. More a way of life than anything. Yet sordidness had haunted Giles all his days. From the very start of his childhood, from the very depths of innocence.

Boys of his age would amble into the school toilets while Giles was fumbling to have a pee.

'Hello, Giles, how are you doing mate!' A bluff, matey slap on the back which practically sent him flying into the urinal. You really needed rubber gloves for that job.

'How are you, Giles! Okay? Coh, I tell you what though, Giles, I didn't half have a hell of a wank last night. Bloody hell, mate, you should have seen it. Shot right out the window, it did. Good job it was open, or I'd have broken the glass. I think me mam must have heard the bed creaking though. Is that you up there wanking? she says. I thought you were supposed to be getting on with your homework! I am getting on with me homework, I says. Yeah, sounds like it an' all, she says. Well, I can do both at the same time, I says. No you can't, she says, you'll make your books all sticky! If you want to go wanking, my boy, you save it up till Saturday, and do it in your own time! So what do you think of that then, eh, Giles? No wanking till the weekends. I mean, bloody hell, mate, it's a bit much, eh, or what? So have you had any good wanks lately then, Giles?'

But Giles's wanks had never been like that. They had somehow, through no fault of his own, taken on a furtive air of sad sinfulness, instead of the robust air of celebration of the quick-ones-off-the-wrist of his contemporaries.

Wanking wasn't discussed in Giles's house. Wanking wasn't admitted to. The place was full of inhibition and a false morality which managed to make natural things unnatural, and clean things dirty. Almost thirty years on now, the feelings of guilt and sordidness were still there. There was something in Giles's upbringing that had left him with the vague feeling that sex was somehow on a par with picking your nose in public.

Giles consulted his watch. He wasn't due back in the office for another ten minutes. Time to make a few more preparations. Time to get provisions in.

As he headed for the chemist's Giles browsed through the Personal Ad and Box Number Code of Conduct: Always arrange to meet in a well-lit place; tell someone where you are going; if possible, bring a friend.

Bring a friend? Threesomes even. Giles pulled his hat down a bit further, and licked his lips. He entered Brownstones, the Small Family Chemist, and looked around for a packet of Jimmy's.

Damn.

He should have gone to Boots, or even to the supermarket. A place where such transactions could remain anonymous. Just bung them into your basket, pay for them at the checkout, and away. These small cosy places were all right for the personal touch. But you didn't always want the personal touch. Sometimes all you wanted from a shop assistant was a little honest indifference.

Giles decided to leave it till another day, and turned to head for the door.

'Yes, sir. Can I help you?'

Double damn.

A tubby Asian man in a white coat with a name badge on it reading MR N. IQBAL blocked his escape route. Quite why Mr Iqbal had decided to call his shop Brownstones rather than Iqbal's was an open question, and one which Giles wasn't going to bother with right now.

Oh well, best get it over with. And he'd bought condoms before. It was all perfectly commonplace. It was the sordidness, the sordidness again. He really must try and overcome it.

'I'd like a packet of Jimmy's!' Giles said. Now how was that for hail-fellow-well-met?

A cloud of mystification crossed Mr Iqbal's face.

'Jimmy's what?'

'Jimmy's – condoms.'

'Oh, of course. Yes, yes, yes. Over here, sir. This way. Now, how many would you like?'

'Em –'

'Here we are, you see.' Iqbal led the way to a rotating display stand. 'Now, we have them in dozens, half-dozens, threes, or if you're trying to give up – ha, ha, ha! – in individual packets of one.'

'I'll take a dozen,' Giles said decisively. To hell with it. If he got the kind of replies to his advertisement that he anticipated, he'd need a dozen at the very least. Probably a gross.

'And what size, sir?'

'Pardon?'

'What size?'

Size. This was a new one on Giles. They had only ever come in one size in the days before his allergy developed. Size? When did this happen? 'Size? But I thought it was sort of . . . one size fits all?'

'Oh, no, no, sir. Not with Jimmy's. Jimmy's come in three sizes, sir, for a perfect fit every time. Now, what size are you, lengthwise, sir? Are you Huge, Massive, or Absolutely Enormous?'

'Em, well, probably just sort of, well, probably just sort of . . . Massive, really.'

'Massive, sir, yes. Me too. We only really sell the Absolutely Enormous to the younger fellows, don't you know. Now, in terms of the other dimensions, are you a Courgette, a Cucumber, or a Rolling Pin?'

'Em, well, a Cucumber, I suppose,' Giles said, translating Cucumber as medium.

'Okay. Here we are then, sir. One packet of twelve Massive Cucumbers.'

'Thank you,' Giles said.

'Anything else, sir?'

'Em – no, thank you.'

'Something for the weekend?'

'I'm sorry?'

'A packet of razor blades, sir?'

'No, I'm fine. There is one thing though. In the past, with other brands, I've tended to come out in a bit of a rash.'

'Ah, in that case sir,' Mr Iqbal said, taking the condoms from Giles's hand, and reaching for a differently-coloured packet, 'what you need is the hypoallergenic. Here you are, sir, that's what you want. One packet of Hypoallergenic Massive Cucumbers. Now, sir, do you need any help with fitting?'

'What?'

'Would you like to try one on in the fitting room?'

'Pardon? No, they'll be okay, I'm sure they'll be fine.'

Chemists with fitting rooms? What next?

Mr Iqbal pointed to a framed certificate up on the wall. It was headed Jimmy's and read *Mr N. Iqbal has completed the Jimmy's Condom Retailer's Course, and is a Registered Fitter and Condom Consultant. Ask about a regular service for best results.*

'Any problems,' he said, 'just give us a ring.'

'Thanks,' said Giles, 'I will.'

He paid for his purchases. Mr Iqbal handed him his change, together with a leaflet titled *The Jimmy's Condom Co. Customer's Charter. Jimmy's Condoms – Satisfaction Guaranteed. Your glands are safe in our hands.*

Satisfaction guaranteed. Rash promises. It was like walking round with a sign reading PLEASE SUE ME.

Giles didn't pretend to know a lot about the Trade Descriptions Act, but he would have hazarded a guess that putting satisfaction guaranteed on a packet of condoms was sticking your absolutely enormous, rolling pin-sized neck out and just asking for trouble.

'Thanks,' Giles said, 'thanks very much.'

'Thank you, sir. Good afternoon. And – enjoy yourself.'

Giles turned to leave the shop. Mr Iqbal smiled farewell at him.

Or had he winked?

Giles walked back to the office, reading the Jimmy's Condom Co. Code of Conduct. *This product has been electronically tested. Do not put on inside out. Keep away from heat. Do not use for balloon modelling. Do not use more than once.*

Do not use more than once? They needed to say that? Good god. Giles had heard of making economies, but how hard up did you have to be?

Hard up. Ha, ha.

As he passed a waste bin, he threw both leaflets away – the one from the magazine, and the one from the chemist's. Cover your tracks, polish away all fingerprints, leave no clues.

SIX

'Saw Doris Number Four last night.'

'What?'

Giles had not heard Roy approaching, and his guilt reflex made him slam shut the copy of *Scene Around* in which he had been gazing at his ad in the personal columns with a mixture of apprehension, wonder, and self-admiration.

'What's that you're reading?'

'Oh, nothing Roy, just seeing what's on.'

'What's on? You? You never go anywhere do you? When did you last bother with a baby-sitter?'

True, Roy, true. It did seem a long time ago.

'Anyway, never mind what's on, mate, it's what's coming off that's more interesting. Har, har!' Roy picked up the copy of *Scene Around* and turned, with the homing instinct of the constantly unfaithful, to the personal ads. 'Yes, I was out with Doris Number Four last night, old mate – I think I'm in love.'

Giles knew what that meant. It meant that Roy hadn't yet managed to get into bed with Doris Four, but had it planned for the very near future.

'Can I ask you something, Roy?'

'What?'

'Are you allergic to condoms?'

'Well, I couldn't say I like them. Dulls the sensation, you know. It's a bit like listening to music with earplugs in. Not that I'm saying you should go sticking condoms in your ears. Har, har. But allergic, no. I mean, you can't afford to take chances with your health, not these days. You can catch anything, anywhere. I sometimes say to myself, Roy, you're playing Russian roulette here with a loaded Doris. You never know, mate, you just never know.'

His eye scanned the personal columns and lighted, almost

instantly, on Giles's ad, which was having its first outing that very day.

'Ha! Look at this one! See this one, Giles, eh? Look, "Married man seeks partner, 18 to 85, for affair." 18 to 85, eh? Bloody hell!'

What? *18 to 85?* That wasn't right. They'd mucked his ad up. He'd be after them for a free insertion.

'Well, he's none too choosy, eh? I mean, nothing like casting the net wide! 18 to 85, you're practically on to necrophilia there if you ask me, eh, Giles? Har, har.'

What did they see in him? What did they –

'Must be pretty desperate though, eh?'

Yes, must be, Roy, more than probably. You could well be right there.

'Having to stick an ad like that in. When they're giving it away for nothing over the counter in Woolies. Dear, oh dear.'

Giles gave a thin, tight-lipped smile.

'Anyway, I came over to say I've been having a bit of success with the software,' Roy went on. 'The Doris Management Programme. It's really like computerized juggling you see, Giles. It's a matter of, like, keeping your balls in the air.'

Giles looked at him. Roy probably kept his balls in the air on quite a regular basis. The amount of taking off and putting on of trousers that Roy did, his balls probably got more of an airing in a fortnight than most people's did in a year. Roy probably had the best-aired balls in the neighbourhood.

'Excuse me – is that mine?'

Lavinia stood by them, like a headmistress in search of furtive schoolboys.

'Sorry?'

'My magazine. I left a copy of *Scene Around* on my desk, and it seems to have disappeared.'

'No,' Roy told her. 'It's his. Unless he nicked it. Har, har.'

He handed the magazine back to Giles, who went to put it away in a drawer of his desk.

'It is mine, but you can have a look at it if you want.'

'No, it's all right. It'll probably turn up. And anyway, I don't think anyone here is employed to read magazines during the firm's time.'

What a toady, Giles thought. Those who so diligently guarded the firm's time reminded him of those serfs in the Middle Ages who so carefully guarded the squire's keep, or the baron's money, not realizing whose side they were actually on, and conspiring in their own oppression.

'I was just putting it away.'

'Good. And why are you at Giles's desk anyway, Roy?'

'I came to borrow his pencil sharpener, Miss.'

For a second Lavinia's eyes flicked around, looking for a pencil sharpener on Giles's desk, then she realized it was sarcasm. She actually coloured; Giles had never seen her blush.

'Yes, very well. Perhaps we could all get on with some work.'

She hurried off in the direction of upper management, doubtlessly to confer on matters of importance. Roy and Giles watched her go.

'Nice arse,' Roy said. 'If you could get a grip on it.'

'Maybe,' Giles said ruefully.

'Anyway, I might be on to a bit of a between-the-sheets with Doris Four this weekend, old matey. I'll keep you posted.'

'Do,' Giles said. 'Do that.' Though the last thing he wanted to hear about was Roy's sexual exploits. What he wanted was a few of his own.

Roy returned to his section to add more touches to the Doris Management Programme. Giles slid open his desk drawer and looked at the magazine inside. He read and re-read his advertisement. Maybe, even as he read it, someone, somewhere, was putting pen to paper, *Dear Box 132, I am a twenty-two-year-old* –

Something wet landed on his flow chart.

Quickly, Giles grabbed a tissue from the box on his desk and wiped it away.

He was mortified to realize he had been dribbling.

Giles didn't want to seem too eager, so he left it a few days before going to pick up the mail from the post office.

A fat envelope awaited him, sent on from *Scene Around*.

'Sign here,' Lenny, the man behind the sorting office counter said, giving Giles a penetrating look. He seemed to suspect that the only citizens who took out post office box numbers, when they had a perfectly good letterbox at home, were those who were up to no good. He was a decent man, soured by public service, as so many are.

It was more by accident than design that the Royal Mail had managed to recruit a seriously dyslexic postman. But now that Lenny Pearson was on the payroll, it was nigh impossible to get rid of him without incurring the wrath of several powerful minority action groups, including Dyslexia in Action, with its famous slogan, 'Dyslexics of the world unite. You have nothing to lose but your chins.' It would also invite a test case for wrongful dismissal which was best avoided, for the legal profession now contained within its ranks as many discrimination chasers as it did ambulance chasers, skirt chasers and whisky chasers.

Nevertheless, dyslexia was obviously a major handicap for a man who delivered letters all day. Not only could Lenny not read street names properly, he had trouble with numbers and postcodes. Threes looked like eights, sevens looked like fours, and on his first day on the job, he only managed to get one letter through the correct letterbox, and that was by accident.

People were on the phone to the sorting office all day, and as soon as Lenny got back to base, the supervisor tackled him.

'I don't know what you're playing at, Pearson, but you'll just have to go back out, collect all the letters you misdelivered, and this time try and get the wood in the right hole! Got me?'

So back out Lenny went, collected the letters, sat on a bench, sorted them all out, and delivered them all over again.

This time, he didn't even get one in the right letterbox.

The supervisor sent him out again.

Lenny was still at it at midnight. The sight of a postman with his sack still delivering at midnight was a source of great mirth for late-night revellers. Lenny had realized by then that he was never going to get it right, so he simply emptied the contents of his sack into the nearest postbox, and went home to bed.

The next morning, he was up in front of the supervisor again. The supervisor had begun to suspect the nature of Lenny's complaint.

'Can you read, Pearson?'

'Yes and no, Mr Oliver, I just see things a bit differently. I'm all right when things are back to front or if I see them in a mirror, but straight on, it all looks like Arabic to me.'

They sent him out with a mirror, so that he could read the envelopes' reflections instead of the envelopes themselves. But this proved so time-consuming that they had to relieve him of his duties.

The supervisor sent Lenny to the sickbay to see if they could find out what was wrong. The nurse pinned a chart on the wall, and asked him to close one eye. She then pointed at the letter X.

'What does that say, Lenny?'

'Tuesday,' he said.

She pointed at the letter B.

'How about that one?'

'Salami,' Lenny said.

She pointed at H.

'Cappuccino,' he said.

'I think you might have a problem,' she said. 'Can you read that sign above the door?' She pointed at the sign reading FIRE EXIT.

'It says gents,' Lenny told her.

'I think I'd better have a word with the supervisor.'

They would have fired Lenny if they could have done so easily.

'Didn't anyone give him a reading test before taking him on?' the supervisor raged. But no one had. Yet, as Lenny himself said, they couldn't dismiss him, not just like that, or he'd have the law on them. It was all in his contract. You only had to read the small print – not that he could all that easily, but his mum helped him out. Yes, he knew his rights. It was all there in black and white. Not that Lenny knew for certain that it was in black and white, as he was a touch colour blind as well, but it was definitely there in grey and mauve. But he

57

knew how to mind his b's and q's all right. You didn't need to dot your r's and cross your m's for his benefit. No, his employers could argue until they were magnolia in the face, but Lenny wouldn't back down. He wasn't afraid of a fight, not Lenny. He wasn't born yesterday, and he wasn't as beige as he was cabbage-looking either.

So it was either keep him on and find him alternative employment, or he'd be round to the nearest industrial tribunal, with all its attendant publicity. Besides, if he left, where was he to go? He'd have the same problems, no matter where he went. Better to stick it out where he was. So he had been transferred to the counter of the sorting office, where, it was hoped, he would be under constant supervision and thus unable to do too much damage.

With someone to keep an eye on him, and by attending day-release classes for English as a Foreign Language, Lenny contrived to do the job with a certain amount of efficiency.

Giles signed for the fat envelope. It was plump with promises, voluptuous with secrets, tumescent with the pleasures to come. He couldn't help but lick his lips as he tucked the envelope under his arm and headed for the door. Out he went, the Giles with the envelope, a close relation of the cat with the cream.

Once outside, Giles suddenly realized that he had nowhere to go, no place to call his own, no place where he could sit and read his letters in peace, without fear of interruption or someone glancing over his shoulder and saying 'What's that, Giles? What've you got there?'

No privacy.

He had no privacy, no private life. Not even at home. Especially not at home. Hardly even in the bathroom; you were lucky to get a crap in peace, that was the plain truth. You couldn't even wash your plonker in the bidet without someone hammering on the door and shouting, 'Giles!' or 'Dad, what are you doing in there?'

'What do you think I'm doing in here?'

'Well, I want to come in!'

'Then you'll have to wait.'

58

'Well, don't stink the place out.'

What could you do? There you were, a functioning meat-eating mammal, with a mammal's digestive system, and they said, 'Don't stink the place out.'

Well, Giles didn't like to be fussy about these things, but he thought, let me ask you just one question, let me ask you just *one* question: how the hell do you have a crap that doesn't stink the place out, when stinking the place out is the very nature of it? That's the job. I mean, pardon me for having a bum.

Yes. He hadn't realized it until now, but he'd had no privacy for years. The girls had been born, they'd grown up, and little by little, day by day, slice by slice, his privacy had vanished.

Even if he fancied a quiet wank, he'd be lucky to get one.

Surely a man had the right to a quiet wank now and then, without fear of interruption. Surely that should be enshrined somewhere in a declaration of human rights. He'd bet it was in America. The right to life, liberty, the pursuit of happiness, and a quiet wank on Sundays.

'What are you doing in there?'

'What do you think?'

'Ah, you're not, are you? Not again!'

Well, I mean to say.

When had he last been alone in the house? When had he last had the place to himself? The chance to have everything as he wanted it, just for an hour. Just a little solitude, just a little privacy, just a little time to be himself.

'Are you doing anything in here, Giles?'

'Just reading.'

'Don't mind if go round with the vacuum?'

'You watching the telly, Dad?'

'Yes. Why?'

'Oh, I just wondered, because my programme's on.'

It was enough to drive you demented. Enough to make you have an affair.

There were twenty minutes of his lunch hour left.

That was a part of it too. It wasn't just the lack of privacy, it was the lack of time, and the accountability that went along with it. Everyone, everywhere, seemed more and more accountable for their time. Where were you? What were you doing? It was like filling in tax returns for the Inland Revenue. Your time was simply not your own. And if you managed an hour to yourself, pretty soon somebody would be asking questions. Where did you go? What were you doing? I called, and you weren't in.

Giles was going to start having to make time, if he wanted this affair. Time, in considerable quantities.

He walked past St Absalom's and went into the cemetery. The weather was still a little sharp, and so the outdoor lunch eaters were not yet abundant. The ones who chewed from packages of clingfilm, sipped from cartons of orange juice and read their papers and magazines.

But not letters.

You used to see lots of people once, not all that long ago, sitting reading and re-reading the letters their friends or relations or lovers had sent them. These days people sat with mobile phones to their ears.

Mind you, even the personal ads had gone hi-tech. You could collect messages from an answering machine if you wanted to. But Giles hadn't wanted that. You could tell a lot about someone from their voice, but you couldn't tell what they looked like, any listener to the radio knew that. The voices of actors, actresses and DJs seldom matched their appearances, and the more honeyed the tones in the sound department, the less they seemed to have in the looks department.

But Giles had his letters. And the moment of truth was coming up. Time to look-see.

With a butterfly-filled stomach, Giles tore the package open. Inside were a dozen or so envelopes, all addressed to Box 132, *Scene Around* magazine. Most were addressed in handwriting of varying legibility, one was typed, and one was laser-printed, hinting at the possession of a personal home computer.

He opened one at random.

A photograph of a large unsavoury moggie with a ribbon round its throat fell out, followed by a sheet of yellow paper, which smelled strongly of cat urine. Giles's suspicions that cat pee was involved were strengthened by the presence of a large paw print on the letter. A spidery scrawl executed with a particularly smudgy biro, prone to ejaculating great globs of greasy ink all over the place, covered the page.

Dear Box 132,

While I was in the hairdresser's recently, a fellow customer drew my attention to your advertisement in the local listings magazine, saying that here was a man who was obviously after some pussy. As an active member of the Waifs and Strays Society, I was wondering – if you are a genuine cat-lover – if you would care to give a good home to Dunstan (photograph enclosed). Dunstan has had a difficult life and came to our notice when he was found lying inside a sack in the estuary mud at low tide, with four heavy bricks tied to his paws, a concrete-filled scaffolding pole attached to his flea collar, and a lead pipe round his tail. We suspect that he may have been an unwanted Christmas present and could possibly have been abandoned.

If Dunstan seems like the kind of pussy you are after, perhaps you would get in touch. Good homes for cats are always needed. Many thanks.

Yours sincerely,

Mrs Angelina Brithe

Giles put the letter down and stared around the cemetery. Not what you'd call a promising start, he thought. He took another look at the photograph of Dunstan, beaming out at him through his furry chops. No, there was no way Giles could fancy him. Not his type at all. He stuffed Dunstan back into the envelope and reached for another letter.

He tore it open and looked warily inside. There was no photograph in this one, and the letter was written on a sheet of paper from a thin-lined A4 note pad. It had been torn roughly out, and one side of the paper was jagged and uneven.

It had also been written in orange ink.

Dear Filthy Bastard,

You are filth. You are all filth, all you filthy bastards who betray their wives. Doing what you do is just filthy, and all you are is filth, doing your filthy things in a filthy way. Of course, you never think, do you, about the damage you do, and the filth you leave behind, about who you hurt, and the lives you wreck, and the families you destroy. One day you will be found out, and then you will wallow in filth forever.

All the best.

Yours sincerely,

Jilted

Giles put down the letter and looked around the cemetery again. He looked at the ivy-clad and graffiti-covered headstones, many cracked and broken, some sagging at odd angles in the earth. There had been passion once too, down there, among the bones, back when the bones had been covered in flesh, and young and passionate hearts had beat within. What did it all matter? No one in the grave felt anything any more. It was quiet, in the end, once it all stopped and the pain was over. He tried to read the inscription on the headstone nearest to him, NATHANIEL ENDICOTT. TAKEN TO HIS MAKER'S BOSOM, 19TH JULY, 1878.

Had he been a filthy bastard too?

Giles glanced down at the letter again. He felt a little shocked. That someone who didn't know him, who had never met him, could be so incensed, so angered, by a simple advertisement in the personal columns –

Why had this person even read the ad? Probably to seek out people like Giles, and to vent her bitterness upon them, as a kind of revenge for her husband's infidelity. Giles was a decent chap. He didn't want to hurt anyone, or break up any happy homes, far from it, it was just ... that Giles felt lonely too.

It wasn't just a meeting of bodies, it was a meeting of souls he needed. That was what was wrong with him and Holly, their souls weren't meeting any more. Marriage itself was not enough. Marriage was not the alleviation and avoidance of loneliness it was supposed to be. It was just another kind of loneliness. It was mixed loneliness – a bit like mixed-sex schools, or mixed bathing or mixed doubles. Marriage was an institution in which men and women came to be lonely together.

Giles wasn't really a filthy bastard. He just felt a bit on his tod.

He scanned the letter. No address, of course. Strictly anon. Pity, really, he would have liked to have written back. Not out of venom, but simply to explain. To appeal to the jury. To clarify the situation, and to promote understanding and tolerance among the peoples of the world.

Oh well, occupational hazard. Everyone took the risk when they advertised in the personal columns that an envelope full of heavy breathing and choice obscenity would land on their mat, or in their rented post office box number. A certain amount of barracking from the sidelines was inevitable in any game, the mating game – or rather, the copulating game – included.

Giles tore the letter up into little shreds, and threw it into the waste bin next to the bench he was sitting on.

Take the charitable view. Maybe Jilted had felt a lot better after writing to him. Maybe she got it all off her chest.

Aunt Sally, that was Giles. A coconut at a funfair. Pick a ball and knock him off. All join in.

He opened the next.

This one was all in pink. Pink envelope, pink paper, with a strong smell of perfume, like a scratch and sniff in a magazine.

'Dear Married Man –' A photograph fluttered out from between the two pages of the letter. It landed on Giles's lap, face down. He hesitated, then picked it up and slowly turned it over.

Bloody hell!

She was gorgeous. Absolutely gorgeous. And young. Young and gorgeous. Bloody hell. Dressed in a skirt so short that you could all but count the goose pimples on her thighs. And what thighs. God! Her legs! Legs that went on for miles, legs that never stopped, legs, and son of legs, and spare legs for emergencies. And there was an indentation of delicious nipple, outlined in her T-shirt. He couldn't see them, but the shape was enough. Nipples like doorbells, nipples like tyre valves, nipples to take gently between your lips, like grapes from a –

Steady, Giles, steady.

Home and heartbreaker.

Just the job!

Giles's mouth had gone dry. People must feel this way when they first realize that they have bought the winning lottery ticket. He read on. 'Dear Married Man, How are you? I have always wanted to have an affair with a married man. I think married men are the best, so attractive and mature and understanding. I have always wanted to lose my virginity to a married man –' *Virginity?* Hang about. Warning bells had started to ring in the distance. Warning bells, coming rapidly nearer. ' – ever since I was twelve.'

Twelve? Twelve! Bloody hell! In less than a second those warning bells had turned into police sirens. Giles was starting to panic, but steeled himself to read on.

'I am almost fourteen now, but look a lot older, as you can see from my photo.' True. True enough. The photograph made her look about twenty-two. Older even. And those legs – 'Perhaps we could get together sometime soon. Maybe I could meet you after school one day.'

School? *School!* Her? In the actual uniform? Bloody hell. Stone the crows. Giles never imagined that reading letters could be so stressful.

'I haven't told my mother that I am writing to you –' No, good idea, love. Best to keep the old low profile, if possible, in these underage sex cases. ' – but I am sure that she would be interested in meeting you as well.'

Mumsie? Mumsie too? What sort of a family was this? How were people bringing up their children these days? This couldn't be right, surely. Fourteen-year-olds passing on their married lovers so that Mumsie could get a bit as well? What was happening to standards? What was happening to morning prayers in schools and religious instruction on the national curriculum?

'Mum is divorced, sadly –' Well, why couldn't she have written in then? She must be quite a looker, if her daughter was anything to go by. And she'd be more the right age. Why couldn't Mumsie have dropped a line? '– but has lots of boyfriends, although I'm sure she'd like to have one more. Please write as soon as you can, as I don't think I can hold out much longer, and Mr Chesterfield, our neighbour across the street, has been trying to get friendly with me, but he's not really my type, I don't think. I could meet you any day after school, or at the weekend. But not on Saturday mornings as that is when I have my hockey.'

Hockey! Good god in heaven.

Giles stared ahead. He simply didn't know about this. This wasn't what he'd imagined at all. He'd lived in this world for thirty-eight years, and had plainly wandered through its streets like an innocent. There were doors he'd never knocked on, and windows he'd never looked through, and now they were throwing themselves open to him, and hands were beckoning him inside. Only he didn't know if he wanted to go.

Lo-li-ta. Light of my life. Fire of my –

What was it? He'd forgotten. He'd read the book once, years ago, and even then had been unable to decide whether Vladimir Nabokov was one of the twentieth century's greatest novelists, or just one of its greatest dirty old men.

Either way, he understood the dilemma now.

But the answer was no. It was a shame, but it was no. No! He was tempted, definitely tempted. Mother, daughter – even granny too, maybe, aunties perhaps, sisters, cousins, au pairs. But no. It wasn't just immoral, it was illegal. You could end up inside for having intercourse with minors. You'd probably never work in computers again. Be blacklisted. Even when you'd done your time, they'd never forgive you, they'd never have you back. Would Lavinia give him his old job back? After he'd served eighteen months for shagging a fourteen-year-old and then nipping round to see her mother afterwards?

Giles doubted it.

65

Would Holly have him back?

Giles doubted it.

He'd probably end up having to top himself in his cell with borrowed shoelaces.

No. Forbidden fruit. Tasty, no doubt. But forbidden. No way back into the Garden Of Suburban Eden after a nibble of fourteen-year-old earlobes like that. Beyond the pale, way beyond. Cast off forever into dull infinity.

Giles sighed. He folded the perfumed letter up and returned it to its envelope along with the photograph of the legs and the indentation of nipples.

Get thee behind me Satan.

And behind him, Satan reluctantly went, still trying to get in a bit of a grope and fumble, but repelled, not so much by Giles's sense of decency, as by his dread of the social consequences.

He would write to her. She deserved a reply. It was a very full, frank, honest and polite letter, after all. Maybe a little card. Something humorous, perhaps. Something from Purple Ronnie about squidgy bums, or a Garfield card, or a Far Side bit of surrealism. She'd appreciate that. And he'd better return her photograph too. Thanks, but no thanks. And he'd maybe give her a word of warning about this Mr Chesterfield from across the road, who sounded like a right old groper. Giles knew his type. People like him were always after other blokes' daughters. You had to lock up your family when men like him got their raincoats on and went for a stroll through the park. He was probably the kind of sad case who put advertisements in magazines.

Yes, he'd do the decent thing and tell her to be careful.

Next!

As Giles worked his way through the replies to his advertisement, two things struck him forcefully as never before. One was that there was a lot of grief, desperation and loneliness in the world, and the other was that there were an awful lot of no-hopers out there too.

And they weren't necessarily born no-hopers either, sometimes they were made. Sometimes people of great potential and ability just turned into no-hopers, for no discernible reason, when they could just as easily have gone on to great and wonderful things.

You never knew your destiny. You could only wait until it arrived. And only then were you in a position to look back, survey the landscape, see the path of your progress, and think, ah yes, that way was bound to lead from there to here. But you could never see it at the time. All you could see while you were travelling was one foot landing in front of the other, as you plod-plod-plodded along.

Yes, there were a lot of no-hopers out there. Only why were they all writing to Giles? Were they trying to tell him something? Did they sense the proximity of one of their own?

Maybe he would have to reword his advertisement to attract a better class of response.

Out of the dozen responses he had received, nine now lay in the cemetery waste bin, one was in his pocket to be answered – Miss Young and Nubile, but sadly underage – and two waited to be opened.

Then he discovered that young and nubile wasn't his only problem.

Old and past it were after him too. And a glance at his advertisement in his copy of *Scene Around* reminded him, *Married man seeks partner between 18 and 85*. Eighty-five was almost in the realms of stiffs. And not the sort of stiffs he was after. The sort of stiff ones Giles had in mind were of a different kind altogether. It was all *her* fault. The girl in the classifieds office. Her with the rings in her ears and the doorbell in her nose. She must have copied his ad down incorrectly.

So he was now prey to every elderly nymphomaniac within a fifty-mile radius. Giles had nothing against sex among the elderly, in fact, he hoped to be at it himself when he got to eighty-five. But certain generation gaps were difficult to bridge, and a 47-year age difference was one of them.

Three of the replies had all come from the same old folks' home, and had been stuffed into one envelope. A Mrs Wiseman, a Mrs Throttly, and a Miss Stavenshaw had formed a consortium and had chipped in together for the stamp, writing paper and envelope in order to cut down on expenses. Mrs Wiseman (72), Mrs Throtly (*78, but sprightly*) and Miss Stavenshaw (*I've never thought that age really mattered as long as there was communality of soul*) had also sent a photograph of the three of them on a day out in Dawlish.

Dawlish must have been having one of its periodical blizzards as everything in the background looked boarded up, and huge waves, the size of houses, could be seen trying to jump over the sea walls.

The three ladies looked like a collection of cauliflowers.

Mrs Wiseman, Mrs Throtly and Miss Stavenshaw wrote that while they did not altogether approve of affairs with married men, they had come to a time in their lives when they could afford to have adventures without too much concern for the consequences. They were therefore prepared to entertain Box 132 on a rota, or a turn-and-turn-about basis, in the visitor's room at the Motley Grange, but they would need a certain amount of notice, as the guest room had to be booked in advance, and the demand for it was high, especially in the summer months.

Mrs Wiseman – who had had three husbands, and had always enjoyed a vigorous sex life – could promise satisfaction. Mrs Throtly – still sprightly – would promise to do her best. And Miss Stavenshaw, who by her own admission had left it a bit late to start, was nevertheless a keen learner, anxious to please, and ready to get down to it at a moment's notice, if someone would just explain to her what it was she had to do.

They all felt that it made a refreshing change to hear from someone who plainly valued the qualities of the older woman, and who didn't write off a good part of the fair sex, just because they were pushing eighty and their legs were going a bit.

'That bloody magazine and their bloody misprints!'

A woman eating a sandwich and reading a copy of *Bella* looked across from her bench in another corner of the graveyard. Giles coloured and tried to convert his exclamation into a cough, 'Ahem, ahem!'

He supposed he owed the three ladies at least the courtesy of a reply. It certainly wasn't his fault that the magazine had put the wrong age limits in his advertisement, but it certainly wasn't the fault of his respondents either. He'd send them a postcard. Something from the National Trust shop, something with flowers on, a bit English garden in flavour.

'To Mrs Wiseman, Mrs Throttly, and Miss Stavenshaw. Dear ladies, thanks, but I am already fixed up, and Dawlish is a bit far for me to come.'

Or was there a *double entendre* there? No, he was getting paranoid.

Hang on. How had they got a copy of *Scene Around* in Dawlish? It was miles away. And why ever were they reading it? They should have been reading *Saga* or *Golden Stitches* or *Gardening Times*, or *Incontinence Pants Weekly*. Why were they reading a right-on listings magazine?

It was a funny old world. A funny, funny old world, the way things got around in it. Funny peculiar, that was. Not much of funny ha-ha in it. But funny just the same. There were mysteries beyond explaining in it, and Giles didn't mean the evolution of monkeys. A funny, funny old world, and an unfair one.

Two to go. They didn't look hopeful.

Letters had an air about them, an odour of what they contained. The envelope revealed the content, as surely as the child was father to the man. Thin brown envelopes brought depressing bills. Fat white ones brought heart-rending demands from charities – they tended to be envelopes within envelopes, envelopes marked *The photographs inside are of a distressing nature*. And so you had to open them, so that you could be distressed. And there they were: dogs with arrows through their heads, starved children, lepers suffering from a disease which could easily be cured with a little help from our friends and supporters. Sight which could be restored with a small donation from the same.

The envelope was the opening bars. Just hum me the envelope, and I'll know the whole tune.

Giles opened the last but one.

'Dear Box 132, I am a widow. This is a photograph of me taken a few years ago. I don't have a recent one, but –'

No recent photograph, but Giles could imagine her as she now was. He suspected that she would be two to three stone heavier than depicted. He didn't know why he thought that, but he did. And how strange it was too, not to have a recent photograph. No holidays then? No parties? No weekend trips to anywhere? No days out? No time away? No occasion to mark? Not this year, nor last year, nor the year before?

He shuddered and put the letter back into its envelope. It was like choosing sides for football. You suddenly felt that here was someone you didn't want on your team. Gut feelings. Sheer, naked prejudice.

He'd send her a card. Say he was already fixed up. Worded so as not to offend.

He tore the last one open.

One thing, he thought, as he took out the letter, one thing that he hadn't really considered, was the general lack of criticism. Apart from the letter in orange ink, the Dear Filthy one, all the replies had been basically unjudgemental.

As the song said, it was just amazing how fair people could be.

They didn't seem to mind that what he was proposing was basically immoral, despicable and undermining of family life.

Maybe it was a matter of birds of a feather flocking together. Maybe it was indicative of a general, national moral collapse.

Or maybe this was going to be the one.

He studied the photograph. Hmm. In her early thirties, he'd guess. Pleasant. Pretty, but not beautiful. Good figure, but not stunning. Not thin, but not plump either. Fashionably dressed, but not flamboyant. Just about right really, just about right. The Little Bear's porridge, just about right.

His pulse rate increased.

Now, what did she have to say?

Dear Box 132.

How are you? What an intriguing advertisement. An affair with a married man? Oh, yes please. And no strings attached either – well, I think that I know about that too. I can't say that I like walking in the country too much, but I am interested in classical music – *very* interested. So why not send me your photo? Then that would be fair. Then maybe we can meet. Your place or mine? Probably mine, I should think. So why not drop me a line, or even give me a call. And you can bring your classical records round. And I'll play you my CDs. I've got some very serious music. *Very* serious indeed. I think you'd like it. Especially the opening bars. Write soon.

    Yours,

    Marilyn

Marilyn.

It sounded promising.

It sounded better than promising.

It sounded perfect.

He'd drop her a line that very afternoon.

Now, did he have time to pop into a photo booth and maybe get a quick snapshot of himself to send to her? Giles looked at his watch.

Good god! Damn and buggeration! He should have been back at work twenty minutes ago. If Lavinia saw him, she'd give him a bollocking. Two bollockings, one for each bollock. Or even three, with an extra one to keep in his pocket.

He grabbed the letters he wanted, threw the rest of the rubbish in the bin, and hurried back to the office.

SEVEN

When Giles got back to the office building, he went and hid in the toilets for five minutes, so that he could make an entrance from somewhere.

Giles, I was looking for you!

Been in the toilet, sorry about that.

That would do.

He sat there, idly trying to separate a sheet of three-ply toilet tissue out into three sheets of one-ply.

And him a grown man.

Me, a grown man, he thought. Hiding in the toilets lest Lavinia should bellow him out for being back late from lunch. It was pathetic. He didn't need telling; he knew. The dry, metallic taste of failure and promise unfulfilled was in his mouth a lot these days. It was one of the reasons he had taken up Orbit chewing gum.

Giles, is that you smelling of peppermint?

Yes, I was chewing gum, sorry about that.

Well, not in the firm's time, please, it looks slovenly.

Life had become one long apology, one long apology for living.

Women were taking over, there was no doubt about that. Men were being turned into mental eunuchs. All they had left were their plonkers, and their Doris Management Programmes. Giles was sure that if Roy had met with the career success he had once expected, he would not be now hunched over a computer screen, trying to work out how to manage all his Dorises and keep four affairs going at once, without duplications, overbookings, or inadvertent neglect.

Little by little, women were on the up. First they got a toe in, then a leg, then a couple of arms, and soon they would take the place over. The company was turning into so many bees' nests, where the queens ruled the roost, the busy females did all the work, and the males were only useful for procreation, and once they had fulfilled that function, were booted out. Booted out to die. For the males in the bees' nests were sad, defenceless, pathetic creatures, without so much as the means of collecting their own food, or doing their own housework.

Yes, men had been emasculated.

The honey bees had taken over. Not like in the old days. It hadn't been a colony of bees then, it had been more like a tribe of chimps, with dominant males and submissive females and everything nicely in its place.

Back to basics, that's what was wanted. Back to chimpanzees, and baboons with big red bums. You knew where you stood then, when the one with the biggest and the reddest bum of all was the best. Back then there had been order in the world, and structure in society.

Creewoooosh!

Giles flushed the loo and went out. Sure enough, Lavinia was loitering by his desk.

'Ah, Giles, there you are. I was looking for you.'

'Sorry, I was in the toilet.'

'Don't you get a lunch hour for that?'

'I thought the lunch hour was to eat your lunch in,' Giles said innocently. Not to go for a crap in, he mentally added. Because if it was for going for a crap in, then logically it would have been called the crap hour, wouldn't it?

'I wanted to see you about this systems spec . . . There's something very wrong with the logic in this, Giles, something very wrong, but I just can't put my finger on it. You'd better come over to my section and we'll go through it together.'

But Giles found it difficult to concentrate. His mind kept drifting off to frame replies to Marilyn, who was so interested in classical music. What should he say to her? Where should they meet? Then it would drift off on another tide, musing over whether an employee was obliged to take a crap in his own lunch hour, or whether making a point of taking it in the employer's time was tantamount to defrauding the company of your labour.

Giles tried to cast his mind back to his interview.

'Yes, Mr West, then of course there is health cover, a contributory pension scheme, three weeks holiday a year, and the hours are from nine to five-thirty, with an hour off for a crap.'

No, no one had said that. It had definitely been lunch. Crap hadn't been mentioned. Not even in terms of a morning or afternoon break.

'And additionally, there's fifteen minutes or so for a crap at eleven in the morning, and three in the afternoon, though we would normally expect you to have it at your desk.'

No. No, there was nothing in his terms of employment about that at all. He was well within his rights to have a crap in the firm's time, as far as he could see. Plainly in moderation mind, you wouldn't expect to make a habit of it. But every now and again, it was quite unavoidable, and if Lavinia didn't like the fact that Giles had to have the odd bowel movement in the firm's time, well, that was too bad.

'Well, Giles? What's wrong with it?'

Giles studied the systems flow chart. Then he saw it. 'Here,' he said. 'That coffee cup ring. You've been counting it as a decision box.'

Lavinia gave him the sort of look normally reserved for things found on the bottom of shoes.

'I suppose that was you.'

'Might have been, I suppose. Sorry about that.'

'Giles, will you please stop saying sorry about that all the time!'

'Yes, I will, yes, it's just a habit I've got into. Yes, I will, sorry. Sorry about that.'

'Giles!'

'Ah, did it again, didn't I. Yes, sorry about – no, not sorry – about anything at all. No.'

'Would you get this system chart redone? Without cup rings on it this time.'

'I'll get it corrected straightaway.'

'Thank you.'

Giles returned to his section and delegated the task to one of his underlings. He didn't have many underlings, just two in fact, and very grateful he was to have them too, though neither Terry nor Sandy looked as if they would remain underlings for long. Bright young things, they were. With ambitions. Both women, of course.

Worrying, yes, very worrying. It would soon be a world of wombs. It was getting to the point where a penis stood for nothing.

He passed Roy's desk. Roy was normally tilted back in his chair, looking round for casual distractions, but not this afternoon. He was hard at work and deep in thought as he fed in commands to the increasingly complex Doris Management Programme.

He saw Giles out of the corner of his eye. 'Ah, Giles. Here, mate, have a look at this.'

A hand of bony fingers grasped Giles by the arm. Giles looked at them in wonder. So these were the fingers whose touch Dorises One to Four – not forgetting Mrs Roy, alias Doris Five – craved. He couldn't think why. Just couldn't see it at all. Fingernails bitten to the quick, ravaged cuticles and yellow nicotine stains – for Roy was a desperate and unrepentant smoker.

It occurred to Giles that the position of Roy's wife, Doris Five, was one of increasingly diminishing status. For every time that Roy took another Doris on, Mrs Roy dropped another place. From Doris One she had gone to Doris Two, to Three, to Four, and now to Five. It didn't show what you'd call a lot of respect. Roy should at least have nominally made her Doris One, as a kind of permanent position, if only out of consideration for her length of service.

'Come and look at this, mate.' Roy hastily looked around to ensure that Lavinia was neither in earshot nor in sight. He plucked Giles by the lapel, and pulled him down to see the screen. 'It's a definite winner this, Giles.'

'Do you think you should be doing this in the firm's time?' Giles asked. The odd crap was one thing, writing a complete Doris Management Programme was another.

'It's working out a treat. This could be the next big thing in software, Giles. This could be bigger than IBM and Microsoft put together. This could be bigger than Windows. It's not just the basic Doris Management, you see. There's a whole realm of possibilities: Doris Management Spreadsheets, Doris Management CD Games, Interactive Doris, Nintendo Doris – you know, like, Doris, the Street Fighter, or even Sonic Doris – Doris the Hedgehog!'

'Roy –'

'As soon as I've got this finished, Giles, I'll show you how it works. Maybe you could come in on it with me. This could make us rich, Giles, beyond our wildest! We could get out of this dump forever. Set up our own software house, Infidelities Limited, or Mine's A Bunk-Up or something like that. I don't know why it's never been thought of before. It's really the simple matter of putting all your Dorises on a business-like footing.'

There was a mad gleam in Roy's eyes. The kind of gleam which, in a more institutional context, had doctors reaching for the Prozac.

'Ah, oh!' Roy had seen something. 'Trouble.'

Lavinia was weaving her way along through the sections, with Roy's desk on her route. With the deft tap of a few keys, the Doris Management Development Programme disappeared from Roy's computer screen, and in its place appeared a national canned beans consumption projection pie chart.

She passed by without comment. Save for a withering *Actually doing some work, are we?* glance at Roy.

'Wonder what she's like under the old duvet,' Roy said when she had gone. 'Probably keeps a ruler on the bedside table for the measuring of plonkers. Has a book of statistics on *Plonkers I Have Known*. Probably gives you marks out of ten, and sends on a typed critique of your performance after.'

Giles tried to muster a smile. But he didn't feel like smiling. His mind kept returning to Marilyn and her strong interest in classical music. Was that significant? Did that mean anything? She had stressed it. Did it mean something Giles didn't know about? Was it streetwise vernacular for something he wasn't *au fait* with? Like a particular kind of deviant sexual practice he might not want to get involved in? Something involving pots of Colman's Mustard, for example. Or courgettes. Or, heaven forfend, Cumberland sausages?

Giles knew about Cumberland sausages from an article he had read in a magazine at the barber's. *(Something for the weekend, sir? No, thanks, they make my plonker go red and swell up. Which reminds me, mental note: must try on a Jimmy's to make sure I'm not allergic to them.)* It was a waste of good bangers, as far as Giles was concerned, but apparently, or so the article claimed, many a young man was afraid to go home at night now, for fear that his wife would be waiting behind the door for him with nine inches of Cumberland sausage in her hand, to put heaven knows where.

It all sounded like a load of old cobblers to Giles, the sort of thing that the features journalists of such magazines made up in order to fill the blank spaces between the photographs of Readers' Wives, snapped in poor lighting from interesting angles, posing suggestively with winking eyes, implying that there was more in their knickers than just a gusset.

It was all a big load of codswallop.

But was it?

Wasn't it?

He decided he'd better check with Roy. Roy was as streetwise as you got. If anyone would know, he would.

'Roy?'

'Yes, old mate.' He was already back at his Doris Management Programme.

'If a woman ever said to you that she was keen on classical music, what would you take that to mean, exactly?'

Roy's fingers hesitated. 'Classical music? Keen on classical music? Well, in my experience, old mate, when a woman says she's red hot on classical music it means she likes listening to orchestras and string quartets and that. You know, a bit of the old boom-tee-boom. Why?'

'So it's got nothing to do with sausages then?'

'Not as far as I know. Why do you ask?'

77

'Oh, no reason,' Giles said, much relieved.

'Right. Well, I'll get on with my programming then.'

'Which one are you seeing tonight?' Giles couldn't help asking.

'Hang on.'

Roy typed a date into the keyboard. A message flashed up on the screen.

Tuesday 15th.
Doris 3.
Real name: Sandra.
>Meet at 8.30 at Wheatsheaf.
>Excuse at home: Playing in darts team.
>Likes to drink: Vodka and tonic.
>Likes to eat: Cashew nuts, but not crisps.
>Status: Married, unhappily.
>Size of husband: Smaller than me, but apparently prone to violence.
>State of play: Two leg-overs and a blow job.
>Location: Back of car.
>Present objectives: Weekend away.
>Things not to mention: Other Dorises.
>Hobbies: Badminton and aerobics.

'And that's just the tip of the iceberg,' Roy said. 'That's just a demo. Once I've got the programme up and running properly, I'll have full files and progress reports on all of them. You'll be able to do projections on the life of the relationship, their star signs, the best time to dump them, the possible consequences of so doing, and all the rest.'

'Brilliant,' Giles said. But it was sinister, more than anything. Sinister and chilling. Big Brother was watching. He was watching Big Doris. But Giles felt that Big Doris was watching too, and that, one day, she would be revenged.

Back at his own desk Giles toyed with a few systems specifications, but his mind was on Marilyn. What to say, where to meet, how to put it exactly, how to respond? Liaisons were minefields of ambiguity, and every word needed to be well chosen, or it might set off an explosion under your feet.

There was another dimension too, now that he had actually received a positive response to his advertisement, and that the ball had started rolling. It was an unanticipated nervousness on his part. A nervousness that was less than terror, but more than mere anxiety.

Fear. That was the best way of putting it.

What if he couldn't go through with it? What if he was really just a one-woman man at heart, for all his longings and pretensions otherwise? What if he and Holly had paired for life, like a couple of seagulls, or a certain kind of duck? And when one died, it would be the end of the other one?

What if?

Well, there was only one way to find out.

'Dear Marilyn, Thank you kindly for your letter –'

No.

'Dear Marilyn, It was great to hear from you –'

No.

'Dear Sexy Baby, Give it to me Hot Stuff, as soon as you can –'

No.

'Dear Marilyn, Well, well –'

Yes. He liked that. It sounded right somehow. 'Well, well.' It had the right racy, insouciant, interested, but not too desperate kind of ring to it. Take it or leave it, that was the way. He was off to a good start. He'd do the rest later.

What was the time?

Three p.m.

God. The unmoving hands of that clock. Office time wasn't real time; it was a time zone all of its own. It was time from the unknown dimension. Two and a half hours still to go. Two and a half hours till the liberty bell rang. How would he get through the afternoon?

Got it! He'd nip off to the loo and try one of his new condoms on, to see whether or not a Jimmy's produced an allergic reaction. It was, after all, important to get the groundwork done now, well in advance. He didn't want to end up jumping into bed with Marilyn, only to find, as soon as he rolled a

Jimmy's over his plonker, that it brought him out in a rash of spots, or gave him an attack of asthma.

It could even kill him.

In fact, sex must be pretty dangerous for asthmatics all round. The wheezing and breathlessness could easily be mistaken for passion. And cries of 'Where's my inhaler?!' could in the heat of the moment, be mistaken for whoops of joy.

No, best to try out the equipment well in advance, and no time like the present.

Giles entered the gents, and found an empty cubicle. He was lucky to get one at that time of day, for mid-afternoon boredom drove many an office worker to the calm sanctuary of a sanitary cubicle for a private sit down. Countless crosswords had been done, countless cigarettes smoked, countless newspapers read; some customers had even fallen asleep, and could be heard gently snoring.

Giles locked the door, dropped his trousers, put his tie into his top pocket – so that it didn't land in anything – and took a Jimmy's out of his wallet. He tore the chewing-gum sized package open and extracted a Jimmy's condom.

It was purple! He nearly fell off the seat.

They might have warned you.

Purple condoms! It was enough to make you ill. Going round with a purple plonker? Was that a turn-off or a turn-on?

The latter, let's hope.

Hmm.

Better put it on then.

Hmm.

Not so easy. The old chap was a bit floppy right then. Giles should have thought to bring a magazine along. Still, never mind. Are we men, or are we beasts? What of the power of the imagination? What about that?

Giles tried to think of amorous adventures and erotic entanglements, but there was something about the clinical atmosphere of the white-tiled cubicle which had the eroticism of a large dose of bromide.

Concentrate. Mind over matter. The power of the intellect.

Ah! Here now! Things were perking up. Giles got ready to put the condom on when suddenly, from the adjacent cubicle, there issued the sound of a short, abrupt, but very loud fart.

Passion killer. Instantaneous. Killed stone dead.

No shame, some people, no consideration for others. Treating the place like a toilet. Disgusting.

After a minute, the cistern flushed, the door opened, hands were washed, footsteps walked away.

Now, how were we getting on? He looked down.

No, no luck. The fish just weren't biting. The old plonker just hung there, like a wet weekend in Bournemouth. Oh well, stick it on anyway, just to see if there's an allergic reaction or not.

Giles put the Jimmy's on. It drooped languidly, like a sock that was too big for him.

Looks a bit like Christmas, he thought, when you hang your stocking up on the end of the bed. Better give it five minutes, that would be more than enough. If there was going to be an allergic reaction, five minutes should be more than enough to trigger it off.

Now, what about composing that letter?

Dear Marilyn, Well, well, you sound like a right old goer!

No. Too crude. Casual sophistication, that was the name of the game here. Urbanity. Mr Smooth.

Dear Marilyn, Well, well. Thank you for your letter. It seems that we may have one or two things in common. I liked your photo — here's one of me.

Yes, he'd have to get his photo taken, or look an old one out. Maybe a new one would be best. Not one of him sitting in a cubicle in the gents with a Jimmy's dangling from the wife's old acquaintance, of course. A photo of his good side. The side which people said made him look like a young Jack Nicholson, crossed with Tom Cruise, crossed with one of the Muppets.

So you are interested in classical music too, Marilyn. That's good. Maybe we could make some beautiful music together.

Yes, good, good, very good. Extra-smooth. Giles liked that.

He was on a roll. It was starting to flow. He took a notebook and pencil out from his pocket and hastily scribbled his thoughts down before they vanished.

– *beautiful music together. Your place or mine – maybe yours would be best. Mine might be a little too crowded for comfort. And I'll certainly bring my CDs round. I have some very interesting little numbers that you may not have come across before.* Yes, yes, very good, Giles thought. The innuendo was flowing like lava. *I especially have one or two little pieces which I hope will give you as much pleasure as they have given me.* Bloody hell, Giles thought, this is terrific. Reading stuff like this was enough to give any woman the hots. It was this kind of correspondence that had them panting for it.

You say, Marilyn, that you've got some very serious music in your collection, well, that's just what I like – the serious and heavy stuff. In fact, I'm not averse to a little bit of Wagner in the night once in a while. How would you feel about that?

Giles noticed that his Jimmy's was a better fit. Yes, it was stirring prose all right.

Maybe, if you're interested in conducting, I could let you inspect my baton.

Coh, bloody hell, Giles, this was the business all right, this was! This kind of erotic literature put *Story of O* well into the shade.

So, let's arrange to meet, why don't we, for a little musical session. Wednesday is always a good night for me. Good, because Holly would presume that he had gone to the sports centre for a squash game, or a swim, or a bit of a lightweight work-out. *Will you write? I'll look forward to hearing from you. Yours, Box 132. PS. I loved your photograph. Your compact discs look very compact to me. I wish I had them in my collection.*

Wonderful.

And people said that the art of letting writing had died with the advent of the telephone. Rubbish. The old skills were still there, you just had to put them into practice.

There was one thing Giles was uncertain of though. It was the Box 132. He couldn't go on describing himself as Box 132 for the duration of all these affairs he hoped to have. People liked to have a name to call you, if only to have something to call out in a moment of orgasm.

Oh god, oh, Giles, oh!

That was all quite acceptable.

But *Oh god, oh Box 132, oh!*

No. Didn't have the same ring somehow. It made it all sound a bit cold and anonymous and mechanical. In fact, it made it sound a bit like sexual intercourse with a swimming pool locker.

He'd need to invent something. Something like ... he looked down. What about Jimmy? Yes, that would be all right. Jimmy what? He looked around the cubicle. Jimmy Trousers? Jimmy Andrex? Jimmy Coat Hook? Jimmy Lavatory Brush? Jimmy Tile?

Yes, why not? Sounded possible. Jimmy Tile. There was that actor, wasn't there, Jimmy Nail. Well, if Jimmy Nail, why not Jimmy Tile?

So Jimmy Tile it would be.

The condom was plainly benign. Giles removed it and dropped it into the loo, then hitched up his trousers. He flushed the loo, then stared down into the bowl. The condom momentarily vanished in a swirl of foam, then it reappeared, grotesquely swollen, as if the turmoil had filled it with air. It bobbed around in the bowl like a warning to passing shipping, heralding the presence of semi-submerged rocks.

Giles waited for the cistern to refill, then flushed again. The condom disappeared into a swirl of foam, but managed to survive its ride down the rapids, and it rose again, somehow fuller than ever with air.

It wasn't going to go away.

It was the condom from hell.

Giles took the toilet brush out of its holder, and poked the condom with it, trying to force it down around the U bend, but it wouldn't go. Now matter how far down he pushed it, it just burst triumphantly back to the surface.

There was nothing he could do. He'd just have to leave it for the cleaners.

He unlocked the cubicle door, and went out to wash his

hands. As bad luck would have it, Eliot of management entered the washroom at that moment and headed directly for the cubicle which Giles had just vacated.

He stopped in the doorway, looked down, and stared.

A large condom seemed to be advancing towards him out of the toilet bowl. An absolute whopper. And bright purple at that.

'Good god!' Eliot said. 'Have you seen this? There's a ruddy great party balloon stuffed down the bog hole!'

Eliot was not a man who had got to upper management by means of airs and graces so much as by forceful action and direct speech.

'It's back-syphonage,' Giles explained. 'They're coming up from product development of that children's toy firm on the first floor.'

'So that's where they're coming from. Here, grab something sharp, man, and we'll spear it!'

Giles found a wire coat hanger on the back of the washroom door. He handed it to Eliot who untwisted it, and, standing well back, speared the offending article. It popped and shrank immediately to a small scrap of rubber.

'Hmm,' Eliot said. 'Mission completed. Thanks for your help. I must send a memo round about this.'

'No problem,' Giles said, and he left Eliot to it.

Sound man, that chap, Eliot thought. Good man in a storm, obviously. Steady hand in an emergency. Must make a note of his name.

Giles got back to his section to find Lavinia standing by his desk. 'Ah, Giles! I've been standing here waiting for you for nearly fifteen minutes.'

'Been in the toilet. Sorry about that.'

'Again? Are you swinging the lead in that toilet, Giles?'

For a moment Giles thought she meant wanking. *(Giles, are you up in that bedroom swinging the lead? You'll get hairs on the palms of your hands and the soles of your feet.)* But Lavinia was plainly unaware of any ambiguity.

'I was discussing the back-syphonage situation with Mr Eliot of management, as a matter of fact.'

The wind fled from her sails. Eliot was *senior* management. She would get there one day, but she hadn't quite got there yet.

'Oh. Oh, well, that's different, I suppose. Now, have you redone that flow chart?'

It was ready – Sandy and Terry had done their stuff – so he gave it to her. He spent the rest of the afternoon swinging the lead: making a fair copy of the letter he had composed in his head to Marilyn. When he had finished, he dropped it into an envelope, addressed it, and then placed it in the post tray, right by the sign which said NOT TO BE USED FOR PRIVATE CORRESPONDENCE UNDER ANY CIRCUMSTANCES WHATSO-EVER. It was just a matter of sitting back now, and waiting for a reply.

Ah! Wait a minute! The photo! He hadn't included a photograph of himself. He grabbed his letter back out of the mail tray, just as the girl who put all the letters through the franking machine was about to take it away.

'Forgot something,' Giles said. 'But don't worry, I'll post it myself, later.'

It was no time for complacency, of course, he had to do things right. And that included having his advertisement reprinted. Only this time, it should go in properly. No '15 to 85' misprints. *Scene Around* owed him a free ad and an apology at the very least, if not proper compensation for the traumatized emotions occasioned by some of the letters. Especially that of the game Mrs Throttly from Dawlish, who had sent on a recent photograph of herself, dressed in Janet Reger lingerie and medical support tights, leaning, in what was presumably supposed to be a seductive fashion, against a tartan shopping trolley.

He picked up the telephone to ring the *Scene Around* small ads department and give them a roasting. Then thought, no, better to go round there in person, and give them a made-to-measure personalized bollocking. The *Scene Around* offices didn't close till seven, and then he could nip into that photo booth on the station platform, post the letter to Marilyn, then home.

Home to loving wife and kiddies.

Giles, he thought, you are a treacherous slug. Slimier than worms, baser than fleas, more repellent than maggots, dirtier than dung flies, a dog's mess of a dog's mess, a cow pat on legs.

Home to loving wife and kiddies indeed. Home to the home that all this may break up and rend asunder. How could you, how can you? The children's lives, the long, faithful, and not unhappy marriage. Moments of great joy – weren't there moments? Many, many such moments. In the old days. Moments of tenderness and real, true, unsentimental, realistic love.

And you'd forget and destroy all of it, and for what? For the few minutes and seconds it took to have an orgasm with a woman who was not your wife. Was it worth it? Is it worth it? Ask yourself that one question, Giles. Is it? Is it worth the risk?

Yes. Oh yes.

Oh no.

Oh hell.

Because it wasn't just the time it took to fill up a Jimmy's with seed for the stony ground. It was much more than that. It was the whole experience. Excitement, lust, newness, freshness, difference. It wasn't just that culmination of desire, not just those final minutes and seconds, but all that went before. Being in an unfamiliar room, with an unfamiliar woman, whose story, whose history, whose aches and pains, whose scent and whose body you did not know. It was to go on a journey, to make a new discovery, to find a new world, a new universe.

The excitement of being with another woman.

Undressing her. Being undressed.

Smelling her hair. Her perfume, mingling with the odour of her body. Lying back with her on the bed. Touching breasts you had not touched before. Wondering at how different they seemed. Wondering that breasts, which were really so much the same, could feel so different. Warm unfamiliarity. Youth returning. Renewal.

Just to live a little before you so soon died.

The faithful and the unfaithful. The true and the untrue. The need for a little drama in your life. Maybe that was all it was. But it was an 'all' which demanded something be done, an appetite which howled for satisfaction.

So in answer to your questions, yes, Giles thought, I am a dog's mess of a dog's mess. And was it worth risking breaking up family and home for? No, maybe not. And was that going to stop him? No, he was afraid it wasn't. And did he feel bad about it? Yes, he did. And would he therefore reconsider, before it was too late?

No, he wouldn't. He couldn't. It was too late already.

After work he called in at the *Scene Around* offices to insist that they correct his advertisement, and they promised him three free insertions by way of compensation for his inconvenience. He had told himself that if he spoke to the girl with the earrings again he would tear her off several strips and give her a right bollocking for messing his ad up. But when it came to it, he couldn't be unpleasant to her. He simply wasn't the type to give bollockings to anyone.

Though he might make the effort for Marilyn.

Then he went on towards the station. He needed to get his mug shots and there was a photo booth on the concourse which would be happy to shoot his mug for him.

At the photo booth Giles gingerly pulled the curtain back, peered in, and sniffed.

No, it smelt all right. No problems there. He sat on the swivel stool and checked that he was at the right level with the dark glass opposite.

He'd had a few bad experiences with station photo booths in his time, had Giles. Sometimes he'd spent as long as half an hour waiting outside for his strip of prints to arrive, not knowing whether to give up hope and leave, or whether they would suddenly appear in the little chute the moment his back was turned.

And no matter what he did to look pleasant for the camera, he usually ended up looking like a cadaver, or a low-grade sex offender. There was something about a photo booth that brought out the corpse and the pervert in you. In fact, they were more like X-ray machines than cameras.

He rummaged in his pocket for fifty pence pieces, then adjusted the seat, spinning it upwards, as if undoing a screw, to make it higher. He didn't want this woman thinking he was vertically challenged after all. It seemed to Giles that women would forgive you for a lot of things, but when it came to having to stand on a box to say hello, they bore a grudge. Even in these liberated times, many women still didn't want to be seen with a man who was shorter than they were – not unless they were his mother.

Not that Giles was short. But it always helped to be taller. (*An extra couple of inches always come in handy, old mate. Arf, arf. Har, har!* Roy would have said. But then as Roy's choice of contemporary reading material was limited to the *Sunday Sport*, *Viz* magazine and the *Evening Argus*, that was hardly surprising. In fact, on his off-duty days, he even wore a T-shirt with Johnny Fartpants on the front. And he had another one with some character on it Giles could not remember much about, except that he had unfeasibly large testicles.)

Schoolboy humour. Men never grew up. It had been like this in childhood. It had been like it in youth. It was like it still, in the onset of his middle years. It would be like it in old age – prostate permitting. It was that obsession with bodily functions and the lower organs. Earwax, spitting contests, how high you could pee, what distance you could hurl a dog's dropping, balls-grabbing competitions, chopper contests, Chinese burns, sucking your arm until it bled, demonstrations of advanced masturbation by older boys who bet you couldn't do that with a milk bottle. Dirty Uncle Ernie who hung around the park shelter, offering juveniles fifty pence to have a shufty inside his fly buttons. Endless obsession, endless preoccupation, and with what? What really was the basis of the great obsession? What did it really do?

It went up and down. It just went up and down.

All day long.

That was what women didn't seem to realize. That there

you were, sitting quietly minding your own business, maybe even in church, or at the funeral of a close and much loved friend. When suddenly – ping! There it was. In the midst of grief, in the midst of study, on a bus, on a train, at the cinema, in the middle of a board meeting, anywhere, any time, whether you wanted it or not. Yes, there it was, at both apt and inappropriate moments. With a twinkle in its eye and a shillelagh under its arm. It was your local friendly erection, just knocking on your door, hoping that it wasn't disturbing you, and hadn't called at a bad moment. But could it count on your vote? Could it rely on your support? Yes, it was universal manhood suffrage, all right, and you just had to suffer it. It was the Monster Raving Loony party in your trousers.

It was the general erection.

It was a bloody nuisance, there was no doubt about that. And yet women wondered why men were so juvenile, so schoolboy humour-ish. Well, you needed that juvenile inside you to survive. It was all right for women. How would they know what it was like to have something flapping about in your undergrowth. Oh, they had their periods and their PMT and the pangs of childbirth and all the ills that female flesh was heir to. Giles wasn't trying to gainsay them their miseries, not at all. He just wanted to make the point that it wasn't so easy to be a man either. And if half of these ball-breaking feminists stopped to think about what life would be like with this thing in your trousers popping up and down every few minutes and waving its arms about like a signal on the railways, they might be a bit more sympathetic. In some ways, it was almost like another person, a little Siamese twin joined at the scrotum. Or maybe it was more like a pet, like having a pet dachshund living in your underpants, and which would unpredictably take it into its mind that it wanted to go walkies. And what could you do then? Nothing. Walkies was where you would have to take it, or it would do wee-wees on you.

Yes, that was it! Giles saw everything clearly. That was what this whole thing was about. It wasn't about infidelity. Morality had nothing to do with this. It was simply about taking your plonker out for walkies. It just needed the exercise, that was all. A little run around with a couple of balls.

Giles smiled inanely, and the camera flashed. He was trying to look charming, but he knew that the result would be either vacuous or absurd. He readjusted his pose for the next shot. He had to get at least one good picture out of this. If musical Marilyn didn't like the look of him, she might call the whole thing off.

Flash!

Better that time. Felt better. Loosening up. He showed a few more teeth and readied himself for the next one.

Giles's other bad experiences in photo booths had been due to foreign visitors. For some reason tourists regularly mistook photo booths for the coin operated super-loos.

Quite why they made this mistake, Giles could not imagine. For a start, the seat had no hole in it, and the short curtains could scarcely afford much privacy. Nevertheless, in the foreign tourist would come, insert his money, spend his penny while flashbulbs popped around him, wipe his hands on the curtains, and then disappear to get on with his sightseeing. Five minutes after his departure, a strip photograph would appear in the little chute outside of a tourist with contorted features, in the throes of some strange exertion. And the booth would be rendered inoperable until the cleaners came round.

And they said travel broadened the mind.

Flash! Flash!

Giles went outside to wait for his photographs, which fell into the chute after a few minutes. He held the strip by the edges. Hmm. Three of them were as he'd expected: he looked like a corpse in need of a good stiff glass of embalming fluid. But the fourth photograph, thank god, presented him in an attractive, almost handsome way. By some fluke of light and angles, the photograph made him appear good-looking, sophisticated, worldly-wise, slightly cynical, and, more important, masterly. Magisterial, almost, like a man who could take command. Like a man who knew what to do with a woman in bed. Not like a man who mumbled 'Well, what do you fancy tonight, dear?' and 'Is it my turn to get on top then, or is it yours?' or 'Shall I do it with my socks on, or shall I try it with them off?' No, he looked like a man with a firm grip, who knew what to hold, and when to hold it, when to give it a good squeeze, and when not to. Not at all like Giles himself with his 'Shall I put my hand there?' and his 'Would you like me to squeeze your bum, dear? Or shall I just grip you by the armpits?' To which Holly might reply 'No, not tonight, if you wouldn't mind, Giles, I didn't have time to shave them.'

Yes, it was all so polite, so polite and non-carnal, so – so English.

They spent most of their sex life apologizing to each other. 'Sorry, Holly, was that your –'

'Sorry, Giles, did I put my elbow –'

'Oh, I beg your pardon, was that my finger –'

'Oh, I really must apologize for what happened earlier, Giles, when your nose got trapped in my –'

'No, really, please don't give it another thought. No, not at all, I quite enjoyed it.'

But the man in the passport photograph wasn't like that. He was a skilled seducer. It was almost as if the machine had photographed the Giles within, the Giles as he would like to be. The man in that photograph didn't apologize. Didn't apologize and didn't explain.

Giles had no scissors with him, so he bent the photographic strip backwards and forwards, until he was able to neatly tear the good photograph off. He took his letter to Marilyn from his briefcase, popped the photo inside, sealed the envelope, and then dropped it into a postbox before going to get his train.

So there.

It was done. *Les jeux sont faites encores, mesdames et messieurs.* The dice were rolling once again. Old snake eyes – old snake hips – was trying his luck.

EIGHT

Giles looked at his fellow commuters on the train. Did they discern any difference in him? Had he grown devil's horns? Were cloven hooves breaking through the black leather of his shoes? No. He was the same as ever. He to them as they were to him: uninteresting, mundane, just one more drop of rain in a sea of faces, incapable of passion or feeling, capable only of wearing a suit, carrying a briefcase, reading a newspaper, and shuttling endlessly back and forth on a train from here to there.

But if he was plotting something, and it didn't show, then what were they up to? What were they planning? Murder? Arson? Robbery? Assassination? You never knew. You never really knew about anyone, least of all yourself. The man who knew his own propensities was a wise man indeed.

The train rattled on. The train he hated. The repetitive journey on which he had spent so many hours of his life, simmering with unfocused anger, ranting internally at the unfairness of who knew what. But now he was enjoying the journey. It was like a day trip to the seaside, from a childhood of long ago.

The sea was calm, the sky was blue, and yet something was bothering him – only what?

Bzzz!

Giles moved uneasily. Where was that noise coming from?

Bzzz! Bzzz! Bzzz! Bzzz!

There it was again. What was it? A wasp or something? He shifted uncomfortably. He rolled up his newspaper, ready to swat, then looked across to where another commuter was rummaging about in his briefcase. The man took out a mobile phone, slid a switch and put it to his ear.

'Hello,' he bellowed, 'George Whimpole speaking. Oh, hello,

darling. Yes, how are you? No, I'm not on the train yet, I'm still at the office as a matter of fact.'

Aye, aye. Giles had overheard every word of it. So what was George Whimpole up to? Lying to his missus down the mobile phone. Another lying bastard in a world of lying bastards. Giles looked across at George and warmed to him with fellow feeling. It was like being in the Freemasons and suddenly discovering a friendly handshake in what you had thought to be a hostile world.

'What – you can hear a train? Oh, no, I don't think so, dear. That's just the coffee percolator. Yes, it does sound a bit like a train sometimes.'

The guard came along the corridor. He shouted loudly, 'All tickets, please!'

'What, darling? No, no. I don't think so. No, not tickets please, no, it's Jenkins in accounts, he just came into the office and said, well, tickle my knees. Yes. It's an expression of his. It means, well, sod it, that sort of thing.'

Next a voice came over the intercom. 'This is your steward speaking. The buffet car, situated towards the front of the train, is now open for hot and cold drinks, snacks, meals, light refreshments and –'

'What? What's that, darling?' the urbane and oily George was saying into his mobile. 'You heard something like a steward speaking? Oh no, no, no. Good heavens, you must be hearing things. No, that was the rep from Seeward and Spreakly, who just put his head round the door. No, he didn't say anything about a buffet car. He said, does anyone like a good cigar. Yes, he's handing them out, freebies. You know what these reps are like.'

At that point, George Whimpole turned his head slightly away from his mobile, and said, 'Thanks very much. Havana, is it? Don't mind if I do. Gave up the cigarettes a while ago, but I still enjoy a good cigar every now and again. I'll put it behind my ear for now. Thanks very much.' Then he addressed himself to the phone again. 'What's that, darling? When will I be home? Ah, yes, now that's a tricky one –'

As Giles listened to the lies tumble effortlessly from George's glib and moustached mouth, he realized what the fly in his adulterous ointment was. And thanks to George, he saw both the problem and solution simultaneously.

Giles's problem was one of communication. In his efforts to protect his anonymity though a succession of box numbers, he had rendered himself directly unapproachable. He could hardly conduct an affair through the post indefinitely. If rendezvous arrangements suddenly had to be altered, news of the changes could take three or four days to reach him. Yet he obviously couldn't give out his home telephone number, and his work number was also out of the question – Lavinia might answer his phone when he was out to lunch, or the call might get put through to the wrong extension.

Immediacy of communication was what Giles needed, flexible response. Those were the minimum system requirements these days to get your affair up and running. He needed to do what George there was doing. He needed a mobile phone. He had to get himself wired for sound.

'Yes, well, I'm just leaving the office now,' George was saying to Mrs Whimpole, who was wondering about the timing of his tea. 'Got a few people to see, calls to make, leads to follow up, that kind of thing. So I can't really see myself getting back to Sussex until quite late tonight.'

Sussex?

Sussex was in the opposite direction.

Giles raised an eyebrow. The train blew its whistle.

'What's that, dear? Heard a whistle? No, just the fire alarm. They test it once a month, that's all. Well, I'll see you later then, shall I? Bye, bye. Yes, say goodnight to the children for me. Fine. Bye then.'

George clicked the phone off, and stuffed it back into his briefcase.

So where was he off to, Giles wondered. Whose boudoir was gregarious George about to spend the dying hours of the evening in, when he should have been home in Sussex?

George looked up from his briefcase, just as Giles was about to look away. Their eyes met. It was a contact which both of them would have preferred to avoid. George, the liar, and

Giles, the aural witness to the crime. But the contact had been made, and something had to be said.

'Lovely evening,' George said.

'Lovely,' Giles agreed. Then he hesitated a moment before adding, 'I don't suppose you know a place to get a good deal on a mobile phone?'

George Whimpole's face brightened. Here indeed was an opportunity to combine business with the pleasure he was bent on. He took a limp piece of white cardboard from his top pocket and handed it to Giles.

'I can get you one,' he said. 'No problem. Let me give you my card. Mobile phones – that's my business! Among other things. I'm in communications.'

'Oh, right,' Giles said. 'Right, I see.'

Yes, he saw all right, he saw that George Whimpole was another lying bastard in a world of lying bastards, and what else could he be in, but communications?

When the train stopped at his station, Giles got off and went to his battered old car in the car park. The guilt and the remorse got to him on the short journey back to the house, but once through the door, his reception soon dispelled them. He was received in his home with all the joy greeting an unwanted, elderly relative, arriving to occupy the spare room for an indefinite period.

'Hello, Ella, hello Lynnie.' He proffered a cheek for kisses which did not materialize.

'Oh, hello Dad, it's you, is it? I thought it might have been someone. Could you close the door, we're watching the TV.'

Onwards, into the kitchen.

'Hello, Holly. Had a good day?'

'No, awful, as a matter of fact. I co-ordinated a whole wardrobe of clothes for that old bat in the Maltings last week, spent ages at it, finally found a colour to suit her – which wasn't easy, believe me – I go round today with the samples, and what has she gone and done? She's had a blue rinse, that's all!'

'Does that matter?'

'Of course it matters. Nothing matches now. I'll have to start all over again.'

'Oh.'

'Yes! Exactly.'

A turn of the back then, a swivel on the heel, and the resumption of the broccoli slicing which she had been doing when he came in. Giles left the evening paper on the surface, and slunk out like a cowed dog.

He went up to the bedroom to change out of his suit. He felt cynical, bitter and disillusioned. How about *his* day? How come no one asked him about that? He stood before the mirror in his underpants, making cynical, bitter and disillusioned smiles. He would keep a few of those in reserve, get the hang of them properly, so that he could deploy them as needed. A man about to be unfaithful to his wife needs a few smiles like that up his sleeve.

Giles took a look at his reflection. He was naked, apart from pants and socks. He took the socks off, as they seemed to spoil the effect. There was something rather unsophisticated about socks. Socks were a downer, wearing them an act of pathos. It was hard to believe that some of the world's greatest revolutionaries had gone about wearing socks. It seemed to undermine the sanctity of their cause.

Hmm.

Not bad though. He turned sideways. Not bad. Pretty flat really, that stomach, for a man of his age. All the squash, probably, and the occasional work-out – nothing too strenuous. Bit of jogging at the weekends as well. Cycling with the kids – until they got too cool for that. He turned, putting his back to the mirror, and peered over his shoulder at his reflection.

Yes. Not bad. Not bad as backsides go. The sort of backside that women would go for, Giles reckoned. He could almost hear them now, squealing with passion 'Oh, Giles, Giles, what a wonderful backside you have! A bum like that should be treasured. It's a real gem.'

Or something along those lines.

It was all in the backside.

But then again, look at Roy, the gigolo of the nine-to-five set. You couldn't say he had a nice backside. It looked more like an old sports bag, with a few items of lumpy kit in it, maybe a cricket bat, and a pair of trainers, and a smelly old towel. But he had no end of amorous success. So maybe it wasn't the backside that did it after all.

But that wasn't the point. No, the point was that if it should come to a showdown where backsides were the deciding factor, well, Giles had the gear. That was a backside to be proud of, that one. In fact, backside-wise, Giles didn't mind saying, his was something of a collector's item.

He put on jeans and a sweatshirt. He did have a very comfortable pair of slacks and a diamond-patterned jumper he was rather fond of, from the Leisure Wear range, but he didn't wear them so much now, at least not when his daughters were in the house. He'd got fed up with the ridicule, with the two girls elbowing each other in the ribs, giggling and snorting like a couple of slow punctures, egging each other on to new heights of mockery and derision every time he changed into his weekend and after-work clobber.

'Got your leisure wear on again then, Dad,' Lynnie would say. *Nudge, nudge, snort snort, giggle giggle*.

'And what is wrong with my leisure wear, exactly?' he once rather foolishly demanded.

'Nothing Dad,' Ella had said, springing – he had thought – to his defence. 'Nothing at all, it's really – really –' *Chortle chortle* '– fashionable!'

Snortedy-snortedy-snort! Each setting the other back off again, the moment she stopped. 'And Dad, Dad –' Lynnie's nose starting to run now, and small tears of hysteria leaking from Ella's eyes.

'What?'

'Dad, Dad, when you go out – seeing you're in your leisure wear – will you be, you know, will you be wearing your . . . Hush Puppies as well?'

Silence. They watched and waited for a reaction. But to be honest, to be perfectly honest, he couldn't see the joke.

'Why? What's funny about my Hush Puppies?'

And that was it. It was round about then that World War Three had broken out, as two thin girls of medium height had collapsed in terminal hysterics on the bed.

He'd stopped wearing the slacks so often after that. It wasn't worth the aggravation. They were still hanging up in the wardrobe though, awaiting their chance to shine. He'd wait till his daughters had gone off on that summer camp and then he'd have a good week in them. They were pretty comfy too, those slacks. And the jumper. And he still didn't see what was funny about his Hush Puppies.

Holly called up the stairs. 'It's ready, Giles! What are you doing up there?'

'Just coming!'

Giles stood in front of the mirror and checked his appearance. Jeans with a smart crease in them, his new sweatshirt with the yacht club motif, the two anchors on the front and the coil of rope on the back. He didn't look bad. Not bad at all.

He took a last look at himself in the mirror. He winked.

You're all right, Giles West.

Giles West?

But no, it wasn't anymore, was it.

You're all right, Jimmy Tile.

Giles West *is* Jimmy Tile (appearing at your local cinema, for one week only).

Giles winked at Jimmy. Jimmy winked back. Giles left the bedroom and went down to the kitchen.

Jimmy Tile was no longer in the mirror. Jimmy Tile was probably round at Marilyn's house, just about to drop his kaks and allow her an admiring glimpse of his posterior before getting down to business.

Marilyn, musical Marilyn.

Just a letter, just a phone call away.

NINE

Within three days, Giles had his portable telephone, and Marilyn had replied. He opened her letter as he left the sorting office and read it as he walked along. The man behind the counter at the sorting office had had a bandage round his head. 'Had an accident,' he told Giles, 'at a pedestrian crossing. Some maniac knocked me over. Went straight through a blue light.'

Giles mumbled his sympathies and hurried off to see what delights the post had brought him. He tore Marilyn's letter open with hands which trembled slightly.

Dear Jimmy, *(That was Giles.)*
Well, well. *(Good start, mate, good start. Read on.)* Make some beautiful music together, you say. Yes, why don't we do that? If you brought your flute along, perhaps I could show you my squeeze-box. *(Saucy stuff, mate, saucy.)* And Wednesday night is a good night for me, too. I'm generally in the mood for a little relaxation by then. Oh, and I got your photograph too. What nice soulful eyes you have. *(All the better to ogle you with, granny.)* So let's arrange a little get-together, shall we? Why not give me a call. Here's my phone number. I look forward to hearing from you and learning all about your favourite tunes.
Yours in anticipation,
Marilyn Crinker

God!
It was paint stripper. It would take the enamel off your saucepans, correspondence like that. It oozed sex, positively oozed it, if Giles – sorry, Jimmy – was any judge.
Jimmy? Jimmy!

Giles suddenly realized that he had unconsciously adopted as his *nom de infidelity* the brand name of his contraceptive – Jimmy. Perhaps that made it more of a *nom de condom* then. He wished he had chosen something else, but it was too late now. Maybe he'd adopt a different name for the next one.

Next one?

Hold on, Giles. This was only meant to be a one-off. Not the start of a new career. A taste of honey, not a pot of it, and your own apiary.

No, quite. Slip of the thought, that was all.

Giles opened and read his other letters as he walked back to the office. His new, lightweight mobile phone, registered in the name of James Tile, sat in his pocket like a brick – the very symbol and substance of his betrayal.

The new replies to his advertisement were disappointing. True, there were no more letters from the over-eighties, but the general standard of response was not encouraging. Giles binned the lot, deciding to concentrate on Marilyn, and not to spread himself too thinly. Maybe his ad needed rewording. He'd attend to that later.

He re-read Marilyn's letter. Beautiful music, squeeze-box, bring along your flute, look forward to finding out your favourite tune – well, you couldn't get more specific than that without getting specific.

So was he going to ring her? Or not? And if so, when?

Giles felt for his mobile phone, but for some reason he didn't want to use it. He spotted a vacant Telecom phone booth, halfway along Rute Street, went inside, took his phone card, and inserted it into the slot. He spread Marilyn's letter out on the ledge before him, and then he –

Should have dialled.

But he didn't want to do it. Not now. The tide came in and a wave of depression washed up the beach. Suddenly it was all useless. Nothing was ever going to make a difference. Not affairs, not sex, not drink, not drugs, not the latest film, the best-looking sunset or anything. Everything that made life worthwhile was worthless.

Come on, Giles, snap out of it, make the call.

But the call meant danger, change, a step out of the rut. Only it was a nice rut. A nice safe rut, to grow old and die in, and which you could follow all the way along to the end. It was almost as if you could see a sign KEEP YOUR HEAD DOWN AND FOLLOW THIS RUT. And if he did, he would be safe. Not very happy, maybe, but safe. Holly would be there, Ella and Lynnie would be there, the annual holiday would be there, the job would be there, growing old together in that domestic discontent would be there.

Make the call, Giles!

He would be giving up so much, losing the security of minor unhappiness, risking what he had, in return for what? Major unhappiness? Greater dissatisfactions?

He replaced the receiver. He couldn't do it, he was not made of that kind of stuff. He was cut from another cloth. The cloth of mediocrity, of middle-class, never-risk-anything, do-nothing mediocrity.

But as he went to open the door he saw a familiar face out in the street.

It was Roy. Roy, with a woman on his arm. And not just any old woman. A new woman. A stunner. An absolute mega-ton bomb.

He'd gone and done it again. He'd acquired another one. He was on to Doris Number Six.

Giles let go of the door, and put his phone card back into the slot. Without any hesitation he punched Marilyn's number, and waited for the ring to be answered.

'Hello!'

'Hello, look, this is –'

'Hello. If this is the number you dialled, then this is the number you've got. If it's not the number you wanted, well, I'm afraid you've dialled it anyway. Either way, if you want to leave a message, please speak after the tone.'

'Oh, hello, hi –' Clumsy now, bloody answering machines. 'This is – *Who the hell was he again? Jimmy Giles? Hammer? Trowel? Grouting? Tile, that was it!* – this is Jimmy Tile. Hi. Got your letter, and I'm just giving you a call. *Suave now, Giles, sophisticated, a little bon mot if you can.* I was just going to suggest that we could maybe meet – how about this Wednesday? *Where? The Wart and Teaspoons? No. Too trendy. He should have planned all this in advance.* In the Cat and Puncture, say, on the Cheltenham Road, if you know it? *Oh, god, why had he suggested there? Dump with a capital D.* At eight o'clock? I'll be wearing – well, no, I don't need to, do I, you've got my photograph, and I've got yours, and very nice it is too. *Oh, compliments, Giles, compliments.* Well, I'll give you my number in case ... well, here it is anyway. This is my mobile – I carry it about with me – it's portable.' He gave her the number. 'I'll look forward to seeing you. And if I don't hear from you before, I'll assume everything's okay. Right. Oh, and I'll –' *Tones redolent of musk and sex and single malt whisky and the seducer's charter.* 'I'll look forward to hearing your squeeze-box, and I'll certainly try and remember my horn. *Flute, Giles, flute! What are you saying?* That is, of course, my trombone – *Trombone? What are you doing, Giles. If she thinks it's that big, she'll run a mile.* That is, my flu –'

Beep, beep, beep!

The answering machine cut him off. He retrieved his phone card, and hurried back to work.

So that was it then. It was done. The bread was cast upon the waters, and even if the vultures hovered overhead, it was too late now. He had his mobile phone in his pocket, his condoms in his wallet, and his excuses at the ready.

Wednesday. Tomorrow. Wednesday at eight. Thirty-one hours from now.

Sex, at last, with another woman. No longer a one-gal guy. Knowledge, experience, understanding. Knowing what he had been missing all these years. A different body, different curves, different contours, different responses.

At last.

He hurried up the steps into the office building. It was happening. It was all his own work. He had initiated an enterprise. He had made a difference. It was going to be all right. Marilyn was going to be wonderful. In and out of bed.

He had a feeling that all this might be a lot more than sex. He had a feeling that it was going to be love.

Giles nodded to Sandy and Terry who, he was pleased to see, were working hard as he entered the section. Lavinia passed and left a memo on his desk.

MEMO

Re Notelets.

  Please note that Notelets are only to be used for notes. Notelets must not be used for shopping lists or personal messages of non-work related nature. If employees wish to use Notelets for shopping lists they may purchase Shop-lets at Ryfield's the Stationer's at a discounted rate, on production of a staff membership card. Shoplets must not however be used for notes, and any notes found to be written on Shoplets will be disregarded. If, for example, a member of staff wishes to buy, say, Twiglets, they must write *Remember to buy Twiglets* on a Shoplet, not a Notelet. If, however, Twiglets were being bought for a staff func-tion, then *Remember to buy Twiglets* should be written on a Notelet, not a Shoplet.

Giles initialled the memo to vouch that he had read it and thought it utterly trivial, and he looked for someone to pass it on to.

  Ah. There was Roy, standing by his desk.

  'Had this?'

  'Yeah, already had it, old mate. Just came over to say –'

  'I know!' Giles said. 'I saw you walking down the street.' He couldn't bear this, he really couldn't. Roy and these women. What did he have? Some sort of genetic equivalent of a dog-whistle, which only women could hear?

  'Doris Six, mate. Met her in the Weasel and Blackboard. I'd just nipped in for a pint, and we got chatting at the bar.'

  The Weasel and Blackboard had once been called The Three Tuns, but, along with many other pubs in the area, it had been taken over, relaunched and rechristened with some absurd name in the hope that it would bring in the younger set.

  It didn't. It brought in Roy.

'I thought you didn't like the Weasel and Blackboard. I thought you used The Compact Disc and Trousers now.'

'No, too trendy for me,' Roy said. 'I'll tell you what though, the Maggot and Hairspray's not a bad place since that new landlord took over. They do you a nice pint of Prairie Oyster in there. Very nutty that. And strong.'

Not only had the breweries renamed the pubs, they had renamed the beers as well.

'No, I tried a half of Prairie Oyster,' Giles said, 'too syrupy for me. I much prefer a drop of Frog's Ankle myself.'

'Yeah. Got a bit of a kick in it that,' Roy agreed. 'Though for my money, if you're having a night out, and aren't driving, the one to go for is a pint of Uncle Oswald's Circumstances or a nice drop of Roger's Hat Pins – that's very smooth.'

'What about Landlord's Truncheon? Are they still doing that?'

'Only in bottles,' Roy said. 'But if you like a drop of the old-style mild, you should treat yourself to a pint of Mrs Wonkin's Bicycle, up at the Coathanger and Walrus.'

'No,' said Giles, 'too noisy for me in there.'

'Only on Saturdays,' Roy said. 'And they've been getting some guest beers in too, from up north. I had a taste of My Little Pit Pony in there, that's good. Then if you're ever in the Haddock and Brainsurgery, you should try this new cider they've got, Granny Grabs Your Pips it's called. Very nice with a bit of cheese. Or there's Farmer –'

It could have gone on all afternoon, and probably would have done, had Lavinia not intervened. She didn't actually say anything, she didn't need to. She just trained her sights on Roy, and she shot him down in one.

'Yes, well then, must get back to work, old mate. Get the old proboscis to the old grindstone, eh? Right.'

Lavinia passed. The ironed and starched edges of her clothes were as sharp as scalpels.

Roy leaned over Giles's desk for a final confidence. 'Yeah, Doris Number Six now, mate. And the Doris Management Programme's coming on a dream. I could probably easily handle another half dozen, no worries. I tell you, when this is up and running, everyone'll want a copy. We'll be able to buy out Microsoft. You've got to come in on this, Giles. We'll make millions. We'll have all the money and women in the world. Bonk ourselves bloody senseless.'

Giles was starting to wonder if Roy hadn't bonked himself halfway senseless already. Maybe a surfeit of Dorises and too many glasses of Roger's Hat Pins were distorting what passed for reality inside his mind.

What was it again that the gods did to those they would destroy?

Oh yes. First they drove them mad. And Roger's Hat Pins and too many Dorises were just steps along the way to insanity. It was knowing where to stop that mattered. Knowing just where to draw the line.

You didn't want to get too tied up.

In any sense of the word.

TEN

There she was: Marilyn. And just as in her photograph. Maybe a little under average height, thirtyish, as Giles had estimated, and pretty, but not beautiful, slim, but not thin, but then not plump either. Yes, she was the Little Bear's porridge, he thought – just about right. Not too hot, not too cold, not too hard, not too soft, not too big, not too small.

Just perfick.

Had Giles been a director round at Central Casting, and had he been looking for an actress to play the girl-next-door who had stayed at home, got married, got hurt, got wiser, got divorced and moved on, then Marilyn was the woman he would have chosen for the part.

She was well-dressed too – casual, but not too casual, trendy, but not too trendy. Her demeanour was conservative, but with a hint of rebellion in there, a smattering of unknown and unpredictable things. But then, Giles thought, there had to be, or she would never have answered his advertisement.

Giles was at the bar when she entered. She came in unobtrusively, yet with confidence, entering a crowded bar on her own plainly didn't faze her. A few heads turned, a few lads nudged their mates. But then Marilyn spotted Giles, perched on a stool, recognized him immediately from the photograph he had sent her, smiled a dissolving smile, and headed straight in his direction.

'Jimmy –'

Who?

'James Tile?'

It couldn't be her then. She was looking for another bloke.

'I knew you from your photo immediately.'

Oh yes, of course. That Jimmy Tile! Giles's alter ego, his doppelgänger.

'Marilyn! Great to see you.'

He got down off his bar stool like a proper gent, and stood a moment, frozen, not knowing whether he was supposed to kiss her, shake her hand, or – in view of the purpose of the rendezvous – give her breasts a squeeze and say, 'Well, everything seems to be in working order.'

Luckily, she took the initiative, and planted a peck on Giles's cheek.

She kissed him.

Actually kissed him. A woman who was not his wife, not his mother, not his daughter and not his Auntie Stottie had actually kissed him. The last time such a thing had happened was when he'd collapsed from heat exhaustion in the street and a passing Girl Guide troupe – most of whom had halitosis – had attempted to give him mouth-to-mouth in order to get their first-aid badges.

The smell of Marilyn's perfumed skin was intoxicating. Giles felt like downing his drink, grabbing her by the arm, running out of the Cat and Puncture with her to the nearest hotel room and getting down to the business in hand right then and there.

But no. Even adultery, even sex with strangers, must have its preliminaries. You can't hurry curry. And Giles didn't know it for a fact, but he supposed that even in the most functional of bordellos, in the most financial of transactions, there were first a few opening words, a platitude or two about the weather, or how your ticket was doing on the National Lottery.

'So you're . . . musical then, James?'

Giles looked blank. Was he *what*?

'Musical?'

Oh *that*. Yes. Giles – sorry, Jimmy – was musical all right. Liked nothing better than a bit of Beethoven. He'd put that in his advertisement, hadn't he, that he was fond of music. Yes, well, you had to say something. You didn't want to seem like a total void. And to be honest, m'dear, Giles would happily be anything you wanted. Musical, sporty, intellectual, cultural, tall, short, black, white, anything, just as long as he could get his leg –

'Can I get you a drink?' he heard himself say. Odd how

carnal feelings sublimated themselves into harmless chat.

'Umm, thanks.'

'What would you like?'

'What are you having?'

Giles looked rather guiltily at his half-pint, wishing that he had treated himself to something a little more sophisticated. 'Em, I'm having a half of – of Woggler's Toenail, as a matter of fact.'

Did they have to give these beers such stupid names?

'Oh, perhaps I'll have a sparkling mineral water,' Marilyn said. 'Keep a clear head.'

Giles reached for his wallet.

Say no more love, say no more. He got the significance of that one, it wasn't wasted on him. *Keep a clear head, eh?* And they both knew what that was for. For the nookies to come. There was a coded message there all right, mate. *Don't drink too much*, she was saying. And Giles wouldn't either. Just another half or so and that would be it. He couldn't do this stone-cold sober, but on the other hand, he wouldn't be able to do it stone-hot drunk. Just enough alcohol to loosen up, and that would be it. He'd better try and demonstrate a little sophistication too. Maybe he'd go on to the shorts. He beckoned the barman over and ordered her a bottle of Sellafield Spring.

Marilyn slid on to a stool next to him. As she did the sliding, her skirt rose up around her rump, exposing two very nicely shaped legs. She put a hand out to steady herself and it landed on Giles's thigh.

'Sorry.'

'That's okay.' *Really, that's okay, really.*

'So, Jimmy, tell me all about yourself.'

Where did he begin?

Which particular card did he deal, from his great big pack of lies? He decided that she would probably never believe him no matter what he said. So he told her the truth, more or less, he just changed the names a little to protect the sober.

'– and just because you want to have sex,' he ended suavely, 'no strings attached, that's nothing to be ashamed of.'

'Exactly, James,' she agreed. 'Absolutely. It's just what I used to say to my husband.'

Giles stiffened. Husband. It came as a blow, and yet he should have expected that word. He had assumed that she was unattached. But it had come to husbands already. And was that big husband or little husband? Was that psychopathically jealous husband, or was that meek, mild and bespectacled itsy-bitsy, teeny-weeny, need to stand on a box to come up to your navel husband? Was that husband as in 'gone abroad for a business meeting and won't be back for a fortnight' or was that husband as in 'might walk in any second and start swinging a claw hammer around'?

'Yes, it's just as I used to say to my husband – well, before we got divorced that is.'

Divorced. Sigh of relief. Get back to Central Casting, she'd passed the screen test, she still had the part. She was divorced. That was better, in fact, that was bloody perfect. Divorcées had their own homes to go to. They could go back to her place.

Aye, aye. Now what was going on under the counter? There was that hand on his thigh again. You could get very fond of a hand like that.

'James –'

'Yes, ahem, Marilyn.'

'I hope you brought your flute with you tonight.'

How to handle this one? Jocularly? Yes. 'Never travel anywhere without it.' Got a smile. That was the right thing to say.

'Shall we have another?'

She'd downed the Sellafield Spring sharpish. Giles glanced at his watch. Another one? But would that give them enough time? Holly would be expecting him back between eleven and midnight, although he could probably safely leave it until one a.m. at a push, but that would have to be the latest.

He had rung her up and told her that he was playing squash after work with Roy. The story was that he and Roy had entered the Squash Software Cup, an intercompany competition which was going to take six weeks of Wednesdays to play.

Whether six weeks of Wednesdays had the edge over a month of Sundays, Giles neither knew nor cared. All that concerned him was that it gave him an alibi. Maybe not a perfect alibi – if any alibi was perfect – but it was the best he was likely to get.

It happened that both Roy and Giles had actually put their names in for the Squash Software Cup, but they had both been rapidly eliminated from the field in the early heats. Roy's failure to shine was due to an excess of Roger's Hat Pins, fornication, and too many late nights spent working on refinements to the Doris Management Programme. Giles's poor showing he put down to his own domestic difficulties and his preoccupation with his box number.

Giles had no fear whatsoever that Roy would ring up for him while he was out and blow the gaff as far as Holly was concerned. Roy never rang up for fear of incriminating himself. The only one ever to ring up was Mrs Roy – presently, though she did not know it, relegated to the lowly status of Doris Number Seven, or was it eight? and falling. If she got relegated much further, she'd soon be up for a transfer.

So Giles did not have to worry that Roy might inadvertently betray him, and Roy did not have to worry about Giles. Giles had every confidence in his friend's total unreliability. You could always depend on Roy to be out of an evening deceiving his nearest and dearest. In that respect, he would never let you down.

Marilyn asked for a dry white this time – she must have decided that a slightly fuzzy head was better than a totally clear one – and Giles had the same. He paid for the drinks and they clinked glasses.

'Cheers!'

'Cheers!'

'To us!'

'To us!'

Repetition, of course, was a confirmation ceremony, a confirmation of mutual intent.

Giles sneaked a look at his watch. 8.20. They'd be out of the bar by half-past if he could manage it, and on their way to her place. Clothes off and into bed by half-nine at the latest. Dressed again and on his way by, what? half-ten, quarter to eleven. Late train, car, and then home by twelve to twelve-thirty. A little later than he'd planned, but never mind. Roy the famous alibi wouldn't let him down.

Ten minutes to kill. He smiled at her.

'So tell me about yourself, Marilyn.' *But not too much.*

So she did.

A little.

'Not a lot to tell,' she began, as people invariably do, apologizing in advance for a mundane and uneventful life, which nine times out of ten proves to be far more interesting than they imagine.

It was a road to self-discovery story. Small town stuff. A village in the Cotswolds which had been too small. A move to the city, which had at first seemed too big, but now she could hardly imagine herself living anywhere else. Love had come along, then marriage, and then a gradual growing apart. Divorce then, followed by a period of loneliness and uncertainty (and probably promiscuity, Giles would have guessed.) Then, after a while, a new confidence, a new self, a new job, a fresh, independent life.

'Marilyn,' Giles said. There was something bothering him. 'Can I ask you a question?'

'Yes, James? What is it?' She looked at him coolly and appraisively.

'I mean, well, you're not like me – no obligations, no commitments. Attractive woman like you – all I mean is, when you've probably got far more choice – scope – than I have, why me? Why my ad? Why – a married man?'

'Because they're so much more obliging, James,' she purred. 'So much more discreet. And besides, when you're a single woman, it's not quite as easy and as carefree as you make it seem. Especially with . . . musical interests.'

There she was. On about the music again. Giles was beginning to wonder if she didn't have a bit of a bee in her bonnet about this. He hoped that he wasn't going to have to spend an hour wading through her CD collection before they got cracking on the real business, and the underwear started flying off.

'Well, shall we go?'

She took his arm as they went out into the street. It was an odd feeling – strange, nostalgic. It was a feeling of youth, of adolescence long ago, the touch of a girl's hand on your arm. Beautiful, poignant, moving.

It wasn't just sex, it wasn't. It was more than that. It was grief. Sadness. Loss. The inevitability of ageing, of slowly turning to stone, the prospect – the certainty – of death. It was about feeling young again.

'You okay?'

'Fine.'

She gestured towards her hand on his arm. 'Do you mind that? Does it embarrass you? Make you feel uncomfortable?'

'No,' Giles said. 'It makes me feel great.'

She hesitated a moment, then asked another question. *Your starter for ten, and no conferring.*

'Does it give you an erection?'

I'm waiting. Your answer, please.

'Yes.'

'Good. Then we're honest with each other.'

'I suppose so,' Giles said, not really sure what she meant. 'Do you have a car?'

'I walked. It's only five minutes to my place. And James –'

'Yes?'

'I'll never tell. You can be sure of that. I'll never tell anyone. I'm not into breaking up marriages or anything like that.'

'No?'

'No. You're perfectly safe with me. This way then – home James!' she said. 'And don't spare the horses!' Giles grinned. He grinned again as Marilyn made an outlandish, exaggerated gesture, as though whacking a horse on the rump with a riding crop.

'Ouch!' Giles mugged. 'That hurt!'

She smiled up at him with half-lidded, lazy eyes.

'Let's go home, James, and put on some music.'

Yes, put it on. And then face it.

* * *

112

Holly was lying on the sofa in the living room when the phone rang. It was twenty-five to nine. Ella and Lynnie were up in their rooms, quiet, but probably not yet asleep. The television was on in front of her, and her hand was down the front of her leggings. She wasn't doing anything with it, just keeping it there. It was a comfort to have your hand down your leggings once in a while. She might do something with her hand later, but for now, just having it down the front of the old leggings was enough. It was nice to have the house to yourself too. Well, not entirely to yourself, obviously, but at least this part of it, this room, this small amount of personal time and space.

Yes, your own personal time and space, your own personal cup of tea, and your own personal packet of chocolate biscuits.

Munch, munch, munch.

She had to swallow her biscuits quickly so that her mouth wouldn't be full when she answered the phone. Typical though, that was so typical! You get settled at last, a bit of time to yourself, girls in their rooms, a nice documentary about women's menstrual problems on the TV, a cup of tea, a packet of chocolate digestives, the old hand down the old leggings, and there you are – the phone rings.

Well, pardon my language.

It wasn't that she couldn't eat chocolate biscuits while Giles was there. She could. In fact he was often on at her to put on a bit of weight.

'I sometimes wonder if you're anorexic.'

But she wasn't? Was she? No.

'Why don't you eat a few biscuits or something?'

But that wasn't the point at all. The secrecy was half the pleasure. The secrecy, the concealment, the privacy of a good pig-out. And Giles wasn't due back for hours yet. There were still the tinned peaches to do. And the yoghurts. And the Häagen Dazs ice-cream. And the Swiss roll. And then the –

And then the phone had to ring. She should have put the answering machine on. It was damned inconsiderate, coming between a woman and her snacks. But when she answered it, it was only someone selling patio doors, and they had all that, so she soon got rid of him and told him he ought to do some proper market research next time, before he bothered people in their homes.

Anyway, another biscuit then. Why not?

Crunch, crunch, crunch.

Have those tinned peaches in a minute too. A glass of wine, even. And a packet of cheese straws, and maybe microwave a bag of popcorn. Meantime, finish these biscuits.

Sounds like the girls are both asleep now. Could turn the TV off for a moment.

Old hand down the old leggings.

Leave the phone off the hook. Maybe just move that mirror a little. Just change the angle a bit so that –

Yes. That's better.

Oh, Giles. Where are you when I need you?

Old mate.

ELEVEN

'Come in, James.'

She pushed the door open and led him into a dim, narrow corridor, with a mirrored wardrobe along one side. She flicked a light switch, and the hall cheered up and welcomed him.

'Nice place,' he said. Other people's houses, like other people's children, should always be praised when popularity was your aim.

'Yes, isn't it? Would you like a drink?'

'Thanks.'

Which way the bedroom? Giles wondered. Then in momentary panic, he thrust his hand down into his pocket. Ah, sigh of relief. *I say, Barman, sighs of relief all round! I've been reunited with my Massive Cucumber. I thought it had gone walkabout, but the prodigal has returned. There is more joy in heaven over the condom returned. I say, I say, is that a Massive Cucumber in your pocket, Giles, or are you just pleased – har, har!* Steady, Giles, you're getting nervous. Yes, just a bit nervous, I'm afraid. Bit of an Arctic blast downstairs, if you get my meaning. Cold showers not necessary. Bit of a tiny little plonker situation just at the moment. All shrivelling up like a duff balloon.

'Go up into the living room, I'll bring the drinks.'

Drinks, yes. Good idea. Revive the flagging member with a good stiff –

Up, did she say? Ah, yes, up to the living room. Yes, the house was on three storeys. Kitchen, dining room and cloakroom on the ground floor, living room in the middle, master bedroom on the top. Or is it mistress bedroom in this case?

Giles –

Yes?

Shut up. You sound like a bloody estate agent.

He entered the living room and looked out over the water-

115

front. The lights from the houseboats moored by the dockside sparkled in the water. Beautiful, wonderful, always fancied a houseboat. When all this is over, I might go and live in one on the Norfolk Broads.

Marilyn entered with a bottle of wine and two glasses. Surely she was about to utter the famous words, 'I'll just go and slip into something more comfortable.'

But no. She didn't know that script.

'Lovely view, isn't it?'

'Lovely.' Maybe she had estate agent proclivities as well.

'Sit down?'

'Yes. Thanks.'

Chair or sofa? Sofa. That way she could sit beside him and put her hand on his thigh again. He sat on the sofa.

She sat on a chair.

Sofa so good, Giles? Har, har!

Sofa not so good.

'Nervous?'

'Yes.'

Who was asking the questions though, and who was answering them?

'Done this before?'

'No. You?'

'Maybe.'

Aha.

'What sort of music do you like?'

'Me? Oh, anything really. Anything and everything. Pop, classical, folk, blues, reggae –'

'Heavy metal?'

'Em, well –'

'I've got a lot of heavy metal, James. We can maybe . . . put some on later.'

Followed by a salacious wink.

And yet she made no effort to turn any music on. So what did that mean, Giles? Put some heavy metal on – wink, wink? You understand what that's all about? Search me, mate. Way above my head. Have a sip of your drink.

Where's she gone?

Giles, she's gone! Where's she gone, mate? She was on that chair a second ago, plain as a pork pie in a – and now she's – bloody hell! What's that? Oh, god, it's a hand. Just a hand. There she is, look, down on the floor, leaning against the sofa, with her hand up your trouser leg, just playing gently with your calf. Well, it is her sofa, I suppose, but all the same.

So what now?

Better respond then, to her opening gambit. Move a few pieces around the board, show a bit of willing. Only what to do? Pawn to where? Or should he move his rook? The right sort of gesture, that was the thing. Only you can't reach much from here, not in this position. Well, just do what you can then, Giles, do your best.

So he patted her on the head. He tried to make it as erotic as possible, but it was difficult to charge a pat on the head with any sort of passion. It was all a bit like taking the dog for a walk. *But that was the idea, wasn't it, old mate? Take the old dog for a walk?*

'Shall we – shall we go – upstairs then?' Giles said. He knew that there was nervousness in his voice, but there was determination in it also, resolution and resolve. There were stirrings down there too, in the faithful, trusty old Marks and Spencer's underpants – good boy, good boy. They probably wouldn't approve mind, neither Mr Marks nor Mr Spencer, nor their assigns and heirs, not of their underpants being the unwitting parties to extra-marital fornication. But at least there was life in them, life in the undies still.

'Just finish our wine, shall we, and then –'

Ping!

Had he heard something? No, it was just a trick of the mind. Or was it? No. It was for real. She had undone the top button of her blouse. What did that mean then? Was that an invitation? Should Giles be slipping the old mitt in at this juncture and giving the old 36-cup the benefit of a good squeeze, tweaking the old nipple, giving the old doorbell a little ring to see who was at home? What was the procedure, exactly? At what pace were you supposed to move? How was a novice adulterer supposed to go about it? Roy would know. In fact, he wished

Roy was here, to give him a spot of advice. *Left a bit, mate, left a bit. Right a bit. Shoot!* Or even if he had been outside the window with a megaphone, bellowing up instructions, acting the Cyrano de Bergerac to his whatshisname – the dim, good-looking one. Well, dim, anyway.

Ping!

There went another button. Time to do it, Giles, this is it. Once this first contact is made, then you're committed, you know that, don't you? This is the boundary, this is the frontier. The sign reads INFIDELITY STARTS HERE. The first touch of the breast, and that's it, Holly betrayed. The marriage irrevocably changed. Finished even. Who can say? The thought is one thing, we all have thoughts, and maybe the thought is as bad as the deed, but the deed is the thing with the repercussions.

The advertisement, the letters, the meetings, all this can be forgiven, tossed away and forgotten as if it had never happened. But not the touch. Not that. Flesh on flesh. Grown-up stuff, big boys and big girls, not playing at mums and dads and wives and lovers now, but this – adults only. Adult as in adultery.

Touch Marilyn's breast, Giles, and neither you, nor she, nor Holly, not Ella, nor Lynnie, nor the unhappy happy home, nor the cat, nor the goldfish will ever be the same again.

The vast consequences of infinitesimal actions.

Ping!

The buttons were going, she was undoing the blouse all the way. She looked up at him. His hand moved. It moved and he could not control it, as if it were under a hypnotist's command. It moved towards her breast.

Ping! Ping, ping! Ping!

The pinging was like wildfire. Just how many buttons did she have?

Ping, ping!

'James, is that your phone?'

'What?'

'Ringing? In your pocket?'

What? God, yes, it was. It was the bloody mobile. The bloody mobile phone ringing. Who the hell was ringing him at this time of night, when he was slap-bang in the middle of committing himself to serious adultery?

'Sorry,' he mumbled, 'meant to switch it off.' He fumbled for the phone. 'Better answer it, I suppose, sorry about that.'

She uncoiled herself from around his feet with a grace that was either feline or serpentine, though which it was Giles did not, right at that moment, have time to decide.

'I'll be upstairs,' she said. 'Come up when you're ready.'

And she was gone then, shedding her blouse as she went, like a snake shedding its skin. *Must have been serpentine.* She turned in the doorway and gave him a look, the sort of look that went straight to your genitals, and inflamed them, until your scrotum swelled up like a haggis. The way a python looked at its dinner. *Serpentine, definitely.*

'Just answer the phone –' And she was gone.

Ring, ring.

'Hello,' Giles said. Who the hell could it be? Who had his number? Apart from Marilyn, nobody he could think of at all.

'Hello? Mr West?'

'Yes, speaking.'

'George Whimpole. How are you?'

Who?

'Whimpole. George Whimpole. Of Whimpole Communications.'

Oh, of course, the lying bastard on the train, the lying bastard who had sold him this mobile phone.

'Hope I'm not disturbing you. Not called at an inopportune moment, have I? No? Good. This is just a courtesy call, as a matter of fact. All part of the aftersales service. Everything fine, is it? No problems with the phone?'

'No, none at all, only I do happen to be a bit –'

'So if I could just ask you a quick question or two then, it would help us improve our service. Now, on a rating of one to ten, how satisfied are you with Whimpole Communications customer attention? Are you very satisfied, which would be ten, moderately satisfied, which would score five, or not satisfied at all, which would be a one, or even zero.'

'Very satisfied,' Giles said. 'Ten! All right?' There, that ought to get rid of him.

'And would you be interested in receiving information about any of our other products? Modems? Fax machines? Novelty pencil sharpeners?'

'Not at the moment, thank you,' Giles rasped. 'I am rather busy. Now if you'll excuse me, I really must go.'

'One last –'

But Giles had cut him off, then turned off the phone so that George could not get in touch again. He could leave a message with the answering service if he had to. Giles downed the last of his wine and headed for the stairs. He looked at his watch as he went up towards the bedroom. It was five past nine. He'd have to be quick.

What was that old song? By that group – The Who. 'A Quick One and Away'? Something like that. Well, that would have to be it then, a quick one, and away.

He came to the door of the bedroom and tapped lightly upon it. 'Marilyn?'

'Come in. Ready for you.'

Here goes then. She was ready for him. And he was ready for her. Goodbye boring brick road. Hello brave new world of sexual adventure. This could be the start of something big. *(Har, har, mate. Who says it's big? Self-praise is no commendation.)* This would put him up on an equal footing with the MPs and the cabinet ministers and those who had mistresses and affairs. The great and the good, the big and the busty. It would put him on a par with Roy.

There was something.

He took the handle, opened the door, and stepped into a world of darkness.

It was odd. Very odd. This wasn't the ordinary darkness of urban night, when the light of streetlamps, and passing cars leaked in from behind the blinds. This was total, absolute darkness, the darkness of long ago, of a cave full of growling wolves, and of Neanderthal man in a corner, fumbling about for his flints to strike a spark.

'James –'

'Yes?'

'You there?'

'Here. But I can't see a thing.'

'Don't worry. Here.'

Where was she? He could smell her perfume. Was she next to him? In front of him?

'Here, give me your hands.'

He reached out to touch her, reaching towards the voice, reaching to touch her hair. But his hand didn't touch hair, it seemed to fall on something else, something which felt cool, cool and moist, with the texture of – what? – leather, was it? Rubber? Almost as if her face and hair were covered in some kind of . . . mask.

Mask?

Here, hang about.

'Here, James, I'll help you, let me.'

'Oh, right, yes, okay.'

His clothes seemed to be disappearing. She seemed to be – well, let's not put too fine a point on it, Giles – taking them off.

Well, that was all right, he didn't mind that.

The jacket, the shirt –

'Kick your shoes off.'

The shoes, the socks, the strides –

My god, the strides! The strides were off now. The Giles West, 32-inch waist, special offer two pairs with the jacket strides had hit the deck. Just standing there in the old vest and pants now. Mr Marks and Mr Spencer – sorry about this.

Where was the bed now? Were they on their way to that?

'Marilyn?'

'Here.'

'It's very dark in here. Can't see much.'

'Yes. I had it done. And soundproofed.'

Beg your pardon? *Soundproofed*? If I can just put my hand up, Miss, and ask a question. When you say soundproofed, what do you mean exactly? Why would you want to sound-proof your bedroom, Marilyn? Do tell.

Ah, his eyes were adjusting now, he was starting to discern

shapes. There was a bed over there, and some other sort of piece of furniture, which looked a bit like a –

'Shall I take your hands, James?'

Bit like a –

'Just slip them in here.'

- like an apparatus.

What was she doing?

'Nice and tight.'

Hang on. An apparatus?

'Is that all right?'

Yes, but now Giles seemed to be, well, a bit, sort of, tied up, really. What had she put his hands into?

'Just move your feet and –'

Snap. Click. Clunk. No imaginary sound effects this time, this was the real thing. And it wasn't a seatbelt either. This sounded like the genuine handcuffs.

Handcuffs?

'Everything nice and cosy, James?'

Em, well, no actually, as a matter of fact. Don't want to be a party pooper, or anything like that, but, I just seem to be a bit immobilized, as a matter of fact, can't really move. Just wondering what's going on.

As a matter of fact, now I think about it, I do have to catch a train.

'Let's just slip these down, shall we?'

Hello. What now? The Giles West buttocks were mooning in the darkness, and Mr Marks and Mr Spencer were down around the ankles. And Giles was bound hand and foot to some kind of contraption. And now that his eyes were used to the light, it wasn't Marilyn he could see anymore, it seemed to be some kind of variation on Miss Whiplash.

'And now we'll put on some heavy metal, shall we, and get a bit musical!'

'Well, actually,' Giles began, rather weakly, not wanting to make a fuss or anything, 'this wasn't quite what I had in mind.'

But his voice was drowned out by the sound of Wagner coming from a set of stereo speakers somewhere in the room.

The Valkyries were on the ride. And the next thing Giles heard was the sound of what could have been a birch twig, or a strip of leather, but certainly something pliable, swishing through the air. And then hearing was no longer of immediate relevance. It was feeling that counted.

'Ahhhhhhhhhh!'

Giles was in no position to count all the aitches in that exclamation, but that there were many could not be in doubt. His buttocks were in searing pain where the strap or the whip or whatever it was had landed. And he could hear another swish approaching.

'Ahhhhhhhhhh!'

Another legion of innumerable aitches. Any more after this had to be avoided at all costs. He shouted out at the top of his voice, 'Here, pack it in, will you! What's the game! What do you think you're doing?'

Wagner stopped. The Valkyries fell off.

'I beg your pardon?'

The lights went on. Marilyn was standing in front of him, all dressed in black leather and holding a whip to match.

'Sorry?' she said. 'Is there a problem?'

'Em – well, yes, actually,' Giles said. 'You see, em, this wasn't really what I expected.'

'What? Amn't I doing it hard enough?'

'No, no, not that at all,' Giles said. 'No. Marvellous arm there. I mean, spin-bowler sort of weight. No, I just – I'm not into this.'

'I beg your pardon?'

'Not into it. Sado-whatsit – all this.'

'But – aren't you – didn't you say – you were – you know, musical?'

'Em, yes, that's true, I did,' Giles agreed.

'Well, then?'

'Only I didn't realize that musical meant musical. I just thought it meant–'

'What?'

'Well – musical.'

'Oh. Oh dear.'

'Yes.'

'How terribly embarrassing.'

'Just a bit.'

'What must you think of me?'

'Nothing at all. Really, no, nothing like that.'

'Oh dear, your poor bottom.'

'Yes, it does sting a bit,' Giles agreed.

'Oh dear, I'm most terribly sorry. Shall I get you a plaster? And a drop of ointment?'

'Well, perhaps if I could just have a sit down on the bidet,' Giles said, 'with the cold tap running. That might take the edge off it.'

'Yes, of course. I'll get you a cup of tea as well.'

'That's terribly kind of you,' Giles said.

'I'll just take off your handcuffs.'

'If it's not too much trouble.'

'Not at all. Now, where are the keys?'

Oh no! She hadn't lost the flaming keys, had she? It was bad enough already. Bloody women lashing you to a bloody apparatus, taking your pants down and giving you bloody belters on your bloody bottom when all you'd done was come round expecting a quiet bit on the side. It really was the limit. Giles was a patient man on the whole, and slow to lose his temper, but this was a bit bloody much.

But he bit his lip and kept his opinions to himself. He was in no position to antagonize anyone, and he didn't need to be told what his options were, he could see them for himself: he had none.

'Now, I'm sure I had them when we started – I'm always doing this – or did I leave them out in the car? I lost them completely once and had to get a man round from Chubb's locks to undo everything – of course I could hardly tell him what we'd been doing, just said it was a little DIY project which had gone a bit wrong. Now, where are they? Ah! Here. Left them under the vase.'

She undid the handcuffs and padlocks, and Giles instantly felt better.

'Now you go and park yourself on the bidet,' she said, 'and

I'll go and put the kettle on, and make us both a nice hot cup of tea.'

'Terrific,' Giles said. 'I could just go for a cuppa after that.'

'Yes, I bet,' Marilyn said. 'The bathroom's that way. Help yourself. Won't be a mo!'

Giles shuffled to the bathroom, his pants around his ankles, walking like a doomed and shackled prisoner in a chain gang.

'Sugar, James?' Marilyn's voice called.

Giles lowered his throbbing buttocks onto the bidet.

'Just milk, thanks.'

Sizzle. Ahh! Clouds of steam rose from the Giles West hot thermal springs. Marvellous. It was almost worth the agony just to have the relief.

Hang on, Giles, now don't say things like that, or you'll be getting into this for real. And what would Holly think if you came back from the out-of-town shopping centre one Saturday afternoon with some planks of plywood and a bit of two-by-four, and started constructing your own apparatus in the en-suite.

Holly! My god, Holly! What was the time?

His watch was still on his wrist. Nine thirty-seven. Was that all? He'd be all right if he didn't hang about. He might even catch the ten-fifteen, and be back not much after eleven.

The bathroom door opened, and Marilyn entered with tea and biscuits on a tray. 'How is it?' she said. She had taken her mask off, but was still wearing her Miss Whiplash outfit, a tight-fitting number made from leather and rubber and which seemed held together by a long, large bootlace. She wore high heeled PVC boots and black tights.

Giles had to admit, despite the ache in his buttocks, that the overall effect was rather erotic.

'I brought up some Rich Tea biscuits,' Marilyn said, 'or there's a Wagon Wheel, if you'd rather one of those.'

'Oh, right, the Wagon Wheel, thanks, if you don't want it,' Giles said, for he noticed that there was only one.

'No, you have it. I eat too many of them as it is. Ought to be punished for it really.'

'Yes,' Giles simpered, but he didn't offer.

125

'You know, I'm most terribly sorry,' Marilyn said. 'I completely misunderstood your advertisement. When you said you were interested in music, I just naturally assumed that well you were *interested in music.* You know.'

'No, my fault entirely,' Giles said, dunking his Wagon Wheel into his tea. 'It's me who owes you the apology. I just shouldn't have been so naive. I just had no idea, you see, that that was what it meant.'

'I thought everyone knew though,' Marilyn said.

'Not me, I'm afraid.'

'Oh dear. I just naturally assumed that you were advertising because you couldn't get any at home.'

'My bottom whipped?'

'Yes.'

'No,' Giles said, biting into his biscuit. 'I'm sure my wife would be only to happy – that is, I'm sure she wouldn't – that is – I don't really know.' Hmm. They were good, these Wagon Wheels. He hadn't had one since he'd been a boy. 'I'm sure she'd be only too pleased to do it – or at least give it a good kick. No, it's just, I've never had sex with anyone else, you see, except her.'

'Oh, how frightfully awful,' Marilyn said, sounding a bit like a gym mistress on Sports Day, consoling stragglers in the egg and spoon race. 'Poor you.' For a moment it almost seemed as if she might offer him a cucumber sandwich. Yes, not a bad idea really. A plate of thinly sliced cucumber sandwiches would cool his bum down nicely.

'So that's what I was after, you see,' Giles said, 'no strings attached.'

'Oh, I see, yes. Oh, dear. Well, I do wish you luck then.'

Ah. That was disappointing. For a moment there Giles had thought that she might offer.

'I mean, I wish there was something I could do to help,' Marilyn said, sitting down on the toilet lid, and stirring her tea with a spoon. 'But I just can't do anything with a man until I've first given him a jolly good spanking.'

Jolly good spanking. So that was what she called it. Most people would have called it manslaughter.

'And, your husband –' Giles couldn't help asking.

'Yes, it's why we got divorced, I'm afraid. I mean, he did his best to oblige, but he got a bit fed up with it really. He said he couldn't really see it as a long-term relationship.'

No, Giles thought, his buttocks would probably have given up the ghost.

'And it began to interfere with his cycling,' Marilyn said. 'So I just said to him one day, look, it's me or that mountain bike. And he chose the mountain bike. I divorced him in the end, on grounds of mental cruelty.'

'Oh dear,' Giles said. 'What a shame. Well.'

'Yes . . .'

It was time to go. They plainly had no further use for each other, the evening was over, and Giles should finish his Wagon Wheel, get Mr Marks and Mr Spencer on, and leave as soon as possible.

'Been mild these past few days though,' Marilyn said. A vein in her breast twitched rhythmically under her laced-up corsetry-work.

'Yes hasn't it?' Giles agreed. 'The gardens will need watering soon too, if it doesn't rain.'

'Well, let's hope there's not a hosepipe ban,' Marilyn said.

No, Giles thought. Though he had a feeling that Marilyn might not use hosepipes quite in the manner that everyone else did.

He swallowed the last of his tea.

It was a funny old world. Oh, it sounded banal, it sounded trite and platitudinous, but it was a funny old world.

There you were, trying to be unfaithful to the missus – nothing personal, you understand, for experience only – and you end up sitting with your bum in a stranger's bidet, while the cold water lapped around two rather nasty weals. And there this woman was, all dressed up in rubber and leather, like one large kinky boot, and what were the two of you doing? Having a cup of tea and a Wagon Wheel.

It was all so terribly English, really, all so terribly civilized. It made you bloody proud to be British, quite frankly, bloody proud indeed. You almost felt like getting your Union Jack out and singing 'Land of Hope and Glory'.

'Top you up?'

Hello. What was she suggesting now?

'Freshen your cup?'

'Oh, no thank you. Not for me. In fact, I'd better be going.'

She brought his clothes in from the bedroom and left him to dress. Although he thought he had switched it off, his mobile phone rang again in his pocket.

'Hello?' Giles said.

'George Whimpole here,' the voice said. 'I don't suppose this would be a good moment to –'

'No,' Giles said. 'It wouldn't.' And he turned the phone off properly this time.

He found a bit of analgesic cream in the bathroom cabinet to put on to his bottom, which was still stinging painfully. He finished dressing and went down, to find Marilyn, changed back into her ordinary clothes, waiting to let him out.

'Well, it's been so nice to meet you.'

'Yes, and you. Sorry about the little misunderstanding.'

'No, really, I should be the one to apologize.'

'Not at all.'

'Well, I hope it doesn't hurt too much.'

'Oh, worse things happen at sea.' *Probably did, and all.* 'I just hope I didn't spoil your evening.'

'No, not at all, not at all.'

'All the best then.'

'Good luck.'

'Bye.'

The door closed behind him. Well, it was all part of life's rich tapestry, he supposed. He walked – no, limped – along the road, heading towards the station, thinking things over as he went.

It was a lesson really, a lesson in what happens when you start on the deceptions. You weave the tangled webs, and more than likely end up yourself where the fly should have been.

More than a lesson, it was a warning. A warning and a narrow escape. The thing to do now was to pack it all in, forget any ideas about illicit leg-overs, settle for what you have, and lead a nice, quiet life.

And yet it all seemed so amusing too. The whole thing – life, death, marriage, children, work, money, the lot. So daft and so immensely amusing. He wouldn't change a thing really, not a thing. He'd do it all over again if he had to. Make all the mistakes and more.

More mistakes. Yes, that was the answer. It wasn't that we made too many mistakes, we didn't make enough of them, mistakes and magnificent blunders.

He had to make up for lost mistakes, before it was all too late.

Holly was already in bed and asleep by the time Giles got home. He was glad, and rather relieved, as he hadn't yet quite worked out a story plausible enough to explain away the two deep, red weals on his backside.

It was going to be the colour of a plum by the morning, red, blue and purple.

He brought in his squash kit, left it in the garage, went into the house, up to the bathroom, brushed his teeth, took two aspirin, and dropped his trousers.

God!

Talk about tramlines.

He slapped a bit more ointment on to it – ouch! The stinging abated, and he got into bed beside Holly, keeping his pants on.

She was breathing heavily. Not snoring, just making a slight noise.

Familiarity, Giles thought, was a terrible thing. Sooner or later it robbed everything of its charm. Familiarity was a depreciating asset, and although the value of things might go up, the regard in which you held them seemed to taper off, until it hit a plateau, and there it remained.

We were so in love once, weren't we?

Dear Holly.

Giles turned his face to the pillow.

TWELVE

'Come over here, mate, have a look at this.'

Giles pretended he hadn't heard, he was busy with work of his own, but Roy was insistent.

'On the computer. This you've got to see.'

Giles got slowly and painfully to his feet and ambled across the office. Roy pointed to his computer screen.

'There!' he said triumphantly.

'What is it?' Giles said.

'It's the Doris Management Programme,' Roy said. 'Latest development!'

'And? So what is it?'

'Doris Spreadsheets, mate! It's bloody magnificent, isn't it? All the data you need, on all your Dorises, all saved and presented in spreadsheet form. And look at this as well, mate –'

Roy tapped the keyboard. The spreadsheet programme disappeared, and a picture of a large segmented and multicoloured pie took its place.

'And what's that?' Giles asked.

'Don't you see, mate! Don't you see? It's Doris Pie Charts! It's coming on, eh, isn't it, mate, coming on a bloody treat. We're really getting geared up here. We'll soon have the lot. The whole Doris Management Programme, and – get this, mate, get this – guess what I'm aiming for next?'

Broadmoor? Giles wondered. 'Dunno,' he muttered, 'what?'

'Multi-media,' Roy said. 'Interactive Doris, mate! Hands-on Doris! On a compact disc. Compact Doris! I might even approach David Bowie or Peter Gabriel or someone, get him to do the music. It's an absolute bloody winner. Has to be. And in stereo!'

'Interactive Doris in stereo?'

'Yeah. It's fantastic, isn't it? Digital stereo. It's Digital Doris, mate! Just what we need! And then we can get it on to the Internet! Have our own Web Site. Doris Pages, mate. And you'll be able to surf the Doris. And download all the latest info and all. Download Doris, mate! It's the shape of the future!'

Giles was getting worried. Roy had his faults, but he was his friend after all. And when even your best friend wouldn't tell you, well, your best friend had to tell you.

'Roy –'

'Yes, mate?'

Giles knew he wasn't listening. He was keying in data even as Giles tried to speak to him, but Giles tried anyway.

'How much time are you spending on the Doris Management Programme, Roy? I mean, are you actually doing any of the work you're paid to do?'

'Sod that, mate,' Roy said. 'When this is up and running, we won't need to work, we'll be billionaires.'

'You do know it's the quarterly reports soon, don't you, Roy?'

'Quarterly, schmarterly, old mate.' His fingers were flying over the keyboards like grasshoppers on speed.

'Roy –'

'Yeah, well, don't let me keep you, mate. Just thought I'd keep you posted. Must crack on now. Things to do.'

'But Roy –'

'I'm busy, Giles! Busy!' He flashed Giles a look. His eyes were going red, his teeth were getting pointed, hair was growing on the palms of his hands.

'Right, okay, Roy, sure thing, mate. I'll leave you to it.'

Giles left the office as soon as one o'clock came, and hobbled as fast as his throbbing buttocks would take him on what was becoming his regular route.

First he popped into Brownstones the Chemists and bought himself a sandwich and a drink, then he stepped out briskly (buttocks permitting) in the direction of the sorting office.

Giles hadn't stepped out briskly for years. And even his aching arse didn't diminish the pleasure he felt at being alive. The mishap with Marilyn had only whetted his taste for adventure. In fact, the very nature of the quest had changed. Sex with the proper stranger seemed less important than simply seeing what would happen. For Giles was having an adventure. He was actually – yes, actually – enjoying himself.

Giles took his letters and his sandwich to the graveyard, and sat down on the same bench as before. St Absalom's church lurched skyward, looking unsteady against the whirling, wind-blown clouds. He took his sandwich and prised it from its plastic bubble. What had he bought? He'd just grabbed the first thing that came to hand, with a carton of orange juice, and taken them to the till.

What did that label say? *Curried prawn and mango chutney with feta cheese and sliced vegetarian sausage on wholemeal walnut olive bread with chives and sun-dried tomatoes, garnished with mung beans and crushed water chestnuts in a hollandaise and banana yoghurt dressing, with low-fat sunflower spread and a pickled gher-kin. Complimentary fresh-breath mint provided.*

What the hell was all that?

That wasn't a sandwich! That was a bleeding lecture!

Giles bit into it. Fortunately, it tasted better than it read. In fact, it was rather good. The only thing that worried him was what was printed next to the Use By date. There wasn't a date there. What it said was *Best by yesterday*. What did that mean? Was it still safe to eat it then? Or had somebody done it as a joke? Or was it a philosophical statement, even? That every-thing you had, you had too late, that autumn was already here, that the rot had already set in. And that everything you did today, you should have done yesterday. The moment was here, and the moment was past. The flowers were dying before you had even planted them, the train wasn't due for another hour, and yet you had already missed it. And the paradox of existence was that it was always, always too late.

You needed to be in Mensa these days just to work out how to eat your lunch.

Giles opened a letter. The handwriting on the envelope looked familiar, and he soon realized why.

Dear Box 132,

We are sorry not to have yet heard from you, and hope

132

that you have not been poorly. You will recall that we wrote to you a short time ago from our nursing home here in Dawlish, the Motley Grange. Very nice it is too. We are all so well looked after. The staff are kind and friendly, and we are very well-fed – though sometimes the tuna salad does taste a bit like Whiskas. And the fees are so very reasonable too – only £950 a week.

I am writing on behalf of us all this time – myself, and my two friends, Mrs Throttly and Miss Stavenshaw. You will remember that we wrote to you under separate cover before, suggesting that you could come down and visit with a view to having a 'bit of fun' as I believe it is called today. (These youngsters! Such expressions they do have!)

It is with regret that I am writing to inform you that Mrs Throttly is no longer with us. It was her habit to go sea bathing every morning – despite her great age and various other infirmities – and was yesterday swept out to sea, Zimmerframe and all, as she was paddling in the shallows. Her body has not yet been found, but her Zimmerframe was rescued by a Spanish fishing trawler, and has been returned to her friends here at the Motley Grange as a memento and a keepsake.

The good news, however, is that Miss Stavenshaw and myself are still interested, and due to a cancellation, the guest room will now be available for the first weekend of next month.

I hope that you will be able to come down and visit us. Miss Stavenshaw is greatly looking forward to it, has bought a new hat, and has been taking her Garlic Pearls every morning, in advance of your call. I myself have splashed out on a new pair of slippers, which I think you will agree, match the carpets rather nicely.

We look forward to hearing from you, and hope that you and your family are all well.

Yours,

Mrs J. Wiseman (widow)

Oh god.

The tangled bloody webs again.

He'd have to write back to them. Explain the misunderstanding. He couldn't go on stringing them along like that, keeping false hopes alive. And he'd better send a card too, for Mrs Throttly, a *Sad to hear of your great loss* sort of thing. A short letter, let them down easy, that would be enough, then end of correspondence. Full stop.

He opened another envelope. The writing on this looked familiar too. 'Dear Filthy Bastard –'

Yes, he had seen that orange ink before. It was Jilted.

He tore Jilted up into tiny fragments and dropped her (or was it even him?) into the bin. He took a bite of his sandwich, and opened envelope number three.

Dear Box 132,

Yeah, great idea! You're on! Don't know why I didn't think of it myself. How about this Thursday, 17th – *Hang on. Eeny meeny miney – the 17th? That was tonight!* – at 8.30 round at the lounge bar of the Mutton Trout – do you know it? – in Colson Street. Here's my photo, too. Hope you like it. Don't know what yours is like, but I'll take the risk. (Only joking, I'm sure you're lovely.) I won't be wearing anything, but I'm sure you'll still recognize me – *Bloody sure I will, if you're going to be sitting there naked in the Mutton Trout* – that is, I won't be wearing a flower in my button hole or anything – though I will have some clothes on – but not for long, eh? Hope you've got somewhere for us to go. Look forward to seeing you.

Love,
Angela

The photograph was of a face as pert and chatty as the letter. Nice. Very nice. Nice figure too. Probably not quite his type exactly. Looked like one of those women he had never really been able to talk to. Who had once been girls he had never really been able to talk to. Who tended to go more for blokes called Darren and Shane, blokes who usually had a few tattoos, and went in for a little light car stealing, when times were hard.

But, breaking down the barriers, that was what it was all about.

Only could he make it? Tonight was short notice. The time lag of the process was the problem. First the letters had to go to *Scene Around*, then they had to go to his box number, then he had to pick them up. By the time the letters were getting to him, he could already have missed his chance.

And then there was that other thing – *Hope you've got somewhere for us to go.*

Well, he hadn't.

Or had he?

The office!

Yes, why not? He could take her there. The cleaners would have gone by the time they got there. And the carpet looked nice and comfy, Giles thought – always assuming that he wasn't the one lying on it. And he had his key card. That was it. No problem. Right.

All it needed was a quick excuse and a phone call home, *Working late, I'm afraid, system crashed, software error, rush job, must get it done,* and he'd be all set. And there was no reason why Holly should disbelieve him. He did genuinely work late occasionally. Not often enough for it to seem suspicious, nor seldom enough for it now to seem unusual.

Right, that was it then.

Angela, the Mutton Trout, 8.30 tonight.

He felt into his jacket pocket, and his hand fell upon the comfort of his Massive Cucumbers. *Have condom, will travel.* He pulled them out of his pocket. The wrappers were already beginning to take on the schooldays' look – the look of the condoms of his youth, carried around for weeks, months or even years, before the opportunity to use them came along.

And the opportunity had been with Holly.

A disaster.

But a wonderful disaster. And gradually, little by little, it had become more wonderful and ecstatic for them both, getting better and better all the time, until one day . . . it got boring, tired, the same. Every night, the same dinner. And then days without dinner. Weeks without dinner. Until now, hardly any dinner at all, and what dinner there was usually needed reheating in the microwave.

And he started to wonder – as maybe she had started to wonder – what it might be like, with someone else.

He opened the remaining two letters.

Dear Box 132,
    Liked your ad. Give me a call if you like the photo.
    Love,
    Martine

Hmm. Very short and business-like. He'd file that for future reference. The final letter was obviously a mix-up, and had gone to the wrong box number.

Dear Advertiser,
    Regarding the collection of Bavarian beer mats you have up for swapsies. I am a very keen beer mat collector, but my Bavarian section is a little bit thin. I would be willing to swapsie ten – yes, ten! – Tasmanian phone cards and two unused Qantas airline sick bags (the old sort) in return for five Bavarian beer mats in good condition.
    What do you say?
    Yours,
    Quentin Stoagley

Yes.

Giles put that letter into the bin.

It cheered you up really. Just when you thought that you were a sad and a pathetic case, up from nowhere popped another case, sadder and even more pathetic than you could ever reasonably hope to be.

The nerd's nerd. The dork's dork. The sad case's sad case. It was a kind of distinction.

He felt quite affectionate towards Quentin Stoagley, but he put him in the bin all the same.

Giles finished his sandwich, took his letters and walked back to the office. His bruised backside seemed better now. In fact, everything seemed better. His head was clearer, his conscience lighter. He had learned not to think about it. That is, not to think of the consequences on relationship, family, hearth and home, of this soon-to-be consummated infidelity with a stranger.

It could lead to divorce, Giles. To pain, distress, misery, a broken family, trauma for the children that the years would never heal – if the psychologists were to be believed.

But it was out of his hands now. Something else, some life force, had taken over. Life was living him. There was nothing he could do to stop the river, he could only swim along with the tide.

On the way back to his office he stopped off at a photo booth and invested in a few more mug shots. He wouldn't want to be caught short.

THIRTEEN

Holly tried to let it all flow away from her. But it was hard to keep your patience. 'Let it all flow away from you,' the instructor had said at the yoga and relaxation classes, 'let all the tension and stress just disappear into the atmosphere. Be calm. Be in control. Be one with the universe.'

Yes, well, it was all right being one with the universe when you didn't have Mrs Trewitt as a client of your Colour Co-ordination Consultancy (Home Visits, Free Initial Assessment) but when you did, you felt more at one with physical violence than anything else.

Three times she had matched Mrs Trewitt up to her books of make-up shades and colour samples. Only each time, just when it seemed they were finally getting somewhere, Holly would return for the final consultation to discover that Mrs Trewitt had been to the hairdresser, and had had her hair dyed yet another awful colour.

In its time it had gone from grey to blue to mauve to hint-of-pink to red to beige to apricot to ash-blonde to auburn to jet-black, from cornrows to plaits to a bun to a pigtail to a beehive to dreadlocks.

But this time Mrs Trewitt had finally done it.

She had gone and had a blue mohican.

'What do you think, dear?' she said when Holly arrived. When she opened the door Holly instantly dropped her book of colour samples. 'You don't think it's too young for me, do you?'

Mrs Trewitt was in her mid-fifties.

'It's very . . . unusual,' Holly said.

'They persuaded me to have it at the salon. Mr Clarence said it would be really me.'

138

'When was that?'

'A little while back. April first, I think. I wasn't sure about it to start with, but I've grown to like it now. Though it gave them quite a start round at the charity shop where I work Tuesday afternoons.'

'Yes, I'm sure,' Holly said. 'And what does your husband think about it?'

'Oh, he thinks it's very nice. He's got a bit of a mohican himself – only the other way round. Instead of having hair in the middle, and none at the sides, he's got hair at the sides, and none at the middle. He keeps calling me Pocahontas! Ha, ha! So what do you think?'

Loads of money, no class, no taste and no real hope of ever getting any, would have been the truth, but Holly didn't say it.

'Yes, very . . . nice. The only thing is, we'll have to start your colour co-ordination all over again.'

'Oh dearie me. Well, never mind, dear, I'm sure if anyone can do it, it'll be you.'

Holly wondered how the Trewitts had made their money. However they'd done it, here they were, in their eight-bedroomed detached house, with more cars than a family could drive. But it wasn't just the material success, they seemed happy.

Actually seemed happy.

Rich and happy, and rather kind and compassionate and considerate too.

It should be against the law.

Holly got out her colour samples and began again. It wasn't just Mrs Trewitt's hair, it was her skin as well. Sometimes it was brown, sometimes white, sometimes pink, all depending on how long she'd spent in the solarium.

It was a thankless job, really. Interesting, nice to meet people, it brought a little money in, and the hours were flexible. But Holly wondered if it really amounted to much. She felt as if she were treading water these days, marking time, just getting on with things, waiting, waiting . . .

For what? To grow old?

And the marriage hadn't been so – had it? No. And whose fault was that? His, hers, anybody's, no one's?

Sometimes she longed to get away from it all, just for a little while, just for a break. It wasn't that she didn't love Giles, she did. But sometimes, just sometimes, she wondered what it would be like to – dare she think it, let alone say it – make love with someone else.

What would it be like to feel the first phase of love again, the passion, abandonment, carnal joy? What would it be like to have a brief affair?

'Cup of tea, love?'

'I'm sorry?' Someone was talking to her. It seemed to be a member of the lost tribes.

'Cup of tea? Before we start?'

'Oh, yes. Yes please. Thank you.'

Mrs Trewitt went to put the kettle on. Maybe, Holly, thought, I should get a mohican haircut too.

If I was another woman, Giles might be another man.

When Giles got back to the office, Lavinia, he was pleased to see, was nowhere around. Roy was still at his computer, and Sandy and Terry were sitting chatting.

Giles headed for his desk. He wanted to tell Roy about what he was doing, about his meeting that night in the Mutton Trout. He wanted to tell Roy that he had joined the big boys, that he could now deal him in, he was in the game. It wasn't faithful old monogamous Giles any more, it was Butch Thrusty, the Leg-over Kid, riding the range armed with only a tattered copy of the Kamasutra, and a saddlebag full of Jimmy's Massive Cucumbers (hypoallergenic).

I'm with you now, Roy. Time to take me seriously.

In other words, Roy, I'm a man too. We all pretend, don't we, Roy, that being a good father and a faithful husband and having the kids at the weekends makes us men. We pretend that, and women pretend that. But we know and they know, Roy, that it isn't true. And we know, and they know, that they'd be off with the bloody Vikings, first opportunity they got.

We know what a woman really thinks, don't we, Roy?

She thinks, look at that big nance in that apron doing the washing up. I'm not married to that, am I?

And she looks at her watch then, doesn't she, Roy, and thinks, I wonder what time the Vikings are coming? I'd better go and get changed.

The Vikings didn't stand around in aprons squeezing bottles of Fairy Liquid, did they, Roy? No, they were like you. They didn't know how to boil an egg or make a cup of tea, they just went round the seas in their longboats with a Doris in every port.

I'm joining the Vikings, Roy, I'm joining them this very night, at half past eight in the Mutton Trout. See, I've got my call-up papers right here in the pocket of my coat, on a letter beginning *Dear Box 132* . . .

Giles would dearly have loved to say all that. But he didn't. For he knew, in advance of disclosure, that Roy would not have been impressed. He would merely have shrugged.

'Oh, aye, mate? That right?'

What was a solitary Doris to Roy, the king of the Dorises? Roy, who got his Dorises wholesale from the Cash and Carry, with discounts for trade.

Giles knew that, somehow, he would never be a man. Because he didn't know what that meant. He had never been able to define it adequately for himself. Whereas Roy did know. Roy had it all sewn up. For Roy, being a man meant lots of Dorises. And Roy had lots of Dorises, so Roy was a man.

But what was Giles? Where did that leave him?

Maybe he would find out tonight. At 8.30. In the Mutton Trout.

First he ought to ring Holly with an excuse. But not here. Not in the office. Not enough Noddy and too much Big Ears in this place.

Lavinia wasn't around. Perhaps he'd slip off to the loo and make a call from there on his mobile phone.

'Won't be a sec. Just going to wash my hands.'

'Okay, Giles.' Terry and Sandy exchanged a look, as if he had said he was off to grow hair on his hands, rather than wash them.

Giles went to the toilet and found a vacant cubicle. He sat on the lid, took out his portable telephone and rang his home number. Holly was out, so he left a message on the answer phone.

'Hello Holly, it's Giles. Sorry about this, but I'll have to work late tonight. There's a bug in a user's system, could even be a virus, and we'll have to sort it out before we can go. Bit like balancing the books in the bank, you know. No one goes home till the last penny's accounted for sort of thing. *Shut up, Giles. You're talking too much. Verbosity, the first sign of guilt.* Anyway, I'll get myself something to eat. Love to the girls, and I'll – well – I'll see you later. Bye.'

It was done. Right. Committed. He was about to put his portable phone back into his pocket when it rang. Now, who could that be? Who knew his number? Apart from – no, it couldn't be, could it –

'Hello?'

'Hello, Mr West. George Whimpole here, of Whimpole Communications. How are you?'

'I'm in the loo, actually.'

'Good, good, Fine, fine. Good weather in there, I hope?'

'What?'

'Where you are, Looe? Lovely place, Cornwall.'

'No! The toilet! I'm on the shanks!'

'Good, good. Yes, Shanks's pony. Can't beat a leisurely stroll after lunch. Is it work that's taken you down there, or a little break with the family?'

'I AM IN THE RUDDY BOG!'

'Oh, muddy, is it? Well, as long as you're wearing your boots. Now, the thing is, I'm sure you must be finding your new portable telephone a major asset to your business. But the point is, can you afford to stop there? Communication, after all, is the name of the game, and unless you're a live wire on the Internet these days, well, business-wise, you just aren't on the ball.'

'Now look,' Giles said firmly, 'if I wish to get on to the Internet –'

'I say – who are you talking to in there?'

Giles looked up. There was another voice. A voice and two eyes peering down at him from the top of the cubicle. It was Eliot of management.

'West, what are you doing in there? I heard voices, thought there was some kind of hanky-panky going on.'

'Oh, Mr Eliot, just a moment –' Giles spoke into the phone, 'Sorry, Mr Whimpole, I'll have to get back to you on that one. Bye for now.' And hung up.

Eliot was waiting outside when Giles emerged from the cubicle.

'Well, West? I take it there is some rational explanation?'

'Eh, yes, Mr Eliot, I was talking – into this.'

He showed him the mobile phone.

'That yours?'

'Yes.'

'You take it into the toilet with you?'

'Em, yes, that is, I have my calls re-routed. So that if I'm not at my desk when someone calls, instead of them wasting time leaving a message, and me ringing them back, the call can be put through to me here.'

'On the jakes?'

'Em, yes,' Giles lied.

'In mid – thing?'

'If necessary.'

'God man, that's bloody brilliant. I don't know why no one's thought of it before. Why, the business we must lose in this company though people being unavailable because otherwise engaged. It's brilliant, man, bloody brilliant.'

'Thank you.'

'And that's your phone, is it? Your own?'

'Em – yes.'

'Well, well. I'm impressed, West, I am impressed. That level of dedication to the job. You don't often come across that degree of commitment in these cynical times. It's all gimme gimme, something for nothing, and how much is the annual bonus. All minimum wages and what have you. Never any mention of minimum work though. But this, West, well, I am most impressed.'

143

'Thank you, Mr Eliot.'

'I shall personally reimburse you for the cost of that phone, and I shall get every member of upper management to follow your example.'

'Oh – I don't know what to say.'

'Mobiles for all, West. Why, this toilet could become a centre of business activity. It'll soon be humming in here.'

Yes, thought Giles, if the air conditioning isn't fixed.

'Yes, I'll send round a memo. We'll call it Don't Waste a Moment. Take your mobile with you and Don't Waste a Moment. Brilliant, West, brilliant. If we had dispatches in this company, I'd mention you. As it is, when the annual salary review comes round, well, you won't be forgotten.'

'Thank you.' The telephone in Giles's pocket was ringing again.

'Ah, well, looks like you've got a bit more work on your plate there. Don't let me keep you.'

'Thank you, no, right.'

Eliot entered a cubicle. Giles answered his phone.

'Hello!'

'Ah, is that Mr West speaking? George Whimpole here again, of Whimpole Communications. We seemed to have got cut off. Now, did I mention, when we last spoke, the importance of a good solar-powered desktop calculator to the modern executive –'

Giles switched him off good and proper and went out into the corridor, the door swinging shut behind him.

Eliot of management was left alone in the gents. Sound man that Giles West. Sounder than he seemed. Mobile phone in the washroom, eh? That was the way to steal the edge on your competitors. Yes, that was the way to get the business all right.

Seemed to have a lot of potential, that man. Maybe he should be given additional responsibilities.

Maybe he should be promoted.

Five-thirty came; three hours to go. Three hours to adultery.

Three hours. Long, dead hours.

Giles stayed in the office a while, tidying his desk.

'Not going home, mate?'

'In a minute. What about you?'

Pointless question, really. Roy went home about as frequently as a salmon returned to its spawning grounds. Homecomings for him were more along the lines of a once in a lifetime thing, and the effort would more than likely kill him.

Roy took a computer printout from his briefcase and consulted it.

'Seeing Doris Number One for a drink before dinner and a quick one in the back of the Espace.'

'The what?'

'Didn't I tell you? Got a new van. Renault Espace. With curtains. Very comfy, mate, very comfy indeed. A regular little old Doris-mobile that one. Then after that, it's dinner with Doris Six. Then drop her off home. Cinema then with Doris Five. Drop her off home. Then a cup of tea with Doris Two – she's working shifts now. Then off home to the trouble.'

Trouble and strife, mate, trouble and strife.

'Yeah, it's all printed out here, see. The programme's coming along nicely. Doris Printouts, you see, old mate. Just the job.'

'Have a good night then, Roy.'

'And you mate. See you. Bye.'

And he was gone, off on his life of Dorises. Roy and his Doris life.

Giles dawdled a little longer. Lavinia went home. (To what? What was Lavinia's out-of-work life? She played for the firm's hockey team, didn't she, and attended courses on self-improvement. Always learning. Always acquiring new skills. After all, knowledge was a marketable commodity. But what of the rest? She must have a private life too. Or maybe not.) The cleaners came, with fag and bucket, ignoring the no-smoking signs, and, for the most part, ignoring the dirt.

And who could blame them. Boring job, boring, exploitative and underpaid. Only doing it because there was nothing else available that suited. Probably the only thing that fitted in with the responsibilities of home, children and husband.

Giles left the office at about quarter-to-six, and nodded to the security guard as he left. Now, that was going to be a problem. How was he going to smuggle Angela past the security guard in two and a half hours' time? Ah, no. They would be gone by then. No problems.

He left the building and went to a near-by card and gift shop which stayed open until seven. He bought a blank greetings card, along with a remembrance card with a solemn black border, and a book of first-class stamps.

He went a few doors along the street and entered a cheap baked potato bar called Mine's A Murphy. He ordered a cup of coffee and a baked potato with cheese. He almost ordered one with beans, but beanz, he remembered in time, meanz flatulenze, and he didn't want that starting up at half-past eight that evening, just as he was getting on to the case.

He opened up the greetings card, found a pen in his pocket, and wrote

Dear Martine,
    Thank you for your reply. Yes, I did like what I saw. Hope you do too. If so, perhaps you could give me a call.
    Love,
    Jimmy Tile

He added the number of his mobile telephone and dropped one of his new passport photographs into the card. He sealed the envelope, then took up the card of remembrance.

Dear Mrs Wiseman and Miss Stavenshaw,
    I was greatly saddened to hear of the death of your good friend, Mrs Throttly. It is a sad thing to be swept out to sea at any age, but especially at seventy-eight, and so unexpectedly as well, since as far as I can remember, Dawlish is not exactly famous for tidal waves. I went there as a child once – or rather to Dawlish Warren, just round the coast – and I lost my beach ball, which, like Mrs

146

Throttly, was also swept out to sea. So I can quite imagine how you must be feeling.

Please accept my condolences and my sympathy for your loss, and I trust that you will be able to find some comfort in the rescue of her Zimmerframe, and that it will bring back many a happy memory to you both.

Regarding the other matter, I am afraid that my initial advertisement was misprinted, and the line '18 to 85' should in fact have read '18 to 55'. I am a great admirer of the older woman, but feel, to be honest, that the generation gap in this instance would be too wide for us to comfortably bridge.

Have you maybe considered putting in an advertisement yourselves? Maybe in *Saga* magazine or *Golden Times*? I'm sure that nobody would think any the less of you for it. Wanting to make contact with others is nothing to be ashamed of, after all.

Well, good luck to you both. I apologize again for the misunderstanding.

Yours sincerely,

Jimmy Tile (Box 132)

He sealed the second envelope.

The cheese on his baked potato had congealed. He picked at it with his plastic fork as it lay on its polystyrene container. Polystyrene container and polystyrene cheese. His fellow diners looked as artificial and as plastic as the plates.

Dead time.

It was never there in films. No boredom, no hanging about, nothing interminable. Straight on into the next scene there. All action and activity.

He left most of the potato and sipped at his coffee.

Suddenly he wanted to go home.

He didn't want to play this game any more. He didn't want to be unfaithful or have experiences or be a man. He wanted to go home to Holly and the girls, and get a cuddle from someone, and not be one of the lonely people in Mine's A Murphy any more.

He wanted to be loved.

He looked around at the diners. Who would eat here from choice? Who would eat here who didn't have to? They were all of them time's executioners in there, killing time with a baked potato and grated polystyrene cheese. Most of them probably wanted what he had – home, family, children.

And he had it. And it wasn't enough. *Wasn't enough, wasn't enough*. Like the rhythm of a train. I *think* I can, I *think* I can. Isn't *enough*, isn't *enough*.

He left and went to post his letters, and then slowly strolled around the city centre. He didn't want to walk too far. If he walked too far, he would start to perspire, and he didn't want to turn up for this assignation in bad need of a shower.

All the practicalities, the things no one ever told you about, the realities of an affair. He went into the late night chemist's and bought a toothbrush and some toothpaste, then went to a public convenience and brushed his teeth. He didn't want to carry a toothbrush and toothpaste around with him, but he didn't want to throw them away either. He put them inside his briefcase.

He went and sat in the graveyard then, but didn't linger, as people passing by were looking at him as though he might be a pervert. His portable phone rang, but he didn't answer it. He knew it was only George Whimpole trying to sell him something he didn't want. He wandered around the precinct then, did a little window shopping. Saw some nice things for the girls, wondered what he could get Holly for her birthday, looked into the travel agents' window and priced a few summer holidays.

What are you doing, Giles? You're on your way to betray your family, and in the next breath wondering about your summer holidays.

Yes, a funny old world mate.

At last eight o'clock came. He made his way to the Mutton Trout, ordered a half pint of Old Rumblefirkin (4.7% abv) and sat in a corner where he would have a good view of the door. By the time he was served and settled, it was 8.17. Thirteen minutes to go. Then twelve. Then ten.

Countdown had begun. He felt in his pocket for his Massive Cucumbers. Yes. They were there. Everything A1, Houston Control. Countdown to lift-off had commenced.

FOURTEEN

He stared at the ceiling, he stared at the floor, he wondered about the other drinkers, he looked at the barman, who had a neck of remarkable shortness and a shaved head of remarkable thickness. The head and neck were perched on broad shoulders, which in turn topped a weightlifter's frame.

'Give us another pint, Jordan.'

Had his mates in as well. Probably giving them cheap drinks, pouring out pints and only ringing up halves on the till.

Giles looked around in more detail. Bit rough, really, the Mutton Trout.

'Give us a pint of Old Rumbly Foreskin then, Jordan.'

Har, har. Arf, arf.

Laugh at bloody anything, some people. Laugh at nothing. Born laughing, probably. Empty, mirthless, sinister laughter. The sort of laughter you would hear as the boot went in, just before you lost consciousness.

The door opened, a middle-aged couple peered in, looked around, decided against it and left. It opened again, and there she was: Angela. He recognized her instantly from her photograph and turned to get a better look – as did every other man in the pub.

She was a state-of-the-art sex bomb, due to go off any second.

The photograph hadn't done her justice. Pert and chatty, the photograph had conveyed, but that wasn't the half of it. She was probably in her mid-twenties, blonde and slim, with an above average-sized bosom, and legs so long they practically came up to her ears.

But it wasn't just the length of the legs, it was the shortness of the skirt. (*Brevity is the soul of tit, old mate, har, har!*) And more than that, it was the tightness of it. It clung to her small buttocks like clingfilm around a couple of peaches in a super-market display.

Jordan behind the bar, and his mates on the other side of it, fell silent. Not even a 'Coh, look at the arse on that!' passed their lips. They just seemed to sit there in silent awe, quietly dribbling into their drinks.

She made a beeline for him. How she knew it was him, Giles didn't know. Maybe the turmoil taking place inside him was displayed on his face. Maybe his psychic aura was branded with the letter A for adultery. But turmoil there was. The turmoil of Mr Average finding himself approached by the Most Beautiful Woman in the Room.

'132?' (It wouldn't have been a bad name for a robot. *Hi, 132, how's it clanging these days, ol' buddy?*)

'Sorry?'

She was at his table.

'Box 132?'

'Oh, yes, I am, yes.'

'Angela.'

'Yes, I recognized you from your photograph, I was just admiring –'

She sat down and crossed one leg over the other, displaying thighs to go to war over. Time spun out of control, the sun revolved around the earth, the jackpot came up on the fruit machine, Giles aged two million years, Jordan and his mates at the bar all got erections big enough to hang flags on and their eyes came out on stalks.

'Well, how are you?'

She had a classless, estuary English accent. Matey, egali-tarian, as good as anyone. Giles wondered if she wasn't dis-appointed in him, but if she was, she didn't say.

'Can I get you a drink?'

'Ta. I'll have a Poached Walnut.'

'I'm sorry?'

'A Poached Walnut. You know. Haven't you ever had a Poached Walnut?'

No, Giles had to admit that he hadn't ever had the pleasure.

'It's a cocktail sort of thing, you know.'

'Oh, right. What's in it?'

She looked at him blankly. 'I don't know. They'll know at the bar.'

'Right.'

Nervously, Giles went up to the bar. Jordan presided; the mates stood impassive and menacing, not exactly obstructing his progress, but not exactly making room for him either. You could see them thinking, what was a bit of crumpet like that doing with a wally like him?

'Yes?'

The bullethead on the bullneck was talking.

'I'd like a Poached Walnut, please.'

For a second he thought they were all going to laugh. But no. Just a faint mutter from somewhere, 'Oh, back on the Poached Walnuts tonight then, is she?'

Was Angela a regular here then? Was this a ritual? Was Giles not the first? Had these young buckos at the bar seen others come and go? What had happened to them? Had they been devoured? Sucked in, and spat out again in little pieces?

'With or without?'

'Sorry?'

'This Poached Walnut. Is that with, or without?'

'Em – with, I think.' He didn't like to ask what. A green-looking solution was being prepared in the cocktail shaker.

'Ice and lemon?'

'Oh, I should think so.'

Jordan dropped in ice and lemon followed by a pork scratching. He went to put the lid on it, but Giles managed to stop him just in time.

'Excuse me, I don't know if you realize, but you've just put a pork scratching in that.'

'So?'

'Well, I mean – in a drink.'

'You did want a Poached Walnut, didn't you?'

'Em, yes.'

'Well, that's all right then, isn't it?'

'Em, yes, right.'

152

Jordan shook up the mixture, strained out the pork scratching, and poured the rest into a cocktail glass. He then picked up a jar, took out a gherkin, and dropped it into the cocktail. Finally, he took a little paper umbrella, stuck it into the gherkin, and pushed the glass across the bar.

'One Poached Walnut.'

'But that's a gherkin,' Giles said.

'Yeah?' Jordan said, challengingly. 'Well, it would be, wouldn't it, in a Poached Walnut.'

Giles supposed it would be in that case, yeah.

'Eight pound fifty.'

Giles suppressed his shock and paid up.

'And there's your mustard.'

Jordan handed him a small jar of Colman's English Mustard.

'What's this for?'

'The Poached Walnut. You can hardly have a Poached Walnut without mustard, can you?'

His mates were sniggering now, and Giles felt foolish and embarrassed. He took his change, the cocktail glass and the mustard, and went back to join Angela at the table. He could feel eyes boring into his back every inch of the way.

'Ta! Cheers!'

She was actually drinking it. Then she spread a dab of mustard on to the back of her hand, dunked the gherkin into it, and took a nibble.

'Is that nice?'

'Lovely. Want to try it?'

'No, I'm fine thanks. Well, then –'

God, he couldn't talk to her. This was going to be difficult.

'Well, then, so, em, tell me a little about yourself, Angela.'

'Oh, yeah. Well, I'm in cosmetics. How about you?'

'Computers.'

'Oh. Have you got a big desk?' she said.

Good! That was something. She was interested in his desk. 'Decent size,' he said. 'What about you?'

'I've got my own counter,' she said. 'It goes all the way round. Does your desk go all the way round?'

No, Giles had to concede that it didn't. She was winning the status battle hands down. Still, forget that. Enough of the small talk. Down to the matter in hand. (*Order, order, members of the committee, if we may now proceed to the next item on the agenda – sex.*)

'So –' he began.

'Married then, are you?' Angela interrupted.

'Yes. You?'

'No. Engaged.'

'Oh.'

'I'm fed up with him though.'

Fed up with him and not even married yet. It started early all right. The rot soon set in.

'You fed up with yours?' she asked Giles. 'Must be, I suppose, or you wouldn't be here.'

He was taken aback at having the question framed so bluntly. Was he fed up with Holly? Well, yes, he was and no, he wasn't. It was a lot more complicated than that.

'It's a lot more complicated than that.'

'What then?'

Well, Giles? What then? What's complicated about it?

'Well –' okay, in for a penny, 'I've never had sex with anyone apart from my wife.'

She looked at him in mid-gherkin.

'Why not?'

'Just never turned out that way.'

'I've only ever had sex with my boyfriend. And half the time he smells of beer.'

'Ah, well, that's not so bad then. Puts us on an even footing.'

'Why? Does your wife smell of beer?'

'No, I just meant us both only having done it with one other person.'

'Mind you, you are a lot older than me. I mean, if I got to your age and had only ever had sex with one person, well, I'd probably shoot myself.'

'I've thought about it,' Giles managed to smile. 'But I thought I'd try this first instead.'

'Well, it just gets on my nerves, to be honest, people taking

154

you for granted all the time. Just expecting you to be there and that.'

'Yes, quite,' Giles said. She was getting a little bit annoyed. Maybe the Poached Walnut had gone to her head.

'You know what I mean, don't you?'

'Oh, yes, yes.'

Her eyes were darting around the bar now, looking at anything but Giles himself.

'So I thought, well, I'm not letting him get away with that. What's sauce for the goose and all that.'

'Absolutely,' Giles agreed. 'Now, I don't know how you're fixed but my office is just round the corner and –'

'And if he thinks he can go out with Charlene Norris and I'll still be sitting waiting for him, well, he's got another think coming.'

'Quite right too. You can be taken too much for granted.' He'd got her measure now. He was hitting the right note, no worries.

'So I thought, I'll show him. And then I saw your thing in the small ads. I always read the personal ads. Do you? Good laugh, aren't they? All the nutters and that. I mean, you've got to be in a bad way if you have to advertise for people to go with you. Don't you think?'

'Oh, absolutely, yes. Quite so.' Don't take offence, Giles, the woman's had a Poached Walnut, she doesn't know what she's saying. 'Anyway, look, I thought we could maybe pop back to my office, if you're still interested –'

'What?' Her eyes flashed a look at him. Was he being too impatient?

'Well, no hurry, obviously. In a bit, in a while, when you're ready. Maybe we could have another Poached Walnut first and –'

'Another Poached Walnut!' she giggled infectiously. 'Oh, I daren't risk that. Do you think I should? Two Poached Walnuts and I'm anyone's!'

She said this loudly, and Giles expected some facetious, or even semi-obscene remark from the lads at the bar, who seemed to have given up on their own conversation in order to eavesdrop on his. But no remarks came. Just a brooding silence emanated from them, like radiant heat.

'Well, look, I can get into my office, and there's bound to be somewhere there we can – very comfy carpet, you know – shag pile –' Oh, god, that was the wrong thing to say!

She was waxing indignant again.

'But they do, don't they? They just take you for granted. Just make assumptions. Seem to think they own you or something and can do what they like. Well, I'll show him what I can do. I will you know.'

'I'm sure you will.'

'I will. In fact, I'll show him now.'

And before Giles could reply, she had kissed him full on the lips.

'There!' she said defiantly.

And then she placed a hand on his crotch and gave it a small squeeze.

'And there!' she said, even more defiant.

'And there!'

She reached inside Giles's shirt and gave one of his nipples a bit of a tweak.

'So what do you think of that?'

'Very – nice,' he said. 'Cheers! Thanks. That is – ta.' But he saw that she wasn't really looking at or even talking to him. None of this had been done for his benefit, none of it at all. It was all directed elsewhere.

She was staring at Jordan behind the bar.

Giles swallowed. Legions of dry biscuits seemed stuck in his throat.

'Angela –'

'Yes? Here, have another one!' She squeezed his genitals again. Perhaps a bit more forcefully than was necessary. 'And one more for luck, to keep the rain off.'

'Thank you. Very nice. Angela, when you say your fiancé – who might that be exactly?'

'Him,' she said, glaring at Jordan. 'That pig behind the bar. Jordan Franklin Consot, that's who. And here, have another one for free.'

Giles crossed his legs and started counting the exits. There was the way he had come in, and there was the door to the gents. And the time to act was now. He didn't like the way Jordan was looking at him.

'I'll be back in a minute, Angela, won't be a sec. Just going to the loo.'

'Okay. But don't be long.' And then, for Jordan's benefit again, she pouted and blew Giles a kiss. 'Hurry back – miss you.'

Miss him?

She didn't even know his name.

Box 132 picked up his briefcase and headed for the gents.

'Why are you taking your briefcase?'

'I keep a special toilet roll in there. I'm allergic to the ordinary ones.'

'Oh, that's a good idea.'

Calmly but rapidly, he headed for the door. He pushed it open, and found himself in a corridor. There were three doors. One marked GENTS, one marked FIRE EXIT, and one marked STAFF ONLY.

Giles pushed open the fire exit door. It would probably set the alarm off, but this was an emergency after all.

But the fire alarm did not go off. Must have been something wrong with it. Not that Giles was complaining. The fire exit door opened on to the side car park. He got his bearings and hurried off around the corner.

Hmmmmph!

Smack-bang into Jordan.

'Oi, you!'

Giles looked round for the others, but no, Jordan was on his own. His mates weren't with him, but then again, he hardly needed them, not against opposition like Giles.

'Oi, you, tosser!'

'Now look, let's be reasonable about this. This is all a big misunderstanding –'

'I don't care what it is. If I fucking find you fucking hanging about my fucking fiancée again, I'll tear your fucking bollocks off and stick one in each fucking ear. All right?'

157

'Fair enough,' Giles conceded. 'Take your point.'

'And here's one for fucking tasters, just so you know what I'm fucking talking about.'

He didn't have a chance. He was in the hands of an expert.

One minute he had a perfectly good nose, the next, blood was spurting out of it, and life had turned into a horror movie.

Giles didn't make a sound. No moan, no groan, no cry. Jordan went back inside. Giles took a tissue from his pocket (*Always have a tissue in your pocket, dear, you never know when it'll come in handy. Yes, Mum.*) and held it to his nose.

No panic, no fear, just this rather awful, tremendous pain in his nose. He felt it between finger and thumb. No, it didn't seem broken. No, just bleeding, that was all.

Who would think it could hurt so much. In films people got hit two dozen times and still got up again. And here was Giles, disabled by one headbutt to the nose.

Well, nothing for it but to soldier on, try and get home, keep the blood off the shirt and think of an excuse, a lamp post walked into, a fall, a door, something.

And tomorrow is another day.

Cools your ardour a bit though, I must say. (*The ardour they come, old mate, the ardour they fall.*)

Seems a bit silly now. Rather stupid. Think I've gone into shock. Man of my age, trying to have an affair. Rather fatuous, actually. Ought to be home with the family. Pottering in the garden, bit of DIY around the house. Get the old weekend leisure wear on, don't you know.

Pain, and you forget everything. Pain and then the meaninglessness of any other desire than the alleviation of it.

Giles made his way home. A few people looked at him, but not many. Just a man with a bloody nose. No one asked if he was all right or if he needed help. Didn't blame them for that though. Best not to get involved these days, when the Good Samaritan was the first to get his head kicked in.

He arrived home at about ten o'clock and Holly was there in the kitchen.

'My god! Giles! What happened to you?'

'It's by dose.'

'But what happened?'

He told her all about the swinging door he had walked into, the one which had caught him on the rebound as he ran for his train.

'They ought to be more careful! I've half a mind to write to them. It's downright unsafe.'

'No, no. Don't worry. No need to write to anyone. I'll be fine. Just an accident, that was all.'

But thank you for your loyalty and love.

She bathed his poor nose.

'Poor nose, oh, poor, poor nose. Poor Giles, poor nose.'

And she took care of him. And helped him undress.

'Oh, Giles, what happened to your poor bottom?'

'What? Oh, that. Got hit with a squash racket. Accident.'

'Oh, and you never said. How brave. What a brave Giles. Brave Giles and poor, poor botty. Poor, poor botty and poor, poor nose. Poor, poor bott-bott, poor, poor nosey-poos.'

'Yes. Yes. That's right. That is right. Yes.'

'Here, let me put some ointment on it. Is that better?'

'That's nice, yes, thanks, that's nice.'

'And a little here?'

'Yes, that's nice too – oh, yes – that's very nice.'

'And here? Is that nice?'

'Yes, that is nice, yes, that's extra-special nice. Extra, extra-special nice.'

'Been in the wars, haven't we?'

'Yes, been in the wars.'

'And how about if we –'

'Yes. Yes. That's nice too.'

'Nose not too painful?'

'No, no.'

'Botty not too sore?'

'No. Botty not too bad.'

'Poor nose.'

'Yes.'

'Poor botty.'

'Yes. Yes. Quite so. Poor, poor botty.'

'Brave Giles.'

'Yes, brave Giles, big brave Giles.'

'And nice Holly.'

'Yes, nice Holly. Lovely Holly, sweet, beautiful, gorgeous Holly. Hol-ly. Light of my life! Fire of my – ohhhhh!'

'Oh, Giles!'

'Oh, Holly!'

Never more to wander, never more to roam, always to be together, sufficient always unto each other. Enough, and more than enough. Forever and forever and forever.

Almost.

FIFTEEN

They awoke from the night's passion feeling inexplicably dissatisfied and discontent, both with themselves and with each other. Love was a vampire, a creature of the night only. It fled from daylight, and evaporated with the dawn. It didn't want to know about getting the girls ready for school, or getting breakfast, or washing and shaving, or catching the train. It slumbered in its lead-lined vault somewhere, the lid of its plush red coffin tightly shut. Love slept all day, and something else took over.

It was called irritation.

Holly wasn't so interested in the poor little botty-bott now. And as for the poor little nosy-wosey, well.

'What did you walk into a door for anyway, Giles? Bit of a silly thing to do, wasn't it?'

Thanks. Thanks for the sympathy.

He examined his nose in the bathroom mirror. Its bark had been worse than its bite, fortunately. It was bruised and swollen, and there were dark rings under both his eyes, but it was nothing that needed surgery. It would clear up in a couple of days.

Ella walked in without knocking.

'Coh! What happened to you, Dad? What did you do – kiss a panda?'

'I had an accident, as a matter of fact, with a door.'

'You should be more careful about where you're going.'

She took a hairbrush and walked out.

No sympathy, no familial affection at all. He could come home with a three-foot tumour growing out of his head and his children would only look at him and say, 'You know that hat doesn't suit you,' and then breeze off, with the callous, indifferent candour of youth.

Not that they were totally insensitive, they were shrinking violets sometimes, easily bruised and dainty flowers. But their sensitivity was only for themselves. Still, they'd grow out of it. It was just the age they were, callously sensitive, indestructibly vulnerable. Oxy and moronic.

He looked at the damage in the mirror.

Learned your lesson, Giles?

But he just felt like laughing. And far from feeling discouraged, he felt rather proud of and pleased with his swollen nose. (*Pleased as punch, eh, mate, and who punched it?*) I mean, say what you like, but Old Giles was having adventures. Life in the old dog yet. Bring on the new tricks, it's not too late to learn them. Yes, despite the poor botty-bott and the poor nosey-wose, Giles, in a strange way, was actually enjoying himself.

He was living.

He was alive.

He sang as he brushed his teeth.

'Giles, you sound like you're drowning!'

'Gno, gust ginging, gat's gall!'

Giles was halfway to the city when he felt a vibration in his trouser pocket.

His first thought was that someone was touching him up, and he lowered his paper and looked around the carriage to see who it might be, and whether he should allow them to continue.

In his many years of commuting, Giles had only been touched up a handful of times – as it were – and most of those were accidental rather than deliberate gropes. In the two cases of unambiguous fondling he could remember, the first offender had been a woman, and the second had been a man. And quite honestly, when you had your newspaper up, you couldn't really tell the difference.

Giles had wondered after that about the whole basis of human sexuality. People said they were heterosexual or homosexual, and that they found the idea of the other totally against their natures.

162

But quite honestly – fair do's – how would you know? As long as you kept on reading your newspaper you wouldn't really know either way.

Personally, Giles had never fancied sex with another man. The thought had crossed his mind occasionally, and the odd opportunity had come his way, but it had never really appealed to him. But he was quite prepared to admit that as long as he kept his eyes on his newspaper, he'd have a hard job – as far as certain practices went – in telling the difference.

It wasn't a hand causing the vibration, however, it was his mobile phone.

George Whimpole! Had to be! No one else knew the number yet.

Right. He'd had enough of it. This was too much. Giles fished the telephone out of his pocket, very aware of the unwanted attentions of his fellow commuters.

'Poser,' someone muttered.

'Ruddy phones,' someone else agreed. 'Can't get away from them.'

He put the phone to his ear and spoke into the other end.

'Hello!' he barked. 'Now, look here Whimpole, I've had more than enough of you and your foot-in-the-door tactics – well, foot-in-the-mouth more like – if I want to buy a –'

'Hello? Hello?'

But it wasn't Whimpole, it was a woman.

'Hello? Is that Mr Tile?'

'I'm sorry?'

'Mr Tile? Mr James Tile?'

'No, I'm sorry, I'm afraid you've got the wrong –'

Hang on though! No she hadn't. How could he forget. Giles West is Jimmy Tile is Giles West. 'No, wait a minute. Yes. Ah, well, yes, that's me, yes. Sorry – bad line – background noise – trouble hearing you – I'm on the train.'

'Well look, it's Martine. I just opened your letter this morning, and I thought, well, no time like the present.'

'Oh, right, yes, right, right.'

Martine, Martine! The brain searched its indexes. Now which one was she? Martine? Oh yes, the short and to the point one.

The no messing about. The direct approach. Just one line. Yes, that was the one. Curt and business-like. With a curt and business-like, but not unpleasant, voice.

'Well, look, why don't we arrange to meet one evening,' she was saying. 'How about an evening next week?'

'Fine.'

'Wednesday?'

'Perfect.' Yes. Squash night. He'd be out with Roy.

'Where?'

'Well –' Not the Mutton Trout for a start.

'How about the Unicorn Hotel?' she suggested. 'Down by the river. I'll book a room, shall I?'

Book a bloody room! Bloody hell, Giles! On the case this one, right enough. Talk about keen!

'Yes, fine, wonderful.'

'Seven-thirty then? In the lounge?'

'Yes, fine, perfect.'

'I'll be wearing a pink suit.'

'Me, too. A suit. Blue, that is.'

'Okay – James.'

'Right. Em, one thing, if I might ask, you didn't say, your letter that is . . . you're not engaged or anything to anyone – like a barman at the hotel?'

'No, no, don't you worry. I'm very discreet.'

Discreet. That was all right. Good, no complications. No broken noses or thwacked buttocks. Yes, discretion was the better part of infidelity. Giles would be in safe, competent hands by the sound of this one. If she was capable of taking the initiative like this, booking hotel rooms and the rest, then it boded well. Organization and decision-making had never been Giles's strong points, he was more the sort of man who chipped in with the odd, quirky idea, and went along with what was proposed.

'Well, I'll look forward to seeing you, James.'

'I'll look forward to seeing *you*, Martine.'

'Bye.'

'Bye.'

'Oh, and James –'

'Yes?'

'Would you mind if I invited a couple of girlfriends along as well?'

'What?' Eh? 'Oh, no. No. Not at all. No.'

Bloody hell! Threesomes! Foursomes! Fivesomes even! Luck's in today, Giles old sport. *(Now there's a turnip for the books, old mate, as the gardener said to the accountant! Har, har!)*

She hung up.

Threesomes, foursome, fivesomes, sixsomes. And all very toothsome too. You're a lucky man sometimes, Giles, a lucky man. Somewhere you have a guardian angel. You land on your feet, butter-side up, every time.

He just had to smile.

Smiling a Cheshire cheese of a smile, Giles put his mobile phone away in his briefcase and became aware of something odd in the train compartment: total silence.

They were all staring at him, as though they had listened to every word. Then gradually their eyes turned back to their papers, and the conversation resumed.

Giles reopened his *Daily Telegraph*. He turned to the inner pages for news of the court cases, to see who had been plotting to murder their spouses lately, and, more than likely, bodging it up. An odd article took his attention.

It was something about the inner city. In an effort to keep kerb crawlers off the streets, a group of militant women campaigners, going under the name of Womb-Bat, had taken to posing as prostitutes. When a man in a car stopped for a chat or to ask the price of French lessons, a crowd of them would rush into his vehicle. Very much the way Giles and Holly had hitch-hiked when they were students, Giles thought. Holly would thumb the lifts, Giles would squat behind a bush and suddenly appear at the last moment to the lorry driver's dismay. Once inside the car, the vigilantes would compel the man to drive to a deserted spot. There they would make him get out of the car, force him at knife point to take off his clothes, and then open up the boot. But far from locking him in it, they would make him remove the tool kit and the car jack, get out the spare, and then they would superglue his balls, and anything else they could get their hands on, to the spare tyre.

Then they would drive off, leaving him stark naked and miles from anywhere, with his private parts glued to a remould.

This was mental and physical torture of some refinement. The only thing for the man to do was to go in search of help. And the only way he could walk, without endangering his privates, was to carry the spare wheel in front of him, with it getting heavier with every step of the way, terrified that he would drop it and then need more than a puncture repair outfit and a new inner tube to put things back to rights.

It must have been quite a sight to see, Giles thought, a stark naked man with the wife's best friend stuck to a Firestone, limping along the slip road from the old trading estate, trying to thumb a lift into town. It was a bit like that old minstrel song 'Oh Susannah', where the singer was off to Louisiana with a banjo on his knee. Well, this was the modern day equivalent: being off to town with a Dunlop on your dick.

Giles could just imagine the reaction of the police too, when they would finally turn up to take you in, as you sat there in the back of the squad car with a wheel on your lap, getting redder and redder as the constables on either side tried unsuccessfully to keep straight faces and not to snort, not even when one of them would say, 'Are you all right, sir? You look rather tyred.'

Then, presumably, they'd have to get the fire brigade to separate you from the wheel with some kind of solvent. And a right bunch of jokers and wind-up merchants they could be – anything to relieve the tedium and stress of a life spent waiting for emergencies. Giles could just picture them running in, brandishing sharp axes and shouting, 'Don't you worry, mate, we'll soon have it off!'

He looked back at the newspaper and read the rest of the article. It said that the victim's car was usually found abandoned, but undamaged, near the scene of his abduction, with his clothes wrapped up in a neat bundle on the front seat and the keys left in the exhaust pipe. A note was customarily left on top of the clothes saying,

DON'T CRAWL OUR KERBS. KEEP THE CITY CLEAN,
OR NEXT TIME IT WILL BE THE EXHAUST PIPE.
YOU HAVE BEEN WARNED!
WOMB-BAT SISTERS.

The police condemned these actions, but they had to admit that as a means of deterrence they were very effective and had reduced kerb crawling considerably – much to the annoyance of those genuinely on the game. None of the assailants had been caught, but even if they were to be apprehended, it was likely that their victims would be too embarrassed to press charges.

Sadly, the article concluded, one or two men had turned into tyre fetishists as a result of their experiences, and had needed to go into therapy. One man even had a court order taken out against him, banning him from going within a hundred metres of his local branch of Kwik-Fit.

Giles quietly extended his sympathies to the male victims of these attacks. It was the kind of thing that could happen to anyone, he thought, to any innocent passer-by. He spent the remainder of the train journey in silent contemplation of modern woman's inhumanity to man. Fancy sticking your bollocks to a radial. It was a bit below the belt. (*A bit below the fanbelt even*, as a certain someone might have said.)

'Stone the flipping magpies, mate!'

It had to be Roy's voice. Couldn't be anyone else.

He had looked up from his coffee as Giles came into the office. 'What happened to your face?'

'I walked into a door.'

'So how's the door? Is it having a couple of days off work?'

Lavinia came bustling down the aisle between the desks with a sheaf of documents in her hand. She had all but given up walking normally; bustling had completely taken over. It infused even the most trivial actions with a sense of urgent importance. She was permanently on a mission.

'Good heavens, Giles, what's that on your face?'

'It's my nose. I had an accident.'

'I just hope none of our clients see you with a face like that.'

'When do I ever see clients? I'm pretty much of a backroom boy, Lavinia, you know that.'

'If you mean you spend half your day skulking in a cubicle in the gents toilet, Giles, then yes, you probably are.'

'No, that's not a backroom boy, that's a bog room boy, har, har! No offence, old mate.'

'I wasn't talking to you, Roy. Don't you have any work to do?'

'Yeah, plenty thanks. Why, did you want some?'

'I have quite enough on my own plate, thank you.'

Lavinia bustled off, handing Giles a memo as she went.

'From Eliot of management,' she said. 'Circulate it when you've read it.'

Giles looked at the memo. It was totally blank. He initialled it anyway and handed it over to Roy.

'Getting bogged down in memos, this place,' he said.

'Yeah,' Roy agreed. 'I've half a mind to send a memo round about it.'

'Good idea,' Giles said, but he knew that Roy never would. He was getting no work done at all, and spending every free minute on The Doris Management Programme.

'Here mate, before you go, cast the wary eyeball on this,' he said. 'Latest refinements, mate, state of the art.'

Like a proud father, Roy showed Giles the progress his programme was making. He clicked on the computer mouse and a picture of a woman appeared on the screen. It was Mrs Roy. Giles knew her at once from her expression of gloom.

'It's Mrs Roy. So what about it? What's she doing there?'

'Don't you see, mate? I scanned in her photo and put her mug shot on disk. Don't you get it? It's Clip-Art Doris, mate! Clip-Art Doris!'

Roy banged the desk in his excitement. Sandy and Terry, in Giles's section at the other end of the room looked round.

'Clip-Art Doris?'

'Yeah. I just used Mrs Roy here because I happened to have her photo to hand. But once you have the full library, you can click on whichever Doris you want, and not only do you get all her facts and info, you get a reminder of what she looks like as well. In fact, you can even print her out, if you want to. Print her out! I mean, you see what that means, don't you, mate?'

'Print-Out Doris?' Giles said, hesitantly.

'Exactly! And then you could fax her! Or send an e-mail. E-mail Doris, mate! Or have her as a screen saver – Screen Saver Doris. Or wallpaper – Wallpaper Doris! Talk about great leaps forward, mate, it's like putting a man on the moon!'

Giles left him to it. He went to his desk and sat thinking of the future. Roll on next Wednesday. Roll on the Unicorn Hotel. Roll on Martine. Roll on her tasty friends. Roll on a good roll on the bed.

And yet strangely, in amongst his anticipation and fantasies, was an inexplicable sense of unease.

The weekend cruised by on low altitude and automatic pilot. Shops, supermarket, car wash, ferrying Ella to her ballet classes, taking Lynnie to her drama. Children with the faces of seasoned professionals practised their dance routines in corners, getting ready to audition for the next panto. Some had already developed monstrous show biz egos, and swanned about in leotards, calling each other darling.

Ella and Lynnie, fortunately, had neither the ability, the looks, nor the co-ordination to take themselves so seriously. Giles had never before been so grateful that his children had so little talent.

Ella danced with all the grace of an ostrich, long skinny legs waving about, feet flapping like a long farewell. In the end-of-term plays, Lynnie came in late on her cues, her singing was flat and her voice was unexpressive.

Yet how they clapped. How all the parents clapped and embraced the appalling amateurism.

And how he loved them then, how Giles loved their gangly

limbs and their awkwardness, how he wished his daughters all the happiness in the world. Pity they couldn't stand him any more. It made it all a bit one-sided. It was a shame they thought of him now as a boring old fart. Only nature's way, he supposed, and, in many ways, that was man's estate: boring old fartdom.

And what did he wish for them?

I wish they will get good jobs, he thought, and meet someone who will love and be true to them, someone who will be kind to them, and considerate –

And who will never be unfaithful, Giles?

Yes, and who will never be unfaithful.

The boy next door?

Well, not the actual boy next door, obviously. Martin Stroud with his spots the size of coconuts, and his collection of Airfix modelling kits.

And I wish they will have children of their own, my grand-children, who will come and visit me, and sit on my knee, and put their arms around my neck, and who won't know that I'm a boring old fart. And who won't find out, not for years and years, until I'm a dead and buried old fart, pushing up the dandelions.

Yes, I wish them fulfilment, and interesting, meaningful lives, shared with those they love, and who love them and who are –

Never unfaithful?

Yes, never unfaithful.

On Saturday evening Beryl Major came and baby-sat while they went to a dinner party at Roger and Deborah Fuller's house. The girls didn't really need a sitter, but Giles liked someone else to be in the house.

'You won't mind if a friend pops round while you're out?' Beryl had asked. That meant the boyfriend, of course, and sex on the sofa. Still, good luck to them, as long as they remembered to draw the curtains this time. Who was Giles to criticize?

He and Holly drove to the Fullers' house in silence. But it

wasn't the comfortable silence which he had with Roy, not the comfortable silence of fellow boozers, but the stiff, almost painful silence of those who have nothing pleasant to say to each other, and so prefer to say nothing at all.

'Right here!'

'You can go left as well.'

'I wouldn't have gone this way.'

'Maybe not. But it's the way I'm going.'

Only who said what? And did it matter? The lines were interchangeable. Identical chips sat on their shoulders, their grudges matched like twins.

It was all right once they got there and the meal had started. Gaiety, laughter, yes, it was better after a few drinks. But what wasn't?

But once it was over, the shutter clanged back down with the closing of the car door.

'How come you can talk to everyone, but you've nothing to say to me?'

'I feel depressed.'

'Oh, *you* feel depressed! How do you think I feel? And anyway, you didn't seem depressed in there. You were the life and soul.'

'I was making an effort then.'

'So make an effort now.'

'You can't always be making an effort. It shouldn't have to be an effort!'

But it was. It was a bloody effort, all right. A sodding effort, like weightlifting. *(The old grab and snatch, mate, har, har!)*

Sunday was newspaper day. The newspaper with its umpteen sections and supplements and reviews. By the time Giles had got through his newspaper, he was too tired for God.

Didn't really believe in him, anyway, He was a bit out of date. Another hundred years, and God would be gone. The Church Of England would still be here, of course, and there would still be Bishops and Archbishops and christenings and funerals and great moral debates. There would still be the clergy – they'd just all be atheists.

The girls did their homework, visited their friends, ran up

171

the phone bill and mooched moodily about. Holly cooked and worked in the garden. Giles caught up on the household accounts, and then went out on his old bike for a cycle ride.

'We never do anything together any more, as a family,' he had once complained. So Holly had organized an afternoon outing for them all one Sunday, a walk around the nearby woods. It was only five miles, she said. She had found the route in *Happy Family Walks*.

They had got lost, and it had started to rain, and the girls had moaned every step of the way.

Giles had turned his back on family activities after that, and had decided to concentrate on individual enterprises.

That was it. It was enterprise culture, every man for himself.

And yet he loved them so much. Loved them with all the hate in the world sometimes, and hated them with all the love. And day by day they grew away from him. One day soon he would go to embrace them, and his daughters would stiffen with embarrassment, become cold and rebuff him completely. And that would be it. It would be over. They would no longer be the children he knew, they would be grown up, their new, mysterious, secret selves.

Then the weekend was over. It was Sunday night with a classic serial on TV. One less weekend to live through; more of the Peter Pan days. It wasn't the Lost Boys who needed a mother, it was all the Lost Days, all the lost, empty, endless, soulless, motherless Sundays, with skies the colour of cement.

And then, with a mixture of relief, regret and resentment, back to work.

'How are you, old mate? Good weekend?'

'Fine. Great. Lovely. And yourself?'

'Marvellous. Fine. Really good.'

Lying bastards all, in a world of duplicitous and lying bastards.

Talking of lying bastards, Giles hadn't had a call from George Whimpole on his mobile recently.

He hoped he was all right.

SIXTEEN

He was blasé now. He'd done it before. The first batch of letters he had scarcely been able to open for the trembling excitement in his fingers. But this lot held no real thrill for him. Giles didn't need them. He was already fixed up. Tonight, at 7.30 or thereabouts, in the Unicorn hotel, he would cease to be a one-gal guy, and become a three-at-once-gal guy, at the very least.

And then once it was done, it was done. Mission completed. Incident over. Back to Holly. No damage.

But what if he got the taste for it?

No. No, that wouldn't happen.

What if he got addicted to it?

No, no, the once would be enough. Just the once, that was all he wanted, just to know the body of another woman, one other woman, that would be enough, that would do. Just to have, well, a basis for comparison.

And meanwhile, the correspondence. He opened a letter at random.

'Dear Filth –'

Ah. One of the regulars. Straight into the bin.

He opened another letter, in another familiar hand.

Dear Mr Tile (Box 132),

Thank you for your letter. We've had such good news I had to write to you as soon as I heard. Mrs Throttly is alive and reunited with her Zimmerframe! She was not drowned at all, but was rescued by a Cornish trawler some days after her disappearance. She had drifted all the way to Plymouth, and was on her way to Westward Ho! when she was spotted clinging to a beach ball (maybe it was the one you lost). She was in good spirits and reasonable health – despite a touch of hypothermia – and was, as you can imagine after several days in the sea, bursting to go to the toilet.

We are so happy that she has been found. She is a remarkable lady. She said that she never for a moment doubted that she would be rescued, and she kept her spirits up throughout her long ordeal by singing show tunes, especially 'Don't Cry For Me, Argentina' which is one of her favourites.

Regarding the other matter – the misprint about the age – please don't give it another thought. In truth, this little correspondence has galvanized us into action. We are going to do as you suggested and advertise for men closer to our time of life in one of the retirement magazines.

Mrs Throttly and Miss Stavenshaw have instructed me to send you their best. Miss Stavenshaw is quite keen now on *losing her raspberry* as she calls it (or was it her apricot?). She also told me to say that she hopes you soon find a *bit of naughty* as she puts it (she really has got quite racy lately, I must say), and I'm sure the rest of us feel the same.

Well, do keep in touch, and drop us a line on how you are getting on.

Yours sincerely,

Mrs Wiseman.

P.S. Mrs Throttly says to thank you for the In Memoriam card. Plainly, it no longer applies, but she hopes you won't mind if she hangs on to it until she needs it. But if you'd rather have it back to send to someone else, please do say.

Giles put the letter down, and gazed around the cemetery. Nice old stick, really. All of them, all nice old sticks. If he ever wanted a nice old stick, he'd know where to find one.

Hmm. This looked different, a new correspondent. Giles sniffed at the perfumed envelope, unable to identify the fragrance, but thought it reminded him of something expensive, one he should know. He tore the letter open.

Dear Box 132,
Hi. How are you? I was interested to see your ad in the personals, and something in it made me think that maybe you could be my kind of man, and I could be the one for you too. No strings attached, you say? Well, that's fine by me. And you like walking in the country as well? Well, best foot forward, is my reply to that.
I am tall, slim, blonde, very sensuous and sensual, and my friends say that I am very attractive.
So why not write back. Or better still, fax me, and we can arrange a date.
Love and sensuality,
Pat

Giles fumbled about inside the envelope for the photograph, to see just what this slim, blonde sensuality looked like. He shook it hard, but nothing fell out. She was either lying about her appearance and looked like an Alsatian in a breaker's yard, or had simply overlooked its enclosure.

Never mind.

He'd keep that one on hold. Just in case tomorrow night with Martine didn't work out, and he'd still have something to fall back on.

The remaining letters were unappealing. Too thin, too fat, too young, too old, too sad, too bad, too many spelling mistakes. Giles realized that he was starting to get choosy, sitting as some grand arbiter of taste and beauty. But it had to be done, someone had to give them the thumbs up or down. *(Peel me another of those grapes, Nero, old matey, and not a sour one this time.)*

Giles got to his feet, and dumped his sandwich wrapper in the bin. Not many of the regulars in today from the graveyard set. Just some peculiar character in a long coat and mirrored sun-glasses. Another nutter, probably. Yes, say what you like about the UK, they did do you a good nutter. The economy

175

might be failing, the country might be going to the dogs, but the good old British nutter went on and on, as reliable as a delay on the railways.

Back at the office Giles found Roy hunched over his computer, tapping in further complexities of coding to the Doris Management Programme. Giles didn't disturb him, knowing how a programmer whose concentration has been broken can turn nasty.

Sandy and Terry were busy on the new stock control system. Giles went to each of their desks in turn, glanced at their work, and nodded sagaciously, murmuring, 'Yes, yes, very good,' and, 'If I may make a small suggestion –' and then left them to get on with it. They thought they carried him, and he knew it. They thought of him as a piece of dead wood, a man who had reached the level of his own incompetence, and who would rise no further.

But it wasn't that Giles lacked ability, it was the interest he lacked, the drive, fire, ambition, and hunger for the fray.

He just didn't care. He hadn't cared for years. It was all so futile in the end. All the elbowing and jostling and office politics. All the backstabbers, all the racing rats, and for what? A piece of cheese, that was all. Sometimes for even only the illusion of cheese. Glittering prizes which were scarcely worth the tinsel they were made from. So was it worth trying to climb the ladder, or were you better off just cultivating your garden outside the bungalow of life? What were these high-flyers after all but nobodies trying to be somebodies, desperate for whatever status and recognition they could grab, hoping that someone might give them a medal – if only for serving their time.

'Memo, Giles – when you've finished daydreaming.' Lavinia left a paper on his desk. He read it, initialled it, passed it on to Terry and Sandy, and eventually it found its way to Roy.

About half an hour later, a second memo landed on his desk. It read

MEMO

I am sick of all these fucking memos. Please initial and pass on.

The memo was not signed, but when Giles looked up to peer around the department, the first face he saw was Roy's. Roy winked and returned to his work.

'What's that, Giles? Another memo?'

Lavinia was back, power-dressed, her legs astride, her hands planted on her hips, brooking no insolence, suffering no fools gladly. She looked like a gunslinger about to let fly.

'Yes, it's just come round.' He handed the memo to her. She read it without expression.

'I see.'

She crumpled the memo up in her hand, then changed her mind, and smoothed it out again.

'May I ask who wrote this?'

'Search me,' Giles said. 'But I thought that the expression of popular sentiment was usually credited to the prolific Anon.'

Lavinia's eyes narrowed. She looked around the department like a lion among zebras, deciding which one to single out for her prey. Then she spotted the one she wanted.

'Roy!'

He looked up, languid and slow-moving.

'Yeah?'

'Would you come to my office for a moment, please.'

'Any time,' Roy said. He uncoiled himself and sloped off after her. He winked at Giles as he passed his desk. Then he followed Lavinia towards her office, a fly shuffling after a spider and the web closing behind him.

He didn't come out for an hour.

The phone rang. It was Holly.

'Hello, Giles,' she said. 'Sorry to bother you at work. Just ringing to ask if you were squashing again this week.'

Giles almost spilled his coffee. Squashing? Squashing what? Squashing who? Was Holly on to him? Had she found out?

177

'Playing squash after work, are you? In this tournament thing with Roy?'

'Oh, yes, yes. That, yes. Right.'

'Then you've got your kit with you, have you?'

For a second his mind went blank.

'Kit? What kit?'

'Your kit – for squash.'

'Oh, yes, yes. That, yes. Thanks. Got it here. Right by the desk.'

Elementary mistake there, Giles, almost gave the game away. Perfectly guilty answer to a perfectly innocent question. Getting careless, you know. Must try harder.

'Okay. What time will you be back?'

'Late–ish.'

'Oh. Okay. I'll see you in the morning then.'

'Right. Bye.'

Giles spent the rest of that afternoon in a state of almost suspended animation. Soldiers must feel like this, Giles thought, in the hours before battle.

He worked late to kill time until his appointment in the Unicorn Hotel. He was still working at five past seven, when Eliot of management strolled through the department on his way down to his Jag.

'Ah, West! Burning the midnight oil, I see.'

'Oh, just tying up a few odds and ends.'

'Good, well, don't let me stop you. Carry on there. Yes. Good.'

He left, impressed more than ever by Giles's capacity for work and his dedication to the job.

'Extraordinary worker, that Giles West,' he said to Kavanagh of auditing, as they went down together in the lift. 'Lives for his job, you know, amazing dedication. Wonder if we shouldn't find something more taxing for him.'

SEVENTEEN

At 7.15 Giles was ready to leave the office, his Massive Cucumbers in his pocket, his sports bag on his shoulder, his briefcase in his hand. He walked the quarter mile to the Unicorn Hotel. When he entered the lounge a cocktail pianist was endeavouring to render popular tunes unrecognizable. The lighting was subdued, and there were many pot plants to contend with. He could not see Martine and so parked himself on a well-lit sofa, facing the revolving door.

People span in and out of the door. Who were they? What were they doing there? What sort of people stayed in hotels on Wednesday evenings? What was their business there? Take this lot now, for example, what was their story?

Four women entered the hotel lobby together. They were all in their late twenties to early thirties, but other than their age and sex, seemed to have little in common. One looked like a professional woman, a solicitor or a barrister, formally dressed in a pin-striped skirt and jacket with a pale cream blouse. An expensive raincoat hung elegantly from her shoulders. The second woman was all swirling dirndl skirts, gypsy tops and head scarves, and could have worked in a health food store or a shop selling aromatherapy products, homoeopathic medicines and crystals. The third woman was small and squat, and very short-sighted if the thickness of her glasses was to be believed, and she had the dishevelled hair and mismatched appearance of the purely cerebral. Giles put her down as an academic, a lecturer in philosophy, maybe, or – perish the thought – that dreaded modern subject, Women's Studies.

Holly had done an evening class in that once.

'So what about Men's Studies,' Giles had objected. 'When do Men's Studies get a look in? When do they start teaching Men's Studies in the universities and polytechnics? Eh?'

'Frankly, Giles, they've never taught anything else.'

That was a put-down, that was. But it hadn't satisfied him. Nor, he felt, had it really answered the question. For it seemed to Giles that the entire Women's Studies curriculum was based on the simple idea that all men are bastards. Discuss.

The fourth woman was different again. She was built like a stoker and dressed like one too, and she was carrying a large, masculine holdall. Her hair was close-cropped, and she wore denim jeans and a denim jacket, along with a plaid shirt and a pair of Doc Martens. She even had what Holly called builder's bum, when the waistband of the jeans hung around the cheeks of the buttocks. Were she to sit down, no doubt a crack of backside would open up like a rift valley.

Now what common cause or purpose could possibly have brought the four of them together, Giles wondered.

The woman who looked like a lawyer went up to the hotel reception desk and asked for her room key. As she waited for the receptionist to fetch it, the others looked around the lobby, in an aimless way – not really looking for anyone, just looking. For a fraction of a second Giles's gaze clashed with that of the stoker's, but she turned her head away and looked elsewhere.

Now, what brought them together, Giles wondered again. The local branch of the Madonna fan club? Some kind of action group? Woman Against Cruelty To Animals? Or some kind of political group, maybe?

The receptionist handed the lawyer her key. The other three women picked up their belongings and followed her towards the lift.

'Which room is it?' the gypsy skirt asked.

'Seventy-eight.'

The lift opened, the four women stepped inside. The lift ascended, and as it did, something drifted out and down through a small aperture between the two doors. Giles watched as it floated and fluttered down to the floor.

It was a feather. A solitary feather. Fancy that. A feather. In the hotel lobby. A feather. Funny that.

'James! James Tile? Box 132?'

He looked up, and there she was: Martine. Dark, pretty,

180

feminine, perfect teeth, in a pale pink suit. Darkly attractive with hazel eyes, she could have been the wife of your best friend, the one you had always desperately fancied and been half in love with. Her loss was your regret.

'Martine?'

'How do you do.'

Handshake or kiss? Mutual confusion which ended up with pecks on the cheek.

'Sorry.'

'No, my fault. Sorry.'

'No, sorry.'

'Sorry.'

'Really, my fault.'

She sat next to Giles on the lobby sofa. Her leg brushed his, and he instantly got an erection. *(In the building trade now are you, old mate, har, har!)*

'Would you like a drink or something?' he offered.

'Em –'

Say no, Giles willed her. Let's get up and get down to business.

'Em – no, I'm all right for the moment. We can always ring for room service after unless you –'

'No, I'm fine, fine!'

'Fine. Then – shall we?'

'Sure, yes, right. You said that you'd –'

'Yes, I have, yes, I booked a room earlier.'

'You must let me –'

Giles was about to say, you must let me pay for half of it, but that sounded a mite cheap.

'You must let me pay for everything.'

'Oh, no, James. No. Let me pay – or at least split it – or it seems like, well –'

Yes, he knew what it seemed like – prostitution.

'Anyway,' she went on, 'let's sort all that out afterwards. Shall we go up to the room?'

Giles's heart pounded with excitement. She was mustard, mate! Absolute mustard. She was the genuine Dijon this one. Never mind the small talk, never mind the story of your life, and 'the long road I travelled that brought me here today'.

181

This was the way to do it. Grab the key, up in the lift, pants off and hit the duvet running. He felt in his pocket for his Massive Cucumber – friend, will you be needed tonight. In fact the way Giles felt, a whole massive greenhouse of Massive Cucumbers might be in order.

Horticulture was never going to be the same again.

'Right.'

They stood. She saw the feather lying on the lobby floor, and she blushed, suddenly clumsy and embarrassed, almost – caught out.

Giles saw what she was looking at.

'It's a feather,' he said. He understood her embarrassment. Feathers – duvets – beds – public place – one and one – two – nudge, nudge. He picked it up and dropped it into a pedestal ashtray.

'Right.'

He waited for her to go to the reception for the key.

'Are you ready?' she said.

'Don't we need the key?'

'Oh, it's in my bag. I was in earlier and didn't hand it back.'

'Ah, right.' Giles understood. It was that old sensitive flower blossoming again. Didn't want the hotel staff knowing any more than they had to.

'Fine, well, lead the way.' He picked up his briefcase and sports bag and followed her to the lift.

They waited a moment.

'Have you ever . . . ?'

'No. Have you?'

'Me neither.'

'Which floor?'

'Seventh,' she said.

'Seven it is.'

He punched seven and the lift whooshed away.

Fly. Me. To the moon.

They got out at the seventh floor and he let her go first to lead the way.

'Which number?' he asked.

'Along here.'

Odd, she seemed a little tense now. Serious and distant. She walked a little ahead of him, then stopped and took his arm.

'Seems strange to be doing this, doesn't it?' she said.

'Yes.'

'Are you nervous?'

'Yes,' he said, honestly.

'Me too.'

'Married?' he asked. He couldn't remember if she had told him or not.

'Sort of.'

Oh yes. No need to say any more. Giles knew what she meant. Very few people were married any more, they were all 'sort of married', especially the married ones.

Seventy. Seventy-two. Seventy-four. Seventy-six. Seventy-eight.

They stopped.

'Here we are.'

Even then, no warning balls rang. Just vague uncertainty muffled by lust. *Now didn't I hear – wasn't someone else – did I hear that room number – and what about these friends – hadn't there been talk of twosomes and threesomes, or –?*

'Have you got the key?'

Martine rummaged for the key in her bag. 'Oh look, I must have left it open!'

The door was slightly ajar.

'Left it open? I'm sorry?' Giles was doing his celebrated impersonation of a charming, pleasant, ready to oblige, ever so slightly dippy Englishman.

'Oh, I looked in on the room earlier,' Martine said. 'Just to make sure we had everything we needed.'

She reached inside the room and brought out the DO NOT DISTURB sign and hung it on the door handle.

'There,' she said.

Giles looked at the sign and arched an eyebrow roguishly. (That *was* roguish, that eyebrow, wasn't it?)

'Perfect,' he said, 'shall we go in?'

She reached out to take his hand.

'Yes. Let's do that. Shall we – Jim?'

Her mouth found his.

'Umm –'

No, not out here in the corridor, he panicked. Someone might see! Please kiss, but don't tell.

They sidled into the room.

(Come into my little rented four-star parlour, said the spider to the fly.)

He noticed how red her nail varnish was. Red as blood.

(How red your little nails are, young granny. All the better to undo your buttons with, my dear.)

He couldn't wait now. He couldn't wait to get into that bedroom and unzip the old kaks and fling them aside with horny abandon. The door began to close. As it did, something tickled his nose, something small and light, floating by on a current of warm air.

It was another feather. Just a feather. Funny.

The door clicked shut behind them. As it did, Martine's voice called out something he didn't understand. Then her hands were all over his body. They were everywhere at once, in his shirt, in the waistband of his trousers, pulling off his jacket and tugging at his shoes.

Her hands?

Hang about.

Shome misthake officer, shurely!

How many hands did she have?

She couldn't have this many hands! That was impossible. She couldn't have two hands inside his shirt and another two hands pulling off his trousers and even more taking off his shoes. No. Come off it. That couldn't be done. She'd need to be a bloody octopus to do that. No, come on now, play the game. Many hands made light work, that was fair enough, but there were limits. And where had they all come from, these hands? Whose were they, precisely?

Then he realized what she had said.

She hadn't said, 'Let me have it, lover boy,' or pleaded, 'Sock it to me, big stuff!' No, Martine's voice had been barking out instructions to certain third, fourth, fifth, and even sixth parties in the room.

'Okay, girls!' she had yelled. 'Grab him and let's do it!'

Giles felt as if he were watching a video, one in which he also had a part. He was a spectator as well as a participant, only he had no control over the flow of events. He couldn't fastforward or rewind. In fact, there seemed to be no way of stopping this video from turning nasty right in front of his eyes. He could only freezeframe – with horror – at what he saw.

Four women had burst out of the bedroom the instant the door had closed, and they had been on him in a flash. The moment he saw them, Giles knew who they were, for he had just seen them down in the hotel foyer. They were the stoker, the gypsy, the lawyer, and the mistress of obscure philosophy.

He didn't even have time to scream.

The four women pounced on him, and grabbed a leg or an arm or whatever they could get a hold of. Martine already had him by the neck. The stoker got him round the torso and held him pinioned. God, she had muscles like ruddy Schwarzenegger. They stripped his clothes from him, every stitch, while he kicked wildly, panic surging inside him, only one thought in his mind: he didn't know who they were and he didn't know why they were doing this, but one thing he did know –

THEY WERE GOING TO DO A BOBBITT ON HIM!

Bobbitt. The case of the American woman who had set upon her husband's manhood, severed it with a sharp instrument, driven off with it, and thrown it out of the car window.

'No! No! No!'

He fought wildly, legs kicking and threshing, until a gravelly voice spoke in his ear. It must have been the stoker. 'Keep still,' she said, 'or we'll do a Bobbitt on you.'

Giles's heart rejoiced. They're not going to do a Bobbitt on me! Whatever they were going to do, as long as he didn't struggle, it wouldn't be a Bobbitt.

Only, if they weren't going to do a Bobbitt on him, what were they going to do? Sell him a couple of raffle tickets for the policeman's ball?

Or –

Oh *no*!

Giles suddenly realized who this unlikely group of women were. He was in the hands of the vigilantes! They were going to superglue his plonker to a car tyre! Only not a spare one this time, no, to one that was still on an axle. Yes, they'd superglue his plonker to the front wheel of a Ferrari, and then they'd drive off with it!

No! Please, no. Wouldn't they please be merciful and just throw him out of the window instead? He couldn't bear to see his plonker speeding off down the road without him. He'd never be able to catch it up, no matter how fast he ran. No, he'd rather take his chances with seven floors of gravity.

Calm down, Giles, calm down. Get a grip of yourself. *(I would if I could, but they've got hold of most of it.)* Be sensible man. Think straight. They can't have a car wheel, not up here in a hotel bedroom. Whatever they're going to do, mate, it won't be the wheel.

'You realize this is nothing personal,' the gypsy said, as they lugged him into the bathroom.

'This is just a warning, that's all,' the mistress of obscure philosophy reassured him, philosophically.

'We don't like to be judge and jury –' that must have been the lawyer who said that. 'But there have to be examples.'

'Men have got away with this kind of thing too often –'

'And for too long!'

'If you can't change on your own –'

'We'll have to help you.'

'Infidelity is not a joke. What is it?'

'Not a joke!' Giles said. 'I understand. I get the message. I'll be good. I won't do it again, I promise. I've never done it anyway. I'm a big failure. All I've done is try. I'm just a wimp!'

'No, you don't get off, not that easily.'

'With your mucky little advertisement in the personal columns.'

'So let this be a warning to you, all right? A warning and a lesson. From Womb-Bat.'

'And next time –'

'And there'd better not be a next time –'

'Next time, no more Mister Nice Girls!'

'So tell your friends that you had a visit from Womb-Bat. And that they could be next on the list!'

'Hold him steady then.'

'Right.'

'Get the glue.'

'Here.'

'And the brush!'

He closed his eyes tightly. It was all he could do. It was best just to close your eyes until the nasty part was over.

Eeeech!

Slop!

Four of them were holding him by his arms and legs over the bath, while the fifth went over him with a brush, laden with – by the smell of it – glue.

'I say, you won't put that on my –'

Slop! Too late. She had. A large dollop, right on the old Giles West gonads. And then it was all over him, up his chest, down his legs. She was a dab hand at the old decorating all right, whoever was wielding the brush. Maybe she'd come round to Giles's house one night and give them a price for repapering the kitchen.

'All right, turn him over.'

Hello. She was pasting both sides. Talk about a thorough job, this was definitely belt and braces this was, belt and braces and rivets, and a bit of gaffer tape bunged in.

'I say, you won't put any of that up my –'

Gluggety-gluggety-glug! Kersplop! Too late. She'd done that bit too. But then, that's the art of decorating, not missing the cracks.

'That's it. He's ready.'

Thank god for that. Ordeal over. They'd go now and leave him alone to have a shower and –

'Drop him in.'

In? Into what?

'All right! Now let's go.'

Darkness, softness, sinking deeper and deeper into a soft, downy bed. It was nice to rest after such a terrifying ordeal.

And nice to be so comfortable. Sticky, but warm and comfortable, sinking into a soft feather bed.

Hang about!

He wasn't in bed. He was in the bath. He heard the light switch get turned off, and then the door slam out in the corridor. He opened his eyes. The gloom gave way to half-light. He reached up, fumbled, found the light cord, pulled, and –

Arghh!

It was awful, terrifying, a living nightmare.

Giles was in the bath with a chicken! A huge, monstrous chicken. It was in the bath with Giles. It would probably peck him and –

Hang on. No. That wasn't right. No, Giles wasn't in the bath *with* a chicken, Giles *was* the chicken!

They'd brushed him with glue from top to toe and dumped him in a bath of feathers.

Giles stood up slowly, hanging on to the towel rail for support. The full-length mirror on the wall revealed the awful metamorphosis.

Giles was a chicken.

He tried to scream, but all that came out was *cock-a-doodle-do!*

EIGHTEEN

Why me?

But then again, *why not*?

At least they'd had the decency to leave a calling card, Giles thought. The absence of an explanation can often offend, and leave the victim confused and bamboozled, and with a sense of personal inadequacy.

The card had been left tucked into the corner support of the mirror. Giles prised it out with a feathery paw, and held it under the light.

WOMB-BAT

THE FEMINIST DIRECT ACTION GROUP

YOU HAVE BEEN WOMB-BATTED!

NOTHING PERSONAL.

BUT KNOW BETTER NEXT TIME.

WOMB-BAT – FOR A BETTER WORLD WITH BETTER MEN

IN IT.

At the bottom of this printed card – probably done on some bus station calling card machine – was a line in biro. It read: 'Next time, think of your wife! Stay faithful.'

Bloody cheek! Giles thought. Bloody vigilantes – who did they think they were anyway, the moral majority? What was this, mob rule? It was none of their damn business what he did. He wasn't standing for this! Oh no, not Giles. He wasn't going to be bullied and intimidated. He wasn't going to let this lot tell him what he should and shouldn't do with his private life and his private parts. Was he a man, or was he a –

Chicken?

Yes, well – he was a chicken, at the moment. It said so, right there in the mirror.

If he had been looking at someone else, he would have laughed. But as it was his own personal tragedy, Giles did not find it so amusing. His head and neck were free from feathers, apart from a few stuck in his hair, but the rest of his body was plastered in them. He had feathery shoulders, feathery arms, a feathery chest, (*Getting a bit pigeon-chested there, aren't you, old mate?*), a feathery waist and abdomen, and a feathery back and sides. The feathers around his hips swelled out like a hula-hula skirt, or like a big, feathery doublet, with a big feathery codpiece poking out at the front.

What time's feeding time, Giles, old mate?

All right, ducky? Have you brought the breadcrumbs?

Ask Giles round for dinner one night, and we'll stick him in the oven.

Say what you want to, you have to admire his pluck.

I bet you get nervous when Christmas comes round, Giles, eh?

What happened to you, Giles, shag a bantam, did you? Har, har!

The demons of ridicule and humiliation danced in the mirror. If anyone he knew was to see him like this – if anyone he didn't know was to see him like this – if anyone at all was to see him like this . . . He burned with shame.

What's up, Giles, old mate? Your feathers have gone all pink. You're turning into a flamingo.

He looked down. He was standing in a pool of feathers in the bath. He raised one leg. Feathers remained clinging to it. He changed legs and looked at the other one. The feathers were stuck on to the very soles of his feet, in-between his toes, and overhanging them at the front. He looked as if was wearing a pair of big feathery shoes, about two sizes too large.

He changed legs, but it made no difference, each was as bad as the other.

Why are you perched on one leg, Giles? Doing the stork now, are you? Here, I hope you're not getting broody, old mate. Are you free-range or what?

The demons waltzed and danced and cackled and broke out the booze.

Then suddenly the chicken smiled a chickeny sort of smile, and laughed a chickeny laugh.

You had to laugh, really. It just looked so bloody ridiculous there, the big bird in the mirror, it just made you cackle out loud.

Cock-a-doodle-do!

Giles did a few cock-a-doodles and scratched about in the bath. Then he waved his elbows up and down, in full chicken simulation, just like that bloke on the telly used to do.

What was the sense in getting worked up about it. Okay, so he'd been made a fool of. No use crying over spilt milk. Just have to pull these feathers off, shower, get dressed and then off home before Holly started wondering where he was.

Right. Shouldn't take him more than ten minutes to get them all off. Giles grabbed a handful of feathers and pulled.

Ahhhhhhhh!

Oh, my sainted bloody, sodding aunt! Ow, ow! He danced round in circles until the pain went away. He'd almost pulled a handful of skin off. What the hell had these feathers been stuck on with? Not a single one had come off.

Right. One at a time then. It might take a bit longer, but he'd get there in the end. He went to the bathroom cabinet and found a pair of tweezers. He used them to grip the stem of one of the feathers and pulled.

Ahhhhhhhh!

The feather came off all right, but the skin came off with it. A drop of blood wept from a tiny wound, and, warmly insulated as he was, Giles suddenly felt chilled and frozen.

The feathers were not going to come off! Whatever they had used to stick them on, it was not going to come off. Giles tried to calm himself. What might soften the adhesive? Water. Warm water.

He turned on the shower, took up the soap, and stood under the water. He scrubbed and scrubbed for five minutes, but to no avail. He tried a small bottle of body shampoo then, and the feathers frothed and bubbled. He rinsed off, tried removing some again, but they couldn't be budged. Every time he pulled one off, a piece of skin came with it.

He turned off the shower, and stood looking at his foggy reflection in the steamed-up mirror.

That was one wet chicken there all right, buddy.

Wet and beginning to get cold. He had to stay warm at all costs. He'd read that somewhere, or maybe seen it on David Attenborough. In order to survive, birds have to look after their feathers. If their feathers lose their insulating properties or their natural oils, they can perish.

Lose their natural oils! And he'd been putting shampoo on them! Quickly Giles stepped from the bath, towelled himself down, and got the hair dryer. He dried himself all over, and his feathers fluffed up nicely. He found a small sachet of moisturiser in the complimentary cosmetics basket and rubbed a bit of oil back into his plumage.

That was better. He felt like a new bird.

He put on the dressing gown that was hanging up behind the door, went to the bedroom, and put on the kettle for a cup of coffee. He wished he had the key to the fridge bar, but he didn't.

As the kettle boiled, he sat and thought about what to do. Plainly he needed some kind of solvent. Now, where was he going to get some at this time of night? It was 8.22, according to the bedside clock. The only solvent he could think of was –

In the office!

Yes! That was it. In the storage cupboard, along with the stationery, there were aerosol cans of solvent, used for cleaning all the computer screens and keyboards. That would probably do it.

Right. That was the plan. Get dressed, out of the hotel, head down, shoulders hunched, back to the office, quick spray with the solvent, feathers off, quick shower in the washroom, wash and brush up, off home, and nobody the wiser.

Getting the quarter mile from the hotel to the office would be the only difficulty, but problems were there to be surmounted. Okay. He took a sip of coffee and instantly felt better. Nothing like a hot cup of coffee to lift a chicken's spirits. Right. Now where were his clothes?

He looked around.

Where were his clothes? Excuse me? Clothes, I say!

They must be out in the corridor. Just behind the door. That was where Martine had debagged him. But no, they weren't there. In fact, they weren't anywhere.

The witches!

They'd done for him. They'd even taken his clothes! They'd left him clobberless.

By the washbasin, Giles sat down and wept. It was understandable. No one could have blamed him for giving expression to his feelings. A chicken is only human after all. Cut us, do we not bleed? Tickle our drumsticks, do we not laugh? Stick us in the oven, are we not done to a turn in an hour and forty minutes?

They'd left him his wallet and his keys and personal possessions, all neatly piled on the hall table. But no clothes. So now what? The gulf opened beneath him. Discovery, publicity, shame, humiliation, the press, TV, a national laughing stock. Oh, god, why had he ever wanted a leg-over? What use was a leg-over when you were Britain's most famous chicken?

Now, wait up a bit, Giles. You have got clothes! This dressing gown for one thing. And what about your sports bag? Did they take that too?

No. They had left him his briefcase and sports bag. Theft was not theirs; theirs was vengeance. Now, where was it? Ah, right. Giles took out his squash kit. He had a choice: the squash kit, or the dressing gown? Which was less likely to attract attention out on the street? The squash kit: he could put it on and pretend to be jogging. Perfect.

Giles pulled the shorts up over his feathers. They bulged rather, but he just managed to get them on. He took out his vest next and pulled that on with some effort. It too bulged strangely with the feathers underneath. Next, he tried to put on his trainers, but he couldn't get them on over his feathery feet. Going to the bathroom, he found a pair of nail scissors in the complimentary manicure set and trimmed his feet with them until he could squeeze into the shoes.

There. Now what did he look like? Did he look more normal? Not exactly. He looked like – what did he look like? He definitely looked like something.

He looked like a very big chicken going out for a jog.

And so what if he did? Was there any law saying that chickens couldn't go jogging?

The next step was to stuff the briefcase into the sports bag, and to loop the handles of the sports bag around his arms, so that he could carry it like a rucksack. This left his hands free to move, but it meant that he would have to carry his squash racket, as it wouldn't fit in the sports bag as well.

How now, Giles? (*Ask the old brown cow, mate.*) Yes, he was transformed. He didn't look like a chicken jogger any more, he now looked more like a chicken from a creaky West End comedy. The sort of chicken who would come in through the French windows and squawk, 'Tennis, anyone?'

Well, he'd just have to live with that. Nerve and plenty of neck, a bit of Parson's nose and a few giblets were all you needed, and you could get away with anything. If anyone asked any questions, he'd say he was doing it for charity. That seemed to be the preferred explanation for irrational behaviour these days. People would see a big chicken coming down the street with a squash racket in its hand, and they would think, 'Aye, aye, it's the Charity Chicken. Probably been sponsored at so much a mile.' And they'd smile and wave and off you went. And little children would say, 'Look, Mum, it's the Charity Chicken!'

Yes. If anyone asked, if he got stopped by the police, he had his story ready. He was the Charity Chicken. That should convince them. You had to get up early in the morning to catch old Giles out. There were no flies on him. Feathers maybe, and a touch of foul pest, but flies, oh, no.

He opened the door and peered out. The outer corridor was empty of both hotel staff and guests. He leaned out further; the coast still seemed clear. He stepped out and let the door close behind him with a quiet thud. His bridges were burned now, he was committed, there was no retreat.

He padded along the corridor. Now, was it to be the stairs or the lift? God damn it, he'd try his luck with the lift. It wasn't sensible, it wasn't rational, but often that was the only way to get away with things: being blatant, up front, and outrageous. Say it out loud, 'I'm a chicken, and I'm proud'.

He punched the lift button and waited. The doors slid open. It was empty. Good. Giles got in and pressed G for the ground floor. The lift sped downwards, but as it approached the third floor, it slowed and came to a halt. The doors opened and a man and a woman stood, waiting to get in. They saw Giles, and with the habitual togetherness of long-married couples, their jaws dropped simultaneously, like cash registers clanging open.

'Holy moly!' the man said. American tourists, Giles thought. Best try to be friendly.

'Going down?' Giles asked.

'What is it, honey?' the woman said.

'Seems to be a chicken. There's a chicken in the elevator.'

'It's all right,' Giles said, 'nothing to worry about. I'm the Charity Chicken.'

'What's he say, dear?'

'Says he's the Charity Chicken.'

'Oh. Has he got a gun on him?'

'Can't rightly say.'

'Is he with Colonel Sanders?'

'You with Colonel Sanders, fella? You from Kentucky?'

'No,' Giles said. 'I'm British. Really, I'm perfectly harmless. The Charity Chicken, you know. Are you coming in?'

'Well – okay.'

They got in gingerly, suspicious but curious. It would certainly make a good anecdote when they got home.

('Yeah, we were staying at this hotel in the ol' UK, when we got into the elevator with a chicken.'

'You got into the elevator with a *what*?')

The lift hummed down to the ground floor.

'You an entertainer?' the man asked.

'Fundraising,' Giles said. 'For charity. The Charity Chicken.'

'Do you know the Easter Bunny?' the woman asked. 'We have a daughter who worked at Disney one vacation as the Easter Bunny.'

'Never had the pleasure,' Giles said. The lift opened on to the lobby and they got out. People turned and stared. The porter dropped a suitcase.

'What the fuck's that?' he muttered. 'It's a giant fucking canary.'

Giles walked rapidly across the lobby floor. The walk turned into a jog as he neared the revolving doors. He pushed hard, span the door round, and then the cool night air hit him. He was out in the street and running.

Back in the hotel lobby, the porter picked the dropped suitcase up, and turned to the two Americans.

'Who was that?' he said.

'That? Why that was the Charity Chicken,' they told him as they went out.

The porter went over to the bellhop.

'You see that?'

'Yeah. What was it?'

'The Charity Chicken.'

'Oh, yeah, the Charity Chicken, right.'

'You heard of it then? The Charity Chicken?'

'Em – might have done. Might have heard something, yeah. Seem to remember something about it on – something or other, yeah.'

'Oh, yeah, I think I did too, now you mention it. The Charity Chicken, yeah.'

Giles jogged on along South Street, and turned right into Jarvis Mews. A bunch of lads on a night out jeered and hollered at him and made clucking noises, but thankfully they didn't give chase. He was nearing the office now and getting hotter with every step. The perspiration trickled down into his feathers.

He climbed over the railings at the end of the mews, and went into the service alley which ran alongside the Hopper and Bryanson building. He stopped to get his breath. There was his office, up there on the fifth floor.

He went to the rear entrance and looked around. He was alone. He tapped the security code into the digital lock and let himself inside. The burglar alarm bleeped, but he cancelled it and quickly headed up the back stairs.

He ran up the steps, two and three at a time, hotter than

ever now, but deliverance was at hand. He tried to look at his watch, but he couldn't see it for feathers. Never mind, time enough to find out the time.

First he had to get that solvent.

A phone rang, just as he was about to open the stationery cupboard. The noise seemed to be coming from somewhere behind him. Yet when he turned to locate it, the sound was behind him again.

It was coming from his sports bag on his shoulders! It was his mobile. Giles shrugged the bag off, grabbed the offending instrument and flipped it on. If that was George Whimpole again, he was going to –

'Hello, James – Mr Tile?'

He recognized the voice instantly, it was Martine.

'You! Why you – you – you –' Clucks failed him.

'Are you all right, Mr Tile?'

'No, I'm not! I'm covered in feathers! I look like a massacre in a hen coop!'

'Yes, well, let that be a lesson to you in future. I'm just ringing to put your mind at rest.'

'Oh?'

'Womb-Bat is intrinsically a nonviolent, nondestructive campaigning organization, dedicated to changing the world through peaceful protest, reasoned argument and friendly persuasion.'

'This is what you call reasoned argument, is it? I suppose you don't realize that my cheeks are stuck together now with the glue. I just hope I don't suddenly get the call, or it'll be 999 time!'

'Yes, well, I'm sorry about that, of course,' she said, but she didn't sound it, 'but maybe you'll treat your wife with a little more consideration in future.'

'Yes, but –'

'And the feathers will drop off in about ten days.'

'But I –'

She hung up. Ten days! He couldn't wait ten days. Those feathers had to come off now! Giles put the phone back into his bag, opened the stationery cupboard, took three large

197

aerosol cans of solvent, and headed for the executive wash-room.

It was working!

The joy, the relief, the release from anxiety and woe. Giles felt like a liberated country, just freed from occupation. He raised an arm, aimed the aerosol at his armpit as though applying deodorant, and pressed the button. *Schwoosh!* A spray of solvent hit him, the glue instantly loosened its grip, and some feathers fell down on to the floor.

The spray stung a little, but Giles was way past caring about that. He'd have a shower as soon as the most of the feathers were off, and wash the solvent away. The worst he could expect was a rash, and that would soon clear up. Anything was better than these damn –

Schwoosh! Ahhh! Now that *was* better. He was starting to look human again.

He stood in the executive washroom, in front of the room-length mirror beside the line of sinks. The feathers fluttered down around him like leaves in the autumn. Autumn had always been his favourite season, and it was even more so now.

Schwoosh! Giles sprayed his watch and the time appeared from behind the feathers. Twenty past nine! And there was still a lot to be done. He sprayed his legs, his back, torso, everywhere, and the feathers fell, or hung loosely from his flesh. He got some paper towels and gave himself a good rub down. Right. Now for the shower.

Giles got into the shower and blessed the day it had been installed. Miners had fought for pit baths, but the executives got their facilities as if by divine right, and with no struggle at all.

He turned the shower on, and luxuriated in the warm water-fall which cascaded over him. Soap, shampoo, towels, talc, everything was supplied, and he took full advantage of it. The last of the feathers fell from him, down into the shower tray. They began to block the plug hole, and he moved them with his toe. The glue was harder to remove than the feathers. It had congealed on him in globs, and had turned rubbery. He rubbed hard at it with a cake of soap, scratched at it with his nails, and pulled at it with his fingers. Gradually it came off and the water washed it away.

He was almost back to normal.

Normal. What a wonderful word that was. And how few things it really applied to.

Feather-free, Giles left the shower, dried himself, and put on his shorts. A large pile of feathers lay on the floor. He gathered them up, took them to a cubicle, and tried to flush them down the pan. As he suspected, they didn't want to go. Well, that was too bad then, they could stay there. He'd had enough.

Giles towelled his hair, checked his appearance, and picked up his belongings. He wasn't much looking forward to travelling home on the train with only his squash kit on, but there was no alternative. He'd just have to brazen it out, that was all.

Feeling a little chilly now that he was bereft of his insulation, Giles headed back down the emergency stairs the way he had come. He hesitated briefly to have a look around the office, which lay quiet, dark and empty, like a theatre awaiting the next performance. All his life, Giles thought, he had been a wage slave, tied to his desk. The wage was called a salary and went directly into his bank account on the first Tuesday of every month, but it represented the kind of security that only left you unfulfilled and discontent. It was enough to give a man the blues. It was enough to make him wake up one morning with his suitcase in his hand, to hear that lonesome whistle blow, and to know that he was not satisfied. And so he fought back as he could. In small ways, in small subversions, undermining the very system which kept him on track. He subverted his own bread, he undermined his own butter, and to do so was the jam that kept him going. Why, he even turned his back on the woman he loved, and went to look for another one. But you had to do something. You had to do *something*. Because if you didn't, you'd be dead. You'd be bound and gagged forever, and have to serve your term in solitary. The nine to five was a harsh sentence, and there was no remission for good behaviour – only for bad.

Giles jogged on down to the station. He was just a jogger now, his chicken-ness had been washed away, and most of his novelty value had gone with it. A few people gave him strange looks as he waited for the train to pull in. A kindly middle-aged lady seemed concerned for his health.

'Aren't you cold, dear? You ought to wrap up. Shorts in this weather?'

'No, I'm okay,' Giles said, 'thanks all the same.'

Thanks all the same. The polite way of saying go away and leave me alone.

He got some more strange looks on the train, but he gave them back, with knobs on. Giles wasn't in the mood to be messed with. You don't tug on Superman's cape, you don't spit into the wind, and you don't mess with Giles West.

Some of the carriage occupants plainly thought that he was a nutter, and so he acted up accordingly. Nutter? I'll give you nutter. He began to growl, make strange noises, and to talk to himself.

The compartment began to clear. Even, Giles noticed, the yobo in the table seat. Yes, even Yobo, Yobo's girlfriend and mate of Yobo were getting edgy. Giles leaned over towards them.

'Gotta time mate?' he growled. 'I've got glue in me watch.'

'N – n – nine fifty-n – n – nine!'

'Fanks!'

Yes. Attack was the best defence. Once it had been safety in numbers, but for the commuter, it was safety in nutters. The more unbalanced you seemed, the safer you were. It was an indictment of the caring society, Giles thought, that the one certain way of getting people to leave you alone was to pretend to be mentally ill.

The train arrived at his station. He got up, growled for luck on his way past the yobo table, and stepped down on to the platform. He jogged to his car and drove home.

The lights were on. Holly was still up. But Giles was prepared for this. He had an explanation ready for his attire. He opened the front door, and went in to the kitchen where Holly was cutting sandwiches for the girls' lunches.

'Hi!'

'Giles? What happened? Why didn't you change?'

'The bastards! They stole my suit! I left it on a peg in the changing room, didn't have the coins for a locker, and the bastards stole it. Huh!'

He blushed.

It was terrible, the lie that brought the sympathy and the tender consolation. Somehow it compounded the felony and doubled the guilt.

Only he was spared that this time. He didn't get any sympathy.

'Oh dear,' Holly said. 'Stole your suit. That is a shame, isn't it? Still, I expect you'll be able to claim for it on the house insurance. Oh well, better go and take the washing out of the tumble dryer.'

And that was it.

That was all you got.

You got your suit nicked and your bollocks covered in feathers, you practically went home in your undies and what sort of a response did you get? They didn't give a monkey's.

No wonder people had affairs.

NINETEEN

Dear Box 132,

You sound like me. Are we the same? Life passes, and nothing changes, and it sometimes seems that it never will. Is that how you feel? Happily married, you say. Well, yes, me too. A happily married woman, with a good husband and children and a career. And this is what we are supposed to want, isn't it, and to be happy with? And yet we aren't happy, are we? Or happiness is not enough. Perhaps we need some danger too. Perhaps we need to gamble with the happiness. We need to live. Do you feel this way too?

Do write and tell me about yourself. I feel I would like to know you better before I can commit to more. But if you would rather not, I will quite understand.

I am hiding behind a box number too. It's easier to be yourself when you are no one. Write soon.

Yours,
PO Box 798

Giles was back on the graveyard shift. He lowered the letter and took a bite of his sandwich (*Edam cheese and sliced strawberries in a blueberry bran muffin with freerange boiled egg, anchovy paste and Nutella*). He was in a reflective mood, and the melancholy tone of the letter chimed in with his own ebbing spirits. It was probably shock, that was all, a delayed reaction to the gluing and feathering, but he felt a bit low today, a bit down on the old uppers.

There was no name at the bottom of the letter either, just another box number. It had been typed out on a word processor too. How appropriate. A box writing to a box. *(Nation shall speak unto nation, and box shall write unto box.)* Completely anonymous, faceless, nameless, no photo, no identification at all. Just lonely soul calling unto lonely soul.

Maybe he'd write back to her. He didn't know. It sounded a bit like one of these cerebral things – Abelard and Heloise, that sort of business, with a whole lot of letters and not much else. He'd had it with the meaning of life. He'd given up on that a long time ago.

He wanted the stuff that spoke louder than words. He wanted action.

He felt a bit itchy from the solvent.

This is to teach you a lesson!

Well, it hadn't. He was made of sterner stuff. A pot of glue up the orifice and a few feathers weren't putting paid to him. He was more determined than ever now to see it through. It was a question of civil rights now, and the freedom of the individual. Come rain or shine, Giles was going to see this through. Right to the bitter end.

The oddest thing was, his conscience no longer pained him. It was as if the attack with the feathers had acted as a declaration of war, and in war, ordinary morality no longer applied.

He had stopped worrying about Holly. She seemed to have no connection with this now. This was between Giles and them, some nebulous them out there he could neither see nor define. Nobody had the right to stop him from being unfaithful. And he had to be unfaithful. He believed it was the only way he could keep the faith.

Giles opened his next letter. Just what he needed to cheer him up – a bulletin from Dawlish.

Dear Box 132,

Good news! Mrs Throtly has had a successful hip replacement operation – her old one was affected by her ordeal at sea. Salt water somehow got into it and it started to squeak so much that we began to call her Squeaky Throtly, which I am afraid was a bit of a tease. But she is all right now, and 'ready to try her new hip out any time'!

203

Miss Stavenshaw is keeping busy too, and has taken up aerobics twice a week, in order to 'get fit for Mr Bonky', as she puts it. I enclose a picture of her in her leotard, which she insisted I send on to you.

We followed your suggestion, and placed an advertisement for gentlemen in the personal columns of *Silver Lining*, the Magazine for the Young at Heart. We have received an encouraging response (Thirty-four letters to date, would you believe!) and are working our way through them.

Well, had better close now, as I have to draft replies to all the *virile grey panthers* out there, 'A bit prostate, but far from prostrate', as one of them says! Hope all goes well with you, and yours. Thanks again for your helpful advice.

Best wishes,

Mrs Wiseman.

P.S. Miss Stavenshaw tells me to tell you that Mr Bonky says you're as young as you feel. She also wants me to ask you if you think that a Mr Bonky T-shirt would be a commercial proposition, as she is working on a design. She already has a slogan: Stay Funky With Mr Bonky. She is even working on a bumper sticker: HONK IF YOU'VE HAD A BONK. But she doesn't know if these ideas are modern enough. What do you think? Can you advise her? You have been so kind already, I hate to ask any more of you, but your opinion would be so gratefully received.

Giles folded the letter up and put it into the pocket of his new suit. He'd have to write back yet again, he supposed. It seemed to be his destiny, to be the man who is nice to old ladies. Even in his youth and boyhood, there had been a plethora of old ladies about the place. Grannies, aunts, great-aunts, great-grannies, cousins removed, cousins transplanted, cousins moved back again. They gave him cakes and good advice, extra pocket money, and nudges in the ribs.

'Don't get any girls into trouble, will you, Giles?'

'I bet he's a terror with the girls!'

Cackle, cackle, cackle.

They were either bawdy and crude, or apparently refined and easily shocked, though he suspected the same bawdy vulgarity was there, under the surface. And Giles had thought that he had long ago got rid of them all, but here they were, back to annoy him and pinch slices of his time when he wasn't looking.

HONK IF YOU'VE HAD A BONK.

The sort of thing his great-aunt Valerie would have come out with. She and her sisters would have sat cackling over it for ages, as the cups rattled against the saucers, and the faces of their long-dead husbands looked down at them from the walls, in sepia-toned disapproval.

'Dear Filth, You just get filthier day by day. Every time your filthy advertisement appears in that filthy – '

Giles screwed it up and binned it. Same old stuff. It was the lack of invention, more than anything. You really needed a bit of variety to make that kind of thing work. If you called someone filthy often enough, it turned into a kind of compliment.

And that was it.

Oh no. One more. A thin one, with a postcard inside. He tore the envelope open and extracted it.

Giles looked at the card thoughtfully. It raised a lot of questions, some of which he could answer easily, some of which he couldn't.

He could guess why they'd sent it to him, that was easy enough. They'd just ploughed their way through the personal ads and had used the box numbers as their mailing list.

But were they expecting him to pay? Seriously expecting him to *pay*? Giles Andrew William West, *pay*? For sex? With women? Were they seriously implying that his charm, looks and body parts were not enough in themselves to sway the balance and find favour?

Well, *were* they? No, he thought not.

He went to bin the card, along with his 'Dear Filth' letter. But he hesitated. 20% discount? I mean, had he had a better offer? Had he had *any* other offer?

Yes, he had! Oh, but yes, he had! In the last batch of letters. Now where was it? He hadn't left it in his other suit? Ah, no, here it was, still in his wallet, crumpled, but readable. He took it out and looked at it again. Ah, yes, it was from Pat. Tall, slim, blonde, sensuous *and* sensual Pat. With a fax number.

And he hadn't replied. But still, it wasn't too late. He'd send her a fax from the office that very afternoon. No time like the present. Strike while the iron was hot.

The fax machine wasn't exactly a secure and confidential means of communication, but there were ways and means, and wheels within wheels. (*Remoulds within remoulds, old mate, har, har!*)

Sometimes Giles felt that a part of Roy had taken up residence in his subconscious. He was there monitoring his activities, surveying his progress, and he couldn't seem to get rid of him.

It was a bit like having worms.

Giles wondered if he had that effect on other people. Did he invade their minds, and police their conduct and thoughts? Did they think to themselves, *What would Giles do? What would Giles say? What would Giles's next suave and confident move be in this situation?*

No. He doubted that even Ella and Lynnie carried his censoriousness around in their minds. They never thought, *What would Dad say?* No, all they thought was *What'd me friends think?* and *Is it cool?*

But Giles had Roy. He didn't want him, but he had him. And he wouldn't seem to go away. Roy, and Mr Bonky, and his great-aunt Valerie, and his dad, and his mum, and a million other formative influences. What would they all think? All put together, what would they say? Would they shout out like the audience at a game show?

Take the money!

No, open the box!

Say yes to Mr Bonky!

No, stay Old Faithful, Giles, stay Old Faithful.

Money!

Box!

Bonky!

Faithful!

It was wrong, it was wrong, it was all damn wrong.

But he was going to do it anyway.

He put his sandwich wrapper into the bin. He might be a potential adulterer, but he didn't leave his litter on the grass. Then he headed back to the office, composing as he walked an appropriate fax to send to tall, slim, blonde and sensuous Patricia.

After all, Giles was, as her letter said, her kind of man.

Giles crossed the vestibule and went to the lift.

'Ah, West!'

It was Eliot of management, after a good lunch. A good two-bottle lunch by the complexion of it.

'Going up?'

'Yes.'

'I'll share your lift. How's your phone?'

'Sorry?'

'Your phone?'

'Yes, fine.'

'That's the spirit. Never waste a moment, and there's never a moment to waste.'

Yes, two bottles and a brandy, Giles guessed.

'Extraordinary thing, you know, West!'

'Yes?'

'Went to the washroom this morning, bloody bog full of feathers. Can't explain it, been bothering me all bloody day. Gave me a bloody shock, I can tell you. Thought I'd done them. Thought it was something I'd eaten. Went pale as a bloody sheet, I can tell you. Felt them tickling the old whatsit, looked down, and there they were. Feathers everywhere. Thought I'd crapped a canary.'

Yes, it was two bottles and a double brandy and the same again, and an illegible signature on the credit card slip.

'Maybe it was a pigeon,' Giles suggested.

'Pigeon? Don't remember eating one of those. Just usually have a piece of toast and a bowl of cereal.'

'Maybe it got into the building through the air conditioning duct, couldn't get out again, panicked, flew into a cubicle, fell into a toilet bowl and drowned.'

'Bloody hell, man! Bloody marvellous! Marvellous feat of reasoning! God, the intellect on the shoulders there! Pigeon in the bog! Yes, that was it, must have been! God! Puts the bloody mind to rest.'

No, it was three bottles and three double brandies, and probably a large martini to start with.

'God. I was drowning the old sorrows, too, there. Well, well. Keep up the good work. You go that way, don't you, and I go this. All the best then eh – what is your first name again?'

'Giles.'

'Giles. All the best, Giles!' Eliot pumped his hand and went on his way. Yes, he would mention that Giles West at the next board meeting. Deserved more responsibility, that man. Bloody head on that man's shoulders. The brain on him. Bloody Einstein's equations, he was.

Feel a bit sick, actually. Had a bit bloody much. Might visit the washroom before Any Other Business.

Point Percy at the pigeon.

*   *   *

There was a memo from Lavinia waiting on Giles's desk informing him that too many memos were being circulated around the office and that anyone who sent unnecessary memos in future would be liable to get a stiff memo about it from her.

Giles read it twice. Then he read it again. Then he held it up to the light. He was starting to wonder about Lavinia, she seemed to have lost her way. All that dynamic energy was being harnessed to strange horses. Three weeks ago, he would have said that she was destined for the top of the greasy pole (*the old oily Hungarian, mate, har, har!*) but now – well, it wasn't that she had mellowed so much as she seemed to have been sidetracked, distracted from her major purpose of company – and ultimately world – domination.

Giles signed the memo and ambled over with it to Roy's desk.

'Seen this?'

Roy glanced at the memo.

'This is bollocks,' he said.

Good old Roy, Giles thought. He could cut right through the bullshit. Giles debated matters endlessly, weighed the pros, counted the cons, dithered, agonized, and still could never make a decision. But Roy had no doubts or uncertainties. Giles was divided and falling, but Roy stood united.

'This,' he said, 'is a *big* load of bollocks.'

He signed the memo anyway, with a flourish, and handed it back to Giles.

'Drinking Friday?'

'Lunchtime? All right. How's –' Giles nodded towards the computer on Roy's desk, his work upon it presently concealed behind the activity of a screen saver, 'the programme?'

Roy winked.

'Had to up the ante a bit,' he said.

What did he mean? 'What do you mean?'

'You know, make a bit of room on my hard disk, make a bit of space in my memory.'

'For what?'

Roy winked again. 'You know – another Doris. Up to Doris Nine now.'

Jammy bugger! How did he do it? How *did* he do it! He was like Mozart with those bloody symphonies of his, bashing them out like they were no more than spaghetti, and there was poor old Salieri, thinking how does the little sod do it. Roy was the Mozart of the Dorises. He was there whistling them up on his magic flute, plucking Dorises out of the air, the way Mozart plucked tunes, conjuring them up from nowhere.

It just made you sick. And jealous. And yet it also filled you with awe and pure selfless admiration. It was a privilege to be in the presence of such genius, and to touch the hems of its garments. Not that Giles ever touched the hems of Roy's garments. In fact, the hems of Roy's garments could have done with a dry-clean and re-tex.

How *did* he do it? *(Answers on a postcard, old mate.)* Giles would have asked him, only he knew the question was pointless. Roy didn't know how he did it. How to do it was the question that even genius could never answer.

It had to come naturally.

'Anyone I know?'

'Who?'

'Doris Nine?'

Roy tapped his beaky nose with a long, nicotine-stained finger.

'Confidential, mate. Don't like to say.'

'Married?'

'I am, yeah.'

'I know that, I mean –'

Giles would have pressed him for more information, but he could see Lavinia bearing down upon them from the far end of the office. She was with them before Giles could slip away.

'Nothing better to do than gossip all day like an old woman, Giles?'

Plainly Lavinia didn't know much about old women. Not if Miss Stavenshaw and Mrs Throttly were typical examples of geriatric behaviour. It wasn't gossip that interested them, it was saying hello to Mr Bonky that kept them going.

'Just conferring with Roy about something.'

'Yes, well, if you could both get on with some real work –
Giles – Roy.'

'Lavinia.'

There was an instant of eye contact between them. It was
almost as if she . . . smiled at him. As if Lavinia smiled – at
Roy.

Giles rubbed his eyes.

No. That wasn't possible. He was imagining it.

He went back to his desk and pretended to work, but was
really composing the fax to be sent to slim, blonde and sensuous Patricia, who felt that he was the man for her.

No. It wasn't possible. Lavinia – Doris Nine? No. It wasn't
possible.

Was it?

A confidential fax proved not to be such a contradiction
after all. As long as you had your own private language of
nudges, winks and insinuations, the most public of communications could be rendered obscure, or at least full of double
meanings – some for public, some for private, consumption.
In ten minutes, Giles had it written.

FAX

Attention Pat.
Re Box 132.
Need to arrange date to network.
Suggest Sock and Handkerchief. Friday, if poss., p.m.
Sixish.
Probable buttonhole. Carnation. Discretion assured.
Possible large order.
Inspection invited. Any trial.
From software to hardware.
Please fax reply a.s.a.p.

Yes. The Sock and Handkerchief was a quiet wine and cocktail
bar in the basement of a building in South Square. Just the
place for an assignation.

He ambled over to the fax machine, with the casual, innocent air of one who is up to no good, and went to dial Pat's number.

'Giles!'

Sod it! Lavinia seemed to come up out of trapdoors in the floor. She crept up on you like a bad cold, and you were suffering from her before you knew it.

'Giles! What's that?'

'I'm sending a fax.'

'Oh, very well.'

She moved on and left him to it. After sending it he loitered around the fax machine, pretending to sort out the paper roll, determined no one else could pick up the reply.

It came back almost immediately.

FAX

Box 132:

Arrangement ideal.

Wondered when I might hear from you.

Sock and Handkerchief perfect. Time just right.

Buttonhole fine. Carnation ideal.

Look forward to early inspection of software, and trust need for hardware will soon arise.

Pat

Cor! He'd got a goer here all right. Giles smacked his hands together in glee. She'd got the message all right. He'd put it across and no mistake. The innuendo wasn't wasted on her. All that about inspecting his software and hoping that the need for hardware would soon arise. Well, you didn't have to be working in the Military Intelligence Code Breaking Section to work out what that lot meant.

So roll on Friday! The weekend and the new life start here!

Only what would he tell Holly? Squash? No. Working late? No. How about a train delay? Yes! Ring her up about sevenish, say sorry, there's been a few cancellations and it's hell on the railways, so I've decided to – to – what? Drink with Roy? Yes, decided to go for a drink with Roy in town in order to drown our commuting sorrows and wait until all the chaos has died down and then get the late train home.

Hunky dory. That would do perfectly. Giles took his faxes back to his desk. His spirits were high, his thoughts were optimistic. Memories of spanked buttocks, Miss Whiplash, punched noses, pots of glue and feathery bollocks had receded to the margins, all pushed aside by the thoughts of the nookie to come.

Giles felt in such a good humour that had he still been a smoking man, he would have sloped off to the toilets for a smoke. He would have loved a cigarette right then. The old Virginia vapours hitting his lungs, the lid coming off his head.

He went and sat on the toilet anyway, just for old time's sake, and sat awhile, staring at the inside of the cubicle door, remembering his smoking days, and which cigarettes had been good ones, and which had been bad. The first thing in the morning one had been awful, and the ones you had when you were streaming with flu were positively painful. But you had them anyway, because you simply couldn't stop.

But some had been good. Some had been great. With a pint, with coffee, last thing at night, after making love, exhaling puffs of smoke and looking up at the stars.

Prinng, prinng!

His mobile phone rang. It had to be George Whimpole. It couldn't be anyone else. Giles took the phone out of his pocket.

'Yes! What is it?'

'Ah! Mr Tile?'

'Yes?'

'George Whimpole here.'

'Look, Mr Whimpole, I don't care what you're selling, I do not want –'

'Oh, no. No, no, no. Nothing like that, Mr Tile. Just called to see how you were getting on. Just rang up for a chat.'

'I'm sorry?'

'A chat. Just a chat. So, how's it going your end, Mr Tile? Everything fine?'

'Yes. Why?'

'Oh, no reason, no reason. Just calling for a chat.'

It came to Giles then. A moment of revelation. Up till then he had thought of George Whimpole of Whimpole Communications as just one more lying bastard in a world of lying bastards. But now he saw that things were far more complex than that. Things rested upon each other, layer upon layer, like the pastry of a Greek pudding.

He was lonely.

He was ringing for a chat, because he had no one to talk to. It was doubly ironic. There he was – there we all were – supposedly in communications. But communications no longer communicated. They excommunicated, they isolated, they distorted and shut people off. Everyone was in their own little compartment, with communications coming in at them from all directions – satellite, cable, fax, e-mail, the Internet. But real human interaction was breaking down, dissolving around us like snow in the rain.

Yes, George Whimpole wasn't just a lying bastard in a world of lying bastards, he was a lonely bastard too. A lying, lonely bastard in a world of lying, lonely bastards. And Giles suddenly saw that he himself was no different. He too was in the club. He wasn't a bad man, he tried to do his best, but it was necessary sometimes to be a lying bastard to survive. And whether the lies made you lonely, or the loneliness made you lie, he didn't know. But that, he saw now, was why he was doing this, it was why he could contemplate these infidelities with such a cold and detached heart.

He was lonely.

And maybe Holly was lonely too.

They had become two lonely people, who somehow couldn't keep each other company any more.

They were all lonely, all of them. Roy was lonely, all the Dorises were lonely, hard-as-nails Lavinia was lonely, Eliot of management and his two-bottle lunch was lonely, Miss Whiplash was lonely, the man at the sorting office who gave him funny looks was lonely.

People crowded into commuter trains until they were so

close they could smell each other's breath. They got as close as they could without physical intimacy, and still they were lonely. They went home and made love to their partners, and five minutes after, they were lonely again. It came round like hunger.

'Where are you phoning from, George?'

'Well, I'm –'

'Yes?'

'Sitting on the loo, as a matter of fact. That is, not doing anything, just sitting here.'

'Yes,' Giles said. 'Me too.'

'It's a bastard, isn't it?' George said.

'Yes,' Giles said. 'It's a bastard.'

He saw the future. We would all live in cubicles and converse over mobile phones. He saw the future, and it almost worked.

They chatted for a while about the weather and the cricket results and the political situation, then both said they ought to go and do some work, and hung up. Giles had only been at his desk a minute or two when Roy came over, not his normal relaxed self, but looking furrowed and anxious.

'Can you come over and have a look at my computer, old mate?'

'Yeah, sure. Why? What's up?'

'Well, I dunno for sure. But I think it's got a bug in it.'

Giles wondered if it was a lonely one.

TWENTY

Friday came, and confidence came with it. *(Tonight's the night. Tonight is the night!)* But for all his internal cheerleading and waving of his inner pom-poms, Giles found it hard to genuinely enthuse.

Probably the best attitude to have really, a take it or leave it kind of thing. He looked at Roy, who sat across the table from him. Enthusiasm certainly wasn't one of his traits. Lugubrious woe interspersed with flashes of sarcasm was more his style.

'So what do you think, old mate?'

They were trying a new pub – the Sniff and Gro-Bag – which had a botanical theme to it, and was heavily decorated with exotic potted plants, one of which seemed to be leaning thirstily towards Giles's pint.

'I'd watch that, mate, it's after your beer. It's probably a Venus lager-trap or something.'

Giles again wondered if he should confide in Roy. But he had kept his own counsel so far, and decided he would continue to do so a while longer. He didn't want sympathy for his failures, he'd be happier with congratulations on his success.

'Another one?' Giles said, drinking up before the plant could get it.

'I'll have something else this time,' Roy said. 'I wasn't too sure about that one, that Muggy Compost or whatever it was. See what else they've got.'

Giles went up to the bar and surveyed the brews on offer.

'Two halves of Olde Slugge Pellettes,' he said. He wasn't risking pints on a name like that. He took the drinks back to the table. The plant seemed to have grown in his absence and it had a tendril wrapped around his sandwich.

'It's after your nosh now,' Roy said.

'It can have it,' Giles said, and he pushed the plate aside. 'It didn't taste much like cheese to me.'

'Finest plastic money can buy, old mate.'

'Dorising tonight?' Giles asked. Roy had recently coined a new word to describe his extra-marital activities. He was always *going Dorising, off out Dorising,* and the most recent one, *it takes two to Doris.*

'Dorising every night these days, old mate.'

'Doesn't your wife *ever* suspect?' Giles said. 'Doesn't she ever wonder where you are?'

'Sure.'

'So where do you say you are?'

'With you.'

'So she thinks you spend every night with me?'

'Mostly.'

'What does she think of that?'

'I think she thinks we're having an affair, old mate.'

'Thanks,' said Giles.

'No problem,' Roy said, and he sipped at his Slugge Pellettes. 'I just don't see how you've never been caught out.'

'The Doris Management Programme, mate.'

'What about that bug in it? I couldn't find anything. You ought to test it more thoroughly.'

An expression of concern crossed Roy's face.

'I don't know, mate. It seems to be all right now, but I've got this feeling – I don't know – like there's a creeping virus or something in there, just biding its time, just waiting to strike.'

'The enemy within?'

'That's the one.'

'Have you virus-checked it?'

'Yeah. Nothing showed up, but all the same . . . Still, worrying over nothing.'

Giles looked over at Roy with the wonder that was his due as a true phenomenon.

'I just don't know how you do it, Roy. I really don't. I mean, how many is it? Nine different Dorises?'

'Well, eight plus the wife,' Roy said modestly.

'All the same. That's more than one for every day of the week.'

'True,' Roy agreed.

'I mean, how many times are you actually doing it, Roy?'

'What?'

'You know – saying hello to Mr Bonky?'

'Oh – don't really know, old mate. I'd have to look it up on the Doris Management Programme. Did I tell you I'd developed a Doris Stats?'

'Doris Stats?'

'Yeah, Doris Statistics, you know, so you can go in for long-term projections and calculate performance-yield and all that sort of business.'

'But how do you handle them all, Roy? How do you actually handle all these women?'

'With delicacy, mate. And one at a time. Har, har! Your round!'

It wasn't. It was Roy's. But Giles went and got them anyway.

'Don't get Olde Slugge Pellettes again,' Roy called after him. 'I wasn't too keen on that either.'

Giles stood and looked at the array of pumps and cold cabinets. What was it to be? A half of Grandpa Tickles the Budgie, maybe? Or how about a bottle of Memphis Ice Levee Delta Slim Mississippi Bud Tennessee Hot Chicken Shit Blues Water in the guitar-shaped bottle – to be drunk with half a chilli pepper and a slice of watermelon while, if at all possible, wearing a porkpie hat? Or maybe they could try a glass of There's a Sheep in My Wellingtons. Or risk a tin of Slow Handclap or a nip of Uncle Tom's Wheelbarrow?

'Yes?' the barmaid said.

Giles was just about to ask for two halves of Rinse Your Socks Out Slowly when, in among the Sherwood forest of beer pumps, he spied an item of great archaeological interest. It was an ancient gnarled handle, and the sign on it read BITTER.

Just bitter. Just plain and simple bitter. He couldn't believe it. He closed his eyes, rubbed them and opened them again. Incredibly, it was still there. He hadn't seen anything like it for years.

'What's it to be then?' the barmaid said. 'There's customers waiting.'

Giles pointed at the pump with his finger, unable to speak for excitement. Then finally he managed to get it out. 'T-t-two pints of bitter, please!' he said.

The barmaid looked puzzled for a moment, but then she saw the pump.

'Oh, bitter, right. We don't get much call for that,' she said. And she took down two glasses from the shelf.

After a couple of pints, Friday afternoon in the office became almost bearable. Alcohol did at least temporarily anaesthetize you against the tedium. But then, of course, the euphoria wore off, and either tiredness or Tense Nervous Headache took over.

Giles put an elbow on the desk and leant his head on it, a couple of fingers strategically placed to hold his eyelids open, so that if he did nod off, he might still appear awake.

He yawned.

Roll on six o'clock. Roll on Patricia in the Sock and Handkerchief.

Roll on.

It was 6.15.

Pat was late, but not yet late enough for Giles to think that she had stood him up. He sat in a booth facing the door so that he could watch the customers enter. One or two slim, blonde and sensual little numbers had shimmied in since he had been sitting there, but none of them had headed for his table, or had evinced any interest in the carnation in his buttonhole.

Behind the bar the two barmen were throwing bottles to and fro. This was all part of the Sock and Handkerchief ambience, where along with your drink and complimentary dish of olives you were also treated to a display of advanced cocktail mixing and bottle hurling.

One of the barmen seemed to be something of a novice however, and had just dropped a bottle of Angostura bitters, which had smashed on the floor to loud applause.

'Seat free, mate?'

Giles looked up. A slim but muscular fair-haired man in his late twenties was standing behind him. He was holding a bottle of beer.

'Well –'

But before Giles could get out the words 'I am meeting someone actually,' the man had already sat down. He took a swig of his beer, wiped his moustache on the back of his hand, glanced up at Giles –

And winked.

Winked?

Just a minute.

'I see you've got your carnation!' the man said.

Instinctively Giles's hand went to hide the flower. Then he realized it was a futile gesture.

'Yes. I'm meeting someone,' he said.

'Yes,' the man said. 'I know.'

Know? How did he know.

'Pat,' he said. And he extended his hand across the table.

'Pat?'

'Pat. You are Box 132, aren't you, mate?'

'Box 132?'

' "The man for me"?'

'The man for you? Me?'

'Sure, I got your fax.'

'I'm sorry,' Giles said, 'look, I think there's been some kind of mistake. I'm waiting for someone else. I'm waiting for Pat.'

'That's me,' the man said.

'I mean, Patricia.'

'No,' Pat said. 'Not if you're Box 132.'

Giles stared across the table, his lower lip dropping in a state of advanced idiocy. Pat was a bloke! A *bloke*! Slim, yes, blonde, yes, good-looking, yes, he could see that. The sensual and sensuous he didn't know about, but then he had never set himself up as an authority on that kind of thing. But one thing was beyond equivocation: Pat was a man.

'I'm sorry, look, I think there's been some dreadful mistake, I – you see, I was expecting a – well – a woman.'

Pat reached for the inner pocket of his leather jacket. He took out a rolled-up copy of *Scene Around*, opened it at the personal ads, and smoothed it out.

'A woman?'

'Em – sort of – yes.'

'"Happily married man seeks affair." That you?'

A bottle of Blue Curaçao smashed to smithereens behind the bar.

'Yes, I suppose so, yes.'

'Well, there you are, mate. Right there!'

Pat plonked the listings magazine down in front of Giles and pointed with a slim, blonde, sensuous and well-manicured finger at the advertisement. It had been placed in the Gay and Bisexual column.

'So what's that all about then?' he said tetchily.

God in heaven!

They'd mucked it up again. Not content with getting the age wrong to start with and entrapping him in a correspondence with octogenarians in Dawlish, the bloody magazine had now gone and stuck him in the Bisexual column! It was that girl with that bloody set of teaspoons in her nose! He'd be straight down there on Monday to give her a bloody piece of his mind.

Giles looked at the Straight listings. His ad was in there as well. They'd included it twice.

Just a second.

He turned to the Flats To Rent section – his ad was in there too. Under a Tenner? Yes, there it was. Cars For Sale? Yup, it was right there. Alternative Therapies? Yes, there he was. Situations Vacant? Yes, that was him. What's On at the Cinema? Yes, Giles was showing. Galleries and Exhibitions? Yes, he was hanging everywhere. The magazine's computer had gone haywire, they seemed to have devoted the entire issue to his ad.

'Look, I'm very sorry about this, but as you can see – some sort of computer error – terrible misunderstanding –'

'So you're not actually gay at all then?' Pat demanded.

'No, afraid not,' Giles admitted. 'More of a misprint, really.'

'Oh,' Pat said irritably. 'Well, that is a piss-off.'

'Yes,' Giles agreed. 'It is.' (He'd had his evening ruined too, after all.)

They sat in silence for a while, both looking downcast and glum.

'I was quite looking forward to this as well,' Pat said. 'A bit of a change like, you know.'

'Me too,' Giles commiserated.

A howl came from behind the bar as a bottle of Crème de Menthe flew through the air and struck one of the barmen on the head. He fell like a dead weight amongst the empties.

'So you're married then, are you?' Pat said by way of conversation, in an effort to relieve their mutual embarrassment.

'Yes,' Giles admitted. 'How about you? How are you fixed?'

'Oh, in a long-term relationship, but we've had a few ups and downs.'

'Ah. And how did you meet?' Giles asked, rather pruriently curious.

'What, Stanley? Oh, I've known him ages. He was the bloke next door,' Pat said. 'Boring, isn't it?'

'Bloke next door, eh? That so?' Giles said. Well, well, he thought, so that's how it was. Life's lottery was the same the wide world over. You rubbed the silver off the scratch cards and the numbers underneath were all the same – and usually they weren't winning ones either, you'd be lucky to get a tenner.

'You wonder if you're not missing out sometimes though,' Pat said. 'Everyone else seems to be getting a bit on the side.'

'Yes,' Giles agreed. 'So how long have you and Stanley been together?'

'Ten years,' Pat told him. 'Though I wonder how I've stuck it, to be honest. He's a right slob. It's not that he squeezes the toothpaste in the middle, he doesn't bloody squeeze it at all.'

'Ten years, eh? Well, well. Any kids at all?' Giles asked automatically.

'Not as yet,' Pat said, bristling a bit, but Giles missed the sarcasm.

'Just got to keep trying, I suppose. You'll get there in the end.'

'Are you trying to be funny?' Pat asked. 'Are you looking for a kick in the bollocks?'

Giles realized his faux pas.

'Sorry,' he backtracked. 'Wasn't thinking. No offence.'

'Oh well,' Pat sighed. 'Another wasted evening – unless you fancy a crack at it seeing you're here. I mean, if you're looking for new experiences –'

'No, it's decent of you to offer,' Giles said hastily, 'but I ought to think about getting home. Can I get you a drink before I go?'

'Well, one for the road then, thanks. Why not?'

Yes, that was the question. Hamlet had got it all wrong. The question wasn't *To be or not to be?*, the question wasn't even *Why?*, the question was *Why not?*. Answer that one, and you've answered them all.

Giles went to the bar. The unconscious barman had been carried off, and they had brought on the substitute. He was balancing a bottle of grenadine on his forehead while juggling three Budweisers. He'd obviously done this sort of thing before. Giles bought two of the Budweisers and took them over to the table. The date had gone wrong, and they drank in polite silence, getting the conventions over with as quickly as possible, anxious to go their separate ways.

It was a funny old world though. And people's similarities were greater than their differences. Yes, that was the lesson to learn. Never mind what the philosophers and the great intellects said. They maybe took a lifetime and twenty-five volumes of small print to say it, but in the end all it amounted to was those selfsame words: it's a funny old world. It was Buddhist in its cryptic simplicity. All philosophy, psychology, poetry and literature could be reduced to that simple but immensely complex statement. It was food for thought to nourish you forever.

It was definitely.

A funny.

Old world.

Giles left Pat and the juggling barman behind him and staggered out into the cool of the night. He didn't want to go straight home – for all he had said in the bar. He felt disappointed, let down, depressed.

He walked aimlessly around, making his way through the town centre, staring at the goods in the shop windows – all the things you wanted and worked for and which made so little difference to your life when you finally got them home.

He bought a *Big Issue* from a street vendor; he spared someone else some change. He wandered vaguely towards the station, in no hurry to get there, then veered off down a side street, for no other reason than that he had not walked down it before. Music blasted from an attic window above him, a group of young people passed, with dogs at their heels, there was the smell of cannabis in the air.

He found himself in a street which was quiet and traffic-free. An oasis of calm and peace in the middle of the city. Children rode up and down on their bicycles and kicked footballs around. On he went.

Where was that station? Oh, it was back the other way now. Still, never mind. What did he care? What did any of it matter?

And that was when he saw it. The answer to his unexpressed prayers. There it was, in all its glory. And suddenly he knew who would do it with good old Giles. He saw it at last. It was the easy way. He should have taken it long ago. No guilt, no recriminations, no repercussions. It was all so simple.

Yes, there it was, just across the street, glowing with warmth and light and welcome and the promise of company. He hurried over to enfold himself in its neon embraces. There in the middle of a parade of shuttered shops was a flashing sign. GOLDEN HANDS MASSAGE PARLOUR, it blinked, GOLDEN HANDS FOR A GOLDEN HANDSHAKE.

And Giles knew that his time had come to press the flesh.

There was little debate in his mind. He just stopped to count the money in his wallet, and then decided that they'd probably take a credit card anyway. The morality of payment no longer concerned him. Morality itself no longer concerned him. He would just be another punter, that was all. Giles the Punter. All right, it wasn't John the Baptist, but it wasn't Attila the Hun either. He was just one more punter among all the punters. Why ever had he not seen that to start with? One more punter on a Friday night, who'd had a bit more drink than he needed, and who wanted some pleasure and bright lights and a little feminine company. But not the sort of feminine company that said 'Can't you take your shoes off?' and 'Have you put the bins out?' and 'When are you going to fix that shelf?'

No. Freedom from criticism, expressed and implied. That was what a bloke wanted. A woman who would be nice to a bloke and who'd tell him he wasn't so bad after all.

Giles checked that he still had his Massive Cucumbers. They were there, and raring to get stuck into it. *(Stick the old cucumber in the mayonnaise, eh, Giles old mate, har de har.)*

He was now at the door of the Golden Hands. Pity he'd thrown that card away that they'd sent him. He wouldn't get his 20% discount now. Still, never mind, he still had his no-claims bonus.

He pushed the door open and went in. He didn't see the car parked across the road, with the two thickset men in it. And he couldn't possibly have seen the two police cars, parked up around the corner.

'Good evening.'

'Oh, hi.'

'And how are you this evening?'

'Em, fine, yes, fine.'

A well-dressed woman in her forties sat behind a reception desk. A large Alsatian dog sat under it. It gave Giles a baleful look, as if to say, 'Here comes another one.'

'Please, take a seat.' She indicated a sofa, placed opposite the desk. Giles sat down, uncomfortable and ill at ease.

'I don't believe we've seen you here before, have we?'

'Em, no, no.'

'No. But not to worry. So you're not a member then, in that case?'

'Eh, no.'

'Twenty pounds membership.'

'Twenty pounds, ah.'

'Covers you for a year.'

'A year, ah. Better – better join then.' He handed over a twenty-pound note. The woman passed him a numbered membership card and a pen and a membership book.

'If you could just put your name there –'

Giles took the pen and wrote Fred Flintstone in the book. The woman leaned over and looked at his signature.

'I'm afraid we already have a gentleman by that name as a member.'

'Ah,' Giles said. 'How about Tweetie Pie? Has he been in lately?'

The woman gave a thin-lipped smile.

'Yes. He was in yesterday, along with Donald Duck, Bugs Bunny, Winston Churchill, Foghorn Leghorn and Baloo the Bear. I think it was some kind of birthday party.'

'In that case –' Giles scratched out Fred Flintstone and wrote Barney Rubble.

'Fine, Mr Rubble,' the woman said. If you'd like to go through to the lounge, I'm sure one of our staff will be very pleased to attend to you.'

'Fine,' Giles said. 'Thanks. I'll do that.'

'In fact I'll get someone to show you –' she rang a bell and a second woman appeared. She was in her late twenties and quite voluptuous. She wore a miniskirt of eye-bulging short-ness and had a name badge on her tiny T-shirt saying CHANTELLE.

'Chantelle, this is Mr Barney Rubble.'

'Hello, Barney,' Chantelle said. 'I'm Chantelle.'

Chantelle and Barney Rubble. It was a match made in heaven.

'Perhaps you could take him through and look after him.'

'Yes, of course, this way.'

Barney followed Chantelle through the inner door and into a pine-clad lounge where a soft porn film was showing on a television set. A Chinese man was sitting watching it, smoking a cigarette down to the filter. He looked like a take-away owner, with the unhealthy complexion resulting from too much time spent near a fryer. He nodded at Giles, who nodded back.

'Not been before?' Chantelle said.

'No.'

'Well, I can look after you, if you want. But there's also Michelle, Wanda, Natalie and Mrs Nettleton if you want to wait.'

It was all rather like getting a haircut. *(Who normally does you, dear? And how do you usually like it?)*

'No, no, you'll be fine – more than fine – perfect,' Giles said. 'But what about –' he gestured towards the Chinese man. 'Isn't he before – I wouldn't like to push in.'

'He's waiting for Mrs Nettleton,' Chantelle explained. The man smiled nervously at the sound of Mrs Nettleton's name. 'This way then, Barney,' Chantelle said, leading the way to a corridor, and Giles obediently followed. She turned to the Chinese man as she passed. 'I'm sure Mrs Nettleton won't be much longer, Mr Flintstone.'

So that was Fred Flintstone. It was a small world. Small old, funny old world. Fancy meeting old Fred in here. He just turned up everywhere, old Fred did.

They passed a succession of doors, from which emanated the metallic sound of televisions, interspersed with occasional grunts.

'I take it you'd like an executive suite, Mr Rubble?'

'Em, yes,' Giles said. 'Fine. And please – call me Barney.'

'Barney,' she said. She opened a door to one of the rooms and let him go in first. Her breasts rubbed impressively against him as he went in. They might not be one hundred percent natural ingredients, those breasts, but they certainly hit the spot.

'I did have a discount card, but I lost it,' Giles said.

'I'm sure we can come to some arrangement,' Chantelle said.

And Giles thought they probably could.

The executive suite was grim enough, Giles was glad he hadn't opted for the non-executive version. *(The one for the manual trades, old mate, har, har!)* The walls were decorated in the same pine panelling as everywhere else, some strips of which had worked loose and were falling away. There was a massage table, a television and a video player, a small shower room off to one side, a dressing gown hanging up behind the door, a table with an ashtray and some bottles of massage oil on it, a sink, some towels, a box of tissues, an easy chair, and no window. The carpet was turned up at the edges like a piece of elderly toast.

They were the most unerotic surroundings Giles had ever been in. He felt no sexual desire at all. Only a sense of *What I am doing here?* and *Let's get it over with and go home.*

'Perhaps you'd like to make yourself comfy while I put on a film.'

She handed him the dressing gown and indicated the shower. 'Make yourself comfy' obviously meant go and have a wash.

'Em, right, yes, fine.'

Wouldn't mind a shower, actually. Might clear his head a bit, wake him up.

As he stood under the spray, he heard Chantelle sorting out video cases in the room.

'Have you seen *Big Ones From Scandinavia*?' she shouted.

Giles confessed that he hadn't.

'I'll put it on.'

'Right.'

He showered and dried himself, put on the dressing gown and went back into the room.

'Well, make yourself comfy then.'

There was that word again. Comfy. What an English adjective. You went and visited your local friendly prostitute, and she exhorted you to make yourself comfy.

He looked at his clothes. Had she been at his wallet? No, he didn't think so. No, it seemed strictly legitimate here. Strictly legitimately illegitimate.

'Why don't you lie down here, Barney?'

Barney laid his weary, Stone-Age bones down, the dressing gown was spirited away and a towel was laid over the Barney bum to preserve his prehistoric modesty, such as it was.

'And I'll do your back.'

Chantelle rubbed oil onto his back as Barney stared ahead

at the goings-on on the video screen. *Big Ones* was a little difficult to follow in terms of narrative thread.

'What's this film about?' he asked.

'Don't really know,' Chantelle said, 'never really worked it out.' She glanced at the set. 'Something about big ones.'

'Oh.'

Ohh!

Oh yes! It was nice to have the weary old bones massaged. It was nice. Everyone should have a bit of this, Giles thought. Him, Barney, Roy, Holly, everyone should have a bit of this.

'Local, are you?'

Chantelle's voice broke his reverie. She seemed in the mood for a bit of a chat.

'Local?'

'Well, I work locally.'

'Married?'

'Em – yes.' Could she mind her own business, please?

'Not getting on with the missus?'

'Em – yes and no.'

'Yes and no. That'd be it.'

She'd seen it all before, obviously. Just as long as she didn't fancy herself Miss Marriage Guidance, that was all.

'Well, I'm sure you'll be able to patch things up.'

Giles began to relax. The serpents of tension uncoiled inside him. The tension fled from places he never knew he had tension. The blood began to surge around his veins.

'Shall I do your front?'

My front? Oh, well, actually, bit embarrassing this – still, nothing you haven't seen before, I'm sure.

'Oh my! We are a big boy, aren't we? Well, well.'

Giles closed his eyes. She probably said that to every one. You could have turned up with a winkle and she'd still have called you Big Boy. But he was beyond caring, beyond self-consciousness and self-reproach. He was Barney Rubble, that was all. He would die one day, and his children would mourn him, and they would never know that any of this had happened. They would never know that once he had been Barney Rubble, and that he had done dangerous and dirty things.

'Would you like any extras, do you think, Barney?'

Well, yes, he probably would. Yes, Barney was finished with the hors d'oeuvres and was thinking of getting stuck into the main course now.

'Would you like to see the menu?'

Eh?

He opened an eye as a card was thrust into his grasp. He looked at it and blinked while Chantelle carried on with the massage, gently rubbing oil into his thighs.

'Hand Shandy – £25,' it read. 'French Fry – £35. Full jacket potato – £50. Potato (with jackets off) – £65. Double-decker sandwich – £150. Pot of Tea – 80p.'

Giles looked at the list. He could more or less translate from the vernacular, but the pot of tea had him beat.

'What's a pot of tea?' he said.

'You know,' Chantelle said, 'it's two tea bags and hot water in a pot.'

'Oh! It's a drink!'

'Yeah!'

'Oh.'

'So is there anything you fancy?'

'I could go for a baked potato,' Giles said.

'Right,' Chantelle said.

And the next thing Giles knew, her miniskirt was lying on the floor.

'I don't suppose you could – take your top off.'

'Baked potato with the top off is another fifteen pounds.'

Ah, ha. There were obviously hidden extras in this game.

'I'll pay,' Barney croaked, 'I'll pay!' Yes, damn the expense, what did Barney care, his friend Giles was paying for everything. Giles's credit card was at his disposal.

The top went the way of the bottom. God! What a body. It was marvellous stuff that silicone, you could make tremendous things out of it. And Giles was getting to be a very big boy now.

'Now, let's not forget our little precautions. Or big precautions, should I say?'

'Actually, I'm allergic to those,' Giles said. 'I brought my own. Just in my jacket pocket there. I've got a Massive Cucumber.'

'Yes, so you have.'

She handed him his jacket and he took his Cucumber out. He was tearing the seal off the packet, and was within a hair's breadth of consummation. It was all about to come true. At long last he was going to make the discovery. He had sighted dry land. It had been a long, hard, tortuous voyage, but Treasure Island was finally in sight. At last, it was to happen, it was all about to come true.

And then –

– and then the door burst open.

And Sergeant Dave Toffer burst in brandishing a warrant.

'This is a raid,' he said. 'You're under arrest.'

Chantelle turned to face him, naked, but livid with rage.

'Fuck off,' she said. 'How dare you come in here?'

'The number of people who've come in here,' Toffer said, 'I wouldn't think you'd be bothered about another one.'

But as for Giles, he turned scarlet all over.

'And you!' Toffer said. 'What's your name?'

'Me?' said Giles. 'I'm Barney Rubble!'

But he had the feeling that Toffer didn't believe him.

TWENTY-ONE

'All right,' said Toffer, 'let's have it again. And this time, nice and slow.'

'But we've already been through it,' Giles said. 'It must be nearly midnight.'

'Well, if we go through it once more, this time I might be able to understand it. Who knows – I might even be able to believe it! Though I don't think it's too likely.'

The police station interview room was as drab and soulless as the executive suite at the Golden Hands Massage, only without out the pneumatic Chantelle and a video of *Big Ones From Scandinavia* to relieve the gloom. The chair Giles sat on was secured firmly to the floor, as was the table under his elbows. A cup of untouched cold tea was in front of him; it had been cold for so long that the milk had separated out.

'So once again then,' Toffer said, 'from the top.'

Giles sighed. Where would Holly think he was? Crushed under a car somewhere? He should ring and tell her. He was entitled to a phone call, wasn't he? But what could he say? That he'd been arrested in a massage parlour about to commit an act which Sergeant Toffer kept describing as being of 'lewd grossness' and that he had been taken into custody? No, he didn't think that would go down too well on the home front.

'From the beginning,' Toffer said. 'And this time, I'll write it down, and then I'll read it back to you, and you can sign it.'

'Right,' Giles said. 'All right. It's all perfectly simple. I suffer from a bad back, you see.'

'Bad back,' Toffer repeated, writing it down.

'And I get this pain in the sacroiliac joints.'

'Sacroiliac joints.'

'And this afternoon it was really bad, so I stopped off for a drink after work for a couple of beers, hoping it might ease the throb.'

'Hoping it might ease the throb? I see. Well, judging from the state you were in when we found you, Mr West, it hadn't eased the throb at all. Quite the opposite. Throbbing away like the train to Glasgow you were, I'd have said.'

'I'm getting to that,' Giles said. 'If I may –'

'Please do,' Toffer said.

'Anyway, the pain was quite bad, sort of going into spasms, and as a result I probably drank a few more beers than I'd intended to, and maybe got a bit woozy.'

'Bit woozy.'

'So anyway, I left the pub and was on my way to the station when I met a bloke –'

'A bloke.'

'Don't remember his name.'

'No. Not unusual. The Unknown Bloke, was he? Yeah, a lot of people have met him.'

'Anyway we got chatting – me and this bloke – and as my back was still bad, I happened to ask if he might know the whereabouts of a late-night osteopath or maybe a late-night physiotherapist.'

'A late-night osteopath, Mr West?'

'Yes, you know, staying open for emergencies.'

'I see. Go on.'

'Right. So anyway, this bloke I met –'

'Whose name you can't remember?'

'That's the one, he said, yes, that he knew of this very good late-night osteopath's just round the back of the station, and he gave me directions on how to find it. So off I went, but I must have got the directions mixed up, because, as I said, I'd had one or two beers too many – but I wasn't driving –'

'Not driving.'

'I was walking. So, anyway, I maybe got a bit lost or confused, or both, and so when I found myself outside of the Golden Hands Massage Parlour –'

'Golden hands for a golden handshake?' Toffer said dryly.

233

'That's the place – well, I naturally assumed that it must be the osteopath's.'

'The late-night osteopath's?'

'Yes. So in I go, and they make me welcome –'

'I'm sure.'

'And that woman came along –'

'Chantelle?'

'Yes, and took me off into this room, you see, and, well, naturally, I just assumed that she was a qualified osteopath.'

'In a miniskirt and wearing a boobtube three sizes too small?'

'Well, I didn't really notice any of that, to be honest, I was a bit preoccupied with the twinge in my back.'

'So then she takes you into this room, tells you to get undressed, and puts on a pornographic video?'

'Apparently so,' Giles agreed. 'Although it didn't seem that way at the time. I was preoccupied with my back, you see, and I thought, well, it did seem odd, but it must be some kind of new therapy – for backs. And that maybe it was an instructional video on how to improve your posture.'

'Yes.'

'So anyway, she gave my back a bit of a massage then, and the treatment did seem to be working, only it did have rather unexpected side effects.'

'Which were?'

'Well, I sort of got this – well, this big erection, to be honest. Not uncommon, apparently, when you've got a bad back. In fact, they do say that if you've got an erection, what it probably means is that your muscles have gone into spasm – in your lower back.'

'I see, yes. Do go on, Mr West. It's a medical education, this.'

'So, as you can imagine, I was a bit put out about that, but then I thought, well, she's a qualified osteopath after all, no reason to be ashamed, so I thought I maybe ought to point it out to her –'

'Your erection?'

'Yes, well, mention it in passing, at least – just in case it was related to my back problem, and she needed to take a look at it. So, anyway, she said that she didn't think it was serious, or anything to worry about, but that she maybe would have a closer peek, just to be on the safe side. And we were just about to do that when you and your officers came in.'

'I see.'

'And that's all there was to it. A perfectly innocent misunderstanding.'

'And so why was it, Mr West, that this Miss Chantelle was stark naked when we arrived?'

'Ah, yes. Now I did wonder about that myself.'

'You did? Yes.'

'And I was going to mention it to her, but I was a bit embarrassed to bring the subject up, and I just sort of assumed that she was a nudist – a naturist, you know.'

'A nudist osteopath?'

'Em – yes.'

'A nudist late-night osteopath?'

'I suppose so, yes.'

'So you weren't about to have sex with her, or anything, Mr West, in return for payment?'

'Me? Sex? With my back? Good heavens!'

'So what were you doing with a condom in your hand, Mr West?'

'Sorry?'

'A condom, Mr West. A Massive Cucumber, to be precise, which you attempted to throw behind a chair when you thought no one was looking.'

'Oh that!' Giles said. 'That! Oh, well, I have to wear those because of . . . because . . . to keep myself warm.'

'Keep warm?'

'Yes. Doctor's recommendation. Otherwise, you see, I get chilblains.'

'On your member?'

'Yes. So what the doctors recommend these days – at least, so I read in the *Guardian* – is a couple of the old condoms on, to keep out the cold, for that extra layer of insulation. Or if you haven't got any of them, maybe an old sock. Or if you've got an old pair of gardening gloves you're not using any more, you can cut the fingers off and have yourself a different willy-warmer every day of the week – plus a few for spares.'

'Is that so?'

'Apparently, yes.'

'Mr West, I'm not a man who approves of strong language, in fact, I am a man of deeply-held religious convictions, and I avoid rude expressions like the plague. But there is such a thing as righteous wrath, Mr West, and I have to say that, quite frankly, I have never heard a bigger load of unbelievable old bollocks in my life!'

'Ah, well, yes, I can understand it might seem a little implausible –'

'Not a little, Mr West, totally!'

'Yes, but –'

'It's got more holes in it than a – a –'.

'Porcupine's pyjamas?' Giles suggested.

'Than I care to think! And as for this erection of yours! I hope you don't expect us to swallow that one?'

'I beg your pardon?'

'A tumescent organ is the symptom of a bad back? Pull the other one, Mr West. You're lucky I don't book you for being in possession of an offensive weapon! You'll be telling us next it wasn't your erection at all, and that you were just looking after it for a friend –'

'Funny you should say that, there was this Chinese gentleman –'

'We know all about Mr Flintstone, thank you. And about Miss Chantelle, your late-night nudist osteopath, we know all about her too, Mr West, oh yes.'

'Is she registered then?'

'Yes, a registered bloody tart! With convictions. She's a well-known prostitute, Mr West!'

'Oh, I see, and so working as an osteopath is just a sort of sideline?'

'No, Mr West, pulling pints of Hand Shandy is her sideline! It's not backs she manipulates. And her real name is Janice Crombo.'

'Oh, well, I was plainly misled then. But I wasn't actually doing anything illegal – was I?'

'Mr West, illegal or not isn't the point. You're a married man, aren't you, Mr West?'

'Yes, I said –'

'With this body, I thee honour, all my worldly goods I thee endow. Nothing in the marriage lines about having a bit of Five Finger Exercise down at The Golden Hands Massage Parlour!'

'I was down for a Baked Potato, actually –'

'I don't care what you were down for!'

'But I thought it was a bit like Deep Heat – you know – Deep Heat – Baked Potato – I just assumed it was something that you rubbed in for your neuralgia.'

'Mr West, look, I am telling you that if you do not co-operate, all it takes is one phone call from me to your home number and your dear loving wife and presumably dearly loved children will find out that their dearly loved daddy-dads has been consorting with known tarts –'

'Well, hardly consorting –'

'On the verge of shagging then! How does that terminology suit you?'

'Well, I –'

'And another thing,' Toffer said gleefully. 'If you believed that you were genuinely at a late-night osteopath's, why did you sign the book under an assumed name? Answer me that. Why did you sign yourself in as Barney Rubble?'

Giles was silent for a few seconds.

'It was my mother's name,' he said. 'And –' But before he could say any more, Toffer had reached out over the table and his hands were on his collar. Toffer pressed his nose close to Giles's, he smelt of beeswax and church incense, mixed with the odours of the police canteen and locker room.

'Listen, Mr West,' Toffer said. 'I'm a man of deep, devout religious principles here. I'm on a mission, you get me? And it's my mission to stamp out vice in this town! So this is your first, last and only chance, you get me? Either you repent right here and now and see the error of your ways, or I pick up that phone and I ring up your ever-loving, and I tell her the lot. You want that?'

'Em – no,' Giles admitted, 'not really.'

'Then there is . . . an alternative,' Toffer said, releasing Giles and sitting back, folding his hands like a priest in confessional.

Giles looked up.

'There is? What?'

'God,' Toffer said.

'Who?' Giles said.

'God,' Toffer said again, and he looked up towards the ceiling. 'God. Up there.'

'Oh, yes. Him.'

'Yes, we have a friend up there who can help us struggle with and vanquish the weaknesses of the flesh. I'm giving you a shot at redemption, Mr West, a chance to extricate yourself from the mire you've tumbled into, to wean yourself from this diet of filth you have obviously become addicted to – from these prostitutes, these Massive Cucumbers, these Baked Potatoes of yours. I'm giving you a chance, Mr West, to come clean.'

And Giles came clean. For what choice did he have?

It was good to confide in someone too. He hadn't told anyone up till now, not even Roy. But he told Sergeant Toffer everything, he spilled all the beans. He told him about the yearning inside, the sense of the days passing, with nothing gained, and more and more lost. He told him about all the women he had never made love to, how there had only ever been Holly, and how he needed to know what it would be like with someone else. He told him about his ad in the personal columns, about his box numbers within box numbers, about the misprint, about Mrs Throttly and Miss Stavenshaw and Mrs Wiseman down in Dawlish, about Dear Filth, and Quentin Stoagley and his Bavarian beer mats, he told him too about Miss Whiplash and the handcuffs, about Jordan and his punch on the conk, about Womb-Bat and the feathery bollocks, about poor George Whimpole, who you thought was just a lying bastard but who turned out to be a lonely bastard as well, about Roy and the Doris Management Programme, about Lavinia and the memos, and then he told him about Pat and Stanley, and how it was the same the whole world over, the great mess of human relationships.

And all the while, Toffer nodded comfortingly and mur-mured, 'That's it – that's right – get it all off your chest.'

And then finally Giles had finished.

'So it's not that I meant anything by it,' Giles said, 'or meant anyone any harm, I was just trying to have a bit of a bonk. I just wanted a bonk, you see. I'm not saying it's right, I'm not trying to justify it. I'm just saying that I'm an ordinary bloke, that's all, who's never ever had a bonk with anyone else but his wife, and I just wanted to live a bit before I died. I'm just a human being, you see. I'm not a bad man, just human. I think I deserve some forgiveness. I think I deserve some understanding.'

Toffer considered the matter.

'I'll tell you what I'll do –' he said, ' – now, I see you live out in Newtham.'

'That's right,' Giles said. Not that he needed reminding, he hated the unravelled suburbia of it, spread out over the green fields like a tablecloth at a boring picnic. Squalid and congested as the inner city might be, at least it wasn't boring. Newtham was just a succession of grey wet days hanging out on a line, unable to ever get dry before the next downpour started.

'Well, I'm just ten minutes' drive away from you, and my local is the Jeremiah Font and Tabernacle.'

'Is that another of those new pubs?' Giles asked. 'What sort of beer do they have in there? Do they do that Moses's Mild in there? I tried a pint of that down at the Snuff and Britches, but –'

'The Font and Tabernacle,' Toffer said stiffly, 'is a house of the Lord! God's true brew is what we serve in there!'

'Ah, a tied house, is it?' Giles said. It was good to find common ground for conversation with a fellow beer-drinking man. 'Now, I've never come across any houses of the Lord. They're mostly Ind Coope round our way, and a few Courage pubs. No, I've never come across Lord's breweries at all, I must say. Is that one of the small independent ones from up in Yorkshire? I know those French Trappist monks do you a nice pint, mind, but –'

'The Lord God is who I'm talking about!' Toffer said. 'I'm talking about matters spiritual!'

'Never been that keen on spirits myself,' Giles said. 'Maybe a glass of brandy after a meal, but on the whole –'

'The Jeremiah Font and Tabernacle, you stupid pillock, is a church!'

'A church?' Giles said. 'Good heavens, and you mean they've got a drinks licence?'

Toffer had him by the lapels again.

'Are you trying to be funny?'

'Beg pardon?'

'No. You just don't know any better, do you, Mr West? You're steeped in your ways, I'm afraid, in your ways of sex and depravity. Well, I'm inviting you, Mr West, to join us at our services at the Tabernacle. To pray with us, sing with us, repent with us, and join our congregation.'

'Eh – when?'

'When? This Sunday, Mr West, next Sunday, for all the Sundays stretching ahead, for as far as the eye can see. I'm inviting you to join us for our Sunday morning service, for our bible classes in the afternoon, for our evensong in the evening. I'm inviting you to come celebrate with us mid-week, Mr West, for an evening of hymn singing and redemption, where we confess the error of our ways, and sing the virtues of home, family, and marital fidelity.'

'Do you go to the pub afterwards?' Giles said.

'Em – midweek, we do, yes,' Toffer admitted. 'The Lord was never against a drink – in moderation. And I'm also inviting you to come with us on our Christian camps in the country, when we all go into the woods together, lunching on roots and berries, and achieve states of mysticism and enlightenment hitherto unknown, while putting up at the local youth hostel.'

'And if I – say I'd rather not?' Giles said. 'Rather not go to church on Sunday?'

'Then I might have to give your wife a little phone call, Mr West, and mention the words "massage parlour" to her.'

'I see.'

'You do? Good! So we'll expect you Sunday then, will we, Mr West?'

'Yes, I suppose you'd better.'

'Good. Then you're free to go.'

Giles stood. He felt tired and battered, both in body and soul.

'What do I tell my –'

'I'd tell her you were out boozing, if I were you, Mr West, had a drop too much and forgot to ring, and just managed to grab the last train home.'

And Toffer spoke as though from experience, as if he too had once known temptation and sin.

'Right,' Giles said. 'I'd best be going.'

'The Lord rejoices, Mr West,' Toffer said, 'at the sinner returned to the fold.'

'See you Sunday.'

'Ten-thirty. The Font and Tabernacle.'

'I'd better be there then, I suppose.'

And Giles let the door swing shut behind him. As he went out into the street, he heard the chimes of the cathedral ringing the hour, ringing the last chimes of midnight.

He began to run. He had five minutes before the last train left the station.

He crept quietly into bed, smelling of toothpaste, but he woke her anyway, or maybe the toothpaste did.

'You're back then.'

'Sorry.'

'Boozing, I suppose.'

'Sorry.'

'You and Roy.'

'Sorry, Holly.'

'You could have rung.'

'Yes, sorry.'

'I was just in the mood too.'

'Were you? Oh.'

'Worn off now.'

'Ah.'

'Night, then.'

'Night.'

A perfunctory kiss. Hardly a kiss at all, more of a mechanism, a reflex. A little bit of clockwork in the night.

TWENTY-TWO

Dear Irma,

I wonder if you, or your readers, can help me with some constructive advice.

My husband and I have been happily married for many years now, and have two lovely daughters, whom we both adore. But over these past few months we seem to have grown further and further apart. We rarely talk, rarely confide, we never go out together, and our sex life is almost nonexistent.

At first I suspected that my husband might simply be having a mid-life crisis, which he would get over in time with our love and support. But no. I then felt that perhaps he was having an affair, for he started coming home late, and acting suspiciously – indeed, he once came home in his shorts and vest, claiming that his suit had been stolen while he was playing squash. I didn't know whether to believe him or not, and wondered if he hadn't been with another woman, but decided to give him the benefit of the doubt.

But now I have finally come to understand the true nature of his problem. I believe he has fallen into the clutches of an obscure religious cult. It is not a group I have heard of before, and my husband clams up whenever I try to get any information out of him. I am not even sure of their real name, but when my husband does talk about them, he describes the cult as Toffer's Bloody Tabernacle.

To be frank, I am very worried and concerned about this. I have asked him who or what Toffer is, but he refuses to say. I presume that he is the charismatic cult leader and that my husband has fallen under his spell – not to say his spiel. The fact that the cult is a 'bloody' tabernacle worries me too, and I am afraid of what might happen in the light of what has occurred within other cult organizations, especially in America.

Strangely though, far from trying to convert the rest of us into cult members, my husband seems to want to keep us well away from his new friends. In fact, when I offered to accompany him to one of his cult meetings, he got very angry, and refused to take me, and said that I should stay well away from Toffer's Bloody Tabernacle if I knew what was good for me.

I did not know how to take this. Was it a warning, or a threat? And if Toffer's Bloody Tabernacle is no place for me, why is it any place for my husband? Have you heard of this cult before? Is it a male organization only, perhaps? Patriarchal, male-supremacist, with no place for women?

It seems to be absorbing more and more of his time too. He has gone – in the space of a few weeks – from being a complete atheist to an out-and-out Toffer's Tabernacle devout. He goes there three times on Sundays and twice during the week. He is even talking of going off camping with them on what he describes as a 'Toffer's Bloody Nuts and Berries Weekend'. Does this mean he is becoming a vegan?

I have tried to discuss these matters with him, but he simply turns a deaf ear. His involvement with this cult is alienating us from each other. I feel I can no longer talk or relate to him on any level, and am even starting to despair for the future of our marriage. There is no one I can really confide in – well, perhaps one friend, whom I write to occasionally – but I feel that our other friends and neighbours simply would not understand.

The last straw – the incident which prompted me to write to you – was last night when my husband returned from another meeting of the Bloody Tabernacle and announced to the family that from now on we were to call him Barney Rubble.

This morning he said that he had only been joking, and that he hadn't meant it, but it all adds to my concern. If they take my husband's very name away from him, what will he have left? And what will it be next? Our savings? Our income? Our marriage?

Can you help, Irma?

Many thanks.

Yours sincerely,

Concerned

(Holly West, Mrs)

P.S. Please do not use my name if you do publish this letter as my husband sometimes reads my magazines, and I wouldn't want him to know that I have been writing to you about him.

Dear Box 798,

You wrote to me some time ago, and I must apologize for not replying sooner, but things have been rather eventful these past weeks, and I have hardly had a minute to call my own. I am afraid that my advertisement has led me into a considerable amount of (unconsummated) trouble, and I am keeping what I believe is called a 'low profile' for the moment.

But how are you? Have you risked all that security yet, and gambled all that happiness? If so, what did it bring? Or are you yet to make a throw of the dice?

Maybe we could meet sometime soon, although things are a little difficult for me just now. But it is nice to write to someone who understands how one feels, and I hope that we can continue to keep in touch. I would value your letters.

Yours,

Box 132

Dear Box 132,

Just a little note from your friends in Dawlish to let you know how things are going. Well, the good news first – I know you won't believe this, but it happens to be true! – at the ripe old age of eighty-two, our dear friend Miss Stavenshaw finally got to say hello to Mr Bonky! Yes! And all thanks to you for putting the thought into her mind. It happened at the visitor's room here in the rest-home, and we were all outside in the corridor listening, ready with the champagne and cake, for the big moment.

It all seemed touch-and-go for a while in there, until we heard Miss Stavenshaw's voice cry out, 'Good heavens, so that's what I've been missing all these years! It certainly tones up your calf muscles!' Well, the residents fairly erupted in a spontaneous display of friendship and celebration. We all gave her a big hand, and shouted, 'Hip, hip, hooray for Miss Stavenshaw!' at the tops of our voices. And then the cry went up, 'Speech, speech!'

So Miss Stavenshaw had to come out in her nightie and give us a few words – which she did very well, too, though not much accustomed to public speaking. Then we opened the champagne and cut the cake and sang 'Jerusalem', and presented her with a nice card we found at the newsagent's, with a badge for her to wear reading CONGRATU-LATIONS. Unfortunately, when she returned to the visitor's room she found that the Major (the one who had answered her advertisement in *Silver Threads*) had succumbed to a heart attack. But, as Miss Stavenshaw said, at least he died with a smile on his face and his teeth in, which is what he would have wanted. She says she has quite got the taste for it now, and will be advertising again.

So there we are, we have to take the good with the bad, I suppose, and the rough with the smooth.

Mrs Throttly and myself have not been quite so lucky as yet in our affairs of the heart, though we have taken

tea with several gentlemen who responded to our advertisements, and have high hopes for the future. I have
met a very nice widower from Sidmouth, elderly but still
active, who works as a shelf stacker in Asda's part time,
which he says keeps him young and outgoing.

Mrs Throttly's hip replacement has taken on a treat,
and has allowed her to take up many new interests –
including windsurfing. She has already been up and down
the bay, and is hoping to make it across to Exmouth soon
– where she has a romantic interest. She has also promised
to take me out on her board, and says that if I can find a
wet suit, she will sail us down to Starcross for a drink in
the Atmospheric Railway – though we might have to get
the bus back, if the wind is against us. Which, at our age,
it usually is.

Well, all the best to you and yours. We all hope that
you are having a good time, and have not advertised in
vain.

Please accept the little gift enclosed as a token of our
thanks and our esteem for your opening up the closed
doors of our golden years. It is a little sachet of pot-pourri
for your sock and undies drawer. Miss Stavenshaw chose
the material, I did the sewing, and Mrs Throttly went out
and stole the lavender from the municipal gardens.

Bye for now then.

Wishing you all that you wish yourself.

Your friend,

Mrs Wiseman

THE NEWTHAM REPORTER AND CHRONICLE

Circulation
15,000

YOUR LOCAL NEWSPAPER,
SERVING YOU

WE ARE THE PILLAR

YOU ARE THE
COMMUNITY

Police Officer up on Serious Charges

'I DON'T KNOW what came over me. I must have been possessed.'

Mr D. Toffer, a sergeant in the police, was today suspended on full pay after being put on remand by local magistrates while charges against him were further investigated and brought to trial. Sergeant Toffer, who is also a lay preacher at the Jeremiah Font and Tabernacle Church, was alleged to have fondled the buttocks of a Mrs Yasmin Patel Biswas, who was standing in the row in front of him in the church. Mrs Patel Biswas had recently moved to the area with her husband, an optician, who said he had seen Sergeant Toffer's type before.

Sergeant Toffer denied any recollection of the assault, claiming that he must have suffered some kind of charismatic spiritual possession or 'blackout' during the course of the service. He said he had often spoken in tongues and that if he had now started groping in tongues, then it was a new one on him. He could only conjecture that Mrs Biswas had radiated an aura of sickness and that Sergeant Toffer had received spiritual instruction for a laying on of hands to make her whole again.

A court date was set for July. An application for legal aid was allowed.

248

Dear Box 132,

Thank you for your letter. I was beginning to wonder if I would hear from you – it seemed such a while since I wrote.

I have reread your thoughts so many times now, that I feel I know you almost like a friend. Maybe I am reading things into them that are not there, but I sense that we have the same ways of thinking and feeling, and must have undergone very similar experiences. It would be nice to meet up and talk, but if this is a difficult time for you now, then I shall quite understand and am happy to wait.

I feel that you have a sensitive nature and that you are a kind, and even shy person. I feel that you are someone I can talk to. Whenever I try to communicate with my husband, he just grunts, and reads his paper. But I feel you wouldn't act that way. Am I right? Or is that just another fantasy?

I would love to hear from you again. Let's keep in touch with each other, if nothing else.

My best wishes.

Box 798

Dear Irma,

This is just a quick letter of thanks for all your help and sound advice. You may remember that I wrote to you some weeks ago as Concerned, expressing my worries over my husband's sudden and apparently motiveless involvement with a cult religious group – Toffer's Bloody Tabernacle. Well, it all worked out exactly as you said. I left well enough alone, and let him go his own way, and sure enough, he became as disenchanted with the cult as rapidly as he had become obsessed by it.

He just came home one night last week from a meeting and said, 'Well, that's it with Toffer's Bloody Tabernacle! It's Toffer's Bloody Wandering Hands more like, if you ask me! Well, stuff that, he can whistle for redemption!' And he hasn't gone back since.

Thank you again for your wonderful advice. I cannot tell you how glad I am that I took it.

Many thanks,
Relieved
(Holly West, Mrs)

Dear Box 798,

Thank you so much for your letter. You seem such a thoughtful, reflective and genuine person, unlike many of the others who have responded to my advertisement. In all honesty, I have had many replies, but they have all – one way or another – led only to disappointment and disillusionment.

Oddly enough, I think I have learnt one thing from my experiences – that it's harder to be a sinner than it is to be a saint. It's easy to be virtuous when you do not have the courage to be anything else. Temptation isn't always something you succumb to, it's something you have to seek out, and it is often easier to be respectable and conformist than it is to have the bravery to seize the moment and chase your dreams.

And yet, paradoxically, the difficult thing in life is not so much to find a fellow sinner as to find someone that you can talk to. The hardest thing to find is a fellow spirit.

Shall we try and meet up sometime? I am much freer now than I was, as many of my commitments have eased off. Wednesday is a good night for me. Or Friday. What do you say? Shall we take the risk and seize the day, before it is gone forever?

Looking forward to seeing you,
Box 132

Dear Box 132,

Thank you for writing again. Your letters always make me smile. Sometimes the thoughts you express are ones which are in my own mind. To see them written down, to know that someone else experiences things as I do, well, I don't feel so alone.

Should we meet or not? Perhaps we should just write to each other and never meet, keep our illusions, stay faithful to our partners, enjoy our secret lives, just knowing that our feelings are not unique. Everything is easier to bear when you know that you are not alone in the world. And marriage can be very lonely, sometimes. The loneliest thing there is.

Or maybe you are right. Maybe we should be brave enough to be a little bit more – or less? – than respectable.

Write to me soon. Tell me more about your thoughts and your feelings, the things that make you happy and sad, your hopes and your dreams.

As for meeting, as I say, I still really don't know yet. But don't stop asking me, please don't stop. And one day, very soon, I may say yes.

Yours, truly, madly, deceitfully,

Box 798

Dear Box 798,

It was such a lovely day today that I took my lunch to the cemetery and sat in the sunshine, and this is where I am writing to you. I know that a cemetery must sound like a gloomy place, but it's calm and peaceful – oddly optimistic and uplifting.

I sat here a while before I began to write, and I imagined another life. Another place, another way and another time. I pictured myself with the wonderful person I imagine you to be. I imagined us together. I wondered why it was so hard to be happy, so difficult to meet the perfect stranger, or are discontentment and sadness and regret just an inevitable part of life and all relationships.

Please let us meet. If only so that I can be a huge

disappointment to you. Not that you will be to me. What do you say? Shall we take the risk? Shall we have the courage to be wicked? Shall we dare to live?

Box 132

Dear Box 132,

Just a card – I thought that the picture would appeal to you. Am I right? I still don't feel certain enough. But ask me again. Ask me again, very soon.

798

Dear Box 798,

The card made me laugh. How about this one? Does it make you say yes? If not, I shall just find another card, and I shall go on asking you. You can't say no forever – can you?

132

Dear Box 132,

Say when and where.

Any sunrise. Any sunset.

I feel like a teenager again.

798

TWENTY-THREE

The Doris Management Programme
Doris Database
>
Do you want hands on?
>Yes.

      ⧗

The Doris Management Programme is working for you!
Thank you for your patience.
10.15 am.
>The following active Dorises were detected on the
system:
Total active Dorises - 9
Number married - 4
Number divorced - 3
Number single - 2
Mean age - 31
>The following dormant Dorises were detected on the
system:
Total dormant Dorises - 4
Total active Dorises giving trouble at this time - 0
>Do you wish to add any new Dorises?
>No.
Press Alt F6 for Schedule or click left mouse button.

      ⧗

The Doris Management Programme is working for you!
Thank you for your patience.
>

Schedule: Doris 1.
>Name: June Sedley.
>On the way in or out: On the way out, but no urgency.
>Points out of 10: Looks - 7. Sack points - 6.
>Drink: White wine.
>Food: Nouvelle cuisine.
>Expectations: Divorce, marriage and children.
>Liable to turn nasty on dumping: Yes.
>Liable to tell wife (ref. Doris 9, Mrs Roy): Yes.
>Suggested ways to avoid trouble: Best to put her off.
>Method: Start to fart while making love. Says husband does this and hates him for it.
>Current objectives: Continue as is for next five weeks, then begin to consume large amounts of roughage. Once dropped, reactivate a dormant Doris to maintain quotient, or recruit new Doris.
>Any other remarks or special requirements: None.
>Reminder needed: Yes.
(Key in R for Reminder and date required.)
>Last meeting: Monday.
>Next meeting: Friday.
>Time and place: The Dust and Nesbitt, East Street, lounge bar, 9 pm.
>Mode of contact: E-mail to office.
>Action automatic or manual: Automatic.

The Doris Management Programme is working for you!
E-mail sent. Rendezvous confirmed.
Dust and Nesbitt, lounge bar, 9 pm.

'Busy, Roy?'

'No, mate. Runs itself. Let your microchips do the walking. Put your feet up and have a coffee.'

'So what's it doing then?'

'Well, it's the complete Doris Management, isn't it, old mate.

All up and running. First week on full auto. One button does it all.'

'You found that bug then?'

'Well, it just seemed to disappear.'

'As long as it's not lurking in there somewhere.'

'Going to make our bloody fortunes this, old mate. Make our bloody fortunes.'

Schedule: Doris 2.

>Name: Francine Thews.

>On the way in or out: Steady as she goes.

>Points out of 10: Looks - 8. Sack points - 7.

>Drink: Orange juice.

>Food: Vegetarian.

>Expectations: A good time.

>Liable to turn nasty on dumping: No. If anything, liable to get dumped.

>Liable to tell wife (ref. Doris 9, Mrs Roy): No. Couldn't give bugger.

>Current objectives: Keep it going.

>Any other remarks or special requirements:
Keen canoeist. Likes you to shout 'Here we go over the weir!' and 'Let's shoot the rapids!' at the big moments.

>Reminder needed: No

>Last meeting: Tuesday.

>Next meeting: Friday.

>Time and place: The Dust and Nesbitt, East Street, lounge bar, 9 pm.

>Mode of contact: E-mail to home computer.

>Action automatic or manual: Automatic.

⧗

The Doris Management Programme is working for you!
E-mail sent. Rendezvous confirmed. Dust and Nesbitt, lounge bar, 9 pm.

'Yeah, nothing to it, old mate, as I say. Piece of cake. Slice of the old Battenberg here, no three ways about it. Got them all on the old e-mail, don't even have to ring them up now. Just fire off a quickie, and there you are. It even fixes up your dates for you, and then gives you a printout after.'

Schedule: Doris 3.
>Name: Hannah Sweet.
>On the way in or out: On the way in.
>Points out of 10: Looks - 2. Sack points - 10.
>Drink: Lager and Ribena.
>Food: Anything, as long as there's plenty of it.
>Expectations: Sex.
>Liable to turn nasty on dumping: No intention of dumping.
>Liable to tell wife (ref Doris 9, Mrs Roy): No. Doesn't know. Thinks I'm a widowed lorry driver from Newcastle who comes down once a week on coal deliveries.
>Current objectives: Keep strength up, eat lots of red meat.
>Any other remarks or special requirements: A drink before and a large bag of chips after.
>Reminder needed: Yes.
(Key in R for Reminder and date required.)
>Last meeting: Saturday.
>Next meeting: Friday.
>Time and place: The Dust and Nesbitt, East Street, lounge bar, 9 pm.
>Mode of contact: E-mail to office number. Works for taxi cab co. Coded message: 'Comfy cab wanted'.
>Action automatic or manual: Automatic.

⧗

The Doris Management Programme is working for you!
E-mail sent. Rendezvous confirmed.
Dust and Nesbitt, lounge bar, 9 pm.

On it went. The Doris Management Programme tripped through the files. Trip, trap, trip, trap, just like the Billy Goats Gruff. Trip, trap, the Doris Goats Gruff went trip, trap. Under the bridge lurked Roy, the ugly Troll with the toll. Trip trap went the Doris Goats Gruff. Doris Goat Four, Doris Goat Five, Doris Goat Six, and Doris Goat Seven. Trip trap. The e-mail tripped and the Troll was trapped.

Rendezvous confirmed. Friday, Dust and Nesbitt, lounge bar. 9 pm. Seven little Dorises, all in a row.

'Can't go wrong, mate, can't go wrong. Make our fortunes this will. We'll retire to California on this lot, old mate, shag ourselves senseless.'

'You sure you've tested this programme, Roy? You sure you'd debugged it all?'

'Debugged and de-bagged, old mate. Have your strides off in no time with the Doris Management Programme. I can see it now.'

Schedule: Doris 8.
>Name: Lavinia Stephenson.
>On the way in or out: Query.
>Points out of 10: Looks - 7. Sack points - 6 but rising.
>Drink: Vodka and coke.
>Food: Small helpings.
>Expectations: Unknown.
>Liable to turn nasty on dumping: Liable to turn nasty full stop.
>Liable to tell wife (ref Doris 9, Mrs Roy): Unpredictable.
>Current objectives: Survival. Involvement reckless.
>Any other remarks or special requirements: This Doris could be dangerous. Ill-advised assignation. Safe extrication a.s.a.p..
>Reminder needed: n.a.
>Last meeting: Sunday.
>Next meeting: Friday.
>Time and place: The Dust and Nesbitt, East Street, lounge bar, 9 pm.
>Mode of contact: Internal e-mail. (Coded.)
>Action automatic or manual: Automatic.

⧗

The Doris Management Programme is working for you!

Eight little Dorises now, eight little Dorises Gruff, heading for the bar in the Dust and Nesbitt, at 9 p.m. on Friday.

And then there was only one to go.

Schedule: Doris 9.

>Name: Mrs Roy.

>On the way in or out: Permanent fixture.

>Points out of 10: Looks - 7. Sack points - 7.

>Drink: Brandy and Appletize.

>Food: Curry.

>Expectations: Numerous but never defined.

>Liable to turn nasty on dumping: Can't afford to dump. Besides, who'd iron shirts?

>Liable to tell wife (ref Doris 9, Mrs Roy): No. Is wife.

>Current objectives: Keep happy, keep in the dark and feed bullshit (ref mushrooms).

>Any other remarks or special requirements: Take out for a drink and a curry on birthday and wedding anniversary.

>Next meeting: Friday, for special birthday treat.

>Time and place: The Dust and Nesbitt, East Street, lounge bar, 9 pm.

Then on to the Ganges of the North curry house.

>Mode of contact: Word of mouth.

>Action automatic or manual: Manual. Print reminder.

REMARKS: Override all other arrangements at this point.

***

NOTE TO ROY: INSERT FAIL-SAFE ROUTINE CODING TO AVOID DUPLICATION OR OVERLAP BEFORE RUNNING PROGRAMME. REMOVE THIS MESSAGE WHEN DONE. DO NOT FORGET!

***

⧗

The Doris Management Programme is working for you!

The laser printer on Roy's desk came to life.

'Here we are, you see mate, it's printing them all out now. Now there you are. Easy as steak and kiddly, old mate. Easy as pie.'

Giles picked the sheet out of the tray and looked at it. It read, *Doris Management Programme. Doris Appointments: No appointments today.*

'That's a relief,' Roy said. 'I need a bit of a rest.'

Next appointment: Doris 9. Birthday treat. Friday. Dust and Nesbitt, lounge bar, 9 pm, followed by curry at Ganges Of The North.

And that was all. The rest of the iceberg was under the water, and the good ship Roy sailed on. And they said he was unsinkable.

'Good god!' Roy said. 'Actually going out with the wife. Well, that'll make a nice change. I haven't been seeing too much of her lately. She'll probably even seem like new.'

'It'll all catch up with you one day, Roy. You see if it doesn't.'

It ought to. If there was any justice. It had all caught up with Giles already, and he hadn't even got to do anything.

'Never, mate, never mind. Foolproof, this programme. Only the innocent have anything to fear.'

Har, har. Old mate.

Giles's heart felt heavy. And yet, it couldn't have weighed any more than usual. Could his heart have put on weight? Could it have grown so heavy that that was the reason he could scarcely drag himself down the street – a heavy heart and leaden spirits.

There must be a word for this, Giles thought. There must be a word which sums up everything I feel. He settled for 'depression.' Yes, that just about covered it. Or maybe 'extreme depression'. Yes, the adjective made all the difference, didn't it, old mate?

Only Old Mate had gone a bit quiet recently. Old Mate didn't seem to have so much good advice. In fact, Giles was starting to wonder if Old Mate knew any more about living than Giles did.

With Sergeant Toffer safely out of the way, Giles's first move was to get down to the *Scene Around* offices, feeling he could now safely go there without the dread of a heavy hand on the shoulder and a 'Hello, hello' in the ear.

Scene Around, yes, he still had a bone to chew with them.

Or was it a bone to pick? Never mind, they'd chew it first, and pick it later. Because if it hadn't been for *Scene Around*'s incompetence, he might never have got into the whole massage parlour mess in the first place.

So he made his way to their offices to register his dissatisfaction and discuss the question of refunds.

Giles pushed open the door to the small ads department. The girl with the purple hair and nose-rings was still there behind the counter. Her nose, ears and top lip had been pierced in several new places since Giles had last seen her, and she was looking more and more like a curtain rail. Maybe that was her objective, Giles thought. Maybe she was slowly heading for a full set of curtains with pelmet and drawstrings – the ultimate in privacy. She would only have to pull her drapes together, and the rest of the world could go away. Or maybe it was a new concept in yashmaks, fitted and supplied by the soft furnishings department in John Lewis.

'Next, please!'

Giles shuffled on down the queue. The man in front of him leaned towards the girl.

'I wish to make a complaint,' he said.

'Oh yes, sir? *(Chink.)* And what seems to be the trouble? *(Chink.)*' The rings on her upper and lower lips clinked together as she spoke.

'I came in last week and paid to put an ad in to sell my lawnmower. But when it appeared, it wasn't in the gardening section at all. It was in the Gay and Bisexual column.'

'I see, sir, yes. *(Clink.)*' She sneezed. *(Clink, clink, tinkle, tinkle.)* She wouldn't have made a bad set of wind chimes. 'Beg pardon. *(Chink.)* Didn't you want to sell it to a bisexual then? *(Chink. Tinkle.)*'

'I don't care who buys it,' the man said. 'I don't care if a gardening transvestite buys it. But if you're looking for a lawnmower, you're not likely to go searching for it in the AC/DC column, are you?'

'Why, is it an electric mower then, sir? *(Chinkle. Tink.)*'

'No, it's a wood-burning lawnmower! What do you think!'

'No need to be rude, sir.'

'Same thing happened to me,' Giles said.

'What, with your lawnmower?'

'No, my ad. Ended up in the Gay and Bisexual when it should have been somewhere else.'

'Same thing over here and all!' a woman in the next queue piped up. 'My husband advertised his moped and it ended up in the Situations Vacant. Well, it's hardly a vacant situation is it? It's a Honda 50.'

'Yes, well, our profound (*tinkle*) apologies, sir. We will give you a full refund. Plus a free (*chink*) insertion. In next week's issue (*tinky-chink!*)' A nose stud fell out. She picked it up and put it back in again. 'We do extend our full (*tinkle*) apologies, as I said, sir. *(Tink.)* But we've been having a lot of trouble with our software.'

'Typical,' the man in front of Giles said. 'They computerize it, and it all goes wrong. Ruddy computers,' he added, and he stomped away.

'Yes, sir? *(Tinkle.)* Are you next? *(Chink.)*'

'No, it's all right,' Giles said. 'Don't bother. It's okay now. I've just remembered something. It's all right.'

'But – *(Tink.)*'

'No, it's all right. My mistake. Bye.'

Giles walked hurriedly from the office and out into the street.

The software! The *Scene Around* listings software! His firm had supplied it. His and Roy's sections had worked on the project together. Giles had been responsible for the design and programming, Roy had been responsible for the testing and troubleshooting. Roy had said he had tested it thoroughly. He had said the system was watertight. He'd said he'd got it up and running and nothing could go wrong. Yes. Ego-free software Lavinia had called it. One team did the design, one team did the testing. That way you didn't end up blind to the defects of your own babies.

But Roy hadn't thoroughly tested it, had he? At least not for every conceivable contingency, or plainly it wouldn't be going wrong. And if Roy could make a mistake like that – if a moped could end up in the situations vacant – well, what

261

else could go askew? And what about the other programmes Roy was supposed to have so exhaustively tested? No, his mind plainly wasn't on his job. It was the Dorises that were doing it. They'd sapped his mental energies. The Dorises and the Doris Management Programme. He was spending time on that when he should have been doing other things.

Well, Giles just hoped that Roy had done a better job of dry-running the Doris Management, old mate. Or he'd definitely be getting an asterisk in the spreadsheets.

But what could Giles do about it? Roy was way beyond a quiet word and good advice, and had been for years. He wouldn't listen to Giles. And even if he would – was Giles his brother, his mother, his keeper?

Nope. Nothing of the sort. He was just his old mate.

He'd maybe try a sensible word in the ear when he got back to the office. *(A phrase in the old aural cavity, old mate, har, har!)* But he knew Roy wouldn't listen. He knew before he breathed a word that he'd be wasting his breath.

And then there was Box 798.

What was he to do with her?

Maybe he should just forget about her and advertise again. It wasn't that Giles couldn't see the potential there. It wasn't that there wasn't a strange sexual allure about her correspondence, there was that and more. And it was the more that worried him. Every other letter he had received had borne the stamp of A.Q.O.A.W. on the envelope – A Quick One and Away. But Box 798 was different. She had the potential to ensnare and entrap him. Her attraction was as emotional as it was sexual. Giles could feel himself drawn to her as to none of the others, and felt a desire to reveal his full and innermost self. No, Box 798 wasn't any old box, she was the kind of box you might fall in love with. Box 798 was a home-breaking, heart-breaking box. You met Box 798 at your peril. He had unburdened too much of himself to her already. He could be heading for serious trouble.

Box 798 was the box you were afraid to open, Pandora's box. Only maybe she would unleash all the good things, rather than all the evils and ills. *(Don't pander to Pandora, old mate.)*

But was this what Giles wanted? Was this really what it meant? Had this really been it all along? Maybe it wasn't sexual adventure alone. Maybe he had wanted more. Maybe that was what was lacking. Maybe what he wanted was to fall in love. That old head over heels, the wonderful sinking feeling.

He took out the last card he had received from her and looked at it again. When and where. That was all it needed. So maybe he would. Maybe he would write to Box 798, suggest that time and that place, that when and that where, that carnation and that buttonhole.

And this time, nothing would go wrong.

He stopped off at a stationer's and he bought a card. He scribbled a message to her and dropped the card into the post.

Friday, at eight o'clock, in the Rosebud.

It was done. No turning back. Live a little before you die.

Friday was the night. Box 132, Box 798. Together they might even add up to something.

TWENTY-FOUR

'Look, you've got to cut down on these Dorises, Roy –'

May as well tell an addict to cut down on the old heroin. Roy tapped at the keyboard, with the speed born of experience.

'It's all under control, mate. No need to wet the old undies. Only I thought I might change the name. Doris Management Programme – not very sexy, you know. A bit short on the old ooh la la. I thought I might change it to Doris Solutions. How does it grab you?'

'Look Roy –'

'Just what I thought. More of a goer, eh? *Sort out the women in your life with Doris Solutions.* I mean, you could see that up on a hoarding somewhere, couldn't you?'

'Roy –'

'It's going to make our fortunes, mate. I've even got a distributor interested in the idea. Bloke I met in a pub, in the communications business. Whimpole Communications. George Whimpole. Big name in cellular phones. He's recruiting new staff to handle it.'

A lying bastard, Roy. A lying, lonely bastard in a world of aforesaid bastards.

'He reckons it's very sound. Reckons there's room in the market. First we thought Doris Solutions. Then Doris For Windows –'

'Roy –'

'Then Doris Artwork, Doris Paintbrush, Apple Mac Doris, Works For Doris, a Doris Screensaver – there's all sorts of spin-offs. I was even thinking of a TV thing. A bit like Blind Date, you know, only called Mine's a Doris!'

'Roy –'

'Or maybe one of those snooker game things – Pot the Doris

or something. And once it all takes off we can introduce a version for women and all. We'll call it Denis – the Doris Alternative. Denis Solutions. A bit like Ken and Barbie, you know.'

He was typing now like nobody's business.

'Going to the pub for lunch?'

'Yeah. Friday, isn't it? Yeah, right. How about trying that new one, the Wodge and Packets, down in Villiers Row?'

'Right. Look, Roy –'

'Can it wait? I am a bit busy, old mate.'

'Yes, don't worry. Okay.'

He had been about to tell him. To confide in Roy about the infidelity ahead, but Roy was too absorbed in his Dorises. (*Hoping to get a bit of a leg-over tonight myself, actually, Roy,* delivered in stroll-on, casual tones. *Are you, mate. Well, well. Join the club.*)

But that was part of the problem. Giles felt isolated, an outsider, not really a part of the brotherhood of man at all, not a fully fledged member of the Leg-over Club.

'Busy, Giles?'

It was Lavinia.

'Just conferring with Roy on a few points.'

'Well, perhaps you could take a look at this. The software package we sold to that listings magazine seems to be corrupting their advertisements. The billing's gone haywire as well. So if you're not too –'

'I'll look at it now.'

Giles took the file, and returned to his work station. As he went he saw Lavinia leaning over Roy's desk talking to him, her hair almost brushing against his face.

How did he do it? How *did* he do it? What did they see in him? He must be using a hormone spray. He probably had a rubdown every morning with Extract Of Bull's Testicles. And as for Lavinia –

– as for Lavinia.

No!

What if Lavinia was Box 798?

*   *   *

265

At lunch time, they sat in the Wodge and Packets over halves of Nutty Cronker. Roy sipped at his beer and took a bite of his Ploughman's Tasty Snodger With Cheese.

'Did I tell you who was on the cards tonight?' he said. 'Going out with Mrs Roy, no less!'

'I know. You said. And that'll make a nice change for you,' Giles said. 'I shouldn't think you see that much of her.'

'Not a lot,' Roy agreed. 'It's a shame, in some ways, that we can't spend more time with each other.'

'Well, maybe once you've retired –'

'Retired! Yeah! Must make a note of that! Pensioner Doris – the programme for the more mature user. But anyway, I always make a point of taking Mrs Roy out on her birthday and on our wedding anniversary.'

'Why's that, Roy? From a sense of duty, or a sense of irony?'

'Eh? No, I mean, fair do's, she deserves an evening out. She's got a lot to put up with.'

Well, he'd said it.

As usual, on a Friday afternoon, the office clock hands stopped revolving. Giles had resolved to ring home at a quarter past three. It had then been five past. An eternity went by, then another. Ice ages came and went. A woolly mammoth walked through the office, a stalactite grew from the ceiling, rocks turned to sand. Then it was twelve minutes past.

Why wait any longer?

'Holly?'

'Yes?'

'It's me, Giles.'

'Yes?'

'Look, I was just ringing to say that I might be home a bit late tonight.'

'Oh!'

'I told you, didn't I? About going out with Roy?'

'No.'

'Oh. Didn't I? I thought I did. Yes, anyway, I promised I'd go out for a drink with Roy.'

A stone-shaped silence rolled down the phone line.

'I thought it was Mrs Roy's birthday today. I was just speak-

ing to her and she said that she and Roy were going out for
a meal.'

Damn! Bugger! What a stupid mistake. *(Never would have
happened with Doris Solutions, old mate. Doris Solutions, for your
every requirement – the antidote to amnesia.)*

'Unless they've invited you along as well, Giles.'

Play dumb.

'Em – who? Who's that?'

'Roy!'

'Roy? No, it's *Ray* I'm seeing for a drink. Did you think I
said Roy? No, Ray. *Ray!*'

'Who's Ray?'

'You know, in computer operations. The one with all the
personal problems. I think he needs to talk to someone, and
he asked me to have a drink with him, and I couldn't really
refuse –'

'Oh. Oh, right.'

That softened the blow. Women seemed to like that. Men
going off and having chats with each other about their personal
problems. Always went down well, a bit of the old shoulder-to-
cry-on.

'It's just a bit inconvenient, that's all, as I have to go out
myself. I'm supposed to be seeing Mrs Trewitt for another
colour consultation tonight. Didn't I tell you?'

'No.'

'I'm sure I did.'

'I don't remember.'

'You remember – she's the one who had the mohican.'

'Oh, her.'

'Yes, well she's gone and had highlights put in now.'

'Highlights, in a mohican?'

'Yes, and nothing matches any more, so we'll have to start
again from scratch. And I was relying on you being here. I
can't leave the girls on their own.'

'Ask Beryl in to baby-sit.'

'Oh. All right. What time will you be back?'

'Late-ish, I'd imagine. I wouldn't wait up.'

'All right.'

267

'Bye then.'

'Bye.'

It was done.

And that was it. He waited to feel something – guilt, remorse. But nothing came. It was how you felt afterwards, that was the test.

Giles went to the toilet to freshen up. He found himself sharing the urinal with Eliot of management, who had been at the good lunches again. Friday was always a good lunch day in management. With a blithe disregard for the no smoking rule, he was puffing on a cigar.

'Ah! West!' he said, shuffling over to give Giles a bit of room. 'We meet at the coalface.'

'Eh, yes,' Giles said. He always felt embarrassed when urinating in company. It somehow seemed to impair the flow. Not so with Eliot, however, who plainly had shares in a water company.

'So this is where all the big knobs hang out, what!' Eliot gave a phlegmy chuckle.

'Yes. Ha, ha. Yes. Very good,' Giles said, as though he had never heard the joke before.

'We can't go on meeting like this – what? Eh?'

'Yes. No. Very good,' Giles said, aware of Eliot's eyes on him.

'Nothing coming out?'

'Eh – not at the moment, no.'

'Tried shaking it? Little word of encouragement?'

'It's all right now.'

Eliot of management looked down at Giles's tackle. Not as big as his own, he was gratified to see. Pretty pathetic stream too. But that was okay. That fitted into the scheme of things. A man in the more senior position should, after all, have the larger equipment.

'I've been thinking, West –' Giles eyed him sideways. God, it was still coming out like a torrent. It was like the Severn Bore. What did he have in there, a bladder or a barrel? ' – of recommending you for promotion.'

What? Who? Me?

'Very impressed with your conduct lately. So, I'm going to recommend you for promotion and a salary increase. Reckon it's time you had more responsibility, your own department. Going to be some changes round here soon.'

'My own department?'

'And your own space in the car park. And you'd better have something to park in it while you're at it. What say you to a BMW?'

'Very nice,' Giles said. 'Very nice car.'

'Good, that's settled then.'

Giles looked at him askance. Did he mean it? Or was it just the good lunch talking? He'd probably forget the whole thing in five minutes.

'Of course, there'll probably be an interview, but I'll be on the panel, so that's just a formality. So – well done!'

'Thank you!'

'Keep up the good work!'

He thumped Giles on the back and went off to wash his hands.

Could Giles's luck possibly be changing?

'Oh, that BMW –' Eliot said.

Ah, here we go, changed his mind already.

'Yes?' Giles said.

'You might prefer a Mercedes.'

And he left.

By 5.35, the office was empty. Even Lavinia had gone, uncharacteristically calling, 'Must get home to change! Off out tonight' as she went. She didn't normally go anywhere – or tell anyone if she did – and was usually the last to leave.

Left alone, Giles had a look at his condoms. The weeks had left their mark on his Cucumbers, and the wrappers seemed cracked here and there. He'd better get a few more before the chemist's closed. Better safe than sorry.

He walked to the chemist's. The lights were on in the window, and illuminated bottles of coloured water gave the place a spurious old world charm. Giles shrugged off a pang of nostalgia for things as they never were, and went in. Mr Iqbal looked up from behind the aspirin, and remembered him instantly.

'Ah! The gentleman with the Massive Cucumber! Have you come for replenishments, sir? Used up all your Cucumbers already? Well, well, well!'

Giles paid for his purchases, and went out. He had only been in the shop a few minutes, but darkness had fallen like a blanket from the sky. Yes, it was the sad hour. They called it happy, of course. In all the pubs and wine bars it would be Happy Hour now. It might even have been Happy Hour all day in some of them. But that was just a false beard and moustache hanging on the face of the day, a thin and unconvincing disguise. And who would need a Happy Hour anyway, if people weren't so sad.

It was a disease of cities – Happy Hour.

The worst bit of adultery in a way was all the hanging about and waiting. If you wanted to break the Ten Commandments these days, you first had to get in line.

Tonight would be the night though. He had the feeling. It was more than intuition, it was a cold-blooded, detached certainty that tonight would be the night.

He took out her last letter and re-read it as he walked. Box 798. The sweet anonymity of her. The abandonment of love in the dark, love with an unknown stranger. Where would they do it? Her place? In a hotel room? Against the wall of an alleyway? How? Like missionaries? Like dogs? How would it be? Sweet? Brutal? Were her fingernails sharp? Did she like to kiss or to be kissed? Whose name would she call him by? His own? Someone else's? The name of a long-lost lover? The first love of her youth?

He turned a corner and then another. Then he saw the Rosebud, at the end of a quiet street.

He was late now. He must have walked the long way, taken detours. Late, but maybe deliberately so. This time he wanted to be the one to make the entrance. Not the one who sits at the bar and scans the door, but the one who comes in and stops, and looks around, and finds the eyes that search for him and thinks *Oh yes*, and steps forward.

Or thinks *Oh no*, and runs.

He was fifteen minutes late, but she would undoubtedly be there, sitting at the bar, alone, but composed. Men would look at her and wonder if they should risk an approach, but no, they would see that she was already involved and waiting for someone. Someone important, someone who mattered. Box 798. Box 132. Together they added up to Box 930. Maybe that was a magic number.

Giles stopped at the door. People pushed by him and went inside. The Rosebud was decorated with posters of Orson Welles in his various guises, and the painted sign was of a sledge on a bonfire. Giles smoothed back his hair and took a deep breath. Another crowd of people brushed past him, and he stepped aside to let them by. He found himself by the window, looking into the bar. Was she there? He looked to see her. And yes, there she was at the bar, sitting on a high stool, reading the magazine she had said she would be reading, and wearing in her buttonhole the flower she had said she would wear.

Yes.

Oh, yes.

It was her. And in a way, he was not surprised. In a way, he had always known it. He had known for so long.

It was his wife.

It was Holly.

Not Lavinia, not someone from Dawlish up on a trip, not Mrs George Whimpole on the Wife's Revenge, not Mrs Roy, not Martine, not Marilyn, nor any of all the Dorises.

It was Holly.

He had advertised for a lover, and the woman who had replied, the woman whose words had touched his soul, was his wife.

Holly. Hol-ly. Light of my life –

He tried to remember the letters she had sent him. Those word-processed, anonymous letters, probably written on his own home computer. Phrases from them came to his mind. *I feel the same. Lonely. Unfulfilled. Life going by. Things I have never*

271

known. Beginning to grow old. No longer so important. Children growing up — I feel the same. I feel just the same.

Holly, Holly, why didn't you say? Why didn't you tell me? I could have tried, I could have made a difference, we could have started over, we could have begun again.

Or could we?

A lump came to his throat. It was hard to breathe and hard to swallow and hard not to cry. The phrases went round and round. Phrases which he had used to justify himself, to persuade himself of the righteousness of his cause. Phrases and sentiments which his wife too had been using — to justify an affair with another man. Another man. Him.

(Well, it's sauce for the goose this time, all right, old mate.)

Roy!

Yeah?

Be quiet! What you think no longer matters. You see I —

Well what? What?

I love Holly.

But that's all right mate. That's all right too. That's good. That's fine. That's allowed.

Giles loves Holly. Holly loves Giles.

That's how it was, you see, the carved heart on the tree. What goes wrong, Roy? What fouls us up? Where does all the love go when it dies? There must be an elephants' graveyard somewhere, a lost graveyard for love, deep in a forgotten forest. Can we bring it back to life, Roy? Is it dead, or only resting? Can we try the old mouth-to-mouth, old mate? Tell me we can bring the love back. Tell me it's so, old mate. Tell me that love doesn't have to die. Tell me that two people can be happy. Tell me that Jack and Jill can live to be Darby and Joan, old mate, and still love and like and value and respect each other. With no regrets. Tell me that love can last, Roy, and that there need be no regrets. Tell me such things are possible.

For that is what I want to hear.

More than anything.

In the whole wide world.

Giles turned away and walked quickly to the end of the

street. He stopped to get his breath and then hurried on. He had to get to the station, he had to get home before her.

The streets were busy with people on their Friday night out. Tuxedoed bouncers stood in the pub doorways, with an eye out for trouble which, hopefully, would arrive soon.

How long would she wait for him? How long before she began to feel uncomfortable in that press of people, her solitude becoming evident? How long before some man, fortified with alcohol, leaned over and said, 'Been stood up, darling? How about a drink?'

And would she? Maybe she would at that. Maybe she'd think to hell with it, why not? Maybe that was what happened, you went off in search of love, and came back with a drunken stranger who had trouble remembering your name.

What would she be doing now? Looking at her watch, at the door, making the drink last? How did it feel to be left waiting? Ah yes, Giles remembered it now, the conflict of emotions – worry and concern mixed with the awareness of rejection. You had been measured and found lacking and stood up.

And they passed by to see you. Oh yes. Giles remembered it. He had been left standing outside a cinema once, a gangly teenager, who gangled more than most. And he had looked at his watch, knowing that they had already missed the film, but that if she came there would still be time for a milky coffee in the Wimpy bar. And then he had looked up, and had seen the girl he was supposed to be meeting. Her face was pressed to the window of a passing bus; there she was, up on the top deck, peering down at him, unable to stay away. Like a cat playing with a mouse, interested in the way it would squirm. Their eyes had met. Only momentarily, but it was long enough for him to see her clearly, and yet brief enough for her to believe that he hadn't seen her at all. She had ducked back out of sight, and in her place had appeared the grinning face of her friend (*me and my friend*) – the friend who could share the joke and spread the laughter. (*She stood Giles up. Did you stand him up? Should have seen him. Still waiting there, an hour later. No! Didn't wait a whole hour did he?*)

Laugh?

He could have wept.

He had seen her the next day in school. *Sorry Giles, really sorry. I couldn't make it last night, tried to get in touch but I couldn't. Sorry. Maybe another time, eh? Stop sniggering, Eileen! What are you sniggering for? Just ignore her, Giles. I don't know why she's sniggering.*

Har, har, old mate, the joke starts early, doesn't it? The old nudge-nudge starts young. It lives long and prospers, does the old nudge-nudge. Har, har.

Giles's heart went out to Holly, alone in a pub full of strangers. Yet what was he getting maudlin about? He'd been all prepared to deceive her, all ready to betray her at the drop of a hat – before the hat even hit the ground. It was a bit late for remorse now.

And what was the use? The feeling didn't go away. It was still there, that pang, that yearning, that sense of a life only half-lived. Time was getting on, how much more would there be? What to do with all the days and years? He had to live, she had to live. And yet what if she –

– found another man?

The pavement wobbled under him, he grabbed a passing lamp post and held on to it tightly.

'Look at him, pissed already!'

He steadied himself and moved on. Well, he'd have to deal with that, as and when. The thing is – the point was – they were men and women now, not boys and girls any more. This wasn't the practice, this wasn't the mock exam, this was it. This was what you got. This was real life, the only life there was.

And people change. They fall out, drift asunder. People get divorced, families fall apart. Juliet turns to Romeo and says 'I'm sorry, but it's all off, I don't love you any more, and besides, you snore.'

And Romeo says 'Fine by me, girl, I never liked your cooking anyway. And you've got cellulite on your thighs.'

He was at the station now and only had to wait five minutes for a train. There were few people on it. It was too late for the commuters, and too early for the revellers; it was the in-between train, a train for those who were neither one thing nor the other, but who were trying to make their minds up.

When he got home, he saw that the curtains were drawn and the light was off in the living room. The fact that the light was off no doubt meant that Beryl the baby-sitter was involved in heavy petting with Derek the boyfriend. Giles made a lot of noise with his arrival, slamming all the car doors – including the boot lid – and coughing and jangling his keys as he made a great pretence of trying to find the right one.

A light came on, and by the time he let himself into the house, everything was decent.

'Oh, hello, Mr West, we didn't expect you back quite so early. Mrs West said –'

'Yes, it's all right Beryl, sorry about that, but don't worry, I'll pay you for the full evening anyway.'

'Oh, thanks very much. Oh, this is Derek, by the way. I hope you don't mind my asking him round.'

'Not at all.'

'We were helping each other with our homework projects.'

'Yes. Well –'

'Well, let me know if you need me again. Any time. You two haven't been going out very much lately, have you?'

'No. Right. Well, thanks again. Bye then, Beryl.'

'Bye.'

'Bye then, Derek.'

Grunt.

Slam.

Silence.

The girls were both asleep. Giles went up and looked in on them, and sighed for childhood lost. He went back down and put on the television but couldn't settle on anything, and kept glancing at his watch. When would Holly come home? How long would she be? And she had lied to him too! That was the thing that hurt. She had lied to him about Mrs Trewitt and the colour co-ordination. He knew he had lied to her, but that didn't seem the same, didn't seem as bad.

Eleven-thirty came, then midnight, then he went to bed.

He had only just put the light off when he heard a taxi pull up outside of the house, then a key in the latch. She must have made some tea, and sat in the kitchen for a while before coming up to bed. There was no glow of light. She must have sat in the darkness, with the thoughts that darkness brings.

He heard her in the bathroom, running the tap, cleaning her teeth. Then the bedroom door opened and she came in. He did not speak, but lay there, as though asleep. He heard her undress and listened as the layers of clothes fell to the floor.

The mattress creaked faintly as she got into bed. She lay still. He could feel her breath. What was she thinking? Where had she been? How had she filled the hours between then and now? He continued to feign sleep.

'Giles –'

'Hmm?'

'You awake?'

'Sort of.'

'Giles –'

'Yes?'

'Have a good night?'

'All right. You?'

'All right.' There was no evidence of disappointment in her voice. No sign that she had just been stood up by Box 132, no sign of despondency, or rejection – who knows, maybe she was even relieved.

Maybe she even knew. That it was him.

There was silence then. It was odd, but she seemed like a different person lying next to him. Maybe it was the fact that she had considered betraying him that she seemed altered somehow, no longer the woman he had known since his teens, no longer the person he had married, but altered by the contemplation of betrayal. Suddenly she seemed mysterious, deep, unknown.

'Giles –'

'Umm?'

'Are you happy?

He took a minute to answer. 'No, not really. Why? Are you?'

276

'Not really.'

'No.'

Her hand touched his back. 'You seem different,' she said, echoing his own thoughts. 'You seem rather different tonight. You've seemed different for a long time.'

'Yes,' he said. 'Yes. I suppose I have.'

'Is it us?'

'Yes.'

'Any regrets?'

'Sometimes. You?'

'Sometimes. It's only human.'

'Yes, it is, isn't it? I mean, do you ever wonder –'

'Sometimes. You?'

'Sometimes.'

He turned to face her, and put his hand on to the curve of her hip.

'Maybe we just need a little time.'

'Maybe.'

'Giles –'

'Yes –'

'It was you, wasn't it? The box number. You were Box 132, weren't you?'

His reflex instinct was to deny it, ask what she meant, what she was talking about. But what was the point? If it was to be finished, it was best to finish it. They couldn't go on like this, not forever.

'Yes,' he said. 'I was.'

'You wrote such beautiful letters.'

'Did I?'

'Just like the ones you used to write. What did you think of me? Box 798?'

He took his time to reply.

'I thought that you were the sort of woman I could fall in love with.'

'Sight unseen?'

'Yes.'

'Were you disappointed?'

'Surprised.'

'Were you?'

'Maybe not. Not really. How did you know it was me?'

'I didn't. Just thought it might be, when you stood me up.'

'Sorry about that.'

'That's all right. So you saw it was me and ran away?'

'Yes.'

There was silence again.

'Were there others?'

'Yes.'

'And did you?'

'No. Almost, but no.'

'And would you have?'

'I don't know. Would you?'

'I don't know. With someone different –'

'Yes, that's it. Curiosity. Maybe we met too young.'

'Yes.'

'Oh, well.'

They shuffled around in the bed, and his feet landed on hers.

'Your feet are warm,' she said. 'They're usually cold. What have you done to them?'

And they were, yes tonight even his feet weren't the usual blocks of ice. Tonight the kaleidoscope had rotated, the pattern had changed. Things seemed new and fresh, never seen quite like this before. Maybe, after all, things could change. Hadn't he read somewhere that after every seven years the body has completely renewed itself? Hadn't he read that about one of the astronauts who had been to the moon? That so much time had gone by that there wasn't a part of him left that had been there, it was all new tissue.

But the memories didn't go, did they? The memories remained. Old thoughts in a new brain. The blossom and the buds were out on the trees, and yet your mind was locked in winter. And maybe that was all part of it too, your inability to discern the difference, to see the changes, to realize that the person you lived with every day of your life was a complete and utter mystery, in many ways still an absolute stranger.

He suddenly felt embarrassed, and then excited – to be in bed, with this strange, unfamiliar woman.

He went to kiss her. What would she do? Would she shout, kick him away, scream, 'Who do you think you are?' But no, she had already moved to kiss him too, to embrace this strange, unfamiliar man she found in her bed, and they met half-way.

Have we been introduced? Or is this the introduction?

Oddly, it was not a kiss he remembered ever coming across before. It was unidentifiable. There was no picture or illustration of it in his *Observer's Book Of Kisses*, no memory of it at all. Even her skin felt different under his touch, softer, more alive.

'Who is it?' he said.

'Who wants to know?'

'Are you sure it's you?'

'Why,' she said, 'who's asking?'

So it was the same for both of them. The familiar seemed new; the light had changed. Perhaps things could now go on forever. He could see no reason why it ever should stop. They could go on into old age, into their dotage, senility, and a double bed in the old folks' home. They had weathered the seas of boredom and familiarity, and docked in the land of plenty, the land of infinite variety, where custom would never grow stale.

So it was the same for Holly. Was that her name?

'Holly, is that your name?'

'No. It isn't. I haven't got one.'

The stranger's hand moved slowly and delicately along the inside of his thigh. He could feel the trace of her long fingernails on his skin. Couldn't be Holly then. Holly bit her nails and could never grow them. Holly, sharp as a holly leaf with hollybush hands. Couldn't be Holly. He reached out and responded, trailing his own fingers along the back of her leg, over her buttocks, and then on along over the base of her spine. Her flesh tingled.

This man – whoever he was.

His fingers moved down, until she moaned softly, gently, losing control.

This woman – whose heart beat like a drum.

Whoever she was.

And they made love, not in any old familiar way, with old familiar responses, but with unexpected twists and turns of their bodies, with a silent, passionate intensity.

Whoever they were.

'Do you love me?'

'I love you.'

'I love you. I'll love you forever.'

And they meant it, when they said it.

I love you.

Whatever that is.

And they held each other for a long time after. And when they woke, it was morning, and their children were in the room demanding their breakfast.

Breakfast and a new day.

TWENTY-FIVE

'Whatever happened to you?'

Roy's eye was several interesting shades of purple. There were sticking plasters on his nose, and he limped painfully, as though his testicles had swollen to twice their normal size.

'I was the victim of rough justice, old mate. They meted it out with no mercy. Kangaroo court, it was, hopping round all over the shop. Mob rule, I can tell you.'

'Where'd it happen? At the football?' Giles said.

'Football my orifice,' Roy said. 'I was Dorised, mate, well and truly Dorised. Hang on, eyes down!'

Roy stared at his work. Giles, on the words *eyes down* naturally looked up, and was confronted by Lavinia, bearing down upon them with a memo. She dumped the memo on Roy's desk, and hissed at him through clenched teeth.

'Memo for you, you bastard! And I hope they still hurt, bastard! And if I get the chance, I'll kick them again! And this time, I'll take a run at it.'

Roy kept his head down and went on with his work. Lavinia straightened up and saw Giles. Her nostrils were flaring like a horse in a race.

'And as for you!' she said to Giles. 'As for you – I suppose you're on his side! You're a friend of the bastard, I suppose.'

'I don't know anything about –'

'But then you would be, wouldn't you. Men! All lying and cheating and covering up for each other. If you're not a bastard yourself, you're some bastard's mate.'

Giles had heard of plumber's mate and brickie's mate, but bastard's mate was a new one. He would have liked to ask a few questions about the exact duties of a bastard's mate, but he didn't need to pose the question, Lavinia was already answering it.

281

'Yes, bastard's mate! You just stand around, don't you, egging the bastards on, and passing them their tools when they need them –'

'I don't know about that,' Giles said. 'I'm not really –'

'Oh yes, and then you go telling them what a good job they've done, once they've plumbed their toilets in, or cemented their bricks together or whatever it is they do.'

'Yes but –'

'Yes, bastard's mate, that's what you are. If he's Hitler, you're Goebbels!'

'Yes, but –'

'Oh, it's no use "Yes, butting" me, Giles.'

'You head-butted me!' Roy chipped in reproachfully. His fingers stroked the Elastoplast on his nose.

'And I should have done it harder!' Lavinia said. She turned back to Giles. 'If anything, I blame you more than him!'

'What have I done? I haven't done anything! I've done nothing!'

'Exactly, Giles,' Lavinia said. 'Nothing! Typical bastard's mate, Giles, just stand about and let it all happen, and never lift a finger!'

'Yes but –'

'Oh, you make me sick!'

And she walked away.

Giles turned to Roy. 'What did I do?'

'Just ignore it,' Roy said. 'She's a bit put out about Friday night.'

'Why, what happened? I thought you were taking Mrs Roy out for a curry on her birthday.'

'Yeah, mate. So did I.'

Roy had been due at the Dust and Nesbitt bang on nine. And as a rule, Roy liked to be punctual. Not early, but punctual. Too early was as bad as too late for him. Timing was crucial in the kind of business operation he was running, and no man can keep nine Dorises on the boil without keeping one eye on the second hand while he's at it.

Mrs Roy had gone home first to change from her job at the council, before coming into town.

'No sense in me coming all the way out to go all the way in again –' *(As the bishop said to the actress, old mate, har, har)* '– I'll see you in the Dust and Nesbitt and we'll have one in there, and then on up to the Ganges of the North.'

'But isn't Edinburgh a long way to go for a curry, Roy?' Mrs Roy had protested.

'No, no,' Roy said. 'Edinburgh isn't the Ganges of the north, Edinburgh is the Athens of the north!'

'I'm not so keen on Greek food, not on my birthday,' Mrs Roy had said.

'Anyway, the Ganges of the North is on Small Street, just round from the Dust and Nesbitt.'

'Oh, that one.'

After work, Roy had gone for a session at the squash and health club. *(Something about that steam room, old mate, something about the way you just sit there, dripping.)* Suitably invigorated, he had made his way to the Shuttlecock Bar *(Members only, and their guests)* where he had a pint of orange squash and a packet of salt and vinegar crisps with a pickled egg in it. *(Delicacy, mate, bloody delicacy. And it's the way they drop your pickled egg into your crisp bag with this long pair of tongs – something about that, something stylish.)*

While he ate his egg and crisps, Roy chatted up the new barmaid, and within eight minutes of making her acquaintance, had arranged to go round to her place on the following Tuesday – when her husband would be out – to give her PC the once over, as the tracking ball kept falling out of her mouse. *(Soon have that fixed, no trouble. Just have to take me shirt off first to get to grips with it.)*

Making a mental note to feed this appointment into the Doris Management Programme (a.k.a. Doris Solutions) at the earliest opportunity, Roy finished his drink, screwed up his crisp bag, and went on his way.

It was eight thirty-nine when he got to the door of the Dust and Nesbitt, but that wasn't what Roy called punctual, no, that was early. So he turned aside and went along the road into another pub, The Midwife And Forceps, which was the nearest pub to the maternity hospital. Several expectant fathers were at the bar, downing a quick one before rushing back to the delivery room to shout 'Push!' and to say 'It'll be all right', feeling all the while that it would be nothing of the sort.

'I just wish I could have an epidural and all,' one young man was saying. He was having a double Scotch instead.

Another young man was asking for a carry-out.

'Have you got any cans?' he said. 'She's refusing all anaesthesia. She says the only thing that can help her now is a large tin of Guinness with a widget.'

It amused Roy to come in here. To see them all starting out on the road he'd travelled, to see them kicking off a new game. With new Roys and new Dorises being born every minute. Yes, it was all part of life's gaudy wallhangings, old mate.

He had a half of Mild and Boompsadaisy (3.3% abv) which he drank in ten minutes, and then he strolled slowly back to the Dust and Nesbitt, pushing open the swing door to the bar.

The Greenwich time signal felled the hour. It was nine p.m. precisely.

It took a second for Roy's eyes to adjust to the light. He glanced around for Mrs Roy – whom he knew from experience would be parked somewhere with her hand around a glass of Appletize and brandy – but before his eyes settled on her, he became aware of other faces staring at him, a long line of familiar faces, each face, and the body belonging to it, sitting atop a bar stool. Nine bar stools. Nine faces. Nine hands waving. Nine smiles. Mrs Roy's among them. Nine fingers beckoning. Nine drinks in nine other hands. Nine voices chorusing 'Hello, Roy! I'm over here!'

He blinked uncertainly, like a man in a haze, and looked again for confirmation.

Yes, there they all were. Nine little Dorises all in a row. Not so little some of them either, old mate. Forceful women, if you know what I mean. Women with a bit of character. Even done self-defence courses some of them. Not the sort of women to be messed about, if you know what I mean.

Nine smiles turning to frowns of perplexity. Nine faces turning to look at each other. Nine dawnings of light. Nine simultaneous understandings. Nine faces turning back to Roy, not smiling now, not one of them. Roy edged towards the door, but fell over a table. Nine faces advancing now, with nine raised handbags.

'I can explain!' a voice cried. 'It's not my fault! It's the Doris Management Programme!'

And then there was darkness.

'So you mean they all turned up in the same place at the same time?' Giles said. 'All nine Dorises? Mrs Roy included?'

'Exactly!'

'And so what happened then?' Giles said. 'After you fell over the table?'

'Then?' Roy repeated. 'Well, I suppose it was round about then that the unpleasantness started.'

'Oh.'

'Yes.'

Roy looked down at his scrotum.

'I've had ice on it all weekend – frozen peas, everything.'

'What have you got down there now?'

'A bag of frozen oven chips, old mate.'

'So what's going to happen? What about Mrs Roy?'

'She's standing by me,' Roy said. 'She's forgiving me, and she's standing by me.'

'But why?'

'She loves me, I suppose.' He shrugged. 'And I love her too.'

'Do you?'

'Yeah. I told her that. Mrs Roy, I said, you're the only one for me. Always have been, always will be.'

'But Roy, what about the others?'

'Don't mean anything, old mate. Never have. Just a bit of fun.'

'So you're a reformed character then, eh?' Giles said, not without a sense of satisfaction. 'So you're giving it all up?'

Roy stared at him.

'You what, old mate?'

'Packing in the womanizing.'

'I can't do that,' Roy said. 'It's me hobby. It's the only thing that keeps me out of trouble.'

Giles just looked at him. He could think of nothing to say. Roy was Roy. And that was it.

'Tell you what though, old mate, if we could just get the bugs out of this Doris Management Programme, I'm still sure it would be a winner.'

'I'll leave you to it, Roy. Must do some work.'

Giles walked back to his desk, taking Lavinia's memo with him, reading it as he went.

MEMO

Lavinia Stephenson will be leaving the company at the end of the month. She is joining a new high-flying firm, Whimpole Communications Ltd., where she will have increased responsibility and will be developing some exciting new software.

We wish Lavinia all the best in her new job. There will be a small get-together in the Snort and Warthog on Greystone Street this coming Friday to wish her all the best and farewell.

In the absence of any volunteers, Lavinia will be coming round with an envelope herself, to collect for her going-away present, and to make sure that everybody signs the card.

Lavinia's present position as leader will be taken over by Giles West. (*What? Eliot of management was behind this. Must be. As good as his word.*)

We take this opportunity to thank Lavinia for all her hard work over the years. She will surely, we hope, pop back to see us from time to time, as we will no doubt miss such a popular member of the team.

Well, you had to say something good about people, Giles supposed. Even the worst of us had our redeeming features. We all had our negative features too, but best not to dwell on them. A farewell note was like an obituary notice: if you couldn't say anything nice, why bother to say anything at all.

He initialled the memo and passed it on.

The memo and the baton. Pass them on. The memo and the baton and the good advice for your children, and the little money you've saved, and the few lessons you've learned, and the iota of wisdom you've garnered from your wealth of experience. Pass them on. All part of the relay race, old mate, all part of life's rich tapestry.

At lunchtime, Giles went down to the sorting office to see if there were any letters. He wanted to clear the decks now, finalize accounts. As he walked through the streets, the usual crowds of sandwich buyers and Diet Coke drinkers milled about. The weather was finer now, and in the parks and the squares, young and old sprawled, reading newspapers, eating their lunches, soaking up the sun.

They closed their eyes and turned their faces to the sky. It was good to be alive. Life brimmed over with possibilities. And winter was far away.

'Box 132?' the man behind the sorting office counter asked, as ever.

'That's it,' Giles said.

'ID please?' More ridiculous formalities. Giles showed him his driving licence yet again. He studied it as if he'd never seen it before.

'Here you are, sir.' He handed Giles his letters.

'Thank you. And I don't think I'll be needing this box number any more, actually, not now.'

'Well, just let it lapse then, sir.'

'Ah, right. Yes. Okay.'

Giles went to the graveyard. Someone was on his bench, and he had to sit on the grass of an old grave mound. It belonged to a Mr V. West (deceased). Funny that. Putting *deceased* on a headstone. Presumably, if he hadn't been deceased, they would never have buried him. At least you hoped not.

Giles sat and opened his letters. (No disrespect to Mr V.

West. And they shared the same surname too. Were probably even family, if you went back far enough. So Giles was sure he wouldn't mind.) There was one from Dawlish.

Dear Box 132,

Just a note to say that Miss Stavenshaw passed away quietly in her sleep last night, after suffering a stroke on Tuesday. Her last words, before she slipped into her final rest, were 'Do say thank you for me, to Mr Box 132. Without him, I'd never have known. At least now I won't die wondering.'

I think that is the important thing too, don't you? Not to die wondering. It's the things we don't do that we always regret.

Your friends,

Mrs Wiseman,

Mrs Throttly

P.S. After the funeral service, we are going to try and get across to Exmouth on Mrs Throttly's windsurfer. We are going to do it for Miss Stavenshaw. Wish us luck.

Giles did.

He wished them luck.

He wished all the luck in the world to everyone in it. He wished well to every enterprise, power to every elbow.

He discarded the other letters without opening them, tearing them into pieces and putting them into the bin. He walked on back towards the office, his lunch hour almost at an end.

He had to get back to work now, yes, back to the old routine. But with a promotion now. And a car. His own space in the car park. Yes, instead of standing in a crowded commuter train, he could sit in a nice comfortable traffic jam at the company's expense.

Holly would be pleased.

Or would she?

He didn't know any more. He didn't know the thoughts and the mind of the woman he lived with, and he didn't want to.

He wanted her to surprise him, to throw him constantly off balance. He didn't know her, he didn't really know anyone. The only way to maintain your equilibrium was to be in perpetual motion, to continually surprise both yourself, and those you loved. And that way love stayed alive, and never grew stale, or got taken for granted. But that way too meant fear and uncertainty, the things which nobody wanted to live with.

But all the same –

Someone held the door open for him.

'Going in?'

He hesitated and then, 'No. No thank you. No, I'm not.'

He turned away from the entrance of the Hopper and Bryanson office building and walked on. At a corner a man was selling copies of the *Big Issue*, and he looked a bit like Sergeant Toffer.

'*Big Issue*, sir?'

Giles bought one, and walked on.

'God bless you, sir, and stay out of the massage parlours!'

He walked on, not knowing or caring where he was going. Maybe he would go into work tomorrow. Maybe he wouldn't. Maybe they would sell up and go and live on the Isle of Skye. Maybe he would give up computers and become a vicar. Or he could open a tattoo shop. Maybe he would grow mushrooms in the basement. There was absolutely no telling.

He wouldn't let it go stale though, not ever again. He would constantly surprise them, all of them, and himself too. After all, there were other things, weren't there? The world was bursting open with possibilities. He'd never really travelled either, had he? That was something else he'd always wanted to do.

He could go away for a few weeks even. Holly wouldn't mind. That was what it was all about, wasn't it? Giving each other the freedom to be themselves, the freedom to grow, to be individuals as well a part of a unit. Freedom and trust, that was it, wasn't it? That was what it was all about. Not shackles and a ball and chain.

He'd get another two weeks holiday a year too, with this promotion. And more money. He could maybe afford a bit of the long haul stuff. South America, for instance, he'd always wanted to go there. What was that trip he'd read about in the Sundays? Oh yes, llama trekking in the Andes. Now, he fancied that. Yes, oh yes. He definitely fancied a spot of the old llama trekking in the Andes and no mistake. Holly wouldn't mind him going, he was sure. She could always take the girls to her mother's. And then he'd have the girls, and she could do what she wanted. And love would stay alive.

Dodgy business on your own though, llama trekking in South America. You'd really want to go with someone. A travelling companion, that was what you needed. But Giles didn't know anyone who'd want to go llama trekking in the Andes. He could ask Roy, but look at the rut he was in, stuck in the Doris rut, and never likely to get out. Just another prisoner in a cell, thinking the bars were windows. No, Roy would never go. He'd need to find someone else.

But who, and how, and where?

Then it came to him.

He turned on his heel, took a left, then a right, until he found himself at the offices of *Scene Around*. He went up to the counter. The girl with the rings was there. She had three new ones in her ears, another one in her lower lip, and two more in her nostrils.

'Yes. *(Clink. Jingle jangle.)* Sir. *(Clink.)* Can I help? *(Clink.)*'

'Yes,' Giles said. 'I'd like to place an advertisement.'

She handed him a pen.

Old mate.

And a piece of paper.

And he began to write.

'Travelling companion wanted –' he began. And then he paused.

For inspiration.

Divorcing Jack

Colin Bateman

'Richly paranoid and very funny' *Sunday Times*

Dan Starkey is a young journalist in Belfast, who shares with his wife Patricia a prodigious appetite for drinking and partying. Then Dan meets Margaret, a beautiful student, and things begin to get out of hand.

Terrifyingly, Margaret is murdered and Patricia kidnapped. Dan has no idea why, but before long he too is a target, running as fast as he can in a race against time to solve the mystery and to save his marriage.

'A joy from start to finish . . . Witty, fast-paced and throbbing with menace, *Divorcing Jack* reads like *The Thirty-Nine Steps* rewritten for the '90s by Roddy Doyle'   *Time Out*

'Grabs you by the throat . . . a magnificent debut. Unlike any thriller you have ever read before . . . like *The Day of the Jackal* out of the Marx Brothers'   *Sunday Press*

'Fresh, funny . . . an Ulster Carl Hiaasen'   *Mail on Sunday*

ISBN 0 00 647903 0

Of Wee Sweetie Mice and Men

Colin Bateman

'A supremely entertaining piece of work' *GQ*

Smooth operator Geordie McClean has succeeded in setting up a gigantic payday (for all concerned) by arranging a St Patrick's Day fight in New York between his hopeless Irish heavyweight champ Fat Boy McMaster and Mike Tyson. Belfast journalist Dan Starkey is hired to write the book of the whole affair.

Dan is trying to persuade his wife Patricia to give their marriage another go, but he has not succeeded before boarding the plane with McMaster and his deeply suspect entourage. If he thought he was leaving the sectarian conflict of his homeland behind him, Starkey is quite mistaken and McClean's outfit soon falls prey to all the old enmities, while developing an uncanny power to outrage plenty of other interest groups at the same time.

Kidnap, romance and mayhem ensue . . . and all before a punch is thrown in the ring!

'Fast, furious, riotously funny and at the end, never a dry eye in the house'   *Mail on Sunday*

'I have absolutely no interest [in boxing], but such are Bateman's skills with narrative and characterization that one is gripped to the last page, whatever one's sporting predilections'
Literary Review

'If Roddy Doyle was as good as people say, he would probably write novels like this'   *Arena*

ISBN 0 00 649612 1

Rogue Female

Nicholas Salaman

A book about living.
Dangerously.

He's shy, retiring and frightened. He's scared he'll be mugged, assaulted or spoken to by a female. Duncan Mackworth is scared of life. So he gets some help. He gets a personal instructor in self-defence. And more.

Duncan Mackworth doesn't know who to expect when he opens the door and he certainly isn't expecting a woman. A woman who will change Duncan Mackworth's life for . . . well, for as long as it lasts.

'Salaman is a crisp, rather droll writer, capable of elegant flourishes at any moment'   *Sunday Telegraph*

ISBN 0 00 649029 8

Flashman

George MacDonald Fraser

'For all their tales of lily-livered skulduggery, the [Flashman]
novels contain a zest for life and a sense of joy unparalleled
in modern literature'   CRAIG BROWN, *Daily Mail*

Flashman, soldier, duellist, lover, imposter, coward, cad
and hero, triumphs in this first instalment of The Flashman
Papers. His adventures as the reluctant secret agent in
Afghanistan and his entry into the exclusive company of
Lord Cardigan's Hussars culminate in his foulest hour –
his part in the historic disaster of the Retreat from Kabul.

This is the story of a blackguard who enjoyed villainy for
its own sake. Shameless, exciting and funny, Flashman's
deplorable odyssey is observed with the cynical eye of a
scoundrel who was honest only in reporting what he saw.
He makes all other black sheep look respectably grey.

'Not only are the Flashman books extremely funny, but
they give meticulous care to authenticity. You can, between
guffaws, learn from them'   *Washington Post*

ISBN 0 00 617680 1

Flashman and
the Angel of the Lord

George MacDonald Fraser

'If only all novels were so clever, and such fun'
CRAIG BROWN, *Daily Mail*

If only Flashman had got on with his dinner, and ignored
the handkerchief dropped by a flirtatious hussy in a
Calcutta hotel . . . well, American history would have been
different, a disastrous civil war might have been avoided –
and Flash Harry himself would have been spared one of
the most hair-raising adventures of his misspent life. If
only . . . but alas, the arch-rotter of the Victorian age could
never resist the lure of a pretty foot and this latest extract
from The Flashman Papers soon finds him careering
towards the little Virginia town of Harper's Ferry, where
John Brown and his gang of rugged fanatics were to fire
the first shot in the great war against slavery.

'If 1994 throws up a more enjoyable novel, I shall be glad
to read it' D J TAYLOR, *Sunday Times*

'Head and shoulders above others who have attempted
this sort of exercise . . . beautifully done . . . an intoxicating cocktail' DAVID ROBSON, *Sunday Telegraph*

'Next to the coming of the new Messiah, the most welcome
appearance one can imagine is the new Flashman book
from George MacDonald Fraser'
STEVE GRANT, *Time Out*

ISBN 0 00 649023 9

The Last Blues Dance

Ferdinand Dennis

Warm, humorous, poignant, *The Last Blues Dance* is a novel about coming to terms with love and loss, belonging and exile.

Boswell Anderson, a reformed gambler and rake, is proprietor of the run-down Caribbean Sunset Café in Hackney, far from his native Jamaica. When his friend, Stone Mason, invites him to a big poker game and the chance to win – or lose – enough money to change his life, Boswell finds the world coming into much sharper focus. In days gone by, the café was famous for its bacchanalian blues dances. Now, its former habitués have all returned to the Caribbean, or dream of doing so. Against this wistful, elegiac background, Boswell must come to terms with his past as well as sorting out the problems of the present, not only for himself, but also for the younger generation of his family.

The Last Blues Dance is a wonderfully engaging novel that weaves together the lives of a rich cast of characters, creating a sense of both community and individuality, tenderness and suspense.

ISBN 0 00 649783 7

Dark Rose

Mike Lunnon-Wood

It was a nineteen-year-old civil engineering student who raised the alarm, drew attention to the first invasion in western Europe by outsiders since the Turkish siege of Vienna was broken by a mixed rescue force of Germans, Prussians and Poles in 1592.

Before anyone knew it, Ireland had been taken over, the surprise pawn in a stunning new game of Middle Eastern politics.

But if the invaders thought they would get away with it easily, they were wrong. As the truth dawns, an extraordinary collection of soldiers, farmers, students and expatriates gets together a Celtic resistance force and heads for a titanic confrontation . . .

With a great cast of characters, packed with action, excitement and suspense, *Dark Rose* is a fascinating portrayal of a world event that couldn't happen . . . or could it?

ISBN 0 00 647591 4